Advance Praise for *The*

"This is a skillfully written first novel with the narrative voice, knack for dialogue, and plot movement of a veteran author."

—PUBLISHERS WEEKLY

"Readers everywhere will identify with these characters' experiences. An incredible story of second chances and seeing the bright light of Christ shine through in the darkest hour. William is using his own second chance at life to remind us of God's love. This is a must-read for anyone who needs a reminder of what God asks of us: only believe."

—PETE WILSON, PASTOR AND AUTHOR OF
PLAN B AND *EMPTY PROMISES*

"*The Reason* will serve to fortify your faith and reassure you of God's constant love and incredible power. If you are not yet a believer, this book will open your eyes to the possibilities of God that can manifest in any and every part of our lives."

—CHRIS SONKSEN, LEAD PASTOR OF SOUTH HILLS CHURCH AND
FOUNDER OF CELERA CHURCH STRATEGY GROUP, AUTHOR OF *IN
SEARCH OF HIGHER GROUND* AND *HANDSHAKE*

"*The Reason* is one of those rare books whose characters reach off the pages and take you by the heartstrings. It demonstrates an unwavering faith in God that was an inspiration to me."

—KIMBERLY BROWN

"*The Reason* will serve as a reminder that God wants us to do our part, to only believe, and to leave the outcome (good or not) to Him because He, ultimately, always knows what's best!"

—JACQUELINE LYNCH, ASSOCIATE PASTOR,
LOMA LINDA UNIVERSITY CHURCH

"*Of Mice and Men* meets *Brian's Song*. *The Reason* is a powerful story that delivers message after message."

—THOMAS LANE

"While I love to read, I'm generally not into Christian fiction. *The Reason* is an exception. It is a gritty story about everyday people that are believable and easy to relate with. It had me both laughing and crying at times as a good book should. I would recommend it to both believers and non-believers alike, but non-believers . . . be cautioned . . . you may have to really rethink and question why you don't believe in the God of the Bible."

—MARK DREW, CALIFORNIA BAPTIST UNIVERSITY

"Pay attention to each and every page or you will miss something. William Sirls is about to take you on an emotional rollercoaster ride that ends in an answer that far too many are still blind to."

—KELLY ANDERSON

"*The Reason* is an outstanding effort to communicate the love of Christ."

—THOMAS AYERS

"A book you will not forget. A clever tearjerker that invites you to think as you turn page after page."

—D. JAMES

"The people in the small town of Carlson come to life fully. They made me laugh and cry. A book as rich and engrossing as *The Reason* can make you forget your own problems."

—PATTI HOGUE

"Draws you in with its richly written characters and maintains an intense, almost eerie vibe throughout the story. *The Reason* is a uniquely compelling tale."

—RUSSELL BRADLEY FENTON

"*The Reason* will grab you at the beginning, wrap its arms around you, and keep you guessing until the end. Have your Kleenex handy and then only believe."

—M. MYERS

"Anyone reading this book will identify with at least one character with an invitation to change."

—James Steere

"May this book turn out to be a blessing to an unheard number of more people as it was to me."

—Michael Stedman

"*The Reason* is an intriguing tale of diverse personalities and problems that will lead you to twists and turns that are entirely unexpected."

—Lorene Miller

"The book started off very well, even had my heart pounding in the opening scene in the church . . . but as soon as I realized it was about Alex having leukemia, I almost put the book down. I have a very difficult time reading/watching books/movies where children are hurt. On top of that, one month ago I lost a best friend to leukemia. It seems that God's timing was perfect for me reading this book! I certainly sense His Hand in it. Looking back, I am blown away by the slim chance that 'I' ended up reading 'your' book. That you ended up being connected with me, when it could have been countless others. There are no such things as 'chances' with our God! I would highly recommend your book to anyone, and will definitely do that. Thank you for letting me have the privilege of reading it."

—Liz Zeller, Director of Biblical Counseling/Director of Growth Classes, Harvest Church, Billings, MT

THE
REASON

WILLIAM SIRLS

THOMAS NELSON
Since 1798

NASHVILLE   DALLAS   MEXICO CITY   RIO DE JANEIRO

Published in Nashville, Tennessee, by Thomas Nelson. Thomas Nelson is a registered trademark of Thomas Nelson, Inc.

Thomas Nelson, Inc., titles may be purchased in bulk for educational, business, fund-raising, or sales promotional use. For information, please e-mail SpecialMarkets@ThomasNelson.com.

Scripture quotations are taken from the New King James Version. Copyright © 1982 by Thomas Nelson, Inc. Used by permission. All rights reserved. From the King James Version of the Bible. And from the HOLY BIBLE: NEW INTERNATIONAL VERSION®. Copyright © 1973, 1978, 1984 by Biblica Inc.™ Used by permission. All rights reserved.

Publisher's note: This novel is a work of fiction. Names, characters, places, and incidents are either products of the author's imagination or used fictitiously. All characters are fictional, and any similarity to people living or dead is purely coincidental.

Library of Congress Cataloging-in-Publication Data

Sirls, William, 1964–
  The reason / William Sirls.
     p. cm.
  ISBN 978-1-4016-8736-6 (trade paper)
1. Clergy—Fiction. 2. Faith—Fiction. 3. Domestic fiction. I. Title.
PS3619.I753R43 2012
813'.6—dc23   2012018427

Printed in the United States of America

12 13 14 15 16 17 QG 6 5 4 3 2 1

DEDICATED TO ALL OF US
WHO NEED FORGIVENESS

✣ ONE

It was the second time in a little under fifteen minutes that the power had gone out at the church, and it was noticeably darker this time. Almost too dark, for the hour.

Brooke paused—waiting for the lights to come back on as they had before—and stared at the three strange shadows that hovered against the fellowship hall's vaulted ceiling. Something about them seemed alive.

She glanced over at her five-year-old son, Alexander, and lowered her earbuds, noticing the howling wind had stopped. "You okay, buddy?"

"I'm not even scared," Alex said bravely. He gave her a reassuring smile and waved the small rag he liked to use when he helped his mother dust.

Brooke turned off her iPod and then pressed the vacuum's power button a few times. Nothing happened. She shook her head and looked back up at the ceiling. The shadows had somehow become one.

The weatherman on the morning news had said they may be getting some storms, but when she, Alex, and Charlie had come up from the house to clean, only plump, white clouds and a relatively bright sun filled the southeast Michigan sky. But it had been windy. *Really windy.*

And now the wind was gone.

"It's too dark," Alex whispered. "Charlie is gonna be scared."

"He'll be okay, baby," she said. "The lights will come back on soon."

"But the sky just did some big thunder," Alex said. "You couldn't hear it with your music on your head."

That changes things.

"Charlie!" she yelled, taking Alex's hand and heading quickly across the room toward the tall double doors that separated them from the sanctuary.

Even though Charlie was thirty-eight years old and big as a tree, thunder absolutely terrified him. Even with his familiarity with the church, all his safe places had surely been erased by the darkness and terror flooding his small mind.

She opened the doors and walked into the sanctuary. It was dark, but not nearly as dark as the fellowship hall. It was perfectly quiet.

"Charlie?" Brooke said, glancing up toward the front of the church. She heard nothing but could feel Alex pulling on her pant leg.

"Look, Mom," he said.

She turned, and her eyes followed his little index finger, pointing at the two paned glass doors that served as the main entrance. Brooke squinted and cocked her head to the side. She had never seen the sky that color before.

She took his hand again, walked to the doors, then leaned against one to push it open.

It was deadly still outside. The air was thick and had a strange smell to it. The clouds were now a dark gray and the sky behind them an eerie crayon green, casting down a steady shadow of the same color over everything she could see.

"We better take cover," Brooke whispered, holding the door. She gazed out at the fifteen-foot wooden cross, centered on the church's front lawn. Beyond the woods, she could hear spirited rolls of thunder approaching off the shore of Lake Erie. There was no way in the world Charlie would have ever come out here, let alone try to make it over to the house.

"I want to go back inside," Alex said, letting go of his mother's hand and wrapping his arms around her leg.

Brooke took a deep breath and tilted her head up again to stare at the sky, wondering how much time they had. She looked down the hill at the house, which now seemed so far away. More thunder sounded in the distance. Louder this time.

"Charlie!" Alex shouted. There was panic in his small voice.

Brooke looked back over her shoulder into the church. She leaned her head against the door and waited for Charlie to jump up from between two pews, as he'd done hundreds of times before during hide-and-seek.

"He won't come out, Mom," Alex said. "You know how he is when he's scared."

"He has to be around here somewhere," Brooke said, taking one more look outside. She picked her son up and stepped back into the church, letting the door close behind them. "We have to find him fast, Alex."

She walked along the length of the back pew and stopped when they hit the center aisle. Brooke could see the push sweeper lying on the floor up near the pulpit. Charlie had obviously abandoned it when he heard the first hint of thunder.

Brooke put Alex back on his feet and tried to listen for Charlie.

She looked back at the main entrance. It had clearly gotten darker, and beyond the door's plated glass, lightning flickered gently, as if God were flashing the porch light for someone who had just missed his driveway.

"Charlie!" Brooke yelled again.

"Charlie!" Alex echoed.

They turned and slowly made their way up the main aisle, taking turns calling Charlie's name and looking for him in the darkness between the pews.

"Maybe he did make it down to the house," Brooke said, glancing back at the front doors. The sky had gone from green to black.

They both flinched at the thick volley of thunder that coincided with a flash of lightning, like an X-ray of the church's front lawn.

"I don't like this," Alex said, sounding on the verge of tears.

"It's okay," she said, still staring at the front doors. She held her hand out behind her for Alex to take. He didn't.

"I'm over here," Alex whispered.

Brooke turned around and could barely see him. He was nothing more than a small shadow kneeling in the pew. "What are you doing?"

"Praying we find Charlie."

Brooke kneeled next to him and struggled to slow her breathing. *Please, Lord, keep us safe*. She put her arm around Alex and pulled him closer. She could feel his little heart pounding against her palm.

Alex squeezed her arm and closed his eyes as she pulled him closer still. She kissed the top of his head as a violent peal of thunder boomed directly over the church.

"No!" Alex cried.

"Let's go," Brooke said, taking Alex's hand. As they rose, she thought she heard something over the rain. It was dark, but she could vaguely make out some of the shadows around them. The pews. The dim outlines of windows. A stack of rarely used folding chairs against the wall. They stepped into the aisle, and Brooke proceeded to look mechanically to her left, then to her right, her head's slowly shifting movements reminding her of a low-end security camera.

She saw little, but she definitely heard something. *Charlie*. He was crying. But the sound of him was drowned out by thunder so loud it reverberated in her chest, and by the wind that had finally returned with a vengeance.

"Make it stop!" Alex begged, grabbing hold of her leg again.

She turned to comfort him and looked outside. Another finger of lightning darted across the grounds, and Brooke flinched as the entire front lawn disappeared into a brilliant flash of reddish-orange light. It was gone before she could shield her eyes, and the deafening blast that followed shook the building, sending them both instinctively to the floor. She draped her arms around Alex.

He was trembling, and she didn't blame him. Whatever had just happened outside was unlike anything she had ever seen or heard. They needed better cover—to get out of this big space.

"Charlie!" she yelled, quickly standing and then picking up Alex. "Where are you?"

There was no response.

"What if he's hurt?" Alex cried.

"What in the world?" she said.

"Do you see him, Mom?"

Brooke squinted at the glass of the front doors.

Something was burning outside. Flames seemed to float in the dark about ten feet in the air, then rapidly weakened under the assault of the constant rain.

"What's that?" Alex asked. As he spoke, the last of the fire went out.

"I think it was the cross," she answered.

"Oh no," Alex said, like a concerned old man. He leaned his head on her shoulder. "Please, let's hurry. Let's find him."

She raised her finger to her lips, gently requesting that he be quiet. As they waited and listened for Charlie, all Brooke could hear was the continuous tapping of the rain on the windows.

"A car's coming," Alex said. Headlights made their way up into the parking lot of the small church.

"It has to be Shirley and Pastor Jim," she whispered. A peculiar clicking sound came from the other side of the building, restoring the power.

Only two of seven lights were on in the sanctuary, offering them no real improvement in their ability to see Charlie, but they both breathed a little easier.

"I like that better," Alex said.

"Me too, little man."

"Can you turn the rest on, Mom?"

"Sure," she said. They heard a humming sound coming from somewhere in the building and looked at each other.

"What's that noise?" Alex asked.

"I think it's the vacuum cleaner over in the fellowship hall. I must've left it on when we lost power."

Alex smiled and she kissed the top of his head again. There was more thunder, but it seemed to be fading. The storm was easing away, and now Brooke was sure she could hear Charlie.

"I hope the dumb lights stay on this time," Alex said. "I wish they—"

"Shh," Brooke said, moving slowly toward the front of the church. One dome light cast a peacefully soothing glow over the altar, an old Wurlitzer piano, and a hand-carved pulpit.

She tilted her head and lifted her hand. She definitely heard someone sniffle.

"We need to find Charlie," Alex said, as if she'd forgotten.

"We just did," Brooke said, running her hand through Alex's bright-red hair. Charlie was up in the nave, lying down between the last two pews, where the choir sat. All she could see of him was the white, size twenty-one tennis shoes on the carpet, sticking out past the end of the bench.

Brooke carried Alex up to the choir stalls and stepped into the row in front of Charlie's hiding spot. She lowered Alex to stand on the seat cushion above Charlie, and they both leaned over and looked down.

Charlie Lindy was perfectly still, flat on his back, with his eyes closed and his hands over his ears.

"There you are, big guy," Brooke said. "It's okay, Charlie."

Alex started giggling. "You big fraidy cat, Charlie!"

"It's okay, Charlie," Brooke repeated softly. "The storm is about over."

Charlie opened his eyes and looked up at them. Thunder rumbled in the distance, and he immediately shut them again.

"It's all right," she said assuredly. "It's going away."

Charlie reluctantly opened his eyes again, and they shifted quickly from side to side. He slowly sat up and lowered his hands from his ears. He smiled at Brooke and pointed at the light switch behind her.

"You got it, big guy," she said.

"You're a big fraidy cat!" Alex laughed, jumping up and down while holding out his arms for Charlie to take him.

"I think we were *all* afraid," Brooke said soothingly as she turned to switch on more lights.

"No!" Alex yelled, his voice echoing off the church's painted white brick walls.

Brooke spun around and found herself staring straight into Charlie's barrel-like chest. His right arm extended firmly out to his side like a thick branch. At the end of that limb, two feet above her head, Alex dangled helplessly facedown as Charlie's mammoth hand held him by the backside of his tiny Levi's. She smiled and put her hands on her hips.

"Okay!" Alex shouted again, followed by a playful giggle. "Okay, Charlie! You're not a fraidy cat!"

Charlie grinned and effortlessly flipped Alex upright to sit on his enormous shoulders. Alex balanced himself by hanging on to one handful of the giant man's cropped blond hair and another handful of his left ear. Charlie's oversized fingers wrapped carefully around the boy's thigh to hold on to him. His other hand slowly lifted, opened, and then revealed a single Tic Tac, which Alex gratefully snatched up.

Brooke was giving Charlie a thumbs-up when Shirley Lindy came through the door. Shirley wore a plastic blue poncho and pulled out tissue to wipe away the small beads of water on her wire-rimmed glasses.

"Hello there, Alexander," Shirley said, looking up at him.

"Hi, Mrs. Lindy," he said. "We couldn't find Charlie and he scared me!"

"Me too," Brooke said. "Where is Pastor Jim?"

"I left him out front," the older woman replied.

"What's he doing out there in the rain?" Brooke asked.

"We have a little problem," Shirley answered, holding up her hand and reeling in her right index finger, silently inviting them to come and see.

Brooke was the first outside as Shirley held the door for a ducking Charlie, who still had Alex saddled comfortably on his shoulders.

A gentle fog had rolled onto the property, and the storm had been reduced to a misty drizzle. Brooke's breath clouded before her mouth and nose. But her eyes were on Pastor Jim.

"Oh no," she sighed. "I saw this happen."

Brooke slid her arms sympathetically around Shirley's shoulders as Alex lowered his chin to the top of Charlie's head.

Pastor Jim knelt in a shallow puddle with his head down and hands resting on the top half of the large wooden cross that lay on the ground before him.

Lightning had struck.

✢ TWO

Twenty-seven-year-old Carla Miller sat quietly on a corner bar stool at The Pilot Inn. She was halfway into her first Bacardi and Coke and wished she could smoke a cigarette. She took a deep breath and ran her finger slowly down the side of her glass. She hadn't had a smoke in over a year and knew the craving wouldn't last long. It felt kind of good to be in control of something, at least.

Despite being one of the area's most popular watering holes, the storm had made it a slow night at The Pilot. The sticky smells of stale beer that usually haunted the hundred-year-old bar and diner were minimized by both a light crowd and a splintered mop handle that propped the back door partially open, allowing rain-fresh air to waft through. Only one of the televisions was on, making it a little darker than usual, and the Guess Who's "No Time Left for You" was playing a little too loudly from the corner jukebox. Carla wasn't sure why she only liked listening to old songs. She guessed that they made her think of her father and the short amount of time she had with him.

She shook it off. This wasn't going to be another one of those nights where the promises she had made to herself once again ended up in small pieces scattered all over the floor of the bar. The song ended to the sarcastic applause of an overweight man in his midfifties. A trucker? A construction worker? His fat, sausage-like fingers held a bottle of Bud Light as he slammed four quarters down on the edge of the pool table, securing his right to play the current game's winner. He glanced back at Carla with eyes as gray and worn as his face, giving her the once-over. It didn't bother Carla. Men had *always* liked her. Though the cigarettes and booze hadn't been kind to her looks, she took a fair amount of consolation in her ability to turn heads.

She rested her chin on the palm of her hand and then looked up. In the long mirror that ran the length of the wall behind the bar, she could see her best friend—her only *real* friend—Brooke Thomas, walking through the saloon doors that separated the two halves of the bar and diner. It was good to see Brooke, but if she was venturing into the bar, it must have been a *really* rough day for her. They had known each other for over ten years now, and Brooke had spent the last two doing a pretty solid job of not meeting Carla anywhere that sold alcohol. *Enable* was the word Brooke liked to use, even though it bugged Carla.

"I hoped I'd find you here," Brooke said, taking off her coat before sitting on the stool next to her. "Busy day at drama central. Went to the free clinic to have Alex checked, then we cleaned the church all afternoon. That was some kind of crazy storm, huh?"

"It was somethin'," Carla responded, hugging Brooke while giving a peace sign to the bartender. "Kathy, let's have two more rum and Cokes. Hold the rum on one." She turned back to Brooke. "What'd you find out about Alex?"

"They want us to come back tomorrow so they can run some tests on him."

"What kind of tests?"

"Blood tests and a couple of other things. Can you go with me?"

"Sure. What time?"

"Have to be there at seven forty-five."

"I'll pick you guys up at quarter after. What are they testing for?"

"Routine stuff," Brooke said, closing her eyes and pinching the bridge of her nose. "You think it's something bad?"

Carla lowered her cheek to Brooke's shoulder and put her arm around her for another quick hug. "I'm sure it's not. Alex is gonna be just fine."

"I know," Brooke said, smiling in a way that seemed a little forced. Her light green eyes begged for more assurance. "But the cross outside St. Thomas won't be fine. Lightning struck it."

"You're kidding."

"No. Wait until you see it."

"Don't worry about the cross," Carla said. "It can be replaced."

"With what?" Brooke said. "Our good looks? We don't have the money to fix it." Whatever happened to Brooke's adopted family—the Lindys—was like it happened to Brooke too. Carla knew she owed them a great deal, but she hated that her friend took on their burdens as if they were her own. She studied Brooke, noticing dark shadows under her eyes, and reached out to rub her shoulder in comfort. But as she did, she caught the eye of a man over by the jukebox, staring hard at her. It wasn't the kind of look she was used to, the soft perusal of a would-be lover. It was like his eyes drilled into her. Saw her. Knew her.

"Check out jukebox boy," Carla said, lifting her hand off Brooke's shoulder.

She nodded toward the man across the bar. He was a little too thin for her liking, had wavy brown hair, and appeared to be in his early thirties. Jeans. Navy peacoat. And boots that told her he was but another construction worker out to blow off some steam. He had a pool stick in one hand and what looked like an apple in the other. And he stared right at them, not politely looking away. Though Carla wouldn't consider him to be an eye-catcher, he had, for some reason, caught her eye.

"Why is he looking at us?" Brooke asked, turning back around. "And why would he bring an apple in here?"

"I'm gonna get him to come over here before we leave," Carla said, flashing him the little smile that never failed.

"Just don't leave with him," Brooke said, giving Carla a warning look.

"What's that supposed to mean?" Carla asked, poking at Brooke's shoulder. "I'm gonna behave."

"Looks like we're gonna find out," Brooke said. "Here he comes."

Carla watched the man lean the pool stick against the wall and put the apple in the front left pocket of his coat. He didn't break their gaze the whole time, and even though God knew she was burned out on construction types, she couldn't take her eyes off him. He sat a few seats down and resumed his stare via the mirror above the bar, making Carla even more curious. Something seemed different about this guy. His eyes were a soft green like Brooke's, yet cast subtle hints of authority. Even though he hadn't shaved in what had to be a couple of days, his grittiness came across as clean and pure. She had never seen anyone quite like him.

"He certainly has your attention," Brooke whispered. "Don't be so obvious."

"He is beautiful," Carla said.

Brooke laughed. "Beautiful? I've never heard you say that about a guy before. He doesn't seem to be your type. Too skinny. Too . . . average."

"Look at him," Carla said. "He's unreal."

"What in the world are you talking about?"

Carla broke their mirrored stare and slowly leaned forward, looking at him, past Brooke. "Hi there," she said softly, in open invitation.

The man casually looked over at her from the side of his green eyes.

"Strong, silent type," Brooke whispered, tapping Carla's leg.

Carla took a neat sip of her drink. She didn't like being ignored. The least he could do was say something back. "Why are you staring at me?" she asked.

The man still didn't move. His head was perfectly still.

"Why don't you just take a picture?" Carla said, waving her hand back and forth in front of her.

"Are you talking to me?" he asked calmly.

"Oh my goodness!" Carla said. "You can talk!"

"You want me to take a picture of you?" the man asked, a hint of a smile bending the corner of his mouth.

"No," Carla said, her voice changing from the curious to the more playful one that she had more confidence in. "I just wondered why you were staring at me."

"I'm not staring at you," he replied casually.

"Oh yes you are," Carla said. She winked at him and hoped Brooke didn't catch it.

"I'm not staring." He gave a little shrug of his shoulders.

"Then what are you looking at?" Was he mental? Or was this part of his game?

The man lifted his hand off the bar and pointed his pinky finger right at what Carla thought was her head. "The TV."

Behind Carla and Brooke, against the far wall, a magician was appearing on a flat-screen television, attempting to crawl *through* a solid piece of glass that served as the front window of a department store. The apple guy had been watching the television the whole time. Carla tried covering her face with her hand as she secretly wished she could steal the magician's thunder by disappearing into thin air.

"I am such an idiot," she mumbled, dropping her hand and ducking her head.

"Sorry," Brooke said to the man, putting her arm around Carla. "Please excuse her. She's a little tipsy."

"No, I'm not," Carla said. "I'm only on my second drink. Two more is my limit."

"Relax," Brooke whispered. "I just saved you."

"That's okay," the man said as if he understood. "It happens."

"Jukebox time," Carla said, standing and looking down at the floor. It was the first excuse she could think of to get off her stool and out of the man's sight. She took Brooke's arm. "Get me and our new friend a shot of Jäger." She was hoping that maybe the drink could, in some way, serve as an apology to the man.

"Okay," Brooke said.

Carla stood a few feet behind the pool table and fed a pair of dollar bills to the jukebox. She laughed out loud. *The only time I really want a guy to look at me, and he doesn't.* She ran her hand through her hair and peeked back toward the bar. Brooke was on her phone, and the guy with the apple was still staring—staring at the television—when she felt a hand settle rudely on her back.

"Need help picking out some real music, sugar britches?"

Carla turned around, and the fat trucker coughed out a syrupy laugh right in her face.

"Excuse me?" she said.

"Who taught you how to pick out music?"

So he didn't like her taste in songs. She ignored him and scanned the jukebox for some more oldies. Maybe she could pick out another classic—something that would stick real well in Truckerman's fat head.

"I have to leave!" Brooke shouted apologetically from the bar. "Shirley called!"

"You just got here!" Carla yelled back, giving the fat trucker a look that suggested pool wasn't the only game he'd lose tonight. She hurried back toward the bar and Brooke yanked on her coat.

"It's Alex," Brooke said, her face alarmed. "I've gotta leave, like right now."

"What's wrong with Alex?" she whispered, hiding her face from the apple man.

"He got another bloody nose. You know how he likes me to be around when he gets them."

"Poor baby. Isn't that like three or four in the last two weeks?"

"More like seven or eight."

She knew it was what had driven Brooke and Alex to the clinic that morning. "Maybe they'll have answers for you at the hospital tomorrow."

"We'll see," Brooke said.

"You gonna leave me alone with this guy?" Carla asked, tilting her head toward the man at the bar. It still looked like he was staring right at them.

"He seems all right," Brooke whispered. "And by the way, he didn't want the shot."

14

"I'll change his mind."

"I gotta go. Be a good girl," Brooke said, leaning her forehead toward Carla's and lifting a delicate brow in silent warning.

"I will. See you in the morning," Carla said.

The two hugged and Brooke left. Carla sat back down and quickly polished off one of the shots that was waiting there. Apple man was still glued to the TV when she turned to him.

"I think I owe you an apology," she said. "I thought you were kind of looking at me and I guess I kind of wanted to talk to you."

He didn't respond again. He just kept staring.

Carla knocked on the bar and raised her voice over Foreigner's "Dirty White Boy." "Will you quit staring at that stupid television? I'm trying to apologize to you."

"I wasn't staring at the television," he said calmly.

"What?" Carla asked.

He carefully crossed his arms. Carla found it difficult to take her eyes off of him while silently wondering what it was about him that she needed to know.

"I was staring at you," he said.

"What?"

"You heard me," he answered. "And I have a feeling you know why."

Carla felt a tiny chill dance across the side of her neck and stop just under her chin. She ran her palm along where she'd felt it and tried to look back at the man. But she couldn't.

"It's not like you to be bashful, is it?" he asked.

She didn't like the way he asked the question. If it was flirting, it wasn't fun. She also knew he hadn't moved, but now he somehow seemed so much closer. Too close.

"You have never been the shy type," he said.

The way he said it was calm and quiet, but some of that authority she sensed in those green eyes had underlined all seven words. She tried to look at him again and couldn't, but now she knew why. She looked down and closed her eyes. He somehow knew her, knew about her past. She heard the legs of a bar stool pushing back from the bar. There was a pause, then evenly paced steps that were clearly made by his tan leather work boots.

He sidled up next to her.

"Tell me why I was staring at you," he whispered.

The man had somehow found a way to take a lifetime of indiscretions and balance them neatly on the point of a needle. Each time she tried to look at him, it poked at her, exposing everything about her while injecting paralyzing doses of shame.

"It's okay," he said.

No, it isn't. It's another bad day, and I'm kidding myself about ever quitting drinking. A four-drink limit was a nice start, but it will never be enough to drown it all out. I'm going to get drunk tonight. And by tomorrow, I will have forgotten about how my conscience let me believe that this guy . . .

Carla opened her eyes. "Look. I don't know who you are or what you want, but let's go back to silent staring. Okay? Better yet, let's just go our own ways."

She edged off the stool and reached out to pick up the other shot of Jägermeister. But as she did so, she felt his warm hand gently take her wrist. That little chill raced across her neck again and moved into gooseflesh that crossed her shoulders and spread down her back.

"That's enough, isn't it?" he asked, guiding her hand and the drink back to the top of the bar. "You're okay."

As he gradually let go of her wrist, for the first time in her life, she felt like she really *was* okay. But that made no sense. She shivered, but oddly wasn't cold. The first tear began to make its way down her cheek, and Carla closed her eyes. She couldn't deny it; she was at complete peace. The bar had gone quiet, and she could feel him still standing next to her. The tear dripped off the side of her chin, and she heard it as it landed on the bar. More tears quickly followed. She couldn't stop them. She didn't want to. Everything was okay. No, *perfect*. Even though she was weeping.

"I would like to show you something," he said.

Carla opened her eyes and the man leaned against the bar and reached into his coat pocket. He pulled the apple out and placed it in front of her.

"What do you see in this?" he asked.

Carla couldn't speak.

"It's okay," he said. "Tell me what you see."

She was mesmerized by the fruit's immaculate shine. She had never seen anything like its perfect shape, and its bright-red color looked as if it had been painted on. It even had a tiny leaf attached to its green stem. It almost seemed fake—as if it belonged in a dining room display at a furniture store. She hesitantly picked it up and held it, confirming that it was, in fact, flawlessly real.

"Tell me," he repeated kindly. "Tell me what you think of it."

She turned it slightly in her hand, and part of the man's refection appeared in it. Her arm fell to the bar, and the tiny hairs on the back of her neck stood on end as she looked at him. She wanted to say more but only managed three words: "It is beautiful."

He tapped on the side of the apple and looked right at her. "What do you think would happen to this beautiful apple if it had a big worm inside of it?"

She paused for a moment, wiping away her remaining tears, leaving smudges of eyeliner on her shirtsleeve. "I don't know. It would eat it up?"

"Yes, it would," he said, placing his hand directly on top of hers. "Forgive."

"Forgive?" she whispered.

"Carla, I want you to learn to forgive."

He turned and slowly walked away from her, making his way out the back door.

Carla picked the apple up off the bar and hurried after him, staring out the window to the rear parking lot. She watched him climb into the cab of an old Ford F-150 and pull away. But one question rang in her mind above the rest.

When did I tell him my name?

✢ THREE

Carla was a few minutes ahead of schedule to pick up Alex and Brooke when she turned her white Dodge Intrepid onto the heavily wooded "Church Road," a grassy, half-mile passage of sand, pea gravel, and white stone that didn't make most maps. Beyond the arrivals and departures of Brooke and the Lindys, the only other traffic the road usually saw was from the few who came to church on Sunday or the occasional jogger looking for a shortcut into the park that ran along Lake Erie.

It was hard for Carla to drive down it without thinking about high school. Back in the day, the cops never bothered coming out here, and it'd been the perfect place to smoke pot, down some Boone's Farm, make out with the boys . . . or more. All that time, she'd never made it down to the end of the road, and it wasn't until Brooke moved in with the Lindys that Carla even knew that there was a church down there. Heck, it wasn't until then that Carla knew the church, the house, or even God existed. It practically made her itch now, passing their favorite parking area, a bare area of grass that nudged into the woods, knowing that when she was doing all those things, Pastor Jim and Shirley were just around the bend. *If they only knew,* she thought.

That made her think about the man last night. Mr. Mysterious. And the apple. When he said *forgive,* was he talking about one of those boys from her high school days? One of the many who used her and then tossed her aside? Or all of them?

Carla made a right into the narrow driveway that led through the trees and to the twenty-acre patch of land, all St. Thomas property. At some point, church members had probably hoped they'd one day need to expand, build a larger sanctuary, a huge parking lot. Sadly, there was little need for that. But Carla was still glad it was here. With the rolling hills, the deep forest, the cute little church and cozy house, it always made her feel at peace when she arrived. Like she'd discovered someplace secret, sacred, hers. Whenever she heard someone say "God's Country," she thought of St. Thomas.

She passed the church's small gravel parking lot and pulled up in the Lindys' driveway. Carla stared at the small white-framed house in front of her.

She wished she lived there. For the thousandth time she wished she was Brooke, with an adorable little boy and an adopted family.

Carla sighed and got out of the car and went to the porch, stopping to look through the front window. Pastor Jim was sitting in the old La-Z-Boy with his Bible in his hand. She suspected he was rehearsing his sermon for Sunday.

Carla smiled and glanced back up the hill toward the church, thinking of him in there, preaching one of his good sermons. Her smile faded and she looked back through the window at Pastor Jim. For the first time ever, she was glad he was blind; she was glad he couldn't see the wreckage on the hill.

Brooke wasn't kidding about the cross. Or what's left of it. The lightning nailed it good. The sight of it made her sadder than she expected.

She took a step back on the porch and remembered the way the cross used to be. It stood so tall, and there was something about its polished wood and placement on the lawn that left her feeling both protected and, in some strange way, even a little afraid. Pastor Jim always told her that it was her choice to go to service, and on the Sundays she chose to go, it was impossible for her not to stop and look at the cross before she walked in. She almost felt like she needed its permission to enter.

But now it'd been blown in half, with the bottom part still stuck in the ground. It looked like a head-high stump with a charred point. Most of the top of the cross lay facedown in the wet sod. A separate piece was a few feet away.

She blew a puff of warm air into her hands and was fighting an unwelcome sense of emptiness when three deer walked gracefully around the corner of the church and stopped next to the cross. That weird sense of being stared at—*just like last night*—niggled at her and she laughed out loud, quickly dismissing it.

Carla stepped forward and grabbed the door handle. She hadn't knocked on the front door in over six years because Pastor Jim and Shirley had always made it clear that she was welcome anytime, and walking right in was a privilege she wasn't afraid to use.

"Hey, hey," she said, stepping in.

"Hello, kiddo," Pastor Jim replied, pivoting the chair in her direction. He was wearing an old T-shirt that fell over a pair of flannel pajama bottoms. He closed the Bible and brushed his salt-and-pepper-gray hair back with his hand. "You're up bright and early this morning."

"I'm taking Brooke and Alex to the hospital."

"I offered to drive them, but the idea didn't go over too well."

"Ha-ha," she said, shaking her head. The pastor hadn't been allowed to drive for years. "By the way, since when is seven in the morning bright and early for you?"

"Seven is pretty early."

"She knows as well as anyone in this house that you're the first to rise," Shirley said, entering the living room from the kitchen. No limp, Carla noticed. *Arthritis must not be bothering her today.* Shirley leaned over and kissed Pastor Jim on his forehead. "This man wakes me up every single morning. I can't remember the last time he slept past five."

Pastor Jim stood and hiked his thumb in the direction of Shirley's voice. "I figured she would be used to it after all this time. You think she's getting ready to trade me in, Carla?"

"I would, if I were her," Carla said.

"Don't tempt me," Shirley said with a teasing lilt to her voice.

"Never gonna happen," Pastor Jim said, holding out his arms

for a hug, which Shirley gladly gave. Carla wished she had someone in her life to hug her like that. The look in Pastor Jim's eyes was usually kind of hard to read, with the gray film that covered them, but right then they said nothing other than *I cherish my wife.*

Brooke came into the room and was dangling a set of keys. She looked like she hadn't slept much. "Who's driving? You or me?"

"I will," Carla said. "Where're Alex and Charlie?"

"Downstairs," Brooke answered, opening the basement door. "Let's go, Alex!"

A series of little footsteps scurried up the stairs. The door opened, and Alex skipped over and hugged Carla's leg. "Hi, Aunt Carla!"

"Hey, pal," she said.

Alex proudly lifted his chin as he let go of her leg. "My nose bleeded again yesterday, but it didn't even hurt. Mom came home, but I was okay."

"That's what I heard," she said, pinching his cheek. "How did you get so brave?"

His hazel eyes squinted, and the freckles that had been sprinkled around his little nose seemed to hunch together. "I don't know, but Mom says I can get some chocolate milk from the store today."

"That's right," Brooke said, holding open his Detroit Tigers jacket. Alex backed into it and put his arms through the sleeves, which were about three inches too short.

"Looks like somebody needs a new coat," Carla said. "Maybe Santa will bring you one."

"No," Alex said. "He's getting me a bike that doesn't have baby wheels on it."

Charlie dipped under the top of the door as he came up from the basement. He smiled and waved at Carla.

"Hey, Charlie," she said.

The big man walked over and handed Brooke Alex's matching Tigers baseball cap.

"Thanks, Charlie," Brooke said. She stopped buttoning halfway up the coat and put Alex's cap on the way he liked it, backward. "We need anything else from the store?"

"Just the Pop-Tarts and two gallons of milk," Shirley said.

"Okay," Brooke said. "We'll be back in a few hours."

"I think maybe Charlie wants something," Shirley added, nodding at her son.

Charlie was holding his Tic Tac container up in front of his face. He stared at it for a few seconds like he had never seen it before. There were two left.

"I think you are right," Carla said.

Charlie opened the lid and poured out the two candies into his other hand. He reached down and gave one to Alex and then leaned his head back and dropped the last one in his mouth. He held the empty container back up in front of his face, then slowly turned his head to Brooke.

"Tic Tacs, Charlie?" Carla asked, smiling.

Charlie took a step toward her and stopped. The top of his head was just under the edge of the ceiling fan. He stuffed two fingers into his front pocket and then took another step toward her. He held out his hand and gave her a nickel and three pennies. His eyes began to blink quickly as a broad grin slowly stretched across his face in what could only mean *Yes, please.*

"Let's bolt," Brooke said.

Carla held the screen door as Alex and Brooke walked outside. She glanced up at the church and then turned back to the three Lindys, who were standing next to one another in the center of the living room. Shirley was smiling at her with eyes that were much easier to read than Pastor Jim's. Despite having a blind husband and a seven-foot, 355-pound son who hadn't spoken a single word in his life, they were sending a message that was loud and clear.

I'm the luckiest woman in the world.

"WE ARE GONNA BE LATE," BROOKE SAID, LEANING HER head against the passenger window.

"They will understand," Carla said. "Quit stressing."

"Easier said than done," Brooke said. "Why'd they want us to come back if they weren't worried?"

"He's gonna be fine," Carla said.

"You okay back there, buddy?" Brooke asked.

"He's out," Carla answered.

"But we just left," Brooke said. She turned and looked in the backseat. Alex was sleeping with his head turned to the side, making his red eyelashes look extra-long. He was snoring lightly, and his little hands held the rubber SpongeBob he scored with his Happy Meal the week before. Though he hadn't been in a car seat in months, he seemed so small back there without one.

"How late were you guys up?"

"Too late," Brooke answered, closing her eyes and shooting up a quick prayer for good news.

It was normally only about a ten-minute ride from the Lindy house to downtown Carlson, but they were stuck behind a train on Old Gibraltar Road, a county-neglected minefield of potholes, gravel, and oily sand. Despite its horrendous condition, the wooded two-mile stretch was the shortest and most commonly used route to North Jefferson Avenue and the city's two banks, one gas station, and string of mom-and-pop businesses that were separated by unoccupied buildings.

At the tail end of North "Jeff" was the hospital and Carlson's number-one producer of unemployed people, a partially functional assembly plant, now operating under the tax-friendly pseudonym of "Auto Trust." Brooke did a two-year stint there before moving on to become a nail tech with Carla at the Downriver Mall in Lincoln Park. Even though the three hundred a week she earned was less than half what she had made at the plant, she liked doing nails and the time it gave her with Carla—as well as less need for child care.

"Pastor Jim didn't say a single thing about the cross," Carla said. "Neither did Shirley."

"How many times have you ever heard them complain about anything?"

"Like, never. What's the plan with it, then?"

"Not sure," Brooke said, turning back around and looking at Alex again. "Pastor Jim said that everything happens for a reason and that God will make something good come from it."

"Of all the places lightning has to hit," Carla said, "why there? Why them?"

"I don't know," Brooke mumbled. She was still looking in the backseat, not at Alex, but at a pile of little plastic rum bottles, like the ones you get when you are on an airplane, that were spilling out of a plastic grocery bag, partially hidden under the driver's seat. She shoved back the urge to lay into Carla. Wasn't the time at the bar enough? She was drinking *in her car*? When? On her way home from work? "What happened with Mr. Mysterious last night?" she forced herself to ask.

"Mr. Mysterious?" Carla laughed. "He actually freaked me out a little bit."

"How's that?"

"Before or after he pulled that apple out of his pocket and put it on the bar?"

"Huh?"

"He also had me crying. Actually . . . I had me crying, but the apple was to tell me to learn to forgive."

"What? I don't get it."

"He asked me what would happen to the apple if it had a worm inside of it. Kind of like I'm the apple and that I need to learn to forgive or it will eat me up."

"That's weird. Forgive who?"

"I don't know."

"Why'd you cry?"

"I really don't know why. Something made me think about all the mistakes I've made in my life. And I sort of tricked myself into thinking that he knew about all of it."

"How many drinks did you have?"

"Just three. I only had one of the shots. Can you believe it?"

I want to, Brooke thought, glancing up at the flashing red lights that were attached to a pair of worn-out posts that looked like they were about to fall over. *This crossing is in serious need of a gate. It's a miracle nobody's ever gotten creamed by a train.* Not that this particular train was going to get anybody. It was dead stopped. She let out a long breath of frustration. *We're so gonna be late.*

"Can you believe it?" Carla repeated, tapping Brooke on her leg. "I didn't hit my limit."

"I'm proud of you," Brooke muttered, looking at what had to be Detroit gang signs scratched repeatedly on the side of one of the boxcar doors, then reading the painted tags. "Guess what, Carla?"

"What?"

Brooke pointed at the train and read words spray-painted in purple and underlined in black. "HUBBA IS ALL DAT."

"Oh yeah?" Carla laughed. She pointed to their right and read huge gold letters. "BOBBY IS A . . . uh . . ." She paused, glancing at the sleeping child behind her. "Something really, really bad."

"I knew that," Brooke said casually, "but more importantly, KRIS R. ROCKS."

"DUKE LOVES EMMA."

"Carla Miller is hot."

"Are you serious?" Carla gasped, grabbing Brooke's arm. "Where?"

Brooke grinned as she watched Carla nervously scan the boxcars. "Just kidding."

"I hate you." Carla laughed.

Brooke plopped her hand on Carla's wrist and smiled. "You love me and you know it."

"I do," Carla said dreamily. She wasn't smiling back and Brooke wondered why.

"What is it, Carla?"

"The way you grabbed my wrist," she answered. "He did that last night at the exact same time I think I was having what the AA people call a 'moment of clarity.'"

"The guy last night?"

"Yeah, and when he did it, everything seemed all right. It was like I had been given another chance. It was like I was being given a choice to do something, and if I did it, all my mistakes would go away."

"Forgive?" Brooke asked.

"No," Carla said as the train finally started to move. "That's what he said, but what I *felt* was something different. I felt like there was something I needed to do, and if I just did that one thing, my mistakes would be forgotten."

"Do what thing?"

"I'm really not sure. Weird, huh?"

"It'll come to you," Brooke said, lifting her hand back toward the train. "Maybe you need to GET HIGH IN JULY."

"You are a dork," Carla said, pointing at a dinged-up freight car as the train began to pick up more speed. "Check that out. One of our little graffiti guys must have taken an art lesson."

Against a gorgeous, colorful backdrop, painted in perfect block letters were the words: ONLY BELIEVE.

"Wow," Brooke said. "I wonder how long it took to do that."

"Don't know. Had to be awhile."

"You can say that again," Brooke said, flipping through Carla's CD holder. "Ever think about listening to some music from this century? Everything in here is from the '60s, '70s, or '80s. We weren't even born when half this stuff came out. Get with the times, girl."

"Quit hatin' on the classics," Carla said. "That's when music was real."

"I'm thirsty, Mom." Alex was up.

Brooke turned around and smiled. He was rubbing his eyes and finishing a yawn. "Hey, buddy, that was a short nap."

He fumbled for his SpongeBob and then looked right at her. "What does it mean that Aunt Carla is hot?"

"Nothing, buddy," Brooke answered quickly. She turned to Carla, who was muffling a laugh.

"Mom, you said, 'Carla Miller is hot.' That's Aunt Carla. Does she have a fever?"

Brooke looked back at Carla, snorted, and they both started laughing uncontrollably. "No, buddy. She's fine."

Carla put the car in drive, and as they made their way over the tracks and headed up Old Gibraltar, Brooke turned the stereo up. She played the air guitar, and they both sang at the top of their lungs with Ann Wilson and Heart.

The song was "Magic Man."

✢ FOUR

M acey Lewis strolled into the waiting room of the free clinic on the first floor of East Shore Community Hospital. It was always busy down here, but today it was packed, even at this early hour. She guessed that the thirty to forty seats in the room were easily a couple dozen shy of what was needed.

Since she wasn't in a rush, for once, she took a place in line in front of the receptionists' window and waited to drop off her file. She didn't mind hanging out here; standing in a room full of colds and sprained wrists practically felt like a vacation, compared to her normal life.

She looked down and smiled at a little redheaded boy standing in front of her. He hid behind what was probably his mother's leg and then peeked back out at her.

"Hi," she said.

He just kept smiling at her. She guessed he was about five or six, and she'd seen his brand of shyness a thousand times before.

She turned around and perused the room. Grandparents, parents, teenagers, and children talked and thumbed through year-old issues of *Time*, *National Geographic*, and *Highlights*. Over in the corner, a school of minnow-sized fish were gliding back and forth in an aquarium, casting a hypnotic spell upon a handful of onlookers.

There was a tap at her hip. A little girl, maybe a year older than the redhead, was looking up at her. She had thick, curly brown hair and matching brown eyes that did more than hint she wasn't quite feeling like herself. Her cheeks were red and raw, and Cheetos residue accented her chapped lips and runny nose.

"How did you get so pretty?" Macey asked.

"I dunno," the little girl said with a tiny voice and shrug. "I like your shoes," she went on, kneeling down and tapping on the light blue logo of Macey's brand-new Nikes.

"Why thank you, sweetheart. I just got them yesterday. I like yours too."

A large woman, wearing a Detroit Pistons sweatshirt, abandoned what appeared to be her two other children and hurried over to apologize for the little girl. "I am so sorry."

"No worries," Macey said. "She sure is a cutie."

"Thank you," the woman said. "She can be a handful, though."

The redhead came out from behind the other woman's leg. He was another cutie. Actually, all the kids in the clinic were cuties, but she hoped to never see any of them again. The boy stepped up next to her and pointed his little index finger at the girl and her mother as they walked away. "She has boogers in her nose."

"Alexander!" the woman said, turning around and picking him up. *Yep, that's his mother.*

"She *really* has boogers in her nose, Mom."

Macey quickly exchanged smiles with the mother, who shook her head in what seemed like a mild form of parental embarrassment. "They tell it like it is, don't they?" Macey said.

"Particularly this one," the woman answered, tugging on the bill of her son's ball cap. She looked like she was going to say something and then stopped.

"Our cross got hitted by thunder," the little boy said.

"What, sweetie?" Macey asked.

"He's talking about the storm last night," the mother said. "Do you mind if I ask you something?"

"Go for it," Macey said.

"How long does it take to become a nurse?"

"Oh, I'm not a nurse," Macey answered, holding up a manila folder. "I'm only down here dropping this off. But I think it's a little over four years."

"Thanks," the woman said. "I thought you looked a little bit young to be a nurse. My bad."

Macey was used to hearing that. She smiled back, knowing full well that with her ponytail and no makeup, she didn't look a day over eighteen. In fact, if she had a dollar for every time someone said they thought she looked too young, her student loan balance would probably be half what it was. Wearing the same comfortable, bright-orange scrubs the third-floor nurses would be wearing that day, she figured she probably *did* look a little bit young to be a nurse.

"It was on fire," the boy said. "I didn't see it, but it was."

"What was on fire? The cross?"

"Yeah," the mother said. "It's in front of our church. It kind of got hit by lightning."

"It got whacked in *half*," the boy said.

"A cross got hit by lightning?" Macey asked.

"And it smells funny," the boy added. "Mrs. Lindy says we can't 'ford to fix it."

"That's not her problem," the mother said. "Shh."

"It's okay," Macey said. "You know it's really none of my business, but the church's insurance will probably cover that. You should check."

"Yeah," the mother said. "We don't have many people at our church. We kind of don't have that much insurance anymore."

A cross they can't afford to fix? What were you thinking, God? I don't understand you. But one thing she *did* understand was not being able to afford things. *Been there, done that.*

"I want to help you fix it," Macey said. The words hadn't made it off her lips before she regretted them.

"Really?" the mother asked, a surprised look on her face.

No, not really. I don't have to be the one who fixes everything. I don't have the time, and wouldn't even begin to know how to help you.

"You can fix it?" the little redhead asked, his eyes lighting as if she were going to orchestrate a miracle for him.

"I'm not sure," she said, smiling, and not sure why it was impossible to say no. "Why don't we find out?"

DR. ZACH NORMAN LEANED OVER THE EDGE OF THE third-floor nurses' station and dropped a stack of folders on the desk. "Will someone please tell me when that noise is finally going to end?"

Kaitlyn knew his question was directed at her, sitting behind the nurses' desk, updating patient records by inputting notes from the rounds into the computer. "If I had to guess, Zach, I'd say the noise will stop when the job is finished." She paused for a few seconds, confident that it wasn't her sarcasm that bothered him. It was the fact that her eyes had never left the pile of charts. She could feel his irritation across the counter.

The noise that Zach referred to was created by the construction workers—working on the hospital's new $28-million administration wing. It was in its twenty-second of twenty-four scheduled months, and Kaitlyn knew that it had been the never-ending bane of the doctor's agitation—the relentless tapping and pounding of hammers, the humming and buzzing of dull saws and worn-out drills, and the painful screech of metal ladders unwillingly dragged from the steel beds of trucks.

"Seriously," he said, snapping his fingers and still waiting for her to look at him. She didn't. "How can you work with all that racket?"

"I ignore it. Try concentrating on your patients, Doc, and quit being so fussy. We've got a ward full of kids today. Let's think about them instead of you for a change, huh?"

Out of the corner of her eye, she saw him cross his arms. "You know, Kait," the doctor said under his breath as another nurse left the station, "I'm really not in the mood today. And by the way, in the halls, I think it's best if you refer to me as Dr. Norman."

"I apologize for questioning your authority, *Doctor*," Kaitlyn said. Her eyes left the chart, and she stared straight at him, exercising a greater authority only the two of them could understand. "If you want to play that way, in the *halls*, you can refer to me as Nurse Practitioner Harby."

He sighed, lifted his hands in surrender, and dropped his elbows on the counter. "Sorry. I've got a rippin' headache. Let's start over. Would you care to join me for lunch, Nurse Harby? My treat."

"I think I'll pass, *Doctor*," she said calmly, picking up the top chart again.

"C'mon, Kait," he sighed. "For Pete's sake, now we can't even go to lunch?"

"Looks that way."

"Isn't today pizza day?"

"Yep."

"You are turning down pizza day?"

She studied him. She knew she should steer clear of him, but she *was* starving and she did love the cafeteria's pizza. And she *had* been a little hard on him, if he had a headache. "Okay. Give me fifteen minutes to check on two patients and I'll join you."

KAITLYN WASN'T SURE WHICH DECISION WAS WORSE— hers to join Zach for lunch or the cafeteria's to serve green beans with pizza.

She rolled her eyes as he fidgeted with his napkin. Of course, pizza in itself was beneath "the great doctor." She watched as he took another bite of his salad before washing it down with a tidy sip of the four-dollar bottle of imported water that he had brought with him.

Everything was beneath Zach. Beneath him and his Mercedes convertible, his Rolex, his eight-thousand-square-foot house, and his seven-figure brokerage account.

It was going to be impossible for her to get through this lunch without explaining for the umpteenth time what had happened to *them* and why she didn't want to be with him anymore.

Though her answer would never change, the way he asked the question always did.

"Do you know how many women out there would be interested in what I have to offer?" he asked.

"Sounds like you already know the answer," she said, peeling little chunks of green pepper off her second slice of pizza. "I'm sure there are way too many to count."

"For crying out loud," the doctor said. "I should just give up."

"That would likely be a good idea."

"Kaitlyn," he whispered loudly. "Just tell me."

"Tell you what?"

His fingers drummed anxiously along the side of his water bottle. "Tell me what I have to do to make you happy. Tell me and I'll do it."

"That was actually pretty good," she said matter-of-factly. "Have you been reading *Cosmo* or something?"

"Don't be ridiculous. C'mon, I'm trying here."

"I just find it interesting that you never even came close to asking me these things while we dated. You always—"

"Hi, kids!"

Kaitlyn was spared by Macey Lewis, who invited herself to join them for lunch.

"Am I interrupting anything?" Macey asked.

"Of course not," Kaitlyn said, offering a halfhearted smile and a subtle look of thanks for a job well done.

"Not at all," Zach added. Kaitlyn knew he was disappointed. There was no doubt in her mind that he would harass her about the intervention later.

"That's some fancy water there, Zach," Macey said, pointing at the plastic bottle. "I'm sure you can tell a *huge* difference between that and the cheap stuff us common folks drink."

"Actually, I can," he said. "You keep up the good work, and you'll be able to afford this stuff someday."

"I'm doing my best," Macey said. "I'm begging you to be patient with me, boss man."

Kaitlyn grinned. Macey was the only person at the hospital who would ever get away with talking to Zach like that. Even though he was the one in charge, he gave Macey all the space she needed on the pediatric floor for one simple reason—she was the most brilliant doctor any of them had ever seen.

"How about that *weather* last night?" Macey asked, squinting and tilting her head toward Zach.

The weather? Kaitlyn thought. Macey either asked a legitimate question or was trying to hint to Zach that it was better to talk about anything other than his relationship with Kait.

"I haven't seen anything like it in years," Zach said, taking the hint with a lift of his chin.

Macey leaned back in her chair. "I sat on my deck and watched the storm for around twenty minutes before I realized I had left the top off my Jeep." She laughed. "My car seat is soaked. I'll have wet-butt for two weeks."

"Wet-butt?" Zach repeated. "Real classy, Dr. Lewis."

"The news said that over half of Carlson lost power last night," Kaitlyn said.

"Lost power and produced one dead cross," Macey added.

"One dead cross?" Kaitlyn asked. "What do you mean?"

"Ran into some people this morning down at the free clinic. Lightning hit the cross at their church and literally cut it in two."

"God firebombs his own house?" Zach asked. He snickered and turned to Kaitlyn.

She didn't like that look. He was also doing his close-mouthed smile that she hated. Even though she only ever went to church for weddings, funerals, or Christmas Eve, her pleas for Zach to join her had gone unanswered. For Zach, science had somehow put God out of a job, so talking about faith was about as important to him as holding hands or sharing his true feelings.

She was glad their relationship was over.

"God didn't just firebomb it," Macey said. "He did it to people who can't afford to fix it either. Go figure."

"Their insurance should help them out on that," Zach said. "Unless Santa Claus is their agent."

"I told the woman the same thing," Macey said. "But it sounds like they don't have any insurance."

"What are they going to do?" Kaitlyn asked. "People are going to pull up to the church and see half a cross?"

"Not for long," Macey said. "We are going to help them."

Zach rolled his eyes. "How are you going to do that?"

"I haven't figured that out yet. I just know I need to help."

"Listen to me, guys," Zach said. "Work with me here on the God stuff."

Kaitlyn clenched her pant leg and held her breath. Zach's "work with me here" was his way of saying, *I'm right and about to prove it. If you disagree, you'll end up feeling pretty stupid.*

"Stop me when I say something you disagree with," Zach said. He pointed at Macey. "Let's say there was an *omniscient* and *loving* God."

"There is," Kaitlyn interjected.

"That *loving* God let that cross get hit by lightning, and he knew they couldn't afford it. So why are you fixing it if God wanted it to happen?" He turned and looked right at Kaitlyn. "Unless, of course, he's just a terrible shot." He laughed over his own joke.

"Maybe God wants us to step in. Fix it," Macey said. "It's a chance to show a kindness."

Zach let out a scoffing laugh. "Don't you have far bigger things to do, Macey? Like save a kid's life?"

Kaitlyn shook her head at him and placed her napkin neatly over the untouched green beans on her plate. "You have such incredible compassion, Zach. I've really missed it."

"What's that supposed to mean?" he asked, glancing between her and Macey. "You guys are missing my point that *God* lets bad things happen. Just look at things we wade through here at East Shore every single day. All I'm saying is if there is a God, he's a bully, I don't like him, and I don't want anything to do with him."

"If God's only a bully," Macey said, "why are you a doctor, cleaning up his messes? Why even do what you do?"

He sighed heavily, clearly growing uncomfortable with the conversation. "There is no God," he said with a shake of his head. "And I help sick kids get better for only one reason."

"Why is that?" Macey asked.

"Because I can."

Macey picked up his bottle of water and gave him a look that seemed to suggest she wasn't all that impressed with it. "Let me hit you with another worn-out question, and then I want to be done with religion for the day." She crossed her arms. "If there is no God, what happens to us when we die?"

"Yeah, Zach," Kaitlyn said, curious to hear his response.

"C'mon, guys," he said. "You're clearly not in the right mood for thoughtful dialogue."

"I want to hear your answer," Kaitlyn said, ignoring his attempt to exit the conversation just when it was getting good. "What will happen to *you* when *you* die, Zach?"

"It's simple," he said, giving her that irritating smile once again. "Remember what it was like before you were born?"

She squinted and looked at Macey, who shrugged. "Of course not."

He lowered his hands and tapped on the table. "Death is just like that."

Kaitlyn noticed that Macey did a little recoil from his answer. She also noticed how oddly quiet it had just become.

Macey tapped back at the table. "We are still going to help them fix that cross."

"Exactly who makes up *we*?" Zach asked.

"Me and whoever I round up," Macey answered, pointing her finger past him and Kaitlyn. "Maybe I can get some of them to help."

Outside the cafeteria window, a handful of construction workers were in the temporary parking lot, sitting in the bed and on the tailgate of a rusty old Ford F-150, laughing and eating their lunches.

"Oh please," Zach said. "Good luck with that."

"I'll help," Kaitlyn said.

"You guys are crazy," Zach said, rolling his eyes and then crossing his arms. His smile went away. "You are serious, aren't you?"

"Yes," Macey said.

"Why?" he asked. "Just tell me why. Don't we have enough to do around here?"

Kaitlyn took his arm and did her best to duplicate his irritating little smile. "Because we can. And if we have the power to help, and a need is presented, doesn't that require any doctor to step up?"

"Touché," he said wearily. He ran his hand along the side of his face and shook his head like he couldn't believe what he was about to say. "Count me in too."

✦ FIVE

L ater that afternoon, Macey sat alone in the quiet of a small laboratory. As she leaned in toward the room's only functional microscope, she was thinking about Zach's statements about death and God. He was wrong, and even though he was a jerk a lot of the time, a big part of her still felt sorry for him. *Such a hopeless, helpless stance, to try and go it alone . . .*

She raised her head and then gently rubbed her eyes before peering back through the lenses at the tiny specimen on the slide below.

The free clinic had ordered the tests, and a computerized whole blood cell counter had already generated the results that were sitting on her desk. Regardless, she still had to be sure.

Though she had yet to prove the machine inaccurate, it was of the utmost importance to her that she saw things for herself.

She held her breath and turned the slide slightly.

Maybe, just maybe, this is the time it will be wrong . . .

It didn't take her long to recognize what she didn't want to see.

Modern science wins again. Wishful thinking loses.

Macey quickly flicked off the microscope lamp and made her way out of the lab toward her small office just a few doors down the hall. She squinted against the harsh hallway lights and struggled to keep the pulse in her head from pounding in direct concert with each step she took.

Another migraine. She looked at her watch. It was only two fifteen, and what was already a long day ahead was about to get longer.

As she opened her office door, she immediately reached for the knob on the wall and turned the lights down. With a simple turn of her wrist, unbearable brightness became a soft, soothing, and therapeutic component of a routine she had developed over twenty years of trial and error at managing the pain. It normally began with dimming the lights, then massaging her temples, taking some medication, and finally putting a cold washcloth on her forehead.

With a little luck, she wouldn't vomit, and a potentially paralyzing headache would hopefully be manageable within three to four hours.

She looked up at the ceiling and tried to keep her head still as she slowly lowered herself into her chair at the desk in the corner of her office.

Macey closed her eyes and placed her hands over her face to slowly massage her temples with the pads of her thumbs. It wasn't helping much. Worse, her stomach was beginning to roll.

When she opened her eyes, she found herself looking directly at a blank calendar on the wall in front of her. The pulse in the back of her head was thickening into a series of hollow *thuds*.

Next to the calendar, on top of a black metal filing cabinet, were a few framed pictures of her and her friends having fun in what she considered to be the good old days: Parasailing a little too close to the coastline with Kimmy Miggs and Samantha in Key West. Skiing with Lauren and Lindsey in Park City; Lindsey was leading them into "the death chute," a two-story drop onto a fifty-degree slope. Bungee jumping alongside a waterfall with Keith, James, Matt, and Doddie in the Smoky Mountains.

Her eyes rested on the last one, a picture of her sitting in an "herbal" club in Amsterdam with the whole gang. She was surprised at how well she still remembered that vacation. They must have burned through a pound of weed that week.

Yep, those were the days when there was time for fun.

Those were the days when she had a life.

That was ten years and $140,000 in student loans ago.

One hundred and forty . . . grand.

Yikes.

Her headache was getting worse. She looked up at the ceiling, wondering if it was really all worth it. She gripped the side of her chair and then reached inside her purse to grab her container of migraine medicine. It felt too light, so she shook it.

It was empty.

"You have to be kidding me," she whispered, glancing at the small clock on the desk. The pharmacy was down on the first floor, and the headache would make the walk practically impossible. Slowly, she laid her arms out on the desk and put her head down on them.

There were four quick knocks at the door. She heard each one as a hammer to the head, but she hoped it was Kaitlyn's signature knock.

"Come in!" she called, immediately regretting raising her voice. It felt like the back of her head was going to explode.

The door opened and then quickly shut.

"You are a savior," the doctor said. "I'm hoping you can run to the pharmacy for me—"

"Dr. Lewis?"

It was a man's voice.

She hastily lifted her head to see a strange man standing in her office. A construction worker, by appearances.

"Can I help you?" she asked, trying not to appear overly startled. And hoping she wouldn't vomit in front of him.

"Actually," he said, "I was hoping to be able to help you." He gave her a small smile.

"Listen," she said sternly. She stood and crossed her arms. "I'm having kind of a rough day. Why are you here, and what do you want?"

The man stepped closer. "I was hoping to help," he said, pulling a folded piece of paper from his pocket.

"Help me with what?" she asked, frowning in irritation.

"With this," he said, holding up a sign.

40

NEED HELP WITH DAMAGED CROSS AT CHURCH
PLEASE SEE DR. MACEY LEWIS, 3RD FLOOR
PEDIATRICS, BETWEEN 7:00 A.M. AND 3:00 P.M.

A wave of relief ran through her, and she smiled thankfully. "Wow, that was fast! I just gave that sign to one of your superintendents after lunch. But shouldn't we leave the sign up? I was thinking we'd need a few guys—"

"I think I can handle it," he said, using a tone that suggested he was probably going to be the *only* volunteer. "I'm pretty good at this sort of thing."

"Sorry if I seemed rude," she said, finding herself oddly drawn to his green eyes. "I'm not feeling too well this afternoon."

"You weren't rude," he said.

She held out her hand to greet him. "I'm Macey Lewis."

"I'm Kenneth."

"I haven't even contacted the minister yet to let him know we'd like to help. I guess I wanted to see if I could gather a group first. You know, before I got his hopes up. So far I have two doctors and a nurse, which sounds like the beginning of a joke . . ."

He gave her a tender smile and lifted his hands. "And now someone with a little construction experience."

"I'm relieved," she said, nodding. "I'm going to contact the minister today and see when we can go over and take a look."

"Sounds good," he said.

Macey shrugged. "I'm not really sure how much I can pay you or what help me and my friends will be. We aren't exactly the hammer-and-saw types, but I guess it's all for a good cause."

"It's for the best cause," he said. "And you don't have to pay me. I *want* to help."

Macey wondered nervously for a second if maybe this guy was just a little too good to be true. She forced a grin and waited before slowly guiding him back toward the door. "I have to get back to work here, Kenneth. Is there a cell phone I can call once I have more specifics?"

"Actually, I don't use a cell phone," he said. "Would it be okay if I just stop by around three tomorrow?"

"That would be fine," she said. "I really appreciate this, Kenneth. Thanks so much for coming by right away."

"I guess I'll see you tomorrow, then," he said, realizing he was being asked to leave.

"Three o'clock," she said.

"I'll be here," he replied. "I hope you feel better."

She smiled politely and then went back and sat at her desk. She flipped open her appointment book to get the name and number of the woman who had told her about the cross. Macey's breath caught when she saw the name.

She blinked quickly and then squinted at the test results she'd just brought with her that were sitting next to the appointment book. A slight chill ran through her chest as the same name seemed to jump off both pages.

Brooke Thomas.

It appeared that she would be speaking with Brooke not once but at least twice over the next few days—once by phone and once again in person.

First, she'd call Brooke to make a plan to see about the damaged cross.

She picked up the test results from the whole blood cell count and looked at the name under "Parent/Guardian." She carefully laid it back on the desk.

She'd also be speaking with Brooke in person, along with Dr. Alisoni from the free clinic, to inform Brooke that her son, Alexander, had leukemia.

What a coincidence, she thought. She looked at the filing cabinet and once again at the pictures of her former life.

And then she glanced slowly back over at the test results and thought about a certain little redhead.

It was all worth it. The long hours. The debt. The headaches. *Kids like Alexander make it all worth it.*

She stood again, confidently snatched the empty pill container off the desk, and walked quickly out of the office to head down toward the pharmacy.

It wasn't until she got off the elevator at the first floor that she realized it.

She lifted her fingers to her temples, and then her palms slowly flattened against her cheeks. She turned around and stared curiously at the elevator door.

Her headache was gone.

✢ SIX

Even though it was a week into October, it was a surprisingly warm sixty-eight degrees. Brooke and Carla were sitting on top of a metal picnic table at Lakeside Metropark, looking across Lake Erie into Canada.

Charlie was down the bank in front of them, standing next to the water, his head teetering curiously to the left and right as he watched a handful of seagulls pace nervously back and forth along the shoreline. A light breeze came in off the lake and filtered quickly through the park, momentarily cooling the Indian summer day.

Alex was his usual arm's length from Charlie, preparing to unload two fistfuls of tiny pebbles into the water. His Detroit Tigers baseball cap was naturally on backward, and his red bangs hung straight across his forehead. Brooke watched him as he teased the dying waves inching toward him on the shore with the toe of his sneaker, getting as close as he could. He tapped Charlie on the side of the leg and pointed at a passing freighter before turning back to her.

"Look, Mom!" he yelled.

"I see it, Alex!"

"Where is it going?" he asked, saluting the ship as he shaded his eyes with his small hand.

"I don't know, baby," she answered. "Maybe Cleveland."

"Cleveland?" He looked at her like it was the first time he had ever heard that word.

"Yeah. It's a city in Ohio."

Alex sent the tiny stones in his fist flying into the lake, then quickly ran up the shallow bank. "Can we go on the swings?" he asked.

"You better hurry up," she answered, smiling and pointing over his head to Charlie, whose broad steps already had him half-way to the playground.

"Wait, Charlie!" Alex yelled, pushing off Brooke's leg before running enthusiastically toward the swings.

"Be careful, buddy!"

"I will!"

Alex eased into a slow-motion tiptoe about three steps before reaching Charlie. He turned around and smiled at Brooke and Carla, holding up a small index finger to his face in the *shh* position, as if requesting their silence.

"Last one there is an egg!" Alex shouted at the top of his lungs. He quickly bolted past the big man and raced toward the swings without realizing that he left the word *rotten* out of his announcement.

"Go, Alexander, go!" Brooke yelled, pumping her fist in the air.

Alex was no more than thirty feet past Charlie, running as hard as he could, when he fell flat on his face while attempting to run through a colorful pile of wet leaves. He appeared to bounce. He didn't make a sound.

Brooke's heart skipped a beat, and she and Carla both stood. Charlie never broke his stride as he reached down and scooped up Alex, along with what appeared to be half of the leaf pile, and hoisted him to the familiar perch of his broad shoulders. They had almost arrived at the swings when Charlie suddenly stopped and turned around. Alex was smiling from ear to ear as they walked all the way back to where he had fallen. Brooke laughed. Her son looked like a human leaf picker as Charlie hung him upside down by one leg to grab the baseball cap that had come off during his fall. Charlie brushed damp leaves off the boy, then set him on his shoulders again.

"Be careful, buddy," Brooke called, taking her seat again beside her friend.

"No need to worry about him with Charlie around," Carla said. "That man is like Alex's own guardian angel."

"Yeah," Brooke said, knowing exactly what Carla meant. "You're right."

Two older kids were already on the swings, and Brooke knew that Alex had probably given Charlie strict orders to make sure he swung the highest of all. As Charlie pushed, at the far end of each arc, the chains of his swing grew slack and the seat lurched. But her son was gloating and scoffing at the other boys' futile attempts to swing as high as he was.

"Not so high, Alexander!" Brooke yelled.

"It's okay, Brooke!" he shouted back, as if he believed that calling his mother by her first name would further impress his competition.

"Brooke?" Carla asked. "Did your little man just call you by your first name?"

"He thinks he's a comedian," Brooke answered. Alex had never called his mother by her first name before, and she was trying hard to prevent herself from laughing out loud when she yelled back to him. "What did you call me, Mr. Thomas?"

Alex's head quickly popped up, and he probably had no idea that he wasn't really in trouble, yet he still seemed to debate about his response. Brooke assumed it was his effort to save face with the other boys.

"Not so high, Charlie!" Brooke hollered.

As Alex swung back to where he would normally be pushed, a gigantic hand appeared across his waist and froze the swing mid-flight. When Charlie finally let go, Alex shook his head in obvious disappointment as he was left to his own swinging abilities, the older boys now easily passing him up.

"Thanks, big guy!" Brooke yelled to Charlie, who waved a massive arm that said *You're welcome.*

"Let's go for a little walk," Carla said. "I need to reflect."

"Reflect?" Brooke said. "You are such a dork."

Carla smiled. "C'mon, let's go."

"We'll be right down there!" Brooke shouted at Alex and Charlie, pointing to the shoreline. "You'll be able to see us! Yell if you need something!"

"Okay, Mom!" Alex yelled back. Despite looking exhausted as he swung frantically to keep up with the other boys, his voice sounded energized, happy.

Even with the warm weather, the lake smelled cold, and the Michigan autumn had hardened the sand, making their footsteps crunch beneath them as they made their way just a short distance down the shore. They walked for over a minute along the shoreline as Brooke waited patiently for Carla, who suddenly seemed like she had something on her mind. Maybe she was *reflecting*.

Carla uncrossed her arms and let them drop to her sides. "You ever wonder how that happens?"

"How what happens?"

"That," Carla said, pointing down in the sand in front of them.

Brooke laughed, and they stopped walking. Directly in front of them was one tennis shoe. It was waterlogged, coated in sand, and its size and faded light-blue Nike logo made it obvious that it had once belonged to a woman. Something about it looked familiar.

"How does just one shoe end up somewhere?"

"Maybe she thought that one went out of style," Brooke joked. She noticed that Carla didn't even come close to smiling. "Are you all right, Carla?"

"That guy at the bar," Carla sighed. "The more I think about him, the weirder it seems. It's like he could see right through me. He touched my arm, and . . . he just knew everything about me."

"I don't understand what you're saying."

"He just touched my arm. I couldn't move and then . . . I can't . . . I can't really explain it. I can't even begin to."

Brooke put her arm around Carla's shoulders, and they walked farther down the shoreline. They stopped for a moment and watched a flock of Canadian geese fly directly over their heads from the park out into the lake.

Carla lifted her left foot and jammed the heel of her shoe in the sand. She covered her ears with her hands and then dropped her arms to her sides in apparent frustration. "My life is a disaster."

"Well, not all of it," Brooke said, studying the mini-whitecaps that came and went in the lake like hundreds of blinking eyes. "You have me and Alex. The Lindys. A job." But her words sounded hollow in her own ears. Carla referred to the drinking. The men . . .

"I don't want to drink anymore," Carla blurted. "I'm not garbage, I don't want to be a bar whore, I'm not stupid, I'm not—"

"You are none of those things," Brooke said, painfully aware of how Carla's efforts to sleep her way into a better life seemed to take turns hammering her self-esteem to new lows. Still, *whore* was just too ugly of a word.

"Yes, I am."

"Who called you these things?" Brooke asked. She winced, quickly regretting the question. Many in Carla's life had called her those things—enough that her friend now believed them.

"I have a lot of rough edges," Carla said, stepping back from the water. She removed a white hooded sweatshirt she had wrapped around her waist and slowly pulled it over her head. "I've made a lot of mistakes, but I know I can do better. I just know it."

"We can both do better," Brooke said. "Mr. Mysterious didn't tell you this stuff, did he?"

"No."

"What's his name, by the way? He kind of looks like a 'Ryan' or a 'Blake.'"

"*Blake?*" Carla said, a smile creasing her lips that Brooke didn't expect. "You watch too much TV, you dope. I actually never got his name. He left about ten minutes after you did."

"All that in ten minutes?"

"It wasn't even ten minutes. I'm telling you that he came over, took my wrist, said a few things, put the apple down, and left."

"And he knew everything about you?"

"No, but it felt like it. He did know my name though."

"He heard us talking."

"I don't think so," Carla said. "Doesn't matter."

It does matter, Brooke thought. She could see something in Carla's eyes that didn't show up too often. It looked like hope, almost like she was on the verge of figuring out how to finally turn things around. If it was only ten minutes with Mr. Mysterious that had Carla wanting to do better, that had her *reflecting* on her life, Brooke didn't care what his name was. She was thankful and liked him.

"Let's do better together," Brooke said.

"Let's do it," Carla said. "I'm gonna quit drinking, not just cut back. And all the people that treat me like garbage . . . I'm not going to put up with it anymore."

"Forgive," Brooke said. "Didn't that guy tell you that? Maybe the people who treat you like garbage are the ones you need to forgive."

"It's not them," Carla said, kicking her toe at the sand. "I know he was talking about my dad."

Brooke closed her eyes. That guy at The Pilot Inn didn't know Carla from Adam, but Carla's father really *was* the one she needed to forgive. *Part of being a parent is making mistakes,* she thought. *But when you leave half your head splattered on a wall for your eleven-year-old daughter to find, it's kind of tough to say sorry.*

Carla said faintly, "The last thing my dad said to me was that he loved me." She paused, then shook her head, her mouth clamping shut. "You just don't do what he did to someone you love."

"Pray about it," Brooke said. "Ask God to help you forgive him."

Carla didn't say anything. She just pointed dolefully down the shoreline.

Charlie and Alex were throwing rocks into the lake. Though they were over fifty yards away, Brooke could still hear Alex laughing and making explosion noises as the rocks he threw hit the water.

As the two women walked quietly back down the shore, the sun moved behind the clouds, reminding Brooke that it was, indeed, still October. She glanced over at Carla and noticed a tear slowly weaving down the side of her friend's face. She took Carla by the sleeve of her sweatshirt and they stopped. "You're going to be okay, Carla."

"You think so?" Carla sniffed.

"I do," Brooke said, her voice holding the same promise and spark of hope that Carla's eyes did. For the first time in a long time, she felt good about Carla. Her declaration was a start. They hugged and started walking again.

Brooke heard Alex laughing. She looked up from the sand, and Charlie was holding him by one arm and one leg, twirling him around in circles from a height most kids would never experience. She smiled. *We're all going to be all right.*

Carla suddenly stopped and pointed down at the sand, only a few feet away from the Nike they had discovered earlier. "When did *that* get there?"

"I don't know. It wasn't here earlier, was it?" Brooke asked.

"No, it wasn't," Carla said. "It's a little creepy, isn't it?"

"A *little*? I'd call it a *lot* creepy."

A baby doll had washed up on the shore, and for some strange reason, Brooke couldn't take her eyes off of it. Most of its red hair had fallen out, and the lake water had stained dark circles around both of the doll's eyes. One eye had been pasted shut, and the other was half open, staring right at her.

"Hey," Carla said. She took Brooke's arm. "It's my turn to ask. Are *you* all right?"

"Yeah," Brooke answered as they started walking again. "I think so."

They took less than a dozen steps when Brooke stopped. She turned back around and looked at the doll. She couldn't stop herself from thinking about the little girl who'd lost it. And she wondered how long the little girl cried, knowing she would probably never see her baby again.

✣ SEVEN

Short-Term Delay
Long-Term Relief
Thank you for bearing with us as we grow.

Macey slowed down and glanced up at the sign. For a fleeting moment she found herself actually agreeing with Zach and his never-ending complaints.

The construction was a pain in the butt.

She looked past the sign into the fenced-in area that once served as the employees' parking lot and wondered if her old spot was even still in there. Maybe it was behind the cement truck, the tons of piled brick, the mounds of shredded plastic and paper, or one of the two mobile homes that now served as central command posts for the various superintendents. Any way she diced it, she had appreciated that parking space when she had it, and wished she had it back every day she had to park two football fields away.

She looked at her watch. The appointment with the construction worker was at three in her office, which was seventeen minutes ago. She shook her head and looked at herself in the rearview mirror.

"Macey Marie Lewis," she said, "you need some time off." Even the thought of a brisk walk made her tired.

She kept giving herself a no-nonsense, you-need-a-vacation look while finding a place to park in the back corner of the temporary lot. She opened the car door and called Kaitlyn. Her cell phone was tucked between her cheek and her shoulder as she carefully repositioned a clear plastic bag over the driver's seat of her black Jeep Laredo.

"Hang on a second, Kaitlyn. I'm adjusting the plastic bag on my seat."

"Uh-oh." The nurse laughed. "The dreaded wet-butt?"

"Not today, thanks to my elegant slipcover. Did you tell him I was running late?"

"Yes," Kaitlyn said.

"Can you tell him I'm in the parking lot and will be up there in five minutes?"

"I can't," Kaitlyn said. "He said he had to go and would try and stop by again."

"Okay," Macey said, walking past a group of huddled smokers and making her way through the revolving front doors of the hospital toward the elevators. "See you in a minute."

Macey closed her phone and exchanged grins with a glowing, red-eyed spider that hung loosely above her from a neatly shaped, white yarn web. The walls leading to the elevators were covered with confetti pumpkins, paper black cats, and a matching pair of plastic, one-toothed witches. The Halloween decor was oddly accented by the scent of roses funneling from the first-floor gift shop.

At the end of the hall, volunteer decorators from the Carlson Rotary had hung an ever-growing flock of tissue ghosts that appeared to swarm above the elevator doors.

She looked up and noticed the lit number 5 above each elevator door. She turned to a bald, overweight Rotary volunteer at his station. "Are the elevators stuck?"

"I think so," the man said, pulling out a pair of silver-rimmed glasses and putting them on. He squinted, his blue eyes looking up. "They've been like that for around fifteen minutes."

"Maintenance must have them all stopped there," Macey said. "It's a little strange they would do that right after visiting hours begin."

The man looked back at all the elevators, then wrapped a rubber band around a twirled piece of tissue, forming a ghost's head. He dropped it on the counter and shrugged. "Who knows what they're thinking."

"No biggie," she said. "I'll take the stairs like everybody else. I need the exercise." She flipped her cell phone open to check the time and then headed toward the door that led to the stairwell. Behind her, all four elevators simultaneously chimed.

"Here you go!" the bald man yelled, pointing at the elevators.

Macey turned around and walked back. "Gotta love that timing."

Four doors all opened at the same time. Each of the cars was empty.

"Take your pick," the man said, holding out an open palm to the four doors.

Macey stared hesitantly at the elevator in front of her before finally entering and pressing 3. She couldn't remember ever being the only person on an elevator at East Shore.

It felt strange.

It *was* strange.

She playfully waved at the smiling man, feeling like a kindergartener saying good-bye to her father from the bus on the first day of school. The doors closed, and the elevator went up.

She exited at the third floor and found herself turning around to watch the elevator doors close. *Something just happened,* she thought. *I don't know what it is, but something strange just happened.*

As she approached the nurses' station, Kaitlyn quickly put a phone call on hold and stood before pointing back over the doctor's head down the hallway. "He just walked back into the visiting room. Go to your office and let me bring him down there."

"Thanks, Kait," Macey said, forming the okay sign before turning around and heading back to her office.

She still had her coat on and was sitting at her desk when Zach came to the door.

"Knock, knock," he said.

"Come in," she said, waving him toward her without ever turning around. "Check this out, Zach."

He leaned over her shoulder, and she held up one of the copies of the map Kaitlyn had printed off, with directions to St. Thomas Church.

"Kaitlyn already told me about the little boy being a part of this cross business and also being a new patient," Zach said. "It's, uh, awkward."

"Awkward isn't the word," she said, shaking her head. "We are going to be working on the cross at their place on Sunday, and I'm going to be acting all happy-go-lucky while the mother won't have the faintest idea how sick her son is. Or that I'm going to be his doctor."

"Until the next morning," he said.

"When I was talking to her on the phone to arrange for our visit, she told me the clinic called and wanted them back Monday morning. You should have heard the worry in her voice."

"Of course."

Macey imagined them all working on the cross. *Hello, Miss Thomas, we are having so much fun working together today. By the way, your little boy has leukemia, but I won't be making it official until the morning, so just try to stay calm and pass me the hammer and saw.*

"I'm not going to say anything until Monday," she said.

"That's smart," Zach said. "And when they ask you why you didn't say anything the day before—*which they will*—tell them it's hospital procedure. Which it is." He pointed at her. "Remember that, Macey. *Hospital procedure.*"

There were a couple knocks on the open door, and the carpenter she had met was standing next to Kaitlyn. He was wearing a tattered white sweatshirt, faded jeans with a hole in the left knee, tan leather work boots, and an old peacoat.

"Hello, Dr. Lewis," he said. He crossed the room and shook her hand, then introduced himself to Zach. "I'm Kenneth."

"I'm Dr. Norman," Zach said, clearly uncomfortable with the carpenter. Macey knew he didn't want another man around Kaitlyn and figured Zach introducing himself as "Doctor" was better than locking horns or making his mark somewhere in her office.

She needed to dish out a quick apology. "I am so sorry I was late."

"No problem at all," the carpenter said. "It gave me a chance to visit an old friend of mine that's up on the fifth floor."

"Great," she said, briefly wondering about his friend. "We are going to meet at the church at eleven on Sunday. Will that work for you?"

"It's perfect," he said, pulling a folded sheet of paper out of his pocket. It was another copy of the map. "And my new friend here just gave me this. I'll be there."

She could practically hear the hair on the back of Zach's neck stand when the carpenter referenced his new friendship with Kaitlyn. She guessed Zach probably wasn't a big fan of the way Kaitlyn was looking at Kenneth either.

"Everyone appreciates what you are doing," Macey said. "The people from the church were thrilled to hear that you volunteered to help."

"And it was great of you to organize this," he said, pulling back the flap on his coat pocket to put the map back in. Macey caught a glimpse of what looked like an apple.

"None of us can save the whole world by ourselves," Zach said, "but we can at least try to do our own little part."

Kaitlyn rolled her eyes, obviously biting her tongue. Kenneth began to button up his coat. "I think I know what you mean, Dr. Norman."

Macey wasn't sure what it was about those light green eyes. Actually, it was something *behind* those eyes that drew her to him. Something innocent, yet powerful.

"Have I met you before, Kenneth?" she found herself asking. "I mean . . . other than my office yesterday, do I know you?"

"Not as well as I'd like you to know me."

She felt herself blushing and let out a little laugh. She wasn't sure how to take that.

Kenneth stepped forward and shook Zach's hand again and then hers. "I have to run, you guys. We will have that cross looking like new."

"I don't know," Macey said. "I think it's really bad."

He walked back to the door and turned around to say it again. "Like new."

"Like new," she echoed. She liked the way he said it, and something about him seemed pretty convincing. "Hey, if you believe it, Kenneth, I believe it."

"Sometimes that's all you have to do," he added.

"Do what?" Macey asked.

Kenneth didn't answer.

Macey waited. They all waited, just long enough for a strange silence to completely fill the room. The carpenter finally smiled at her, then shifted his eyes straight toward Zach. He was still staring at Zach when he finally answered.

"Only believe."

There was another uncomfortable pause, and Macey turned to Zach just in time to catch a fleeting glimpse of something she had never seen before. It certainly wasn't his light brown hair, which was neatly combed back. It wasn't his crisp white dress shirt. It was practically perfect—same as his red tie, black slacks, and six-hundred-dollar matching belt and shoes. But she had seen it, and knew exactly what it was.

Even though they were in her office, this was Zach's territory; nobody ever dared to try and push Zach Norman around at East Shore Community Hospital. Still, she knew he had just been rattled. And the carpenter had somehow done it with just two words.

She glanced over at Kaitlyn to see if she was picking up on the same thing. No dice. Her nurse friend was still looking at Kenneth like he was a movie star or something.

"See you guys on Sunday," Kenneth said. He did a quick little wave, took another long look at Zach, and then left.

Kaitlyn peeked out of the office, down the hallway, and ran her hand across the back of her neck. "I had the weirdest feeling standing next to him."

"Never would have guessed by the way you were gawking at him," Zach said.

"You're kidding me, right?" Kaitlyn asked. "You were gawking at him too. In fact, I've never seen you so speechless, Mr. 'Do Our Little Part to Save the World.' Spare me."

Zach finally uncrossed his arms and whirled his index finger in a little circle like he didn't want to listen to her. "He's too young for you."

"Whatever, Zach," Kaitlyn responded. "Seriously, though. I felt like a little kid next to him. And it had nothing to do with his looks, Zach."

Zach clapped his hands together and held them in front of his chest. "Listen, let's move beyond it. My alma mater is playing Wisconsin Saturday and I have killer seats. You guys want to go?"

"I didn't know the University of Control Freak had a football team," Kaitlyn responded. "But I couldn't go anyway. I think I'm covering Jo's shift."

"C'mon, guys," he said, gesturing toward Macey. "I was going to set you up with a buddy of mine from Detroit Medical. He's a prince."

"Sorry. I'm working too," Macey said. "I have to catch up on some stuff." She felt like she was *always* catching up on stuff.

"Catch up next week," he said. "Find somebody else to cover Jo's shift, Kait. The game will be fun."

"I can't, Zach," Macey said, honestly regretting it. *First chance at a date in two years and it's a double with a guy my BFF can't stand and his buddy. So much for that.*

"If I find someone for Jo, can you set me up with the prince, Zach?" Kaitlyn asked.

He gave her a frustrated sigh. "Are you telling me I should take someone else, then?"

"Hmm," Kaitlyn said. "With Macey out, wouldn't that make the prince available?"

"Come on, Kaitlyn," Zach replied, patting her on the shoulder. "You know I'm even better than some prince."

"Do I?"

"Of course," he said, grinning in a way that let Macey know the bulk of his feathers were back in order. "Who would take a prince over a king?"

✦ EIGHT

Next to the stove, the digital clock made its dinner-bell sound, letting Jim know it was 5:30 p.m. and time for supper at the Lindy house.

He finished drying his hands and leaned back against the kitchen sink. "The news said it's supposed to be a beautiful day tomorrow," he said.

"That's what I heard too," Shirley answered. "Midfifties and sunny."

"A perfect day, in my book," he said as Shirley wrapped her arms around his waist and leaned her head against him. There weren't many better feelings in the world.

"My best friend once told me something," Shirley said. Her cheek came off his chest, and he knew she was looking up at him. She nestled in again. "He told me every day is a perfect day if you just take the time to look."

"That's my girl," he said, smiling proudly. He leaned down and kissed the top of her head before resting his chin on it.

She lightly pinched his elbow. "Your wheels are turning, James Lindy. What is it?"

"How many people do you think our doctor friend is bringing with her tomorrow?"

"I don't know. Why are you asking?"

"Three others," Brooke said, walking into the kitchen. She had spent the last two hours cleaning the basement, and Jim knew her maternal stress and worry were in full bloom. There hadn't been a fifteen-minute span when he didn't hear her come up the stairs to check on Alex as he slept on the couch. "I think another doctor is coming, along with a nurse and a carpenter."

"So around nine of us altogether, then?" Jim asked.

"Something like that."

"Just curious," he said. "If you had to guess, how much do you think it would be for all of us to have lunch at The Pilot Inn?"

"I think we can afford that," Shirley said. "That'd be so nice."

"I'll chip in," Brooke said absently.

Jim knocked on the counter. He could tell she was distracted. "Stop worrying about Alex, Brooke. I promise you, he is going to be all right."

"Maybe." Brooke sighed. It sounded like she turned away. "You guys ate lunch at eleven?"

"A little earlier," Shirley answered. "Alex ate a little bit of his fried bologna sandwich and then went to lie down."

Brooke paused. "So he's been asleep for six hours? He hasn't slept like this during the day since he was a baby."

"Maybe he's going through a growth spurt," Shirley tried.

Brooke took a deep breath and quickly exhaled through her mouth, making a noticeably labored *huh* sound. "Something is wrong with him. I know it."

Jim felt Shirley let go of him. He guessed that she was hugging or putting an arm around Brooke before she said, "You're going to worry yourself sick. There's nothing to do until we know more."

"If it will make you feel better," Jim added, "maybe we can ask one of the doctors to have a quick look at him tomorrow."

"I just don't like it," Brooke said. "If everything's okay, why would they want to see him on Monday?"

"There could be a hundred reasons, many of them no big deal," Jim said.

"Right," Brooke said. "You're sure he'll be okay, Pastor Jim?"

"I wouldn't say it if I didn't believe it," he said.

"I'm sorry for being such a downer today," Brooke said.

It was Jim's turn to put his arm around her. "You are not being a downer. We are here for one another."

"Yes, we are," Shirley said. "And don't forget, we also have had a little bit of experience with a child who had some rough turns through hospitals. Do you know I couldn't hold Charlie until over a month after he was born?"

"No," Brooke said, her tone horrified. "That's terrible."

They never talked much about those early years. About the umbilical cord wrapping around Charlie's neck—depriving his brain of oxygen for a "detrimental" length of time. *Hypoxia.* Those were the two words Jim remembered most. *Hypoxia* and *detrimental.* And endless days, walking hospital hallways, feeling helpless . . .

Jim laced his fingers together and tilted his head toward Brooke. "Charlie wasn't supposed to live past age five. When he turned ten, we pretty much quit listening to the doctors, but not a day has gone by when we didn't thank God for our sweet son. Just remember God's in charge, Brooke. Alex is going to be fine."

"I can't imagine Charlie as a ten-year-old," Brooke said.

"That was twenty-eight years ago," Shirley said. "Heavens, where has the time gone?"

Jim shook his head and smiled. "Charlie was little then, at ten. A pip-squeak of a mere six feet in height."

Brooke laughed and Jim was glad for the sound of it. He hadn't heard her laugh in days.

"I don't know where I'd be without you," Brooke said. "Thanks, guys."

"We don't know where we would be without you and Alexander," Shirley said.

"I'm gonna wake Alex up," Brooke said. "By the way, Dr. Lewis said she hasn't been to church in years and is way overdue. She said she and her nurse friend may be coming to service in the morning."

"Praise God," Jim said. "That's certainly good news. I can barely wait to meet them."

BROOKE RETURNED TO THE LIVING ROOM AND SAT next to Alex, who was asleep on his stomach and facing the back of the couch. She slid her hand up under his shirt, and he seemed unusually warm and sticky. As she rubbed his back, tiny, pin-sized red dots appeared and disappeared on his skin in the shape of her hand. She looked over at Charlie, who was completely ignoring the television. He kept looking at Alex and then at her. Back to Alex, then back to her. It made her uncomfortable. *Something's wrong, isn't it, Charlie?*

"C'mon, Alex," she said. "Wake up, sweetheart. Shirley's going to make some mac and cheese for you." She rolled him over, and he squinted up at her. His red bangs were darkened in sweat, like a new paintbrush that had just been dipped in water.

"Where were you, Mom?" he asked faintly.

"I was at work this morning, buddy. When I got home, you were sleeping, Mr. Sleepyhead."

"Mr. Sleepyhead?" He giggled. "Where's Charlie?"

Charlie leaned over Brooke's shoulder, his eyes wide and worried, peeking at Alex. He smiled and nodded his approval, seeming to draw comfort from the fact that his friend was at last waking up.

Alex held up his hand, and Charlie high-fived him. He lowered his arm and rolled back over again. As if he would go back to sleep the second she let him.

"C'mon, buddy," Brooke urged.

"Pea butter samich too?" he asked, his eyes still closed.

Brooke managed a small laugh. "Peanut butter sandwich too. It's done, buddy, c'mon."

When they walked into the kitchen, Alex reached up and grabbed a cookie off a plate on the counter.

"Uh-uh, young man," Shirley said. "Not before dinner."

As Alex apologized and put the cookie back, Brooke nudged Shirley and said, "At least he's getting his appetite back."

"He's just fine," Shirley whispered. "Mark my words: growth spurt."

"I think you're right," Brooke said, watching Shirley empty the balance of the noodles into a bowl for Charlie. She then ran a knife through the center of five peanut butter sandwiches—four and one half for Charlie, and the final half for Alex.

Brooke took Alex's bowl and lightly tapped a few sprinkles of pepper on top of the macaroni and cheese and retrieved Alex's preferred eating utensil. He wouldn't dare eat his favorite meal with a fork, and he really didn't like pepper, but two-handing the Batman spoon and stirring the cheese and noodles until the little black specks disappeared had to be just as much fun as eating the food itself.

The five of them sat at the table and held hands. Pastor Jim cleared his throat. "Let's pray."

Brooke peeked at Alex, right next to her. His eyelids fluttered as he forced himself to keep his eyes closed. She gave his hand a little squeeze, and he squeezed it back. Sitting next to Alex was Charlie. Brooke looked down at the giant fist that held and covered her son's entire hand and forearm. She noticed how Charlie's thumb was almost as long as the space between Alex's wrist and elbow, then closed her eyes.

Pastor Jim thanked God for the food, their family, their health, and their visitors from the hospital who would be coming tomorrow.

The prayer ended, and Brooke opened her eyes.

"Pastor Jim," Alex said. "You have a boo-boo on your head."

Brooke noticed the scratched, marble-sized bump that was partially hidden near Pastor Jim's hairline, wondering how she'd missed it in the kitchen.

Shirley reached up and lightly touched her husband's forehead. "What happened?"

"Old track injury," he said, tapping his finger lightly on the bump. "Javelin catching."

Brooke laughed, causing Alex to giggle. Shirley didn't.

Pastor Jim leaned his head back. "It's funny. I don't know how many times I've tried it, but I just can't seem to walk into the garage with the garage door closed."

"Oh, honey," Shirley said sympathetically.

"It's all right," Pastor Jim said, grinning. "I'll most likely live. I thought I had left the garage door open. It must have swung shut."

"Uh-oh," Alex said.

"Oh, honey," Shirley said again.

"What is it, buddy?" Brooke asked, turning to Alex. His eyes were wide with a mixture of fear and excitement.

Blood was spilling out of his little nose.

✢ NINE

*Z*ach was in that room again.
    He was trapped.

She couldn't breathe.

He was running frantically back and forth on the cool white carpet.

He looked and looked but couldn't find her. Only he could save her. He was her only chance.

Time was running short. Time always ran short in that room.

At last, he could see her again in the window—that clear, thick, icy window.

Her face, that beautiful face.

Her hair slowly bounced and flowed freely around the top of her head and the sides of her chalk-white cheeks. Her face pressed against the window and slid slowly against it. Her eyes, her frightened blue eyes, blinked repeatedly in a desperate panic.

Her hand was gliding back and forth across the window. She knocked. She wanted to come into the room.

He placed his own hand over the outline of hers and watched her lips speak words he couldn't hear—words that no one could hear.

She pounded on the window. He pounded, clawed, and kicked at the window too, but it wouldn't open. It wouldn't break. He needed just a little more time.

She drifted back from the window, her form disappearing into the darkness beyond.

He screamed her name and popped up in his office chair.

Sweat rolled off his forehead and the sides of his neck as his heart knocked rudely at the inside of his chest.

The dream. The cursed dream.

It was back.

MACEY REMOVED HER LAB COAT AND HUNG IT ON THE wooden coatrack she had inherited with her office. Kaitlyn had already kicked off her tennis shoes and was sitting on the couch, her legs folded beneath her.

"I'm starving," the nurse said.

"Me too," Macey responded.

"I barely saw you today," Kaitlyn said, giving herself a foot massage. "You were a pretty busy girl for a Saturday. You really were catching up."

"Too busy to eat lunch."

Kaitlyn put her right shoe back on and began to massage her left foot. "Soup and salad down at the corner café with two huge Diet Cokes. What do you think?"

"Sounds perfect," Macey said. "Let's get out of here."

Zach was standing in the doorway with his arms crossed. The edge of his mouth tilted toward his right cheek as he lightly bit down on the inside of his lip. "Would you ladies like to join me for dinner?"

Kaitlyn put her other shoe back on. "Nice of you to knock, Zach."

"The door was open."

"What are you doing here?" Macey asked. "Your plans for the game fall through?"

"Yeah," Zach said, his tone vague. His eyes shifted to the window. "What do you say? Dinner? My treat?"

Macey looked over at Zach and wondered what he would do if she said yes and Kaitlyn said no, but he didn't look like he was in a joking mood. In fact, something seemed different about him. Today's dress shirt had a few unthinkable creases in it, and there was a small tuft of hair curling around the top of his right ear. She wasn't quite sure what was wrong, but the mighty Dr. Norman actually appeared to be having a bad day.

"You all right, Zach?" she asked.

He straightened up and frowned a little. "Yeah. Why?"

"You look a little gray."

"You do look a little pale," Kaitlyn added.

"I'm fine."

Kaitlyn leaned forward and crossed her arms. "Thank you for asking us for dinner, but we already made plans."

Macey flicked the desk lamp off and turned around. "But you are welcome to join us, Zach."

Kaitlyn smiled at him. "The corner café—your favorite."

Macey grinned at Kaitlyn, knowing that the odds of Dr. Norman wanting to eat at the little run-down café were the same as him wanting to eat pizza in the cafeteria. Besides, it was rude of him to ask *them* to dinner when all three of them knew that he only really wanted to have dinner with Kaitlyn.

"I think I'll pass," he said. "What time are we meeting at the church tomorrow?"

"We decided to go to the service at ten," Macey said, suspecting Zach's motivation for going had probably expanded into keeping Kaitlyn away from the carpenter. "But we are going to start on the cross around eleven."

"Good," Zach said.

Macey grabbed her coat off of the rack and folded it over her arm. "What'd you do with your tickets to the game?"

"I gave them to Dr. Timmins," he said.

"I didn't think Jerry liked football," Macey said.

Zach shrugged. "I'm not sure if he likes football or not. The tickets weren't for him."

Kaitlyn stood and picked her own coat up off the other side of the couch. "I saw Dr. Timmins give the tickets to that cute little Mr. Springsted."

"That's right," Zach said.

"Oh," Macey said. "You mean that little old man security always chases out of the chapel after-hours?"

"That's him," Kaitlyn answered. "The one who used to buy his wife flowers every Friday and put them by her bedside."

"*Used* to buy?" Macey said sympathetically. "Oh no, that's terrible. I heard that she was in a coma for, what—six, eight weeks? Poor thing."

"Twenty-two weeks," Zach corrected.

Kaitlyn crossed her arms. "Mrs. Springsted was in a coma for twenty-two weeks and got flowers *every* Friday."

"Yeah?" Zach said, squinting at her.

"That's about twenty more times than I got flowers from my old boyfriend over three years."

"Well, it looks like Mr. Springsted doesn't have to buy them anymore."

"Zach!" Macey said. That statement was a little cold even for him. "That's awful!"

"What?" Zach asked. "What's awful?"

"Are you serious?" Macey puffed. "The poor woman is dead, for Pete's sake."

"What are you talking about?" Kaitlyn asked. "You really *were* busy today, weren't you? You didn't hear?"

"Hear what?"

"She didn't die," Zach said.

Kaitlyn took Macey by the arm. "Mrs. Springsted walked out of here yesterday."

"She *walked* out of here?"

Zach leaned against the doorway. "Her husband came to visit her yesterday, and she was sitting up in the bed when he walked in the room."

Macey grabbed her purse off her desk, went to the door, and waited for a punch line. "You guys are pulling my leg. After twenty-two weeks in a coma? That's impossible."

"Call it what you want," Kaitlyn said. "She walked out of here yesterday."

"Twenty-two weeks?" Macey asked again. "But her mind, her strength, the atrophy—it's impossible!"

"It happened," Kaitlyn said. "Carrie Armstrong told me that Mrs. Springsted was as sharp as a tack and walked as if she had just awakened from a little nap."

"It's amazing," Macey said, looking back and forth at them. They were telling the truth. She had never heard anything like it. "First thing Monday, I'm going up to Seven to hear the story from Dr. Timmins. I love stories like this."

"He doesn't work on Seven," Kaitlyn said. "He hasn't worked up there in a couple of months."

"What floor is he on now?"

Macey suddenly felt as if something had brushed against the hairs on the side of her neck. Thousands of goose bumps marched down her back and arms. She thought about that strange and lonely elevator ride and how she tried to figure out why maintenance would be working on the elevators during the busiest part of the day. She could still see the same lit number, frozen above all four doors before the elevators had come down to answer her call. She remembered getting off that elevator, feeling—no, not feeling, *knowing*—something had happened.

She knew, before they said it, which floor Mary Springsted was on when she came out of her twenty-two-week coma and went home. The floor Dr. Timmins worked.

She knew.

Five.

✦ TEN

Macey closed the passenger door of her Jeep and leaned over to check her hair in the cracked side-view mirror.

"Did you want the window rolled up?" Kaitlyn asked.

"Just leave it like it is."

The air was cool, and although a lazy fog stretched out over both the parking lot and most of the grounds of St. Thomas, the sun was starting to peek through the clouds behind them, hinting at a beautiful day ahead. The faint sound of a piano filtered through the damp air and down the hill from inside the small church. Macey threw her purse over her shoulder and walked around the front of the car.

"It starts in four minutes," she said, putting her coat on. "We better move it—and by the way, you look nice, Kait. Very churchy."

"Thanks, but I honestly can't remember the last time I was in church."

"It's been awhile for me too," Macey said, picking at a strip of pesky lint that clung to the arm of her coat. "I hope the building doesn't crumble when I walk in."

"You actually think Zach is going to show up here?"

"Trust me," Macey answered confidently. "He will be here. Particularly since I told him that you promised me that you would lighten up on him a little."

"You didn't tell him that," Kaitlyn said. "Shush."

A slight frost had glazed the lawn, and the air was sprinkled with the fresh scent of wet pine needles. The two women were making their way up the narrow walkway leading to the church when the cross emerged through the fog.

"Wow," Macey said, stopping and staring in disbelief. "How is anybody going to be able to fix that thing?"

The cross was history. Its bottom portion was now a dew-darkened, six-foot-high, splintered stump, looking like it still grabbed for what was once its upper half—like an arm that had been severed at the elbow.

Phantom limb, she thought, conceding that the cross was beyond repair.

Had she seen it earlier, she would never have volunteered to find someone to fix it. *It's impossible.* She studied the tiny drops of moisture that glistened like pieces of broken glass on the cross's top side that rested in the wet grass, serving as a temporary playground for three robins that chirped and pranced playfully around it. She studied the quickness of the birds' pipe-cleaner legs and figured maybe they were discussing their pending vacation south. *Vacation*, she thought. *I wish I could get away for just a few days . . .*

"It's ruined," Kaitlyn said. "To get that even presentable, let alone fixed, is going to take a serious fund-raising campaign. Maybe we could at least get this dragged out of here today."

"That's probably the best way to go," Macey said, shaking her head. "I'm going to buy them a new cross."

"I don't think anyone expects you to do that, Macey. C'mon."

"Hi, Dr. Lewis!" Brooke called from the front door of the church. She was wearing a cream-colored dress, a black cardigan sweater—the edges of which looked a bit frayed—and shoes that the doctor figured were reserved exclusively for Sundays. Brooke held the door open. "C'mon in, you guys; service is about to start. We'll see to that old cross later."

As they entered the church, Macey was overcome by a sense of quaintness and warmth. She couldn't help feeling *welcome*. Just being there felt right, and she was glad. Someone tapped her lightly on the shoulder, and she turned and witnessed the largest hand she had ever seen.

"This is Charlie Lindy," Brooke said. "He is Pastor Jim and Shirley's son."

Macey looked up—and then up some more—before quickly realizing that the largest hand she'd ever seen belonged to the largest man she'd ever seen. He was wearing a navy blue suit with a slight tear in the breast pocket, giant-sized white tennis shoes, and a dark gray clip-on tie that was slightly crooked and only came to the bottom of his ribs. She guessed his height at close to seven feet as her hand and wrist disappeared into his gentle handshake. His blue eyes blinked innocently as he tilted his enormous head, encouraging her and Kaitlyn to take two church bulletins from his other hand.

"Hello, big guy," she said. She found it difficult to break eye contact with him, knowing something was wrong with him and that she was unqualified to help him. It made her feel a little sad.

"Hi, Charlie," Kaitlyn added, looking up at him as he greeted them back with another quick nod of his head.

"Would you guys like to sit with us?" Brooke asked, pointing toward the second pew.

"Of course," Macey answered, quickly scanning the rest of the church. There were twelve to fifteen other people. Flowers were neatly tucked in vases beneath each stained glass window. Hymnals and Bibles were all straight and tidy in their compartments behind the pews. It was clear to her that these people were doing their best on a limited budget. No insurance, she remembered. Now it all made more sense.

As Brooke led them up the aisle, Macey noticed a tiny pair of eyes peeking over the edge of the pew. The little redhead slowly rose to his knees and leaned forward against the back of the bench to completely face them. He had on a short-sleeve dress shirt and a small, dark gray clip-on tie—a miniature replica of Charlie's. His short, red hair was gel-spiked and slightly brushed to the side. Those freckles that surrounded his nose bunched together as he instinctively smiled when he spotted his mother approaching. Macey could still see his name on the medical chart. *Alexander Robert Thomas.* Within twenty-four hours he would be her patient.

"Guys," Brooke whispered. "This is Dr. Lewis and her friend Kaitlyn."

"Hi!" Alex shouted.

"*Shh*, buddy," Brooke said, apologetically raising a finger to her lips.

"He is so cute," Kaitlyn said softly.

"That's my son, Alex," Brooke said, "and that's my friend Carla."

"Hi, everybody," Macey said, recognizing Carla from the visiting room. She was one of the people standing in front of the aquarium.

Brooke pointed to the piano. "That's Shirley, and Pastor Jim will be out in a minute."

The piano stopped playing, and everyone stood. Macey looked at Alex, and they exchanged playful grins before he took refuge behind his mother's leg.

Charlie came and joined them at the end of the pew. The music resumed with "I've Got a Friend in Jesus," a song that Macey remembered from her childhood. She and Kaitlyn opened the hymnals and each pretended to mouth the words, too embarrassed to have the other hear her voice. Macey secretly admired—maybe even envied—Carla's singing voice. It was lovely, in tune.

Kaitlyn nudged her, and they both looked at Charlie, who also held a hymnal and was swaying, not singing, along with the song. Alex continued to smile mischievously and stare both of them down before adjusting Charlie's hymnal. It was upside down.

As Pastor Jim came up the center aisle, Macey quickly realized where Charlie had gotten at least a portion of his height. She guessed that the minister was about six foot four, and she also admired how thin and clean-cut he was. He walked confidently in his white and burgundy robe while singing heartily in a deep baritone.

When Pastor Jim turned around and faced the gathering, Macey felt like a weight tugged on her heart. She could see his ravaged eyes from the second pew. He was clearly blind.

"Good morning, friends," he said, emitting a welcoming smile. "Please, let's greet one another."

She watched as he walked forward and to his left to the first pew and held out his hand. It was taken by an older man, likely in his seventies, and close to a foot shorter than the minister.

"Good morning, Alton," Pastor Jim said. He then turned his head to the frail, bluish-haired woman next to Alton. "Good morning, Pauline."

Macey felt as if she had made eye contact with him as he stepped back into the aisle and to the second row.

"Good morning," he said, "looking" right at her.

"Good morning," she said into sightless eyes.

"I'm Pastor Jim," he said kindly. "Thank you so much for being here today."

"Thanks for having us," she said, wondering how in the world he knew they were standing there. "I'm Macey Lewis, and with me is Kaitlyn Harby."

"Hello, Kaitlyn," he said, taking her hand as everyone else in the church appeared to be shaking a hand, saying hello, or hugging someone.

When Pastor Jim returned to the front of the church, Macey noticed him look at Shirley, who lightly tapped on what had to be the highest note on the piano. *She's letting him know that she's there.*

The minister nodded, then smiled at his wife before closing his eyes. "Let's pray."

During the prayer, Macey felt like she was breaking one of God's laws by looking around the church again. Bowed heads were absorbing the minister's words of hope, love, and thankfulness. Little Alex was leaning against Charlie. Brooke's hands kneaded the top of her thighs, as if anxious. Carla had her arms crossed and her legs were jittering nervously against each other. Macey looked back up toward the piano and at Shirley.

She also had her eyes open.

Macey watched the way the woman was looking at her husband as he neared the end of the prayer. She was fixed in admiration, soaking up every word he said, as if she *felt* each one. Shirley clearly loved her husband. They were the real deal. How long had it been since she'd witnessed such love and devotion?

The prayer ended, and Brooke went to the pulpit and started reading from Isaiah 53. Macey grabbed a Bible, but Brooke was done reading by the time either she or Kaitlyn could even find the book of Isaiah.

Carla stood. Apparently she was going to read something too.

Alex had recaptured Macey's attention with a bashful smile as he crossed his arms and leaned back to let his tiny legs dangle over the edge of the bench. She figured he wasn't used to seeing strangers at church, and when she winked at him, he unsuccessfully tried to wink back, closing both eyes.

Alex slid over in the pew and tapped Macey on the leg. "My grandpa and grandma are in heaven."

"So are mine," she whispered.

"Really?" he asked.

"Really," she said.

Carla went to the pulpit for the New Testament reading from Matthew 18. She cleared her throat and then read what appeared to be smoothly and confidently: "'Assuredly, I say to you, whatever you bind on earth will be bound in heaven, and whatever you loose on earth will be loosed in heaven. Again I say to you that if two of you agree on earth concerning anything that they ask, it will be done for them by My Father in heaven. For where two or three are gathered to—to—um—to . . .'" Carla stuttered and paused like she had a piece of dry clay stuck in her throat.

Macey glanced up at her. Carla had stepped back from the pulpit and had her head slightly lowered. Her arms were straight down at her sides, and she was looking out at the congregation like an ashamed little girl who had been reprimanded by her mother for not cleaning her room.

Macey ran her hand across the back of her neck and listened. *I can hear it.*

Pastor Jim had turned his head toward Carla, then toward

Shirley. Macey knew he had to be wondering what was going on, as did everyone else.

They can hear it too.

It was that strange and uncomfortable silence. The same one that was in her office the other day. It poured into the small church, surrounded them.

Kaitlyn nudged her and then nodded—not at Carla, but over at Brooke, whose pretty green eyes had lit up with a pleasant smile that dimpled her cheeks. She was looking behind them.

Macey turned around to see what Brooke was staring at.

It was the construction worker. He was sitting in the back row.

He was unshaven, dressed in work clothes, and sat perfectly still. He was leaning forward, resting his forearms on the back of the pew in front of him. But his eyes were only on Carla.

"Small world," Kaitlyn whispered. "Looks like our new friends already know one another."

"Yeah," Macey said, lifting her arm and giving the carpenter a subtle little wave hello.

Kenneth didn't even glance in her direction. He only gave what appeared to be a confidence-boosting nod of encouragement to Carla, and by the time Macey turned back around, Carla's voice had pierced through the silence in the room like a shot out of a cannon as she resumed the reading.

⌖ ELEVEN

S ure, Dr. Norman," the woman said. "I could probably swing by there to take a few pictures."

Zach held his phone to his ear as he sat in the parking lot of CC's Sporting Goods. The driver's side door of his three-week-old Mercedes was open, and he was relishing the new-car smell that seemed to be enhanced by the clean, fall air. He eyed the ruffled, white packing paper that was hanging out of an empty shoe box on the passenger's seat that read "Red Wing Shoes—Since 1905." As he wiggled his toes, he was pleasantly surprised at how good the boots felt, considering their affordable $76.70 price tag, which was almost $400 less than his previous footwear purchase.

"I think it would be great press for the hospital," he said, pulling the car door closed. "I can see it now on the front page of the *Carlson Herald* this coming Wednesday—'East Shore Professionals Nurse Cross Back to Health.'"

"That sounds pretty good," she said.

"Unless you can think of something better," he added, confident she couldn't.

"I think your idea sounds real good," she said. "I'll put something together for you."

"I would owe you big time," he responded, fully aware that he was playing a bit of a bully, but sometimes a guy had to be that way to get things done. He didn't mind playing the bigwig from East Shore, which happened to be the paper's largest advertiser. It had all kinds of perks.

"Okay," she said. "What time do you want me out there?"

Zach smiled and started the Mercedes. "Hang on a second, Shannon," he said, setting the phone down on the car seat. He just had to check it. He carefully listened and noticed that he could barely hear the car's engine. It was perfect. He picked up the phone. "Church ends at eleven. How about eleven thirty?"

"Okay, Dr. Norman."

"You're the greatest, Shannon. Thanks again."

"THIS GUY IS GOOD," KAITLYN WHISPERED AS PASTOR Jim's voice resonated throughout the small church toward the end of his sermon.

"Awesome," Dr. Lewis responded.

"I'm asking you to be thankful," Pastor Jim said, stepping out from behind the pulpit.

Macey glanced over at Charlie, who was giving a small piece of white candy or a mint to Alex. She watched the giant man squint at a tiny clear box that he held up in front of his face. *Tic Tacs*, she thought. *Those are Tic Tacs.*

"Be thankful," Pastor Jim repeated.

The way the minister said it actually had Macey *wanting* to be thankful.

She watched him pause as he slid his right foot carefully forward on the carpet, feeling for the top of the two steps, before he walked down in front of the first pew. The minister stopped and waited again before lifting his hands to close his sermon.

"Friends," he said, talking barely loud enough for everyone to hear. "I'm asking you to think about something. When you go home today, ask yourselves if maybe—just maybe—you spend too much time worrying about what you *don't* have, when you should be taking the opportunity to be thankful for what you *do* have." He smiled, then walked back up the steps and turned around.

Shirley began playing the piano, and the whole congregation stood.

"He is so right," Kaitlyn said.

"Yes, he is," Macey agreed, once again looking around the church. Old Alton had put his arm around Pauline, and most of the people were still nodding their heads in agreement with the message that the minister had delivered. She looked back at Pastor Jim and privately wished he could see the good he had just done.

"Zach's here," Kaitlyn said, holding up her cell phone. "He only texted me seven times. Good thing I had my phone on mute."

"I'll go out there and bring him in," Macey said.

"You gonna have cookies and punch?" a little voice said. It was Alex.

"You really have cookies?" Macey asked. "*And* punch?"

"Really," Alex answered. The little guy actually looked surprised that she was impressed with the menu.

"I gotta have some then," she said, reaching down for a high-five, which he gladly gave. "I'll be right back, but can you help me with something?"

"Help you with what?" he asked.

"Can you take my friend here to the cookies and make sure you guys save one for me?"

"There's a lot," he said. "Charlie can't even eat all them cookies." He scooted by her in the pew and held up his hand for Kaitlyn. "C'mon, I'll show you where the cookies are."

"You'll do that for me?" Kaitlyn asked, using the voice she reserved only for kids. She leaned over and took his hand. "Awesome!"

As Macey watched Alex lead Kaitlyn toward what looked like a small reception room, she thought about how much she loved that voice Kaitlyn had just used. How much she appreciated her friend. Kaitlyn did so much more than deliver medications, shots, and food that the kids didn't like. The kids loved Kaitlyn, and so did just about everybody at the hospital. All the staff on the third floor knew that she understood the difference between hope and hype, and that it wasn't uncommon for her to stick around after her shift had ended, normally to relieve tired parents who desperately needed an hour or so to go home and catch up on personal matters. They also knew that during some of those same hours, Kaitlyn had held the hands or stroked the heads of dying children, assuring them that they were not alone as they let go.

Brooke tapped her on the shoulder. "Did you enjoy the service, Dr. Lewis?"

"It was excellent," Macey answered, watching the carpenter dip into the reception area. "I'm so glad I came, and please call me Macey."

"Sorry about the little pause we had," Brooke said. "Me and Carla met that guy who was sitting in the back the other night. She was a little surprised to see him show up here at church, of all places."

"Is she all right? It looked like she regained her composure pretty well."

"I just talked to her," Brooke said. "She was laughing about it. She said she looked up and saw him sitting back there and freaked out a little bit."

"He is the carpenter volunteer from the hospital," Macey said. Somehow it relieved a little of the responsibility she felt over that irreparable cross out front. Kenneth wasn't just the guy she'd brought along to hopefully save the day; they knew him too.

"Seriously?" Brooke said. "What are the odds of that?"

"Speaking of volunteers," Macey said. "Excuse me while I run out and get the last one. He's outside."

"Okay," Brooke said. "See you in the fellowship hall and then we'll see what we are gonna do about the cross."

"Perfect," Macey said, heading toward the door.

She went outside, and Zach was leaning on the wooden handrail that led down to the parking lot.

"Looks like you dressed for the occasion, Zach," she said, glancing at her watch. "And you're here early to boot."

"Where is Kaitlyn?" he asked.

"She's inside."

"Is church over with?"

"Just ended," she answered. "Spiffy new boots there, Zach."

"Thanks, I just picked them up."

She looked at his designer jeans, which were neatly cuffed over the top of the boots. She also noticed how well they matched the gray Tommy Hilfiger sweatshirt that appeared to have never been worn. At the very least, it was a gallant effort on his part to resemble a man of manual labor. Regardless of what his intentions were for being there, she appreciated his efforts to actually show. "Thanks for coming, Zach."

"The newspaper will be here in about twenty minutes or so to take a few pictures," he said. "It will look good for us."

She shook her head as he walked up a few steps, blindsided by his news. "What's wrong with helping somebody just for the sake of helping, without telling the whole world about it?"

"Nothing," he said sharply. "But what's wrong with giving some credit where credit is due?"

"Credit?" she asked.

"Good PR for the hospital certainly wouldn't hurt us," he said, looking at the cross like a motorist who had slowed to gawk at a fatal car accident. "But whoa. Who are we trying to kid here? That thing is done."

She glanced again at the cross. The splintered pieces looked even more tattered and hopeless now that the morning dew had dried from its remains. The three robins were gone.

"Kenneth said they will have it looking like new," she said. "Remember?"

"Yeah. Right. It isn't going to happen."

"If not, I'm going to replace it."

"Whatever," he said indifferently. He sounded like he was having a bad morning.

They walked into the church, and Alex and Charlie were the only two left in the main sanctuary. Alex was jumping up and down behind the pulpit, and it looked like Charlie was putting hymnals back in place behind the pews. They both stopped what they were doing and looked back at the door.

"There's my patient," Macey murmured.

"Cute. But holy cow," Zach whispered back, staring at Charlie. "Will you look at the size of that guy beside him?"

"He doesn't speak. That's the minister's son."

Alex sprinted down the main aisle and put on his brakes in front of the two doctors. "Hi, Docca Lewis. Your friend is eating a cookie." He looked up at Zach and squinted his eyes. "You weren't at church."

"I'm sorry, buddy," Zach said, talking to Alex while staring up at Charlie.

Macey rested her hand on Alex's shoulder. "Alex, this is Dr. Norman. We work together."

Alex poked Zach on the leg. "My grandpa and grandma are in heaven." He pointed at Macey. "She already knows."

Zach didn't say anything, and Charlie's tie unclipped and fell softly to the ground. Zach picked it up and handed it back to him. Charlie smiled and slowly stuffed it into his pants pocket.

"C'mon," Alex said, poking again at Zach's leg and then quickly pulling his hands behind his back. "Even though you didn't go to church, I'll ask if *you* can have some cookies too."

Alex led them through a door in the side of the chapel into the reception room while Charlie followed. At the center of the room sat a folding table covered with a stained white tablecloth, a half-gallon can of Hawaiian Punch, and a plate of what had to be fifty chocolate chip cookies. The wall to their left was lined with metal folding chairs, while the opposite wall featured an old maroon couch accented by a scratched and faded coffee table.

They walked over toward Kaitlyn, who was standing in the far corner speaking with Kenneth.

"So there's my lady," Zach said.

"Ex-lady," Kaitlyn said, frowning in confusion.

What's that about? Macey wondered. *Trying to stake your claim, Doc?*

Zach nodded at Kenneth. "It appears we have our work cut out for us with that cross."

"I'm pretty sure we will get it straightened out," Kenneth said, opening his hand in the direction behind Zach and Kaitlyn. Pastor Jim and Shirley were approaching.

"Hello, friends," Pastor Jim said. "On behalf of the congregation of St. Thomas, welcome and thank you so much for being here today."

"I loved your sermon," Macey said.

"Why, praise God," he replied. "And thank you for your kind words."

"Thank *you*, James," Kenneth said. "Your words were from the heart. They were beautiful."

"You folks are too kind," the minister said, tilting his head curiously toward Kenneth.

"That's Kenneth," Macey said.

"Hello, Kenneth," Pastor Jim said. The minister was holding a Styrofoam cup of punch, and the short sip he took didn't take much of the curious look off his face. "It's funny for me to hear anyone call me James, with the exception of my wife. Around here, I'm mostly Pastor Jim."

Alex walked into the middle of the group, tugged quickly at Pastor Jim's pant leg, and pointed at Zach with his other hand. "Pastor Jim, that man wasn't at church. Can he still have some punch?"

"Why, of course he can." The minister laughed.

Alex looked up at Zach and pointed over at the cookies and punch as if he had just brokered a successful deal. "You can have punch if you want now."

Shirley ran her hand across the top of Alex's head as she looked at them. "I don't know what we would do without your help today. It's beautiful how people can help one another in times of need."

"Yes," Pastor Jim agreed, lifting his hands. "'Bear one another's burdens, and so fulfill the law of Christ.'"

"Sounds like that's from the Bible," Kaitlyn said, as if she were both asking a question and giving the answer.

"Galatians 6:2," Kenneth said.

"Yes, it is, and yes, it is," Pastor Jim said, nodding and smiling. "Somebody knows the Bible pretty well to get the chapter and verse on that one. I'm really impressed."

"Let's hope he knows as much about carpentry as he does the Bible," Zach whispered.

"He'll give it a go," Macey said, taking a bite out of a cookie and glancing over toward the punch table at Brooke and Carla. They were whispering to each other, and she had no doubt who it was about. It was clear that Pastor Jim wasn't the only one who was impressed with green-eyed Kenneth. "And if he can't fix it, we'll be here to help make it right."

✦ TWELVE

T hanks, Shannon," Zach said, handing the *Carlson Herald*
reporter a bill from his pocket, folded in a small square. "I
wanted to give you this."

"What's this for?" She stared at it in confusion.

"Something to show my appreciation for you coming out on
such short notice." *As in, a hundred bucks' worth of appreciation.*
"Make it look real good, Shannon."

"I can't take this," she said. "I'll make the article look good
anyway."

"Call it a tip. Take it," Zach said, glancing over at the cross. It
didn't really matter that they hadn't even started on it yet, let alone
had absolutely no chance of fixing it. What did matter was that he
looked pretty good in the group picture she had taken and it was
great press for the hospital. He pointed at the bill in her hand and
nodded. "I insist you have that. I'm sure you had other plans for
your Sunday morning."

"Well, uh, okay. Thank you, Dr. Norman," she said, taking the
bill and pressing it into her front pants pocket.

"Let me know tomorrow how it's going to read," Zach said as
they walked down the steps toward the others, who were gathering around Kenneth's pickup truck. Shannon might have run the
story and picture without the tip, but he knew that now she'd feel
obligated to send him a draft to review. He smiled in satisfaction.

Kaitlyn put her hand on the top of the old Ford's tailgate. "My
brother drives an F-150 and loves it. Do you like yours, Kenneth?"

The carpenter closed the driver's side door and turned to her.

"It serves its purpose, Kaitlyn, but I don't see it making it through the winter."

Zach shot a quick glance into the back of the truck. He was a little surprised that it wasn't a complete mess. "Congratulations. This is the only pickup I've seen from the East Shore job that doesn't have a case of empty beer cans scattered in back."

"Not much of a beer drinker," Kenneth said, shrugging his shoulders.

"I'm going to need some of this stuff to do my deck in the spring," Macey said, pointing at four brand-new gallons of lacquer in the back corner of the truck bed. "That's a pretty big cross up there. Think we have enough?"

"We can always get more," Kenneth said. "Let's see what happens."

Zach watched Brooke sneak a long stare at Kenneth, who was smiling innocently over at Carla. There was something about that smile that made him really uncomfortable.

Brooke pointed toward the house and said to the women, "Let's move out, ladies."

"Where are you guys going?" Zach asked.

"We need to change," Kaitlyn answered. "It's gonna take all of us to move that cross."

Macey pointed to Pastor Jim and Charlie, who had changed clothes somewhere in the church and were walking toward them. "Looks like the men are ready to go, but you're welcome to join us at the house, Zach."

"Very funny."

"Try not to get your new boots dirty," Kaitlyn added, drawing a little laugh from Macey that he didn't like one bit. As the women left, the thought of jumping in his Mercedes and heading over to the club for a quick nine holes passed through his mind. It was a little too cool for golf, but he needed this grief like a hole in the head.

He walked around the back of the truck and turned to watch Kaitlyn walk across the lawn with the others.

"She's a nice lady, Dr. Norman," Kenneth said.

"She's with *me*, pal," he answered, not caring how it sounded. Kenneth was nowhere near as good-looking as he was, and Zach probably paid more taxes in a month than the carpenter made in a year. But there was something vaguely threatening about him. *Why?* Zach thought, puzzled.

"No worries, friend," Kenneth said, hands up. That little smile the carpenter had shared with Kaitlyn was back. *Maybe he's just waiting for the right chance to make a move on her . . .*

Pastor Jim and Charlie were standing to the side of the truck. Zach would much rather have taken them over to CC's for some new outfits instead of dinking around with the cross. The minister had on a pair of Wranglers that had to be ten years old, his white high-top Reebok tennis shoes were even older, and his Honolulu blue Detroit Lions sweatshirt had a bleach stain on it the size of a softball. The big guy had on gray cotton sweatpants with a matching top that could probably cover the hood of the Mercedes. His tennis shoes weren't quite as old as the minister's. *But probably a size twenty.*

"Charlie and I would like to do our part," Pastor Jim said.

"I wish I had more like you, James," Kenneth said.

"You wish you had more like me?" Pastor Jim asked. "More blind guys?"

"More willing hearts. And you see better than most."

Pastor Jim paused as if considering his words. "Are you a supervisor over at the construction site?"

"Something like that," the carpenter answered. "Let's get a few things out of the truck."

"Hey, Shirl," Jim said, turning around and putting his hands in his pockets. "Charlie and I—" He stopped and tilted his head toward his left shoulder and waited a few seconds. "She's not here, is she?"

"She went back to the house a few minutes before the rest of the women did, James."

"Yes, to change her clothes," the minister said humbly.

Kenneth took Charlie by his sleeve. "You, my Nephilim-like friend, will be a big help."

"What do you want me to do?" Zach asked.

"Can you grab this?" Kenneth asked, reaching into the truck bed and handing him a rolled-up extension cord.

"I certainly hope so," Zach answered, taking it.

"And this." Kenneth grinned, handing him a power saw to take in his other hand. It was a lot heavier than it looked.

He handed Pastor Jim a fifteen-foot piece of coiled rope and another extension cord. Kenneth guided Charlie to the side of the truck and pointed at a shovel, a pick, and a sledgehammer. He lightly touched Charlie's left hand, and Charlie reached down with it and scooped up all three by their handles. The carpenter then tapped on the end of a five-foot-long metal spike, which Charlie effortlessly grabbed with his other hand before stepping away from the truck.

Kenneth slammed the Ford's tailgate closed and grabbed a utility belt and buckled it around his waist. The four cans of lacquer were all that remained until Kenneth grabbed two in each hand by their handles.

"To the cross," Kenneth said, pointing in front of them.

"To the cross," Zach echoed as the four men made their way up the hill. He kind of liked how valiant it sounded.

ALEX SLID A CHAIR OVER TO THE KITCHEN WINDOW and was looking out at the men as they surrounded the cross. "Can I go outside, Mom?"

"Baby, you better stick with us for now," Brooke said, lifting him up and returning the chair to the table. "Do you guys want a cup of coffee before we head out?" she asked her guests.

Macey and Kaitlyn shared a glance. Shirley wasn't changed yet, so they had a few minutes. "A little caffeine would be perfect right now."

Brooke smiled. "It'll make us better workers. How do you take yours?"

"Cream and sugar would be great," Kaitlyn said.

"Black," Macey answered.

As Brooke poured, Macey quietly took in the friendliness of the décor in the small kitchen. There was a chipped cookie jar on the far counter, an ancient waffle maker that had seen plenty of use, two ceramic angels, and four stained pot holders with the word *Love* embroidered around the edges. A half dozen of what had to be Alex's crayon masterpieces hung on the front of the refrigerator, held firmly in place by an impressive collection of M&M-sized magnets. Most of the drawings featured the same two stick figures—one quite small with bright-red hair, and the other a huge one with an oversized head. On the other counter next to a stacked set of plastic bowls was a plaster of paris square with what looked like a man's handprint in it. Typed on a blank business card glued at the base of the handprint were the words CHARLES PAUL LINDY—AGE 9—LOUISE GIVENS ACADEMY.

"I love this kitchen," Macey said. "It's so homey."

"Me too," Brooke replied, lifting a white paper sack of sugar from a narrow pantry before struggling to tear off its top. It wasn't ripping properly.

"Let me help you with that," Kaitlyn said as she walked over to the sink. She glanced out the window and laughed, covering her mouth, forcing herself to stop. "Macey, come look at Zach."

Macey stood and went to the kitchen window. "When do you think Zach Norman last had a shovel in his hand?"

Carla joined them. "Is he your boyfriend?"

"Ex-boyfriend," Kaitlyn answered. "Things didn't quite work out. Is it that obvious?"

"Maybe a little," Carla said.

"Men," Shirley said, shaking her head as she entered the kitchen. "If that man had his head on straight, he'd make sure a cutie like you never got away."

Kaitlyn smiled and poured some sugar into the container Brooke brought over.

"Speaking of men," Macey said, "Brooke mentioned that you guys already knew Kenneth before today?"

"Sort of," Carla said, giving Brooke what Macey thought was a confused glance. "It was only for a few minutes, but our meeting was, uh, amazing, really. I've never met anyone like him. So I went a little brain-dead when he showed up today." Macey studied her—she wasn't acting enamored; more like she was simply trying to figure out exactly what happened when they met.

Kaitlyn sat back at the table. "It's funny you say that. I feel a little weird being around him, but in a good way. It's kind of hard to describe it."

Carla nodded. "He's not the most handsome guy in the world, but there is something about him that's just . . . *beautiful*."

"Here we go again," Brooke said, laughing.

"Mom says *I'm* handsome," Alex said.

"You sure are," Macey said.

"Yeah, I know," Alex said.

"You're also very modest," Shirley added, grimacing as she leaned forward in her seat to put on her other shoe. She slowly sat back up and smiled at Macey. "Dr. Lewis, you seem like a natural around kids."

"I work with kids every day, Shirley."

"Oh," Shirley said. "What kind of doctor are you?"

Kaitlyn pressed her tongue to the back of her front teeth and gave Macey a look that only could have meant, *You had to know this was coming.*

"I practice pediatric oncology and hematology."

Carla tried to help Shirley out. "That means she works on kids' rear ends."

Kaitlyn put her hand on top of Carla's. "Actually, that's *proctology*, Carla."

Carla covered her mouth. "Duh, what was I thinking?"

"That's okay," Macey said. "I help kids with cancer."

"And she's the best," Kaitlyn said.

"I don't know about that, but I do my best."

"That must be terrible," Carla said. "Working with sick kids like that."

"Actually, it's just the opposite. It's incredibly rewarding."

"I couldn't imagine that," Brooke said. "I mean, the stress of it all."

"What do you guys do?" Macey asked. The needle on her irony meter was buried all the way to the right as she began to mentally rehearse one of tomorrow's top questions from Brooke, which was certainly going to be, *Why didn't you tell me Alex was sick yesterday?* Suddenly, she was hoping they could wrap up things here in the kitchen and head back down to the cross.

Brooke tapped on the side of her coffee cup. "Me and Carla do nails. We work over at Clippers in the mall."

Shirley sipped at her coffee, and the steam left a thin film of fog on her glasses as she looked at Macey. "You look so young to be a doctor."

"I'm thirty-four," Macey said, "but I hear that quite a bit. Brooke thought I looked too young to be a nurse."

"That's not much older than we are," Carla said in admiration.

"I'm just glad I'm out of school and into my job," Macey added. "I love my job. There's nothing I'd rather be doing."

"That's like me. I really do like doing nails," Carla said, "but you won't see me pulling up here in a new Mercedes."

"Yeah, well, it'll be a long while before I can afford one of those either. Med school loans are my constant companion for a while."

"Med school loans and dealing with dying kids?" Carla said, shuddering. "No thank you. I don't know how you do it."

"Honey, let's not talk about kids with cancer," Shirley declared. "If we're all ready, maybe we should head back down to join the men . . ."

"I'm sorry," Carla said apologetically. "I probably shouldn't have said that."

"That's okay," Macey said.

Kaitlyn reached her hand out to Carla like a queen presenting it to be kissed. "What could you do with this nurse's nails, Carla?"

Dr. Lewis winked, thanking her nurse friend for changing the conversation, and then said, "Maybe we should head on down. They probably think we ditched them."

"Mom," Alex said.

All eyes moved to him and Macey's heart dropped. *Nosebleeds. Just one of the many signs of leukemia.*

JIM WISHED HE COULD BE OF MORE HELP.

He was standing next to Charlie, about ten feet from the cross, patiently listening to the men and the sounds of their shovels as they stabbed at the ground. All he had really done so far was listen in as Kenneth instructed Dr. Norman and Charlie.

It had been dry and windy since the big storm, and apparently the muck the cross had fallen into had hardened, leaving it stuck in the ground. As he understood things, it sounded like Kenneth and Dr. Norman had managed to get a makeshift noose under the very tip of what was once the top half of the cross. As soon as they could get their shovels under at least *some* of the wood that had become embedded in the soil to lift it, Kenneth would say something to him and he would have Charlie, who was hanging on to the other end of the rope, pull as hard as he could to drag it out of the way. It sounded like a good plan, and regardless if it worked or not, he was thankful for his new friends and their effort.

"This ground is hard as a rock," Dr. Norman said. "And I still don't see how we are going to get these halves of the cross to stay together, once we get it upright."

This clearly wasn't the doctor's cup of tea, but God bless him for being here. Perhaps some words of encouragement would be one way he could assist. "I'd like to offer something, if you don't mind," Jim said. "From the book of Mark."

"Go for it," Kenneth said.

Jim raised his right hand. "'For the earth yields crops by itself: first the blade, then the head, after that the full grain in the head.'"

"Good timing," Kenneth said. "Chapter four, verse twenty-eight."

"Man, you are sharp on the Scriptures," Jim said. "How long have you been a man of God?"

"Forever," the carpenter answered. "What does that verse from Mark mean to you, James?"

Jim wondered why Kenneth kept calling him James. He sort of liked it, and as he thought about his answer, he could smell Tic Tacs in Charlie's hand.

"I was taught that it asks us to focus on God's harvest and to enjoy the journey toward reaching our goals as much as finally reaching the goal itself. To me, it means to enjoy every moment of your life and to be thankful, because each second that you live is a gift from God."

"I like that interpretation, James."

"Thank you, Kenneth. It's nice to know the Scripture can make—"

"Ow!" someone cried, followed by what could only have been the sound of a shovel falling to the ground. "Man that hurt!"

"What happened?" Jim asked. "Are you all right?"

"I'm fine," Dr. Norman said, not sounding like it.

"Let me have a look at that hand," Kenneth said, followed by the sound of another shovel falling to the ground and a few footsteps.

"I'll live," Dr. Norman said.

"But you're bleeding," Kenneth said.

"It's okay," Dr. Norman insisted. "I'm the doctor here, sir."

"That you are," Kenneth said. "But you should still probably run over to the house and get that cleaned up."

"We have a first-aid box in the kitchen," Jim said. "How did you hurt yourself, Dr. Norman?"

"I tried jamming my shovel down," the doctor said. "And the only thing that moved was my palm down the wooden handle."

"I'm sorry," Jim said. "Got yourself a splinter, eh?"

"Pretty good sized," Dr. Norman said. "I am going to run over to the house real quick. Looks like the gals are still there."

"And two of them a doctor and nurse," Kenneth said, a smile in his voice. "I wager a man could find all the medical care he needs in the Lindy home today."

"I'll be right back," Dr. Norman said.

It became quiet without Dr. Norman around. Jim hoped that the man's hand wasn't hurt too badly; he needed those hands to make his living. *I trust you, Lord, to see to his healing.*

"Tell me when you want Charlie to pull," Jim said. "He's pretty strong. You know he could beat me at arm wrestling when he was eleven?"

"I'm sure he could," Kenneth said.

"Just say when," Jim said, turning his head to Charlie. "I know he wants to help too."

"Let's hang on a second here," Kenneth said. "I think we're going to try something different."

"Whatever you think is best," Jim said. The sound of the front door closing at the house echoed up the hill toward them. There were a few footsteps and someone took his arm.

"Ready to get this done, James?"

"Yes, sir."

"This shouldn't take long now."

"Really?" Jim asked, loving the young man's confidence. From what Shirley had described, he couldn't imagine this taking less than all day. "What do you want me and Charlie to do now?"

"You and Charlie may want to step back a little."

"Why is that?" Jim asked, feeling someone take him by the elbow.

"This way," Kenneth said, guiding him and Charlie back from the cross. "You guys ready?"

"Ready for what?" Jim asked. "What should we do?"

Kenneth didn't answer. Charlie was breathing faster.

From directly in front of them, Jim heard what sounded like small pieces of wood cracking, as if a large animal were walking across fallen branches in the distance on a quiet night in the woods.

Charlie gasped and put both his arms around him at the same time the noise stopped.

Jim sensed that Charlie was trying to protect him from something. "It's okay, son. It's okay."

"You guys all right over there?" Kenneth yelled.

"What was that noise?" Jim asked.

"Hang on!" Kenneth yelled. "James, why don't you and Charlie cover your ears? This will be done a little quicker than most expected."

"Do like this, Charlie," Jim said, holding a hand over each ear, showing his son what to do.

But Charlie wouldn't let go of him until he took Charlie's hands and put them over his ears for him.

The noise grew louder.

Jim could hear the stress of bending wood. It sounded like someone was pulling on or trying to break a thick limb off of a tree. "What is that?" he yelled, hanging on to Charlie.

Charlie grunted and then shrieked in terror at the first snap. Jim instinctively ducked and covered his head as if something were about to fall on them.

Snap! Crack! Snap! The wood seemed to cry out as the carpenter stretched, split, broke, and . . . *What is that sound?*

Charlie picked Jim up by the armpits and swiftly carried him back at least another thirty feet.

"Charlie!" he cried, alarmed at the panic in his child. "What is it, son? What are you doing?" Charlie trembled and breathed rapidly, almost in a pant. He knew Charlie was terrified, and there was no doubt in his mind that his son was desperately trying to shield him from something.

"What's going on?" he yelled. "Is Kenneth hurt?"

Charlie's grip burned into his arm as the final ear-piercing snap ripped through the air, followed by a quick series of muffled sounds that Jim couldn't identify. *There is a row of wooden cars, and someone is gently opening and closing their wooden doors—it is definitely wood joining wood. It almost sounds like someone is doing a huge jigsaw puzzle made of soft wooden pieces.* There was no more cracking, bending, pulling, snapping, or breaking.

Charlie was still shaking as silence enveloped them. Footsteps approached.

"Kenneth?" Jim asked. "What on earth was that?"

"*That* was your cross being repaired, James," Kenneth said.

"Repaired?" Jim sputtered. "It's *done*?"

"Good as new," Kenneth said.

Jim blinked, wishing, more than ever, that he could see. *Even a little bit, Lord.*

"Is Charlie okay?" he asked, still feeling the sting of Charlie's grip and the distinct smell of what he thought was urine.

"Something frightened him," Kenneth said calmly. "He had a little accident. But he's going to be fine. You both are."

"Oh," Jim said, realizing that Charlie had wet himself. What in the world . . . ? An accident? His son hadn't had an accident in thirty-four years. Numbly, he reached out a hand, found Charlie's shoulder, and patted it. "It's okay, son. It's okay."

KAITLYN WAS WRAPPING ZACH'S HAND WITH THE GAUZE that Shirley had retrieved from the hallway bathroom. "You're lucky this isn't worse, Zach."

"I didn't plan on it," he said with a flirty smile. "But maybe I would have, had I known it'd get you to hold my hand again."

"What's the prognosis on the cross, Doctor?" Shirley asked.

"I don't like to be the bearer of bad news, but I don't see us finishing today," Zach said. "With only a handful of tools and four cans of varnish—I don't know—even with all the tools in the world, I just don't see it. That lightning really did a number on it."

Shirley sipped at her coffee as a half-dozen lines stretched across her forehead. "It's okay. James knew it was bad. We are still extremely thankful that you'd even try to help."

Macey leaned against the table. "Shirley, I'll make sure the cross gets replaced. Nobody deserves it more than you guys."

"Oh, honey, thank you, but that's not your responsibility. What with those med school loans you mentioned—"

"Please. It'd be an honor to help," Macey said, imagining for a second that the two ceramic angels on the counter were looking at her. She noticed the unusual silence fill the room. It wasn't that uncomfortable silence, but a *good* silence.

Zach broke it. "I'll split the cost with you, Macey."

"We'll go thirds," Kaitlyn said.

Brooke stood up and hugged Shirley. "You know I don't have much, but what I have is for the cross."

"Me too," Carla said.

Zach seemingly saw his chance to floor the women, primarily Kaitlyn. "Ladies, forget it. I'm paying for the whole thing, and that's all there is to it." Macey could almost hear him wondering if it was tax-deductible as soon as the words were out of his mouth.

"Well, let's go see if we can salvage it before we start scouring the Internet for crosses," Macey said. "Everybody ready?"

"I think so," Shirley said, standing up and taking her cup to the kitchen sink. "Oh my word!"

"What is it?" Brooke asked.

"Thank you, but your kind offer won't be necessary!" Shirley said, leaning closer to the window. "Come look at it, Dr. Norman. It's beautiful!"

Kaitlyn reached her first and looked out the window. She glanced back at Zach. "Nice try, Zach."

"Nice try with what?"

"Why didn't you tell us the job was done?"

"What?"

Brooke and Carla were now looking out the small window too. "Looks pretty good to me," Brooke said.

Zach joined the others as they stared at the cross up on the hill. His mouth gaped, and he slowly parted the women and craned his head forward, his face only an inch from the glass. He swallowed audibly. "It's impossible."

"Right," Kaitlyn whispered as the rest of them quickly headed toward the front door.

"But . . . but . . . it's impossible!" Zach repeated, staggering back from the window before joining Macey at the door.

THE CARPENTER WAS PUTTING EQUIPMENT BACK INTO the truck when they all walked up. Charlie was sitting in the back of the truck with his legs hanging over the tailgate. He had a newspaper draped over his lap.

Pastor Jim hugged Shirley, and she kissed his cheek. "How does it look?" he asked excitedly.

"Magnificent," Shirley said. "It looks brand-new."

"Praise God," Pastor Jim said. "It must not have been as bad as I thought."

Kenneth took him by the arm. "Let's just let that last coat of finish dry, and it should be all set."

"Last coat?" Zach asked. "You didn't have time to put *one* coat on it."

"Tricks of the trade," Kenneth said.

Macey noticed that Zach couldn't take his eyes off the cross. "It—it's perfect!" he yelled. "You could not have possibly—"

"Yes, it is, Dr. Norman," Kenneth said, joining them.

Macey looked at Zach again, then up at the cross. As Shirley said, it was magnificent—standing high and shining in the sun as the wet lacquer provided the perfect finish.

"It's unreal," Brooke said.

Carla stepped forward and proudly said, "I had a feeling he would fix it."

"It's impossible what they did!" Zach muttered, almost complaining. He rambled halfway up the hill and stopped. He had a look on his face that Macey had never seen before. He looked crazy.

Brooke pointed at Charlie, who was walking toward the house. "Where's he going?"

Kenneth shrugged and then smiled. "His dad mentioned that we were all going to get burgers and fries when we were done. I think he's going to change."

"Let's get a close-up of the cross," Shirley said excitedly.

"Take me with you," Pastor Jim said.

"You guys did a great job, Kenneth," Macey said, her elbows up on the side of the truck, gazing up the hill in a bit of disbelief herself. *They really fixed it.*

"Thanks," Kenneth said, closing the tailgate on the truck, rattling the tools and the cans of lacquer as tiny flakes of rust from the bed fluttered to the ground.

Macey looked back up at the cross. It really was impeccable. She glanced over at Zach. The look on his face practically scared her. Zach could be obnoxious, but he wasn't crazy. The scent of lacquer drifted down the hill toward them, testifying to a fresh application. She looked back in the truck bed again—at the cans of finish.

She could hear Brooke, Carla, Shirley, Kaitlyn, and Pastor Jim celebrate as they walked up the hill to closely examine the risen cross, but she couldn't move.

She couldn't take her eyes off the seals on the cans—*all four of them.*

"Only believe, Macey Lewis," Kenneth said, throwing a tarp over the tools and cans of finish. "Remember?"

✦ FOURTEEN

All three TVs in the bar half of The Pilot Inn featured the four-and-one Detroit Lions leading the Green Bay Packers seventeen to seven in the third quarter. The Lions' unusually good start to the season had made Sundays at The Pilot a weekly party, and thousands of southeastern Michiganders were uttering three words that had never made sense in the same sentence before: *Super*, *Bowl*, and *Lions*.

"I don't ever remember it being so busy in here," Carla said, not sure if she spoke loud enough to be heard.

"Football is bad for my ears but good for my wallet," Kathy said, leaving the bar to lead them into the diner. "It makes up for the slow days." They walked through swinging doors and into a lighter, brighter rectangle of a room, devoid of TVs. Five of the booths were occupied, folks enjoying their lunch. The diner portion of The Pilot did a decent business, but not nearly what the bar did.

"I guess so," Carla said, watching the buxom, five-foot-ten, 195-pound woman effortlessly slide one table toward another so they could all sit in the center of the room, between the booths. Carla swore Kathy was part bull, and Carla had seen the friendly hostess/waitress/bartender turn into a bouncer several times when someone misbehaved at The Pilot, even knocking a man out cold with a single punch when he tried to skip out on his bill.

"Everybody watch their fingers," Kathy said, pushing together the last two tables and then pulling out an order pad. "Sorry about making you the center of attention," she said. "This is the best I can do with so many of you."

"This is perfect," Carla assured her, looking back at the swinging doors that led to the bar and wishing for a little rum and Coke.

"I want chicken strips," Alex said.

"We've got those, little man," Kathy answered. "And as you all know, we also have the best burgers in the state."

Brooke was giving her order when she handed Charlie a handful of quarters. Carla figured the big guy must have spotted the video games and remembered how much fun he had the last time he was here. Charlie stood and left the table with Alex at his heels.

Kaitlyn, Zach, and Macey were sitting with Brooke, and at the adjacent table, an empty seat was to the left of the carpenter, who sat across from Pastor Jim and Shirley. Carla decided to take it.

"This is fun!" Shirley said, surprisingly loud over the dim tune of Willie Nelson's "Always on My Mind" playing on the jukebox in the bar next door.

"Hey, Pastor Jim," Carla said, glad to see the Lindys out and having a good time. She pointed at Shirley. "Try to settle her down. We don't want to get kicked out of here."

Pastor Jim put his arm around Shirley and pulled her toward him. "If she gets kicked out, I may just try my luck around here with one of those other women next door."

Shirley smacked him playfully on his arm and shook her head.

Pastor Jim shifted in Kenneth's direction. "Just point me toward a keeper, Kenneth. Then watch me work."

Kenneth reached across the table and tapped Pastor Jim on his arm. "I think you already have a keeper, James."

"I guess I'll probably hang on to her," Pastor Jim said. "I'd be in the dark without her!"

"Not even close to your best blind joke," Carla said.

"Forgive me," he answered sheepishly, giving Shirley another squeeze.

Kenneth turned slightly toward Carla and spoke so low, only she could hear. "Can you forgive him?"

"It was only a joke," Carla said, tightly gripping the metal napkin holder in front of her. She could feel its cool touch in her palms as she angled it just right to see his reflection. "He makes blind jokes all the time. And by the way, you tripped me out when I looked up and saw you sitting in church."

"Look at me, Carla," Kenneth said.

She slowly turned her head toward him and found herself immediately locked into his clear green eyes. Soft and understanding. She could feel her abdomen tighten as the overwhelming feelings she had the other night returned. *He knows everything about me . . . and he's not talking about me forgiving Pastor Jim for his joke.*

"Can you take these for me, handsome?" Kathy asked, holding five standard bar glasses in her hands behind Kenneth.

Kenneth reached up and took the glasses without breaking eye contact with Carla. A memory flashed in her mind—her father standing in the doorway to her bedroom, smiling at her with such tender care. She remembered his last five words.

"I love you, baby girl."

Carla abruptly stood, looking toward Kenneth, but unable to see him any longer. Only her dad. "No, I can't forgive him," she mumbled. "And I never will."

MACEY WASN'T SURE WHAT TO MAKE OF THE WAY ZACH was behaving. He seemed listless, rising to stare at the historic pictures on the diner walls, as if they were the most intriguing things he'd seen all week. When he returned to the table, he was quiet, fiddling with his cheap napkin ring, making it spin. "You're sure quiet, Zach. You feeling okay?"

"I'm all right," he said.

"No, you're not," she said, leaning toward him so she could whisper. She shot a sidelong glance down the table to make sure no one else was paying attention. "Tell me, Zach. How did he fix it so fast?"

"Like the minister said, it must not have been as bad as we all thought."

She could tell that Zach didn't believe his own words. He was acting like a man who knew that ghosts didn't exist, trying to explain the ghost sitting right in front of him.

"You sure?" she asked.

"Yeah, I'm sure," he said, giving her a drawn and tired look. Not the physically exhausted sort of tired, but that expression normally reserved for people coming out of four-hour calculus exams. She knew that he couldn't rationalize what had happened.

"Zach," she said, trying to get him to focus.

He tilted his head as if he hoped she had an explanation. They stared at each other and seemed to silently agree that something unusual was going on.

Zach finally looked away. "It wasn't as bad as we thought," he said again. "There's no other explanation, Macey."

"I guess you're right," she conceded. He *was* right. There really was no other explanation. But it was destroyed. It looked so bad. *And, yes, ladies and gentlemen, let's not forget about those four cans of lacquer. Surely a weather-beaten, lightning-singed, fifteen-foot cross would soak in at least one of the cans.* She turned her head to find that Kenneth was staring right at her. And then he gave her a slow, knowing smile.

She quickly looked away at Alex and Charlie. Alex was standing on a chair in front of an arcade-type game at the end of the diner, methodically controlling the jaws of a tiny metal crane toward a specific prize. Charlie was looking back—*staring*, actually—at Kenneth. He seemed baffled—fearful?—maybe even awestruck by the carpenter. Charlie looked at Kenneth as if he were a magician who'd made an elephant disappear into thin air. Or took a completely destroyed cross—shredded, split, and burned by a lightning bolt—and made it brand new. Better than new—considering the layers of lacquer that magically covered the cross in a matter of minutes.

She turned her head back toward Kenneth, who was again

looking at her like he knew what she was thinking. *Nice work, Kenneth*, she thought. *His dad couldn't see you fix the cross, and he can't talk about it. Good one there, pal. Just who are you and what are you up to?*

BROOKE RETURNED FROM A VISIT TO THE RESTROOM, next door in the bar. "Guess who's here," she whispered to Carla.

"Don't even say it," Carla said, now playing the crane game, trying to nab the tiny stuffed tiger that Alex had missed—and was so sad about. He and Charlie had moved on to an ancient Pac-Man machine in the corner while Carla took a shot at it.

"I never even thought about him being here on a Sunday," Brooke said. "We should have known, with the Lions playing."

Carla sighed, lost her concentration and the tiger too. She turned toward her friend. "Is he drinking?"

"Has been for a while, from the looks of him." Brooke knew what Carla feared. Tim Shempner, Carla's ex-fiancé, was pretty good at losing his temper, and when he was drinking, he was one of the best. The innocent victims of his drunken bouts of anger were normally smaller and weaker targets, with his favorite one being Carla. When they were together, Carla showed up with a black eye or sporting suspicious bruises more times than Brooke cared to remember.

"Maybe you should get out of here," Brooke said. "Kathy wouldn't mind if you went through the kitchen. I'll bring you your burger."

"Did he see you walk through?"

"I hope not," Brooke said.

"I'm not going to let Shempner push me around anymore," Carla said. "Remember what I said at the park?"

Brooke looked back at Pastor Jim and Shirley, and then at the other table. "That's great, Carla, but the last thing we need today is a scene in front of everybody."

JIM WAS TRYING TO FIGURE OUT WHY ALL OLD DINERS seemed to smell the same, when he heard Shirley clear her throat.

"I'm amazed how good the cross looks, Kenneth. You certainly are gifted with tools. We never imagined it could be repaired so quickly."

"It's sometimes difficult to believe things," Kenneth said, "particularly when you don't see them with your own eyes."

"I don't know how we can ever repay you," Jim said.

"Your joy and gratefulness are thanks enough," he answered.

Jim smiled. "Where are you from, Kenneth, if you don't mind me asking?"

"A little bit of everywhere," Kenneth said.

Hmm, Jim thought. *A wanderer.* Times had been tough for many. Maybe Kenneth had had a difficult time holding a job and went wherever construction led him. Jim found himself hoping the hospital construction would keep him around for a good long while.

"It'd be nice if you could come to our harvest party on Saturday," Shirley said. "You'd be welcome to bring a date if you wanted."

Jim let out a little laugh. "Shirley, I'm sure the man has other plans for the weekend."

"I don't, actually. I'll be there," Kenneth said over the cheers of The Pilot Inn regulars next door. It sounded like Detroit kicked a field goal.

"Wonderful!" Shirley said. "That goes for you guys too!"

"What goes for us too?" He thought it was Kaitlyn speaking.

"We're having a harvest party this Saturday at the church," Shirley said. "Come if you don't already have plans. Kenneth is coming."

"Sounds like fun. I haven't been to a church party in ages." That was definitely Macey.

"Wonderful!" Shirley said again. There was nothing his wife liked better than a bunch of guests to look after.

"Maybe then we can have our friend tell us how he patched that cross up so fast," Macey said. "What do you think, Kenneth?"

"Maybe I will," Kenneth said. "I think Dr. Lewis is onto me, James."

Jim smiled. "Sometimes the Lord works in mysterious ways. Even through us!"

"He certainly does," Kenneth agreed.

"By the way," Jim said, "after the young lady from the newspaper took our picture, why didn't you give her your name? I was just curious."

Jim felt a warm hand on his shoulder and figured it was Kenneth. "'Take heed that you do not do your charitable deeds before men, to be seen by them. Otherwise you have no reward from your Father in heaven.'"

"Matthew 6:1," Jim said, recognizing the verse his men's group had just studied a couple of weeks ago. "A hard lesson for most of us." Hadn't he even enjoyed a flash of pride when he could identify the chapter and verse as easily as Kenneth seemed able to do? "We all like a little recognition. But good for you, for living it out."

"I had a feeling you'd get that verse," Kenneth said. "I'm thinking I can stump you with another though."

"Possibly," Jim said. He held up his hands and then pointed his index fingers at Kenneth. "But as Alex would say, bring it on."

"'Do not be afraid; only believe, and he will be made well.'"

"It's Luke 8:50," Jim said, not feeling prideful but fortunate. He'd been reading the Bible since he was about seven, and when he finally lost his sight for good, he ended up with a steel-trap memory and a braille Bible to boot. By the grace of God, he was pretty sure he'd memorized most of Scripture over the years, and even spotted something the carpenter had missed.

"If you don't mind me correcting you," Jim said, "the verse ends with '*she* will be made well.' I think you may have accidentally said '*he* will be made well.'"

"Tell her," Kenneth said. "It's very important that you remember that. *Please* don't forget to tell her."

"Tell who?" Jim asked, sitting back, confused.

"Tell her to only believe, and *he* will be made well."

"Tell who?" Jim repeated.

The carpenter remained stubbornly silent.

"A puzzle?" Jim asked, drumming his fingers on the table. "Something you want me to figure out on my own? I won't forget the verse, it's Luke 8:50. But who to tell?"

There was a little pause and then a warm hand took his wrist.

"Give it a day or so," Kenneth said. "I think you'll figure it out."

"WHAT DO YOU THINK YOU GUYS ARE GONNA BE FOR THE harvest party?" Carla asked. "We don't have much time to figure it out."

"Adults are dressing up too?" Kaitlyn asked. "I have no idea. After years of working with kids on the hospital ward, I have a few options. What are you going to be?"

"I haven't decided yet," Carla said. Most of her costumes were a little too suggestive to wear to a party at the Lindys'. She clearly remembered being here at The Pilot last Halloween . . . she just didn't remember where she woke up on November first.

"I'm going to be Dorothy from *The Wizard of Oz*," Brooke said. "Alex is gonna be the scarecrow, and Charlie is gonna be a big tin man."

"He is perfect for that!" Macey said, sitting up straight in her chair and taking a deep breath. Next to her, Zach was reaching into a bowl of Goldfish crackers with a pained expression.

"Look at me," Zach said. "I'm so hungry that now I'm eating this garbage."

Alex wedged himself between Macey and Zach and was staring at Zach. "Hey, mister," he said in his small voice while tugging on Zach's sleeve.

"Hey there, sport," Zach said.

Alex pointed at the small bowl of Goldfish crackers. "Why are you eating those?"

"It's a little snack before the food comes," Zach answered. "Want some?"

"No way," Alex said, pointing back at the half-filled bowl of tiny golden crackers. "Mom says there is pee on those goldfishies. People don't always wash their hands after going to the bathroom, and then they get pee on those."

Carla hid a smile.

"Alexander!" Brooke said.

"But you said that there—"

"Enough, Alexander! I'm sorry, Zach."

Zach choked down the ball of half-chewed pulp in his mouth. "It's all right," he said, picking up his glass of water. He studied the cleanliness of the glass and then took a drink.

Alex looked wide-eyed at Zach. "It's pretty gross, isn't it?"

Zach nodded his head in agreement and set his glass back down.

"Sorry about the wait, everybody!" Kathy said loudly, placing a huge tray of Pilot Burgers on the crease that brought the two tables together.

"Where is mine, Kaffy?" Alex asked.

Kathy put a plate of chicken strips in front of Alex to his delight. "And these are for you, Alex."

"No sauce for me," Alex said, lifting his hand to the stocky waitress the way a little Roman emperor would address his subjects.

"You can keep my sauce too," Macey said.

"Shall we join hands real quick before we eat?" Pastor Jim asked.

The nine joined hands all the way around both tables and Pastor Jim began the prayer.

"Lord, thank you for bringing us together today, and thank you for the additional blessing of new friends, and for showing us that regardless of what obstacles we face, we can come together and—"

"Well, if it isn't The Pilot bimbo!" someone called. The other customers in the diner immediately fell silent. Everyone in their party looked up to the swinging door as a drunk man weaved his way toward them. "Here I was thinking it was just your sweet little friend I saw, but no! You're in here hiding too!"

"Who the heck is that?" Zach whispered.

At the sound of Tim Shempner's voice, Carla felt like she'd just stepped out into the snow, barefoot.

Even most of the bar seemed to fall silent on the other side of the doors, with the exception of the televisions. Carla reluctantly looked up to see her ex, clearly drunk and walking aggressively toward their table. He wore a plaid shirt over a gray T-shirt, hanging over dirty jeans. It looked like he hadn't shaved in three days, and his grease-stained fingers were resting across his beer gut.

How did I ever think he was cute? Horror flooded her chest at the thought of what was about to come down. *Why didn't I go when Brooke suggested it? But I'm done, right? Done with putting up with stuff like this?*

Even though you couldn't smoke in the bar, a half-finished Newport hung out of his mouth, and when he arrived at the table, an inch of dirty gray ash broke off and fluttered down to the floor.

Carla stood, determined to hold her ground. "Not today, Tim. Go back, now. Back to the bar and leave us be."

"Only if you come with me," Shempner crooned. "Or are you gunning for one of these poor fools to buy you a rum and Coke so you'll go home with them?"

"Please, Tim," Carla said, turning in embarrassment to Pastor Jim and Kenneth, now standing.

Shempner dropped a heavy hand on Charlie's shoulder and then glared at Brooke. "Oh, lookie here, everybody. They brought the big retard with them today! The preacher's boy!"

Charlie reached in his pocket to seek the refuge of his Tic Tacs. He pulled them out and offered one to Shempner, who mindlessly slapped the container out of Charlie's hand, scattering little white pieces of candy across the table and floor.

Charlie stood to retrieve the small plastic container, and

Shempner grabbed his arm and squeezed it. "You stay put, boy! I didn't say you could leave! Sit down!" Charlie froze.

Shempner laughed then, so hard tears streamed from his eyes.

The rest of them remained silent. Pastor Jim took a step toward him. "Why are you doing this, Tim?"

"Shut up, fool." All trace of humor abruptly left his face. He looked savage, mean. A shiver ran down Carla's back. She recognized that face.

Kenneth calmly crossed his arms, drawing her attention. *Do something,* she thought. *Please, do something.*

Charlie turned cautiously toward the safety of Pastor Jim and Shirley. He smiled gratefully at the mere sight of their faces.

"Hey, retard!" Shempner screamed. "Are you deaf too, boy? I said, sit down!"

"Please, Tim," Carla pleaded. "Let's go outside and talk things over. C'mon . . ."

But Charlie spotted the tiny plastic top of his Tic Tac container on the floor directly behind Shempner. Excited by his discovery, he jerked forward, but before he could reach it, Shempner slapped him firmly across his left cheek.

Charlie stood straight up and covered his face with both hands. "No!" Alex screamed.

"He was coming after me!" Shempner cried. "I've got witnesses!"

Brooke stood. "No more, Tim!"

Shempner stepped closer to Charlie and lifted his hand, causing Charlie to flinch. Shempner then let out a crazy laugh and lowered his hand. "Turn the other cheek, preacher's boy!"

Pastor Jim started to step forward, but Kenneth grabbed him by the arm, bringing him to a stop.

Charlie held his hands over his face. He was trembling and peeking through his fingers down at Shempner.

Carla edged between them and slowly pulled Charlie's arms down. "Shh, shh," she soothed. "It's okay. I won't let him hurt you anymore, Charlie." He had a red handprint on the side of his face. Two tears slowly trickled down his cheeks.

Shempner let out a scoffing noise. "I should kick the tar out of both of you!" he screamed, stepping back toward Charlie.

"Just try, Tim!" Carla cried, turning to face him. "Just try, here, in front of all these witnesses you're so fond of noting. Hopefully it will land you in jail where you should be!"

"Why, you . . . ," he sneered, pulling back a fist.

"Twenty seconds, Tim! You have twenty seconds!"

It was Kathy. She barreled through the doors and came up behind Shempner, two-handing an aluminum baseball bat, waving its top back and forth as if she were waiting for a curveball. "You leave within fifteen seconds or I'll start playing T-ball with your head."

Kenneth took a step toward Shempner. "I think she means business, friend."

"Shut up. I'm not your friend."

"You are down to ten seconds, Tim," Kathy said.

"You gonna take this whore's side, Kathy? You know what she did to me."

"Five seconds," Kathy said, the barrel of the bat trembling. "Don't ever show your face in The Pilot again."

"If me and my buddies quit drinking at this dump, you would go out of business."

"I'll take that risk," Kathy said, lowering the bat. She stepped right up next to him and whispered something only Carla could hear. And after she finished, Shempner straightened, gave her a long look, then turned around and slammed through the saloon doors.

Kathy gave them all a self-satisfied smile. "Sorry about that, folks. I'll see that he doesn't return. Please, go back to your meal. It's getting cold."

Carla just stared at the saloon doors, wondering why she couldn't ever send Tim Shempner off like that. As Kathy walked away, the waitress's words played over in Carla's mind:

"Don't stay away forever, Tim. I'm begging you. You know who my friends are. Come back just one more time, and I promise that you'll walk funny for the rest of your life."

Carla could hear Alex crying. She turned and he was clinging to Charlie's leg. Charlie picked him up, and Alex kissed the man on his cheek and hugged him. "You okay, Charlie?" Alex asked.

Carla took Charlie's hand and looked up at him. "I am sorry he did that to you, Charlie." She reached up and wiped the tears from his cheek, feeling the weight of his pain and embarrassment, and then stroked Alex's arm. "It's okay, Alex. Charlie is all right."

But it felt anything but right. It was all wrong.

And it was all her fault. *All my fault. Is there nothing I don't screw up? What did Charlie ever do to hurt anybody? And little Alex . . .* Tears clogged her throat.

She looked down the table. As if it wasn't already horrifying enough, she was about to lose it, in front of everyone. The doctors, the nurse, Kenneth.

The carpenter stared into her eyes, but she quickly looked away. *Forgive him? Who? Tim? Not in this lifetime.*

Who was Kenneth to come here anyway? Judging her?

What right did he have?

THEY ATE QUIETLY AS THE PACKERS SCORED ON THE LAST play of the game to beat the Lions twenty-one to twenty. By the cheers, those in the bar had all but forgotten the drama next door.

"I'm sorry you had to see that," Shirley said to the others at the table. "Carla has had such trouble with him."

Jim noticed that Carla didn't respond. Was she offended by his wife's words?

"You all right, Carla?" he asked.

"She's still in the restroom with Brooke," Shirley said. He could hear the doctors and Kaitlyn talking in low tones at the end of the table.

"Oh, right," Jim said. "I'm thankful it didn't get any worse."

"It isn't your fault," Kenneth said. "And everybody is okay, including Charlie."

"Praise God," Jim said. "I've prayed for Tim before. I hope something happens to help him find his way."

"Hey, James," Kenneth said. "Let's let it go and try to enjoy the rest of this day. Let me see you smile. Remember that new cross."

He was right. They couldn't let evil overshadow the light of this amazing, grand day. Jim grinned and held out his hand, warmed when Kenneth took it. "I'm glad we met, friend. I feel like I've known you forever."

"I feel like I've known you forever too," the carpenter said. He paused, still holding his hand. "And, James, I need you to remember to do something."

"Oh, don't worry," Jim said. "You want me to tell someone about Luke 8:50."

"I'm not talking about 8:50 anymore," the carpenter said, pulling his hand away. "When it happens, promise me that you will never tell anyone about it."

"Tell them about what?"

"About 7:14."

"From which book?" Jim asked, hearing Carla and Brooke return to the table. He thought he could smell liquor and swallowed a wave of disappointment. Did the girls have to turn to liquor? Even when they'd faced hardship? He opened his mouth to say something at the same moment he felt Kenneth's warm hand wrap around his wrist once again.

"Give it a little time," the carpenter said, lightly squeezing his wrist before letting go. "I think you'll figure 7:14 out too."

✢ FIFTEEN

arla's head was pounding.

She turned over on the couch and opened her eyes. The living room in her small apartment was completely dark and silent. She could smell rum and the ashtray on the coffee table only a few feet away. *Please tell me I didn't start smoking again. I was doing so good.* That failure was quickly drowned out by sickening memories of The Pilot Inn.

Tim Shempner.

Charlie.

The carpenter.

Her father.

It can't get any worse. I can't take this anymore.

The booze was wearing off, and she vaguely remembered spilling what had been left in the bottle. Carla pulled her T-shirt up over her face, trying to forget what she'd been drinking to forget. The anger. The doubt. The shame.

She lowered the shirt, then gripped it again to pull it back up to her nose. It had a funny smell to it. Smoke, sweat, a man's cologne? Worse, it was the only thing she had on.

Was I with somebody last night? What am I doing on the couch?

Carla sat up—light-headed. Her throat was dry and she swallowed, licking her lips with a thick tongue soaked in liquor, smoke, and a hint of something that let her know she'd also gotten sick. She couldn't remember the apartment ever being this warm—what was the thermostat set at, ninety?—and she wiped the sweat off her neck. She heard a clanking sound, followed by a toilet flushing.

Whoever he is, he's still here.

Her mind raced, trying to remember. She wanted a cigarette. Maybe there were some in her purse. She reached over on the table and there was nothing there. No purse, no table. She squinted in the darkness. She lifted her legs off the couch and put her feet on the floor. Something seemed different about the carpet.

Why is it so hot in here?

She stood and made her way across the floor, holding out her arms in front of her to protect herself, feeling for a wall, for anything. She angled toward the moonlight that was coming in from a window and stopped.

This isn't my apartment.

A light came on behind her and she turned around, startled. A skinny little girl, maybe around six or seven, was standing there. She was wearing a nightie and had straight blond hair.

"You need to go home. This is not your house."

"Sweetie," Carla said, staring in disbelief. She didn't have any idea where she was or who she came with. "Who else is here?"

The little girl pointed behind her to the hallway. "Just Daddy."

Daddy. Something about the way the girl said it stabbed Carla.

The little girl pointed and frowned. "Why are you wearing Daddy's shirt?"

Carla looked at the T-shirt she was wearing, then glanced over at the couch. It looked like she had used her coat as a pillow, and in the light cast from the bathroom, she could see that she had thrown up all over the armrest. Her jeans and underwear were on the floor.

"Mommy comes home from work right before I go to school. I'm telling her that you puked on the couch. That's bad."

"Your mommy lives here?" Carla asked. She felt like she was going to be sick again.

"You aren't supposed to kiss Daddy. I saw you. That's bad and I'm telling Mommy that too."

Not supposed to kiss Daddy.

Carla closed her eyes and thought about the carpenter. *He*

knows. He knows it all. She leaned toward the little girl and whispered, "Honey, please don't ever say—"

"You're not supposed to," the little girl repeated. "Only Mommy is supposed to kiss Daddy."

I know, Carla thought. *Only Mommy is supposed to kiss Daddy.*

"You are bad," the little girl said. "Go away."

Carla smiled at her and nodded. Her smile faded. This was it. It all had to end. The little girl was right.

I really am bad.

And I really need to go away.

MACEY KNOCKED AND WAITED WHILE STUDYING THE thick brass nameplate on the office door that read "Percival J. Timmins." She took a quick sip of her coffee and found herself wondering if there was anyone who had been at East Shore longer than Jerry Timmins. In his thirty-five years at the hospital, Timmins had established himself as a no-nonsense doctor; a straightforward, what-you-see-is-what-you-get human being; and a devout Christian. She liked him, as most people did.

The door opened and Timmins smiled. "C'mon in, Dr. Lewis."

"Hello, Jerry. Thanks for taking the time."

He glanced at his watch and then guided her to a chair that was angled to the side of his desk. "I'm usually not busy at this hour." He smiled again. "Zach Norman taking care of you down there on Three?"

"As well as can be expected. Zach actually called in—he isn't feeling well."

"Really?" Timmins said. "Our model of health called in sick? That's a first."

"Yes, it is."

"I'm gonna close this window," he said, walking swiftly toward the other side of the room and then cranking a small handle at the windowsill. "It feels like we're going to have an early winter."

"I'm still trying to figure out where summer went," Macey said, admiring the agility and speed that Timmins still possessed. She guessed him to be around five foot nine, 160 pounds, and he was still in what she thought to be excellent shape. Despite being sixty-six years old, he didn't have a gray hair on his head, and he kept that hair in a tight brush-cut, not unlike the one she assumed he had during his two tours as a medic in Vietnam, doing what he referred to as "patching up wounded teenagers."

She glanced around the office. The faint aroma of Lemon Pledge accented the spotless office that she already considered to be military-clean. Behind the desk she noticed a photo she'd not seen before of a handsome young man in a military officer's uniform. "West Point?" she asked, pointing at the photograph.

"Yes," Timmins answered. "That's Michael. That was taken about eight years ago."

"You must be proud."

"As proud as a father could ever be," Timmins said, pausing. "We lost him in Iraq."

Macey clenched her teeth and gave herself a swift internal kick for not remembering that Timmins had a son who'd been killed in action. "Oh, Jerry, I'm sorry."

"Don't be," he said calmly—almost too calmly, she thought. "Michael's with God."

"With God," she repeated.

"Yes," Timmins said. "You know, Macey, we don't always understand why, but certain things happen for a reason. Including what happened to Mary Springsted."

"Yes," Macey said, straightening up in her seat. "I mean— twenty-two weeks in a coma, and she just gets up and walks out?"

"Just like that," Timmins said, snapping his fingers crisply.

"But, Jerry, five months in a—"

"Just like that," he repeated. "Mr. Springsted walked into his wife's room around twenty minutes after visiting hours started and then immediately came running out, screaming like a madman, yelling for us to come. Carrie Armstrong and I rushed down there, and when we entered the room, little Mary Springsted was sitting up with her legs hanging over the edge of the bed." Timmins shrugged his shoulders and then crossed his arms. "It's that simple."

"Simple?" Macey chirped. "She was in a coma for five months. *Five* months."

"Mrs. Springsted was speaking with perfect clarity and said she wanted to get out of bed. Carrie and I asked her to lay back down so we could examine her, but she'd have none of it. She stood right up and looked at us like the suggestion of an exam was nuts. Why? Because she felt perfectly fine."

Macey tugged nervously at her ear. "That's absolutely unreal."

"Agreed. But I assure you, it was most real."

"But her mind . . . her muscles, the atrophy . . ."

"I know."

Macey sipped quickly at her coffee again. "Twenty-two weeks? It's impossible, isn't it?"

Timmins grabbed a peach-colored mug off of his desk that had the words "I love Grandpa" printed in dark blue letters on its side. "How about a warm-up?" he asked.

She handed Timmins her cup, and he walked toward a small kitchenette in the corner of the office. "And then there were the bedsores," he said.

"Bedsores? What about them?" She knew it was a chronic problem that doctors and nurses faced when treating comatose patients; the skin simply began to break down.

Timmins picked up the pot of coffee that was next to the sink and then immediately put it back down. "They were gone, Macey. Gone."

"What do you mean, they were gone?"

Timmins turned around and brought his hands to the sides of his face. He suddenly seemed uncomfortable. He took a deep breath, and his cheeks puffed out as he exhaled. "I'm telling you, Dr. Lewis, that we treated her bedsores every single day. And then came that day, the day she woke up. They simply weren't there anymore. They were gone."

Macey brought her hand to her chin, reminding herself of *The Thinker*. "Jerry—how do you explain it? What you are describing seems impossible."

"But it's not impossible. This isn't some secondhand story. The fact remains that it happened, and I *saw* it happen. Mrs. Springsted stood up, and her husband said they were leaving and that nobody was going to stop them."

"Keep going," Macey said, noticing an open Bible next to a magnifying glass on the desk.

"Mrs. Springsted finally agreed to let us take a look at her." Timmins paused for a few seconds and then shook his head again. "I really don't know what to say, Macey. She was fine—mentally and physically. As Carrie said, it was like she had just awakened from a short nap."

Macey blinked, slowly. She thought as highly of Carrie Armstrong as a nurse as she did about Kaitlyn. "Okay, Jerry, tell me—what is your medical explanation? What are you going to put in her file?"

"Explanation?" he said. "Well, it's not entirely unheard of for someone to come out of a five-month coma. You know that."

"I understand, but for her to *walk* out the same day? That's inexplicable, right?"

"In my thirty-five years, I've had six patients come out of comas longer than three months, and I've read about dozens of others. In each and every one of these cases, you're looking at months of physical therapy, and normally an equal—if not greater—amount of mental and emotional rehabilitation. I really don't believe that you will find a single documented case anywhere of someone just getting up and walking out the same day, let alone . . ."

"What?" she asked.

Timmins shifted in his chair. His brow was furrowed, as if he were deciding if she could handle the truth.

"Jerry?"

He looked her straight in the eye. "Let alone waking up in *better* physical condition than when they entered the hospital."

"Until Mary Springsted?"

"Exactly," the doctor said. "I'm telling you right now that Mary Springsted walked out of here not only in better shape than when she arrived, but in better shape than she had been in for over a decade."

"I don't know what to say," Macey said, leaning to the side of her chair. "How do you explain *that*?"

Timmins took a deep breath. "I believe that man—Mr. Springsted—was down on his knees at the chapel literally every single day, praying. He prayed and prayed, and then prayed some more that God would heal his wife." Timmins brought his hands together. "And I believe his prayer was answered."

"You really think that's what—"

"I *know* that's what happened."

Macey grinned, but she wasn't really sure why. "That *God* did it?"

"Yes," he said. "Another one of those unexplained parts of that plan we don't understand—that we can't understand."

Macey held her coffee with both hands and bit down lightly on her bottom lip. "I don't think I'd tell Zach Norman that, Jerry."

"Why not?"

"I'm not sure he would believe you."

Timmins nodded and then looked down in a way that she found peculiar. "Sometimes things happen to people, and they choose not to believe."

"What do you mean?"

"Let's just say if Zach asks, I'm still going to tell him what I believe really happened."

Macey got up and walked over to the window, catching herself trying to spot the old Ford pickup. "But *medically* speaking, what do you tell Zach?"

"Nothing different than I've told you. That there are things that are bigger than medicine—and as much as we docs hate to admit it, bigger than us." Timmins tilted his head, and the corner of his mouth rose. "Other than that, what happened to Mary

Springsted is impossible. There is no other explanation other than God."

Macey felt a wave of religious claustrophobia. It was all a bit much. "So, what is Mrs. Springsted's follow-up?"

Timmins smiled. "I'm sorry to impose my beliefs on you, Macey."

"That's not it, Jerry."

"The Springsteds said they'd think about coming back in on Wednesday to let us check Mrs. Springsted out, just to make sure everything is okay. But they won't be here."

"Why do you say that?"

"I think they agreed to Wednesday just so we wouldn't give them a hard time about leaving. But I'd be very surprised if they come back. Mrs. Springsted looked too good, and if you'd just lost five months to this place, would you be anxious to return?"

Macey smiled. "Probably not."

"Mr. Springsted looked like he was ready to burst at the seams, yelling and practically pushing us out of the way to dance his wife down the halls."

Macey looked at her watch. It was 7:57 a.m. "Jerry, I have to be at the free clinic in a few minutes. Plan on me bothering you some more about this."

"It was a pleasure having you up here, Dr. Lewis. Don't be such a stranger in the future."

"I won't," Macey said, standing and walking to the door before stopping to turn around. "Jerry, you said Mr. Springsted was yelling? After it was all over?"

Timmins grinned and held up his hands. "Yep."

"What was he yelling?"

"He kept saying that they didn't need to come back. That they didn't need doctors, nurses, medicines, and that they didn't even need the hospital. Mr. Springsted kept yelling that there was only one thing they needed to do—"

Macey could hear her name being called over the paging system at the same time Timmins finished speaking.

"That's me," she said. "I'm sorry, Jerry, I didn't catch what you said. What was the only thing Mr. Springsted said they needed to do?"

"Only believe," Timmins said.

Macey felt her throat close. The McDonald's cup slipped through her fingers. It was hard to breathe, and she felt her heart pounding at the walls of her chest.

All she could see was the carpenter's face.

"Are you all right?" Timmins asked, taking her by the elbow.

"I—I'm sorry," she said in a small, breathless voice, belatedly remembering she'd dropped her cup.

"Don't worry about it," Timmins said, patiently guiding her back to the chair.

She struggled to catch her breath and then leaned forward in the chair. She stood again and walked slowly over to the windowsill. Dr. Timmins was right.

"There are things that are bigger than medicine."

"Macey?" Timmins said softly. "What is it?"

She turned the handle until the window was a little over halfway open and took in a deep breath of cold air before looking hesitantly over at the new wing—and then slowly down at the parking lot. She knew he was out there somewhere. Right here at East Shore.

"And as much as we docs hate to admit it, bigger than us."

Timmins brought her a Dixie cup of water. "Here you go."

She took the water and was leaning against the windowsill as she heard her name being called again over the paging system. She could feel the sock on her left foot, soaked in coffee, uncomfortably sliding around the inside of her brand-new tennis shoe, and glanced down. The Nike logo on the shoe was now stained a dull coffee-brown. She didn't care. She glanced at her watch again. It was five minutes past eight when she was paged a third time to the free clinic.

Brooke and little Alex Thomas were waiting for her.

✢ SIXTEEN

Alex liked the fact that he didn't refer to his mother as *mommy* anymore.

After all, he thought that *mommy* was little-kid talk, and he was almost six—almost big enough to play with the big kids. He knew because his mother had not only told him that next year he'd be getting a lunch box with a thermos, but she'd also said that the big yellow school bus would be coming to get him in front of the house to go to first grade every single day except Saturdays and Sundays. For the *whole* day.

As he got older, there were more and more things that Alex learned about his mother, including what to not talk about. He had always done his best to avoid using words like *grandma*, *grandpa*, *dad*, and *father* around her because they seemed to make her sad. Sometimes there were other words that he thought put her in bad moods, like *money*, *laid off*, and *car payment*. But today he thought that there was a different one that was making her worry. The word was *list*.

Why would Mom worry about a list?

It didn't make sense to him. He thought lists were good. He knew it wasn't the shopping list Mrs. Lindy sometimes gave his mother when they went to the store and came back with food. And it sure wasn't the Christmas list like the one they made when his mother asked him what he wanted from Santa (even though he figured Santa must not have read the whole list). He knew that the list that was worrying her was different. It was special. The list was special because Dr. Alisoni said that a *special list* was coming and for them to all wait in this room until the *special list* came.

He didn't like it when his mother worried—and he could tell she was *really* worried. Her feet were tapping on the ground, she was pinching at her forehead, she was eating the ends of her fingers, and she also was asking Mrs. Lindy lots of questions he didn't understand. He had a plan to make her feel better, though. He'd found something he thought was cool, and he was going to distract her from thinking about the special list by showing it to her and making her laugh.

"Look, Mom!" he said excitedly, pressing his small foot down on a funny silver garbage can peddle, making its lid open and close. "I can make it talk! 'Hi, Mrs. Lindy,'" he said in a funny voice.

"Oh, you're good at that, Alexander," Mrs. Lindy said, sitting right next to Mom.

"Hey, Mom," Alex said, holding the lid open and looking curiously into the can at the trash inside. "How long before we can go home?"

"I'm not sure, baby," Mom answered, biting on her fingers again. "I'm worried, Shirley. What do you think it is?"

Mrs. Lindy blinked real slow and shook her head at Mom. "I don't know. Let's just see what the special list says, honey."

Mom rested her chin on her hand. "I can't understand a word Dr. Alisoni says. How am I going to decipher what a special list has to say?"

"Brooke, honey, just trust. God sees us here. He'll help us."

"But why even bring in a special list?" Mom said. She was making that worried face again.

Alex's foot came off the foot lever, causing the lid to clank heavily as it fell shut, and he moved over to a cool painting of a yellow-haired clown with big, square teeth who was getting lifted off the ground by a whole bunch of balloons. His eyes moved over to the next painting, and he took two big steps sideways to stand beneath it. "What's this say, Mom?" Alex asked, pointing at the words.

Mom didn't answer, but Mrs. Lindy did. "It says Norman Rockwell."

Alex figured the painting had to be done in what Mom called the *olden days*. In the painting he could see an old rocking chair with a blue seat. Next to the chair he could see a scale. Alex remembered that he weighed forty-six pounds now. In front of the scale there was an old-fashioned shoe and a big mitten on the floor. He thought they really looked funny, and he wouldn't want to wear them. Then there was the boy he guessed was around nine or ten, standing up on another chair and squinting at a piece of paper that was stuck on the wall. He didn't like the boy's T-shirt that didn't have sleeves on it, and he noticed that the boy's pants were pulled partly down and that he could see his—

"What the heck?" Alex said, laughing. "Hey, Mom! I see that kid's bare butt!"

"*Shh*," Mom said.

"It's right there in the picture! Look at it, Mom! His butt!"

"*Shh*, I see it, baby."

He knew why she didn't laugh. He was pretty sure it was that list. He looked back at the rest of the painting, and his head swiveled curiously back and forth as he studied it. There was a doctor in the painting who was tall, reminding him of Pastor Jim, but not as tall as Charlie—nobody was as tall as Charlie. The man was turned around and holding something in his hand. Alex looked closer at the man's hand. *What are you holding?* he thought. *A crayon? No, it's a pencil. No, a pen. No, it's—uh-oh . . .* Alex's eyes widened, and his stomach suddenly felt sickish.

"Are you okay, buddy?" Mom asked as Alex stutter-stepped back quickly from the painting. He didn't answer. He pointed frightfully at the picture.

"Alex?"

"Alexander?" Mrs. Lindy said.

"He has a shot, Mom! This is a *shot room*!"

"No, it's not, buddy," Mom said.

He continued to point at the painting in terror. "Mrs. Lindy! It's right there!"

"That's just a painting, Alexander," Mrs. Lindy said.

He removed his Tigers ball cap and rubbed his head nervously, still not quite sure how this couldn't be a shot room. "Are you *sure*?"

Shadows appeared under the door, followed by grown-up voices.

"Someone is here," Mrs. Lindy said.

"Come here and sit on my lap, silly," Mom said.

Alex skipped quickly to his mother, who picked him up and spun him around on her lap. She wrapped her arms around him, took his cap off, and lowered her chin softly to the top of his head.

"I want to go home," Alex said nervously, looking back at the shot doctor in the painting.

"We have to wait for the doctor," Mom said as someone knocked and then opened the door.

Dr. Alisoni walked into the room, followed by Kaitlyn, and then Dr. Lewis.

"Macey and Kaitlyn!" Mom said, tapping on Mrs. Lindy's arm. "Boy, am I glad to see your friendly faces." She nodded at Dr. Alisoni.

"Good morning, everybody," Dr. Lewis said, smiling in a way that Alex liked. "How did that cross look this morning? Still standing?"

"It looks perfect," Mom said. "Pastor Jim and I went out and touched it to do a reality check. It's hard to believe how good it looks."

"James can't wait for the congregation to see it," Mrs. Lindy added.

"It certainly is good news," Dr. Lewis said. Alex was looking at the doctor's feet, noticing that one shoe was a lot darker than the other. She kneeled in front of him and held out her hand for a high-five. "And a special hello to you, Mr. Alex."

"Hi, Docca Lewis," Alex said, grinning bashfully and smacking the doctor's open hand. "Mom says you guys are coming to the party Saturday. I like SweeTarts if you want to bring some."

"I could maybe bring some," Dr. Lewis said.

Alex wondered why nobody else was talking. He glanced over at Mom. She seemed worried again and was looking at Dr. Lewis. In fact, *all* the big people were looking at each other. It got *real* quiet.

"It's you, isn't it?" Mom said. "You're the special list?"

Dr. Lewis ran her hand through Alex's hair and stood. "Yes, I am."

Now nobody was talking and it got *super-duper* quiet.

"But didn't you say yesterday that you worked with kids who have—"

"Brooke," Dr. Alisoni interrupted. "Maybe we should—"

"Alex has it?" Mom asked. Alex squirmed out of her arms and stood up to look at her. Her chin was shaking real fast.

"Yes," Dr. Lewis said.

"You okay, Mom?" Alex asked. He was beginning to think he might have to get a shot after all.

Mrs. Lindy grabbed Mom's hand. "It's okay, honey."

"No. No, it isn't, Shirley."

"Please, Brooke, let's just see what Dr. Lewis has to say."

"Why didn't you . . ." Mom stopped talking and wiped her lips. She looked back up at Dr. Lewis, then down at Alex. "Why didn't you tell me this yesterday?"

"It would not have been appropriate, Brooke. And for that, I am sorry."

"Shirley," Kaitlyn said, "I'm really glad you are with us today. Maybe you and Alex wouldn't mind stepping into the next room with me for a little bit?"

"Certainly," Mrs. Lindy said. She put her hand on Mom's shoulder. "Brooke—"

"Not Alex," Mom whispered, looking down and then burying her face in her hands.

"Not me, what?" Alex said, really scared now. "I feel good, Mom. I don't want a shot."

Kaitlyn smiled and leaned down in front of Alex. "Hey, buddy, why don't you and Shirley follow me?"

"Am I going to get a shot in there?" Alex asked. *Maybe if I run when they open the door—*

"No, sir," she answered believably. "But let me tell you, there are some *really* fun things to do in there."

Alex looked at Kaitlyn and then back at Mom. "You okay, Mom?" he asked again, facing her and then plopping his hands on her knees when she just stared at the clown painting, her eyes wide and blank.

"Let's go," Mrs. Lindy said, gently taking his hand. "We'll be right next door, Brooke. It's okay, honey."

As Alex followed Mrs. Lindy and Kaitlyn out of the room, he watched his mother's mouth slowly move, but nothing was coming out. Her eyebrows looked funny and her bottom lip was starting to move real fast again like her chin. It *had to be* that special list. In fact, he knew it was, and it was dumb and he didn't like it. Not one bit.

DR. ALISONI STEPPED FORWARD TO KINDLY EXCUSE HIM-self in his best broken English. "Miss Thomas, Dr. Lewis tell me you meet her already before. I leave you now to let her discuss Alexander with you."

Brooke didn't say anything, and it seemed to her that Dr. Alisoni didn't walk out the door but melted through the wall. She wanted out of the room too—out of the bad dream. This couldn't possibly be happening.

Macey sat in the chair next to Brooke, who immediately stood, wanting to run away from it all. Brooke's heartbeat became a dull *thud*, a foreign body in her chest, distant, not her own. Her mouth felt like it was coated with windblown sand, and her legs wobbled like rubber garden hoses, unable to support her weight. As she collapsed back into the chair, she felt stuck—a trapped animal—glued to this room, this awful place, this now-soundless box of panic and horror. She was suffocating in the cruel moment, waiting to hear the actual words formally announcing that Alex had cancer.

"You said you worked with kids . . . who have . . . have cancer," she said, her words spilling out slowly. She already knew, but for some strange reason she found herself needing to hear it again. Hear it straight. "Does Alex . . . have cancer?"

Macey looked right at her. "Yes, he does, Brooke."

Brooke felt a cold finger tap lightly on her heart as she recoiled from the force of the answer. *Alex has cancer. My Alex. Alexander, my son, has cancer. Capricorn, Aquarius, Aries, and Cancer. Cancer. This is a nightmare happening right here and now. Please, God, not this . . . Cancer is for old people. Alex is only five. Only five!*

"Brooke . . . ," Macey said.

Brooke grabbed at her own pant legs and squeezed tightly. *Wake up,* she thought. *Please wake up, Brooke. This is really not happening—this terrible thing that you occasionally hear about. It's one of those awful things that happens to other people's children—not Alex.* She lifted her hands to her ears and could feel herself starting to shake. "Please, please, not Alex. What am I supposed to do? Please help him. Please help us."

Macey put her hand on Brooke's shoulder. "We will, Brooke."

"I can't believe this is happening," Brooke said. "Why am I not crying right now?"

"Brooke," Macey said, "I don't have children, so I can't fully understand what you are feeling. What I can tell you, though, is that you are going to have a lot of different feelings. This is new to you. This is a lot at once—and I know it is scary."

"Where?" Brooke asked. "Where is the cancer?"

"Alex has leukemia."

"Leukemia?" Brooke repeated faintly.

"Brooke, I'm telling you right now. We are going to beat this."

Leukemia? Brooke asked herself. *Yeah, Brooke. Leukemia. Just like in the sad movies, where the ending isn't always happy. Alex has leukemia.*

"Brooke, leukemia is—"

"Hang on a second," Brooke said, rubbing her eyes. She started to think about Alex's costume for Saturday's harvest party. He knew what he was going to be, but he didn't have his costume yet. He also didn't have a bike without training wheels permanently attached, his first baseball glove, or his first adult tooth. Alex did, however, have *leukemia*.

"Brooke, what are you thinking about right now?"

Brooke looked at the doctor. "Is he going to die?"

"When I said we are going to beat this, I meant it."

"I don't even understand what leukemia is."

"And Alex doesn't either," Macey said. "And he won't. But what he *will* understand is that he doesn't feel well during many parts of his treatment. And the way he feels is going to get a lot worse before it gets better. I saw firsthand the wonderful support group Alex has, and he is going to need all of us. And when I say us, I mean you, me, Pastor Jim, Shirley, definitely Charlie, Carla, and our whole pediatric oncology group here. Together, we *will* beat this."

Brooke stood and closed her eyes, turning away from Macey. *Why? Why? Why?*

It wasn't the first time she had asked herself what terrible thing she possibly could have done to deserve something like this. She couldn't stop herself from thinking about the past.

She was a little girl, not quite a year younger than Alex. It was the night that *home* had changed forever. The night a highly intoxicated police officer drove south on northbound I-75 into oncoming traffic. He walked away from the resulting accident physically unscathed.

Mommy, Daddy, and their 1979 Harley Davidson Roadster had not.

Now this. *I can't do this, Lord. Not again. Not again!*

"Why? Why us?" Brooke said, sitting down. "What in the world am I supposed to do now?"

"For starters, continue to be the great mother I saw yesterday," Macey answered. "And, Brooke, there are going to be *lots* of steps—lots of steps and lots of tests, then more steps and more tests. It's a complicated process, but I promise you you'll know what we are doing every step of the way."

Brooke shook her head. "I'm so afraid."

"It's normal to be afraid. It's normal to be confused."

Brooke put her elbows back on her knees and leaned forward to rest her forehead on the heels of her palms. "This can't be happening. This can't really be happening. Please, God."

"Look at me, Brooke," Macey said, kneeling in front of her.

Brooke raised her head. She could feel the tears streaking down her cheeks. "Please, Macey. Please tell me this isn't really happening."

"I'm going to tell you again," Macey said confidently. "We're going to win. We will beat this. But we all have to do our parts."

"I will do anything for him," Brooke said through her tears.

"I know you will," Macey said. "Alex isn't the only one we're going to be doing tests on. We'll be starting Alex with something called a bone marrow aspiration to determine—"

"A what?"

"A bone marrow aspiration," Macey repeated. "Leukemia is a cancer of the blood cells, and the bone marrow is where the majority of our blood cells originate. We are going to need to remove a tiny sample from Alex to make a final diagnosis."

"Final diagnosis?" Brooke asked hopefully. "Is there any chance he doesn't have it?"

"I would say no."

"When do you want to do this aspiration thing?" Brooke sighed. "Is it going to *hurt* him?"

"Excellent question," Macey said, standing. "Most kids have a tendency to fight any invasive process. I don't want to use the word *hurt*, and I will never mislead you. But I will tell you again that there will be times during the various parts of his treatment when he will be uncomfortable—extremely uncomfortable. But we'll do our best to minimize his discomfort."

"You said Alex won't be the only one you need to do tests on. What do you mean? Who else?"

"The most likely candidates for a bone marrow match for Alex would be siblings, which he doesn't have, right? Even half siblings?"

"Right. As far as I know . . ."

"Then along with trying to find a marrow match through a donor registry, we are also going to want to run tests on you and Alex's father."

"His father?" Brooke winced. "What does *he* need to do?"

"Are you in contact with the father?" Macey asked carefully.

"No," Brooke said quickly. "Can't we test me first to see if I'm a match? Alex doesn't even know his father."

"We will certainly test you, Brooke. But is there a way to get in contact with Alex's father? We need *all* possible biological matches as soon as possible. Time is a card we want to play well."

Brooke wondered how much bad news this windowless room had played host to in the past—this room with the clown paintings and the little boy who was about to get a shot. *If only Alex had been so lucky.*

"Alex's father . . . ," Brooke said, wiping her cheek and then looking around at the walls. They suddenly seemed so much closer together. "Doesn't know he's Alex's father."

"That doesn't change the fact that he may be the marrow match we're looking for—that Alex is looking for. It's extremely rare for a parent to be a match, but I want to make sure we have all of our options on the table."

Brooke could hear fate knocking. It was loud, impatient, and pounding mercilessly on a door she had kept so neatly locked for over six years now. But it had to open. It needed to open for Alex.

"He was my boss at the plant," Brooke said. "There was a party for a big contract we had won. We were both drunk and it ended up happening. That was it. Just that one time. Not a single time before or after."

"That's all it takes," Macey said. "Regardless, you have a beautiful son."

"We both felt really stupid about what happened and never

talked about it. When I realized I was pregnant, I was afraid to tell anybody who the father was."

"Even him?" Macey frowned.

"He was married," Brooke said. "He was a really nice guy and we both knew it was a mistake. I could only imagine the kind of problems it would cause with his wife, and I knew he'd get fired from the plant. I didn't know what to do."

"So you decided to go it alone?"

"Yeah," Brooke said. She hesitated. "I'm sorry for dumping this on you."

"I asked you about Alex's father and you're telling me. It's all right. You can tell me whatever you want."

Brooke crossed her arms and leaned to her side. She knew Macey meant it.

"I was living at my aunt's house when I found out I was pregnant. She and her third husband weren't doing too well at the time. She kept asking and asking and asking who the father was and I would never say. A few months later she and I were taking a walk at the park over near the church that runs along the lake. My aunt asked me if Frank was the baby's father."

"Was Frank your boss at the plant?"

"No," Brooke said. "My aunt's third husband."

"Oh," Macey said. "No wonder she kept asking you who the father was."

"I thought she was kidding and laughed at her."

"What happened?"

"She hit me with something," Brooke said. "I don't remember, but it was probably part of a branch. It broke my jaw and my nose, and I guess she hit me again in the back of the head after I was on the ground."

"That's awful," Macey said. "How far along were you?"

"Four or five months," Brooke said.

"What happened?"

"My aunt left me there."

"What?"

"Other than Alex, it's the best thing that ever happened to me."

"H-How?"

Brooke sighed and shook her head. "The only other thing I can remember about that day is that someone was carrying me, walking really fast, and he had blood all over his hand. I had no idea that it was my blood, *but that hand* . . . I can still see it, the way it crossed over the tops of *both* of my legs. I'd never seen a hand that *huge*. And then I saw the cross and blacked out again." She paused and looked at Macey. "It was the same cross you came to salvage at St. Thomas."

Macey squinted and then her eyes rounded sadly like she was about to cry. She shook her head slowly back and forth as if to fight the tears, then became still. "It was Charlie, wasn't it?"

"Yeah," Brooke said. "I'd lived in eleven different places by that time. I was twenty-one years old and I had finally made it home."

"That's beautiful," Macey said.

"Yeah," Brooke said again. "But you're right, I decided to go it alone. Just me and Alex, Batman and Robin. I grew up without a father, Carla grew up without a father, and what better father figure could you ask for over Pastor Jim?"

"He's an amazing man."

"The Lindys wanted us there and I wanted to be there. The five of us don't have much, but we have each other, and now this happens. Why?"

"It's going to be okay," Macey said.

"What do we do now?"

"We have Alex come back in here."

"Good," Brooke said, thinking about how Alex somehow now seemed so much younger than five. She wanted to hold him, cuddle him.

"And, Brooke, we are *not* going to explain to Alex that he is sick or even ever use the word *sick*. We are only going to focus on how everything we do is going to make him better. We keep it all positive."

"Okay," Brooke said.

"We'll do the bone marrow aspiration on Alex tomorrow as an outpatient," Macey said. "But for now, I want you to go home and prepare some things for us."

"Okay," Brooke said again.

Macey put her hand on Brooke's shoulder. "I want to know everything about Alex's personal preferences. What he likes to eat, what television shows he likes, what books he enjoys, what makes him laugh, what makes him cry—everything."

"What am I gonna do?" Brooke whispered. "I'm so scared."

"Here's what you are going to do," Macey said. "You are going to do two things."

Brooke looked at her, and the doctor had a reassuring smile on her face.

"One. You are going to watch him get better. And two . . ."

Brooke knew what "two" was before the smile faded off Macey's lips.

Fate had quit knocking. That door she'd kept locked for six years had just been kicked open, and on the other side was a man named Ian Tobias Jr.

Alex's father.

Possibly a donor match.

Brooke needed to talk to Ian right away.

✝ SEVENTEEN

My sugar really is feeling a little low right now," Jim said aloud. He casually crossed his arms and then patiently listened for someone's approval.

Nobody said a word.

"I had one at five this morning," he added boldly. "Another one won't hurt."

He put his hands on the edge of the kitchen sink, turned his head wishfully toward the pantry, and then began feeling a little embarrassed, realizing his voice held the pitch of a nine-year-old and the sincerity of a used-car salesman.

He dearly wanted another strawberry Pop-Tart and was having one heck of a time persuading anyone in the house that he should go against his doctor's recommended limit of only one per day. Truth be told, there was only one person he really needed to convince—himself.

He was home alone.

"Shirley?" he yelled, secretly hoping there would be no response. He got his wish. She had been gone for over two hours but apparently still wasn't home.

"Don't mind if I do," he said, reminding himself of Wile E. Coyote and quietly tiptoeing to the pantry door before coming to an abrupt halt.

"Charlie?" he said, turning his head cautiously toward the living room door. "You there, son?"

Once again, there was no reply. There weren't three taps on the kitchen table, three knocks on the living room or bedroom wall, or three tugs on his shirtsleeve, Charlie's way of answering him.

About an hour earlier he had heard the front door close and figured that his son was back up at the church, standing out in front of the cross again. Like he'd apparently done five other times, through the night and early morning hours.

Jim timidly reached down to the second shelf of the pantry and was already feeling a little guilty by the time his fingers found the small cardboard Pop-Tart box. It seemed a little light. He shook it and laughed under his breath.

"Thank you, Alex," he said. "Thanks for looking out for Pastor Jim."

Alex had put the empty box back in the pantry.

Jim dropped the box in the trash and poured himself another cup of coffee before sitting back at the table.

"Charlie?" he called again, running his hand across the soft leather cover of the Bible in front of him. "Charlie?"

He took a light sip of his coffee, set his cup back on the table, and then slowly opened the book. He dropped the heel of his palm to the base of the inside cover, then patiently began to guide the top pad of his index finger over and across the series of tiny raised dots on the page.

He'd been impressed with Kenneth's uncanny ability to recall and quote Bible verses. What had impressed him more, though, was the young man's ability to seem even more convincing when he *misquoted* a verse.

Jim flipped anxiously through the braille pages to the New Testament before feeling his way to Luke 8:50.

He stopped and ran his finger across it.

"'Do not be afraid; only believe, and she will be made well.'"

Why would Kenneth say "he" will be made well?

"And who am I supposed to tell?" Jim asked the empty house. He drummed his fingers on top of the kitchen table, shoving away the thought of Alex, back at the hospital.

And what did he mean when he said I'm not supposed to tell anyone about 7:14? The least he could have done was tell me the book.

He'd gotten as far as Isaiah 7:14, checking each book, when there were three knocks on the front door. *There's my boy.* "Hello, Charlie," he said in greeting. "I was wondering where you were, son."

Charlie's big shoes pounded across the living room floor in deliberate steps, moving him quickly to the table. Jim could hear Charlie's labored breathing as his son's enormous hand landed on his shoulder. The three light tugs on the sleeve of his sweatshirt meant that Charlie wanted his father to follow him.

"What is it, son?"

Three harder tugs almost pulled him off the chair. Whatever it was, he knew it was important to Charlie, so he stood and said, "I'll follow you, Charlie. Let's go."

Three light squeezes on his shoulder meant "okay."

As the two Lindy men made it out the door, Jim could tell that Charlie was anxious.

He also knew it had something to do with the cross.

ZACH WAS BACK IN THE ROOM.

He was trapped again. Only he could save her. She couldn't breathe, and time was running short. He yelled for help, but nobody could hear. They never heard him in that room.

Please, she can't breathe out there. Please . . .

He slid across the cool white carpet. He needed to find that window. She would be in the window. He could save her.

He found the window.

There! There she is! I can save her . . .

She wanted in so badly, but she couldn't get in. She never could. He kicked at the window. She clawed at the window. He kept kicking. She kept clawing in panic, leaving tiny strings of scratches on the smooth, frigid glass. He punched at the window. She still scratched. He continued to punch wildly with both fists.

Please! Please let her in. She can't breathe . . .

He kept kicking and punching at the center of the window. Why wouldn't it ever break? Just once?

She stopped clawing and then stared at him. Her brown, curly hair flowed and feathered in slow motion at the sides of her face— that beautiful face. He kicked one last time. She didn't move.

Don't stop trying. Please.

But his words were silent, as well as unanswered. As always.

As she fell back into the darkness behind the window, he stepped back.

He could see them—the hands. The hands were on her shoulders. They were the wrinkled and weathered hands of an old man. Zach put his face against the cold window and looked closer at the hands on her shoulders. Then he looked back at her face. The panic in her eyes was now gone . . .

Behind her, an arm's length away, another face was almost visible. An old man's face. With shining white hair and a majestic beard, accented by fiery red eyes . . . Zach couldn't look away as the face moved closer to him, shoving the girl behind him. The closer the face came, the younger it became. The glowing red eyes were developing an oval shape, and the color softening into a light green. The beard was gone, and the white hair darkened like dusk shadowing a snowy field.

The man slowly turned and wrapped his arms under the girl's limp body to effortlessly pick her up. The hair on top of his head was now almost completely brown. The man put his hand over her face, that beautiful face, and closed her blue eyes. Her head dropped back and bobbed lifelessly as he held her in his arms. The man tilted his head and kissed her on her forehead before turning around to carry her off into the darkness.

No! Stop it! Bring her to me! Help her! Come back!

Zach pressed his face back against the window one last time. Tears flooded his cheeks, which he frantically wiped with his bloody knuckles.

Please stop!

The man did what he asked. And then the man looked back at him, over his shoulder.

Please don't take her! Help me!

The man's stare drifted through the darkness, directly through the window and into his eyes.

It was then that the boy recognized the man.

It was that construction worker. It was Kenneth.

Zach Norman screamed and sat up in his bed. He was trying to make sense of his dream, remember where he was, when the phone rang. He edged across the sweat-drenched sheets and picked up the receiver. "Amy?" he said desperately.

There was a pause. "No, Zach, it's Macey. Who's Amy?"

Zach cradled the phone between his ear and his neck before rubbing his face, trying to wake completely.

His fingers and cheeks felt like they were freezing, even as he sweat.

The ice . . .

CHARLIE TOOK JIM BY THE HAND AS THEY STOOD OUT in front of the church and carefully placed his fingers against the cross. Jim felt the smooth wood surface and could practically taste the scent of the lacquer that gently wafted from the cross by the breeze.

"The cross is like new, isn't it?" he said softly. "It was hit by lightning, and the carpenter fixed it yesterday. Remember? It's okay, son."

Charlie then lowered his father's hand down off the cross and placed what felt like three pieces of broken twig in it.

"What's this?" he asked, rolling the pieces across his open palm.

Charlie snatched the broken pieces away and quickly placed a single twig in Pastor Jim's hand.

"What is it, Charlie?"

Charlie tilted the twig straight upright in his hand.

"What are you doing?"

Charlie took the broken pieces and put them back in his father's hand, then quickly replaced them with the unbroken piece of twig.

"Yes, Charlie, he fixed it. He did a good job; I know."

He could feel Charlie shifting the twig in his open palm from flat to upright, flat to upright.

It was clear that Charlie was struggling to understand how the cross was now standing before them after being in ruins just the day before.

"Don't worry, Charlie, fixing the cross is a *good* thing. The carpenter—it's what he does, son. I'm not quite sure how he did it; I'm just glad he did."

Charlie kept lowering and tilting the twig in his hand.

Jim let out a little laugh, admiring Charlie's persistence. "I'm pretty sure you're trying to tell me they fixed it real fast, huh, Charlie?"

Behind them, he could hear the gravel stirring on Church Road.

Brooke's car was approaching the driveway to the church.

MACEY WAS LOOKING OUT HER OFFICE WINDOW, HER eyes continuing to bounce off the roofs and bumpers of each and every vehicle in the parking lot as she once again searched for the old Ford pickup. Her heart began racing a bit in odd anticipation of spotting it, and she suddenly wondered if she really wanted to find it. The truth of the matter was that the idea of actually seeing the truck made her more than a little nervous. She was practically afraid.

Only believe.

"There's some strange stuff going on around here, Kait."

"You've been pretty quiet," Kaitlyn responded, sitting attentively on the couch, looking comfortable in her baby blue scrubs, the third-floor nurses' assigned uniform of the day. "Is it Alex that's getting to you?"

"Among other things," Macey said, catching herself sounding apologetic. "It's just been a strange couple of days, that's all."

"Speaking of strange," Kaitlyn said, "I still can't believe Zach called in sick."

"He called in *late*," Macey said. "He'll be in around noon." Macey pictured the lost look on Zach's face at The Pilot Inn. She was certain that he'd always been able to make sense of everything around him—until yesterday. She knew how he felt.

"I couldn't imagine him ever missing a whole day of work," the nurse said.

"Kaitlyn?" Macey asked faintly. She glanced down at her coffee-stained Nike, took another cautious look out the window, and peeked back down into the parking lot. "Has Zach ever mentioned the name Amy to you before?"

"Amy? Not that I can recall. Why?"

She turned around and crossed her arms. "Old girlfriend? Relative?"

Kaitlyn opened a manila folder labeled "Alexander R. Thomas" and placed it neatly on the coffee table in front of the sofa. She seemed surprised. "Not that I know of. Why are you asking?"

Macey dragged the chair from her desk over next to the couch and sat down. "Because I called him earlier, and he answered the phone by yelling 'Amy' at the top of his lungs. It actually scared me a little. It wasn't like him."

"*Amy?*" Kaitlyn asked. "I don't ever remember Zach even saying that name before."

Macey looked at her and nodded at the folder. "Aspiration tomorrow morning for Alex at six forty-five."

"Wait a minute," Kaitlyn said, putting her pen down. She paused, then reached over and tapped Macey chidingly on the arm. "That's not fair."

"What's not fair?"

"Do *you* know who Amy is? Was it someone he dated while he was seeing me or something?"

"I don't have the faintest idea who Amy is," she said, raising her hand and extending two fingers. "Scout's honor." She looked at Kaitlyn and couldn't tell if her friend was more disappointed in Macey for not knowing who Amy was or in herself for allowing anything to do with Zach to actually bother her.

"I'm sure it's nothing," Kaitlyn said, grabbing the folder and fidgeting with it before opening it up. "It looks like our little red-headed cutie may be missing the church harvest party on Saturday."

"Let's see how he responds to his first round of treatment," Macey said. "I told Brooke that if he feels up to it, he can go."

"He might," Kaitlyn said. "You can tell he's going to be a little trouper."

"I think you're right."

"What about us?" Kaitlyn asked. "We still going? Or is it weird now?"

"We said we would, so let's," Macey answered.

"Sounds good," Kaitlyn said, closing the folder and leaning back. "You know what, Macey?"

"What?"

"I know Amy wouldn't be a relative. Zach is an only child, and I've met all his cousins."

Macey rolled her eyes and then grinned playfully at her friend. "Still not over him, are you? No matter how hard you protest?"

"Oh, please," Kaitlyn said, laughing unconvincingly. "Over what?"

✦ EIGHTEEN

harlie turned around and waved at Alex, wanting him to come. *Now or never,* Alex thought. But he didn't like it.

Charlie was *way* down the dirt path that went from behind the church and into the haunted woods.

Alex had never been down the trail by himself, and walking any of it without Charlie protecting him didn't seem like too much fun.

Charlie lowered himself to one knee and opened his arms for him to come.

Alex lifted his left foot and stepped tentatively onto the crackly leaves and dirt that marked the beginning of the path. He quickly pulled it back as if he'd just stepped in burning hot lava. He put his hands in his pockets and began to wiggle his toes in his tennies. He noticed that his shoes were getting tighter and tighter, but that was okay, because Mom said he'd be getting new ones pretty soon.

As he continued to stare down the path at Charlie, he was beginning to feel more and more like a fraidy cat. Didn't he just take a vow of courage with Nurse Kaitlyn? He promised he'd try his best not to be afraid of things. Promised. What would Nurse Kaitlyn say if she saw him now?

'Course, she didn't know *Looney Cooney* was out here somewhere. Mrs. Kipler had *said.*

Webster Cooney was a very scary man. Mrs. Kipler told Mom at church that Looney Cooney had *gone nuts* and was *off his rocker.* She also said that Looney Cooney drank water right out of the lake and that he also came out at night to kill animals with his bare hands to eat. But it all ended one night when Looney Cooney was *drunk off his butt.* That was the night when his house burned all the way to the ground with him still in it. And that was when she said the scariest thing of all!

Even though Looney Cooney died, Mrs. Kipler said that people walking on the shore at night still saw him every once in a while, drinking from the lake and walking around in the woods. Alex knew it had to be true, because even though Looney Cooney's house and rocker may have burned to the ground, every once in a while, when it was real windy outside, he could still hear the rocker creaking back and forth in the woods.

Alex looked back up and noticed that Charlie had moved a few steps closer. He still wasn't close enough, but Alex thought about going for it.

But what if burned-up Looney Cooney is out there? What if he got up off his rocker and came and got me before Charlie could save me? What if . . .

The longer he stared at the path, the more he thought that the leafless branches of all shapes and sizes leaning over the path were waiting—just *waiting* for him to move, *waiting* to reach down like bony little fingers to snatch him up and drag him into the darkness of the trees forever. He slowly lowered his head in despair, quietly hoping that Charlie wouldn't be too disappointed.

"Can you come get me, Charlie?" he pleaded, looking down at his tennies in defeat. "Please?"

He couldn't hear anything.

He was afraid to look back down the path.

And then he could hear the leaves moving. Charlie was coming.

"I'm sorry for being a fraidy cat," he said.

Charlie lifted him to his shoulders, and Alex wrapped his arms around his neck. Alex was a little mad that he had called himself a fraidy cat, but felt instantly brave with Charlie there. "Try to get me now, Looney Cooney!"

Charlie ran really fast for a superlong time until they got to the spot in the woods that didn't have any trees in it. Pastor Jim said that God carved it out like that. There wasn't any wind there, but it was sunny. The grass was real long, and there was part of an old wooden picnic table that Pastor Jim started to make, but then he couldn't see anymore and had to stop. Now that Looney Cooney was behind them, Alex began to drum playfully on top of Charlie's head while telling Charlie about the hospital people.

"Hey, Charlie," he said. "Nurse Kaitlyn says that I'm going to be going to the hospital a lot." He noticed that his hand was almost the exact same length as Charlie's ear and smiled. "She showed me a cool trick where she can pull her finger off and put it back on."

Charlie stopped next to the old picnic table, lifted Alex off of his shoulders, and carefully set Alex on his feet on top of the lone bench.

"Hey, Charlie," Alex said. "Nurse Kaitlyn has puppets too. One of the puppets is called Mr. Brave. Nurse Kaitlyn says that I can be just like Mr. Brave if I want to be."

Charlie went into his pocket and pulled out his Tic Tac container.

"I asked Nurse Kaitlyn if I was going to get a shot, and she said that even if I do, that Mr. Brave will be there with me, and that it will only hurt for a little bit, and that sometimes shots are good and not bad." Alex paused and lifted his finger to his chin. "I think that's what she said."

Charlie tapped out two Tic Tacs.

"Hey, Charlie," Alex said, snickering. He jumped off the table into the soft grass. "Pull my finger."

Charlie tugged on Alex's index finger, and Alex farted, sending himself into a hysterical bout of laughter.

"Hey, Charlie," Alex said, still giggling. "You gotta try that one sometime."

"HOW LONG DID MACEY SAY IT WOULD BE BEFORE SHE thought Alex would be better?" James asked, sitting patiently at the kitchen table with Shirley and Brooke.

"They're going to start chemotherapy this week," Brooke explained timidly. "And then test him weekly."

"For how long?"

"Until he goes into remission," Brooke said, covering her eyes with her hands. "Alex is going to be getting chemo. Can you believe this?"

Shirley could see the drawn expression across Brooke's face. She hadn't worn any makeup that day, and she had a pair of light purple lines under her eyes that darkened with stress. Shirley put her hand on top of Brooke's and said, "Why don't you try to rest for a little bit?"

"I can't," Brooke said.

Shirley could tell James was having difficulty absorbing the news. He'd always been able to offer the right words of comfort in times of trouble. But this was hitting home—too close to home. She watched him close his eyes and knew he was silently asking God to help him find the right words.

"Why me again, Pastor Jim?" Brooke asked, her voice without any trace of energy, and clearly defeated. "My parents—my life— now Alex. It's not fair. It isn't fair."

Shirley edged her chair closer to Brooke and put her arm around her.

Brooke looked at Shirley, and Shirley could see the hopelessness in her eyes.

James rested his hands on top of his Bible. "Brooke, it's important that you understand something. God has a plan. And you and Alex are part of that plan. He will be there for you."

"Well," Brooke said dryly, "I need him now. Right here, right now. Tell me, Pastor Jim. Where is he?"

"We all need him," Shirley said. "And though you may not feel it, he is here right now."

"What do I do?" Brooke asked, her voice starting to quiver. "Please tell me what to do."

"Only believe," Shirley said.

"Believe what?" Brooke asked, shaking her head in dismissal

before getting up from the table. "That this, *this* is part of God's plan?" She looked to the window and shook her head again.

Shirley looked at James as if he was missing an unseen cue, but he had already risen to his feet. "You only need to trust in God."

"Trust in God?" Brooke shrieked. She said it in a way that Shirley didn't like, but understood. "Why were my parents killed? Why would Alex have leukemia? Please tell me why. And I don't want to hear about Peter, Paul, Job, or someone else right now. Tell me *why*."

James reached for Brooke's hand, and she responded somewhat reluctantly. "Brooke," he said.

"What?" she said quickly.

"Brooke," he repeated. "You know that God doesn't keep us from tests and trials."

"I never would have guessed, Pastor Jim," she said sarcastically. "He doesn't keep us from tests and trials? Really?"

"No," James answered, giving Brooke's hand a little squeeze of encouragement. "He helps us get through them."

"Well, I don't feel his *help* right now," Brooke snapped. "Where? Where is he?"

"Please," Shirley said, standing up and holding both palms toward the ceiling as if she were holding up an invisible tray. "Just trust him, Brooke. God loves you more than you can imagine."

"I have to go," Brooke said, crossing her arms and rolling her eyes. "I'll be back."

James lowered his voice. "Brooke, please. Shirley is right. Trust him, no matter how it *feels*."

Brooke shook her head. "I want to believe in everything you two are saying," she said. "But this is a little much right now, okay?"

"Honey," Shirley said, "we know it's hard for you right now. It's hard for all of us."

"I'm sorry, I have to go," Brooke said again, heading quickly out of the kitchen and toward the front door. "I'll be back in a couple of hours—unless, you know, my car blows up."

"Brooke," Shirley said. "That's not what you have learned."

"Not now," Brooke responded, her eyes starting to fill with tears.

"What can we do?" James asked. "Tell us."

"Looks like nothing," Brooke said, wiping her eyes and closing the door behind her.

James bowed his head. "I didn't know what to say, Shirley. For the first time in my life, I couldn't find the words."

"Come here, James Lindy," Shirley said, sitting back down at the kitchen table. He walked up next to her, and she grabbed his sleeve and lowered the side of her face to his arm. "We're hurting too. It steals your breath, such news, let alone our words. And you know as well as anyone, James, all we can do is pray. Pray for Alex and pray for Brooke, and remind her to only believe that things will turn out."

James kissed Shirley on her cheek and walked out of the kitchen before making his way down the narrow hallway to the bedroom. Shirley walked slowly to the sink and turned the water on to rinse the morning dishes. She looked passively out the kitchen window and could see Brooke in her car, leaning against its steering wheel. It appeared that she was sobbing. "Oh, you poor thing," she whispered.

She shut the water off and turned around to head outside. When she looked up, she found James standing in the doorway to the kitchen. The blood in his fingers seemed to have rushed to his nails as he squeezed his Bible with both hands. His face was flushed, his eyes were squinting almost painfully, and Shirley noticed he seemed to be shaking.

"James?" Shirley said, rushing toward him and grabbing his arms. "Your sugar."

"Shirley," James said, his voice sounding weak and labored. "You just said it."

"James Lindy, you get on the couch right now!" Shirley pleaded, grabbing the phone off the wall. "I'm calling 9-1-1."

James reached out and found her arm. He took the phone from her and hung it back up. "My blood sugar's fine."

"You're shaking!"

He turned around and ran haphazardly toward the front door and flung it open. "Brooke!" he shouted at the top of his lungs.

"She's in her car," Shirley said, frowning and coming up beside him. Was he delirious?

James let go of the door and hurried outside. When he hit the end of the porch, he missed the top step and fell hard to the ground, landing facedown, square on his elbows.

"James!"

He raised his head and quickly got to his knees, and then, slowly, to his feet. Shirley could tell he was struggling to catch his breath when he yelled again, "Brooke, wait!"

"She's pulling out of the driveway!" Shirley yelled, helplessly watching James run across the lawn, falling again and bouncing right back up while protecting his Bible like a running back not wanting to fumble the ball. She'd not seen him run in over a decade.

"Brooke!" he screamed again.

"James, you're bleeding," Shirley said, walking as fast as she could toward him on the lawn.

"Brooke Thomas!" he bellowed.

"What is it, James?" Shirley asked.

He dropped back down to one knee to catch his breath. His pants had a tear at the other knee, and his elbow was bleeding. He lifted his head, wiped his mouth with his shirtsleeve, and then turned his head toward her.

"James?" Shirley said. "You're a mess. What are you *doing*?"

He slowly stood and held out his hand. Tentatively, Shirley took it. He inhaled deeply and leaned his head in the direction of the cross.

"Only believe, Brooke!" he yelled.

"She's gone, James," Shirley said. "She's halfway down the road."

"Only believe," he said again, letting go of her hand. He took a couple steps toward the driveway and stopped. Then he held his hands up in the air and turned around. He was smiling.

"Only believe . . . and *he* . . . will be made well."

☦ NINETEEN

They were deep, deep, deep into the forest. Farther than they'd ever, ever gone, when they reached an old, rusted barbed wire fence. Alex's skin got the goose bumps all over, and he rubbed his arms as he walked beside his big friend.

He looked back down the path they'd come. "We better go back now, Charlie. Mom will be worried. But let's go out to Church Road and walk down that, 'kay? I don't wanna go back down the path."

Charlie nodded.

Alex picked up a big piece of bark from the ground and threw it as hard as he could at one of the rotting fence poles. It burst into a kajillion pieces. "Did you see that? That was cool!"

Charlie nodded, smiling.

"I hope Mrs. Lindy went to the store and got some macaroni and cheese. Are you hungry too, Charlie?"

Charlie's big eyes lit up at the word *macaroni* and he nodded his head in agreement.

"Look at *this*!" Alex yelled, pointing down into a bunch of mushrooms that were growing at the side of a dead tree. "It's *ginormous*!" The green and white cap was the size of a plate. Alex reached down to touch it, but a tan boot stepped in the way. Alex pulled his hand quickly to his side, then looked up in surprise.

Kenneth was standing there.

Charlie snatched up Alex and then took a few steps back, carefully cradling him in the crook of his massive left arm.

"It's okay, Charlie. It's just Kenneth!" Alex said, frowning at his big friend and wondering why he was acting like a fraidy cat. Alex looked around the woods and then back to Kenneth. "What are you doing out here?"

"Keeping you two away from those mushrooms," Kenneth said, taking a small step toward Charlie, who took a big step back.

Kenneth looked up at Charlie. "Hello, Charles Paul Lindy."

Charlie's head tilted back and forth. And then he smiled at the carpenter.

"Charlie likes hearing his name like that," Alex said. "Pastor Jim does that too."

"Hey, Alex," Kenneth said, taking another step closer to them. Charlie didn't move. "Mr. Cooney is a very nice man."

"No, he's bad," Alex said. "Looney Cooney killed animals and ate them and burned up in his rocker and died."

"Tell me something," Kenneth said, holding out his arms for Charlie to pass Alex to him.

"Tell you what?" Alex asked, reaching for Kenneth.

Charlie waited. His head teetered back and forth again.

"It's okay, Charlie," the carpenter said.

Charlie held Alex out and Kenneth took him. He tapped Alex lightly on the chin and said, "Tell me how those things make Mr. Cooney bad."

"I don't know," Alex said. "But he died."

"That doesn't make him bad, does it? Everyone dies, in time."

Alex looked at Charlie and then poked at Kenneth's chest. "But I dunno if he knew 'bout Jesus."

Kenneth squinted and lowered Alex to the ground, crouching beside him. "What do you mean?"

Alex looked at Charlie and back at Kenneth. Could Kenneth really not know? Didn't *everyone*?

The carpenter smiled. "Tell me," he said.

"Jesus died for us," he said.

Kenneth stared at Alex for a few seconds and then smiled. "How do you know, Alex?"

"Pastor Jim tol' me. Tha's how we get to *heaven*. Do *you* know Jesus, Kenneth?"

"Oh yes," he said, getting that warm look in his green eyes that Alex liked. It made him just want to look and look at them. "He and I go way back."

"But I don't really get how he died and came back again."

"You will, in time," Kenneth said, standing and running his hand across the top of Alex's head. "Everyone will, in time. You guys want to race? I know a shortcut."

"Yeah!" Alex said. "You'll never beat me and Charlie!"

"You think so?" Kenneth said. "Why don't we find out?"

"Let's do horsey back," Alex said, pulling on Charlie's pant leg.

Charlie lifted Alex over his head, on top of his shoulders. Alex loved being up there. It was like he was on top of the world!

Alex reached his arms over to hang on to Charlie's thick neck. Charlie held his legs. Alex's big horsey was ready to go. "You ready?" Alex said to Kenneth.

"Ready when you are," Kenneth said, standing next to them.

Alex clicked his heels gently on Charlie's chest and yelled the magic words: "Giddy up, horsey!"

Fallen branches and dry acorns *pop, pop, popped* under Charlie's feet as he ran through the red and yellow leaves at the base of a narrow hill. Alex smiled as they moved through the woods, keeping a safe lead over Kenneth, who was right behind them. As Kenneth came closer, Alex squealed and Charlie ran faster and faster. Alex laughed as they ran up the side and over the top of another small hill. Then Charlie began to slow down.

"Giddyap," Alex said, not wanting Kenneth to catch up. But instead of going fast again, Charlie came to a stop. "What's wrong, Charlie?"

Panting, Charlie lifted his left arm and pointed toward the fence.

Alex saw it. The woods suddenly seemed smaller and much quieter. The only noise in the woods was Charlie catching his breath and Kenneth walking up behind them.

"Oh man," Alex said sadly. "What happened to it?"

But he could kinda see what happened. A little deer had tried to leap over the barbed wire and one of its rear hooves got caught on the top of the fence. It hung upside down, with its tongue hanging out and its body twisted on the other side.

"Let me down, Charlie," Alex said. "I want to see it closer."

Charlie followed his instructions and carefully lowered Alex. They both stood and stared at the dead animal.

"Why did it have to die, Charlie?" Alex asked. "It doesn't seem fair to die like that."

Charlie was still. His arms were hanging straight down to his sides, and he bowed his head at a slight angle like a child who had just been scolded. His eyes shifted back and forth between the deer's tongue and its lifeless eyes. He looked like he was going to cry.

"Something was eating at it," Alex said, noticing a patch of black blood on the deer's side, all dried up. "Its fur looks yucky."

Alex inched a few feet closer, shuffling slowly through the leaves. He stopped again, almost hoping the deer would wake up and run away. He turned around and looked back at Charlie and Kenneth.

"C'mon, guys! Let's go closer," Alex said, going back to Charlie and tugging on his pant leg so he'd lift him up. He wanted to see the deer. But he'd feel better if Charlie would hold him.

Charlie remained still. Alex looked up and saw he was about to cry. "It's okay, Charlie. Don't cry."

"He'll be all right," Kenneth said.

Charlie's eyes never left the deer as he lifted Alex and moved them a little closer. The closer they got, the faster Alex's heart raced and the tighter he hung on to Charlie. Alex didn't like the way the deer's eyes were, open but not seeing. Blank.

"I feel bad for that deer," Alex said, lifting his head to see little puffs of light dust that were coming off of Church Road as a black car approached from the distance.

"Its foot got broken on the fence," Alex said, noticing a tiny broken bone sticking out of the deer's hoof. He turned to look back up at Kenneth. "There's a bone; you can see it."

"I know," Kenneth said.

Charlie still didn't move.

"Can we get it off the fence?"

They all looked up at the road as the fancy black car hummed by them. It caused a small tornado of leaves to swirl off the ground in tiny circles behind it as it made its way toward St. Thomas. Alex thought the driver was the man who ate the crackers with pee on them yesterday. Dr. Somethin'. But he was more interested in the dead deer.

Still holding Alex, Charlie snapped a branch off of a nearby tree and then slowly approached the dead deer as if he were protecting him and Alex with a wooden sword. He tapped at the deer with the branch, and Alex didn't like the hollow way it sounded. Charlie poked it again as if he were making sure the animal was dead. He put Alex down and then carefully lined up the end of the branch with the deer's trapped hoof. He gave it a firm shove, ripping its skin from the rusty brown wire. It tumbled over and into a bunch of tall, dry grass.

Alex took another look into the deer's lifeless eyes. Charlie scratched at his chin, wiped a small tear, and then leaned over and picked up Alex to place him over the fence.

"Don't cry, Charlie," Alex said again. "Maybe that deer went to heaven. Maybe she is okay."

Charlie straddled and then pulled one leg carefully over the fence.

"She sure is stinky," Alex said, holding his nose. He backed away and reached up for Charlie to lift him again. He stared down at the little deer. She looked smaller, now that she was off the fence. "I wish she didn't have to die hangin' up like that."

"Me too," Kenneth said. "But she's fine now. Better than you can imagine."

Alex stared at the little doe. She did look more peaceful-like now that she was down in the tall grass.

"I'm tired, Charlie." A nap on the couch right now sounded really, really good to him. Right after a bowl of macaroni and cheese.

JAMES'S LEG TWITCHED AS IF SOMEONE WERE HOLDING the open flame of a lighter against his bare knee. "I'm telling you, I *know* that Kenneth was talking about Brooke and Alex."

"How could he know?" Shirley asked, delicately patting James's wound with a cotton ball soaked with antiseptic.

"I don't know. Maybe he heard Brooke talking about the hospital visits. But that's why he switched the Bible verse to *he* from *she.*"

"Sit still, James Lindy," Shirley said sternly, taking another bandage out of a small cardboard box and tearing off its paper cover.

James briefly held his hands up in surrender before dropping them to his lap. He rubbed the top of an oval-shaped bandage that she had just applied to his elbow, making sure the edges would stick. "It's too much of a coincidence."

"Why don't you ask him when he comes to the harvest party on Saturday?"

"I will. You know I will."

Shirley looked curiously out the kitchen window. "James, that same fancy black car that was here yesterday is parked out in front of the church."

"Fancy black car?"

"I'm pretty sure that it's that doctor," Shirley said, hesitating before putting her glasses on to look again. "It's Zach Norman. He is going up the walkway to the church."

"Maybe he's looking for me," James said, rising dutifully to his feet. "I better go over there."

Shirley's palms were on the edge of the sink, and she went up on tiptoe. "Now he is walking across the lawn."

"Coming here?" James asked. "Why didn't he drive over here?"

"I don't think he is coming here," Shirley said. "He just stopped."

"What's he doing?"

"Nothing," Shirley answered, shrugging. She stepped back and then turned to James. "He is just standing in front of the cross, looking at it."

ZACH TURNED AROUND AND ACKNOWLEDGED CHARLIE and Alex as they approached him from behind. "Hey, guys," he said distantly. He then turned back to the cross.

"What are you looking at?" Alex asked innocently, the tiny freckles beneath his eyes huddling together as he squinted to look up past the cross and into the sky as if he were missing something that was flying over.

"It's awesome," Zach answered.

"What is?" Alex asked. "What does that mean?"

"The cross," Zach said, placing his palm firmly on it and oddly feeling as if it were alive in some way. "It's a miracle."

"Yes, it is," Pastor Jim said loudly as he walked across the lawn from the doctor's left. His arms were crossed to shelter himself from the breeze, and the bandage on his elbow had come undone, hanging halfway off, flapping with each step he took.

Zach didn't respond.

"Yes, it *is* a miracle," Pastor Jim repeated. "The Lord blessed us with the work of our friends' hands."

"Yeah," Zach said politely, knowing that there was a little more to the cross's resurrection than what the good minister believed. He didn't really expect Pastor Jim to be able to explain what had happened—mostly because he himself couldn't explain it. In fact, looking at the cross again today convinced him of what spooked him the most, and that was his high degree of certainty that *nobody* could explain it.

"Is there something I can help you with, Dr. Norman?" Pastor Jim asked.

"I guess I just wanted to see it again," he said as Beethoven's

"Symphony No. 9" flowed softly through the half-opened driver's side window of the Mercedes. "That's all I really needed, Pastor Jim." What he *really* needed was what no one could give, and that was the answer as to exactly how the carpenter did it, because what he did was, by a strict definition, impossible. It was, in fact—and he found himself thinking it again—a *miracle*.

"See what?" Pastor Jim asked. "The cross?"

Zach nodded again. "It really happened, didn't it?" He slid his hand a little higher on the smooth side of the cross. "He really did this."

"What really happened?" Pastor Jim asked, his forehead creasing in confusion.

Zach had no words to answer. That was part of the problem. There were no words to explain it.

Charlie stepped closer to them and placed his hand above Zach's on the cross. They looked at each other and exchanged what Zach felt to be some type of glance of mutual understanding.

"You—" he said to Charlie. "You *saw* it, didn't you, big fella?"

Charlie looked innocently into Zach's eyes.

"Are you all right, Dr. Norman?" Pastor Jim asked.

"I'm not sure," Zach said, keeping his right hand on the cross while lightly rubbing his forehead with his left. "To be honest with you, sir, I really don't know."

Alex stepped between Zach and the cross and poked at the doctor's leg before looking up at him. "I was at the hospital today. Nurse Kaitlyn was there."

Zach didn't even acknowledge Alex. He didn't mean to ignore him; he just couldn't look away from Charlie.

"Would you like to go inside the church and talk?" Pastor Jim asked warmly. "Maybe I can help. I don't see real well, but I think I'm a pretty good listener."

"I appreciate it, Pastor Jim," Zach said, his hand fluttering off the cross as he turned to the minister. "I may take you up on that sometime—sometime soon. But I'm running late as it is, and I need to make another stop before I get to work."

"I understand," Pastor Jim said. "Just remember that I'm always here."

"I like Nurse Kaitlyn," Alex said impatiently.

"She is a very nice lady, Alexander," Zach said. "I like her too."

"There's a dead deer on the fence back in the woods," Alex said, somber and earnest in his reporting. "Its toe got stuck, and it stinks, and something ate its stomach."

Zach didn't say anything, smiling at the cute little redhead. *Poor kid. Rough go for him ahead. Leukemia could—*

"It went to heaven," Alex said confidently.

"Heaven, huh?" Zach said quietly, his smile melting. Did dead deer go to heaven? Did anyone? "I have to go, you guys. I'm really sorry to have bothered you today."

He took a hand out of his pocket and placed it back up on the cross one more time, only a few inches below Charlie's hand, which was still resting there. Something about touching the cross made him feel good. It reminded him he wasn't losing it—it'd really happened.

Charlie suddenly dropped his hand over Zach's, and Zach was startled. He thought that Charlie was looking at him like he wanted to say something.

"I'm tired, Pastor Jim," Alex said quietly. The pastor picked him up and kissed him. Alex rested his head on his shoulder.

Zach took his hand off the cross, patted Charlie on the shoulder, and then zipped up his jacket. At least he wasn't alone. Charlie knew something really bizarre had happened here too. "See you later, guys."

"You're welcome here anytime you like, Dr. Norman," Pastor Jim said. "Anytime you like."

"I appreciate it, Pastor Jim," Zach said, turning to offer his hand to Charlie. Slowly, they shook hands, and Zach looked into his eyes. "I know you can't do it, so I'll say it for you, big fella. It's a miracle. A true-blue miracle. You know it and I know it, and somehow, that makes me feel better."

✢ TWENTY

Zach double-clicked his key holder, which chirped to confirm that the Mercedes was securely locked behind him. He dropped his hands to his sides and then looked up to read the copper block letters that arched above the wrought iron gate—the sole entrance to St. Victor's Cemetery.

He'd heard that the last of the 150-year-old cemetery's 6,500-plus plots had all been claimed a good twenty years ago, which was one of several reasons its upkeep was no longer on the top of anyone's to-do list.

"Here goes nothing," he said, firmly shoving on the rusty gate, which swung open with an obligatory creak that magnetically invited him onto the gravel walkway within the cemetery grounds.

Zach closed the gate behind him and then looked around. None of it was familiar anymore. He hadn't been to the cemetery in over twenty years, and the lack of maintenance had left it looking like an abandoned set of a low-budget horror film. Tumbleweeds piled against the highest gravestones. Weeds were overtaking everything. Half the grass was dead and gone and not coming back with spring.

He buttoned up his coat, lifted his shoulders, hid his hands in his pockets, and walked slowly down the first of countless rows of tombstones, his head moving back and forth, trying to remember any visual clues about where it was. His confidence in just happening upon the tiny headstone was pretty low. Were there two trees? A hedge? A huge angel tombstone somewhere close? He shook his head. He couldn't be sure of anything.

He stopped abruptly and glanced at his watch. He was supposed to have been at East Shore fifteen minutes ago. He had already called in late for the second time that day, which would make it the second time in his entire career as a medical doctor that he had done that.

His cell phone rang, and he took it out of his pocket. It was Kaitlyn. She hadn't called him in over three months, and as surprised as he was—as much as he really *needed* to talk to her—he knew he couldn't. Nothing could interrupt him now. He had to find the grave.

The phone quit ringing, and he put his hands back in his pockets while quickening his pace down another row, and then yet another, aggressively scanning names on what had to have been over a hundred headstones.

He couldn't remember where it was. Maybe he'd purposefully forgotten it, part of his effort to banish the memories of that torturous winter . . .

Zach's eyes swept over the balance of the cemetery and he felt completely lost. An overwhelming sea of headstones, dead grass, and patches of dirt sprawled in all directions.

"Needle in a haystack," he muttered, shaking his head.

Gingerly, he sat down on the cleanest half of what looked like one of the cemetery's original cement benches. Part of the seat's back had crumbled to the ground, and the rest of the bench was nothing more than a nasty collection of bird droppings and stress cracks.

He could hear someone talking.

To his left, halfway up a shaggy hillside, an elderly man with flowing white hair was on one knee, removing dead flowers from a pot at the head of a tombstone. The grave appeared to be one of only a few receiving any form of regular maintenance. *Probably because he's doing it himself.*

Zach thought the old man seemed familiar as he watched him gently tilt the flowerpot upside down, remove a handkerchief from his breast pocket, and wipe the outside of the pot clean. The man then opened a cardboard floral box and carefully arranged an assortment of flowers in the pot before neatly centering it back at the head of the tombstone.

He scanned the grounds again and noticed that they were the only two people in the entire cemetery. He looked back at the man, who now appeared to be talking to the grave. *I wonder if anyone is listening,* he thought.

Zach glanced again at his watch, conceding defeat, and decided to head back to the car. There were simply too many graves. He brushed off the seat of his pants and turned to walk back to his car when it caught his eye—a cross.

About five hundred feet away, the top portion of a metal cross jutted up over the edge of one of the cemetery's many small and unkempt hills. Zach quickly stood on top of the bench, causing a softball-sized chunk of its edge to collapse, but it didn't matter. He had to get a better look at the cross. He shaded his eyes as the early afternoon sun glistened off it.

He wanted to touch it, be near it, just like the one at St. Thomas. Not later, but *right away.*

Zach jumped off the bench and walked quickly, trampling directly across the tops of several graves as his eyes never left the cross. *Hurry,* he thought. *Get there.*

He picked up his pace, becoming increasingly filled with a new sense of energy and purpose as to why he had come to the cemetery. There was no doubt the answer was ahead.

The more he focused on the cross, the more he was drawn to it. The more he was drawn to it, the faster he went—faster and faster, closer and closer—until in the end, he was running.

His coat was restricting his arms, and he unbuttoned it as he ran. He freed his right arm and lowered his head like a halfback, picking up more speed as his coat waved off his back and left arm like a thick cape. The cross was getting closer.

Zach dropped his coat behind him, free, faster now.

The reason—the purpose he was there—was getting closer. He cut across into the next row of headstones, hoping to shorten the distance, when his left foot banked awkwardly off the edge of a partially buried flowerpot. A horrific bolt of pain shot up his leg, throwing him flat on his chest, directly on top of a grave. He bit his tongue, and the wind was knocked out of him.

You have to be kidding me, he thought, turning over, searching for air that his lungs couldn't take in. He tried again for a shot of air, and he managed a small breath, followed by a deeper one. Slowly, he sat up, doing a mental body check. Nothing broken. Just bruised.

Way to go, Norman—you've totally lost it. This is insane. Running? Why?

He thought about the word *insane* and how frighteningly well it described his thoughts and feelings over the last couple of days. Very little of it made sense to him. He shivered, glanced back to see where his coat landed, and saw it spread out across the top of a grave several rows down. He looked over his shoulder at the cross, still strangely distant. What religious taboo had he committed by running across the tops of all those graves?

He leaned back again on his elbow, took another deep breath, and caught the name on the tombstone only a foot or so from his face.

"Pardon the intrusion, Andrew Hood," he said.

He brushed his hair back from his eyes with the heel of his hand. "And hello there, Robert and Karen Thomas," he added, reading the two names that shared a single headstone directly across from him. He wondered what happened to them. They'd died the same day.

"Needle in a haystack," he said again, looking around at all the headstones. "I'm sorry, Amy. Please forgive me for not being able to find you."

Somewhere within these grounds was the body of his dead sister. Not that she likely looked the way he remembered. After all of these years, he imagined she was nothing more than bones and dust inside the pink dress she was buried in.

The funeral.

He could still see the emotionless expression on his father's face as Drake Norman looked at his dead daughter, too young to be wearing makeup. Her curly brown hair splayed out across a small satin pillow.

And then there was *the stare.*

He remembered his father's arms crossed and the peculiar tilt of his head. That stare stayed fixed on Zach long after Amy's casket was closed for the last time. And it said many terrible things that words could never convey. *You failed. She was your responsibility, Zachary. How could you let it happen?*

He'd never forget it.

Zach swallowed hard and rose, brushing off the grass. He put his head in his hands and closed his eyes.

"I am so sorry, Dad," he said. "I am so sorry, Amy. Please, please forgive me."

"It wasn't your fault, Zach."

He instantly recognized the voice. He slowly opened his eyes, and the carpenter was standing four graves down, the tip of the cross glimmering directly behind him in the distance.

Zach nodded. "I knew it. I knew you would be here."

Kenneth stepped closer, walking slowly yet purposefully around the back of the headstones before cutting back to the side of the grave he sat on.

Zach crossed his arms and looked into his eyes. "I've been thinking quite a bit about you. That was some nifty work with that cross yesterday."

Kenneth nodded.

Zach looked away. "I have a feeling that one was just for me."

"Maybe it was, Zach."

Zach lowered his chin. "I tried to find out who you are. I called your employer to get some background on you. They wouldn't give out any information."

"That's not important," Kenneth said. "But, Zach, you need to know that what happened to Amy wasn't your fault."

"What do you mean?"

"You know exactly what I mean."

Zach stared at him for a long moment. "Who are you, man?" he whispered.

"I am—"

"It *was* my fault," Zach said sternly, his whisper evaporating. "It was *all* my fault."

"Says who?" Kenneth asked. "Your father? Don't you think it's time to let it go?"

Zach's hands clenched into fists. He could see her flowing hair behind that window—*outside that room*. He knew it was all his fault. Hadn't he relived it over and over in his dreams? "She wanted in so badly. I couldn't open that window."

The carpenter remained quiet.

Zach continued, his voice weakening and his fists starting to shake. "I kicked it, I punched it . . . and she scratched at it and scratched at it. She wanted in. I tried. I did my best."

Kenneth was perfectly still. "Yes, you did."

"How do you even know what I'm talking about?" Zach asked defensively. "How did you know my sister's name? Tell me. Please tell me."

Kenneth didn't respond.

I'm losing it, totally losing it. Here I am, spilling my guts to a carpenter . . . But that wasn't true. There was something special about the man. Something that let him see everything, know everything. You could see it in his eyes. Zach combed his hair back with his fingers and crossed his arms. "I just want the nightmare to stop."

"I know it hurts," Kenneth said, stepping to the foot of the grave to face the headstone. "But we both know it's not only a dream but a memory—an instant replay that has been torturing you for a long, long time."

"It isn't fair," Zach said. He could still see her small hands pressed against the window like it was happening now, right before him. "I was supposed to be watching her. It should have been me."

"It wasn't your fault, Zach."

"The carpet—it was so cold."

"It wasn't carpet. It was snow."

"I was trapped."

"No, you weren't, Zach. *She* was trapped."

"No!" Zach yelled. "I couldn't open the window!"

"It was ice you couldn't break."

Zach looked quickly at the carpenter. *How does he know?*

"Do you remember the ice?" Kenneth asked softly.

"Yes! It wouldn't break!"

"It was a foot thick, Zach."

"I couldn't break it!"

"You were a boy, Zach. Twelve."

"I should be here, not her," he said, his hand pointing in a circle around the cemetery. "Why couldn't it have been me? Amy never hurt anyone."

"It wasn't your time, Zach. It was Amy's time."

Amy's time?

Zach covered his face with his hands. The carpenter's answer was just a little too cliché. It made Amy's life sound like an expiring gallon of milk, like it was stamped with some predetermined date that was never up for negotiation.

"You're wrong," Zach said, pressing the heel of his palm against his forehead. "Amy had on brand-new skates. It was the first time she'd worn them . . ." He closed his eyes and shook his head.

"Take your time," Kenneth said.

"I saved money from my paper route to buy her white figure skates for Christmas. She had always worn my old black hockey skates. She never complained about them; it's just that all of her friends had the white ones—the pretty ones. I couldn't wait to give them to her, so I gave them to her early, and we went out to the lake. You should have seen her. She was so happy."

"Yes, she was," Kenneth whispered.

He paused over the carpenter's strange remark, but by now he was too immersed in the story to stop. He had to get it out. "I heard the ice break, the only place it was so thin—the *only* place. Every other place it was rock solid. She fell straight through the ice—I mean *straight* through . . . and the current . . . it took her farther, and then . . ."

"Zach," Kenneth said.

Zach's breathing was fast and rapid. He wanted to cry, but he didn't remember the last time he had—maybe he'd forgotten how. "Her face—I could *see* it under there, under the ice. I tried so hard. She was looking up at me, clawing at the ice. I couldn't—I tried everything—I just couldn't break it." He lowered his head, staring down at his hands, shaking violently.

"Everything happens for a reason, Zach. *Every single thing.*"

"Reason?" he said. He was suddenly welling with hate, and he fixed his resentment on Kenneth. "What reason could there possibly be for Amy to die? Tell me why an innocent, ten-year-old little girl falls through the ice and drowns. Please tell me *that.*"

Kenneth stepped around the grave but remained silent.

"Tell me!" the doctor yelled at the top of his lungs, the *me* echoing through the cemetery.

"Why don't you tell me something?" Kenneth whispered, touching Zach's shoulder and pointing in the direction of the cross with his other hand. "Tell me what you feel when you look at that."

"The cross?" he asked. The hate seemed to drain out of him, leaving him hollow, weak.

"Tell me what you think about when you look at it. Tell me what you feel."

Zach hesitated for a moment, needing to understand why he suddenly felt so peaceful. He thought about the carpenter's question and then answered, "Oddly calm. But I'm so confused. No, more like *bewildered.* It makes me think about the cross yesterday, at the Lindys' church, and *you.* I've gone over it dozens of times in my mind, man. It's insanity. I went back to St. Thomas this morning. Just to look at it. It's impossible, any which way I try to explain it."

Kenneth lowered his hand from the doctor's shoulder and said, "You know what, Zach? You don't *have* to understand everything, and you don't *have* to be the one who is always in control."

"Yeah, I do."

"Listen for a second," Kenneth said. "Truly listen. You don't have to understand everything, and you don't always have to be the one who is in control."

"Why not?"

"Because, regardless of how you feel, and what you think you've experienced, you can't—and you aren't."

Zach shook his head and thought, *Who in the world is this guy?* "I don't understand you, man. I'm not even close to understanding."

The carpenter grinned in a way Zach wasn't sure he liked—but maybe it didn't really matter, because this was just another weird day in a series of weird days.

"What are you looking for here at the cemetery, Zach?" Kenneth asked. "Why are you here?"

"I guess I'm looking for Amy's grave."

"Why?"

He started to say something and then stopped. He finally looked at Kenneth. "I'm really not sure. I can't find the grave anyhow, and I have—"

"How would you feel if I told you Mr. Hood isn't dead?" Kenneth pointed to the grave beside them.

"What?" Zach said in irritation, reading the man's name on the granite headstone. "That's his grave."

"Let me try that again," the carpenter said. "Would you understand or believe me if I told you that Amy was more alive than ever?"

"No," Zach said, unable to block the memories—the police yelling and pointing, ordering people to stand back; the whining, whirring sound of the chain saw opening up a square in the ice; the frogmen pushing Amy's lifeless body out through the hole in the ice and onto the frozen lake like a stillborn baby.

"No?" Kenneth asked. "Why not?"

"No," he repeated, trying to block out the figure skates, the wet clothes, the matted hair, and the strange, practically light-blue color of his sister's face. "It's impossible. I *saw* her." He shook his head and pinched his temples. "Much as I wish I hadn't."

"Let me try another one, then," Kenneth said, squatting down into a catcher's position and tugging out a few blades of dead grass from the grave. "Would you believe it if someone told you that a cross cut in half by a bolt of lightning could look like new in a matter of moments?"

Zach studied the carpenter suspiciously out of the corner of his eye. "That's not fair."

"Why not? Did it happen, or did it not?"

"Normally I would say that it's impossible, but in this case I *know* it happened. I was there."

"But Amy being more alive than ever is impossible? What's the difference?"

"I just told you," Zach said. "I *saw* it. I saw the cross only a few minutes before *and* after it happened. Seeing is believing."

"Zach," Kenneth said quickly, "if you told someone what happened yesterday with the cross, what would they say to you?"

"They probably wouldn't believe me. They'd think I was nuts."

"But you understand why they'd think your story was a little tough to swallow."

"Of course," Zach said. "But that doesn't change the fact that it happened. I saw it with my own two eyes."

"Tell me, then," Kenneth said, putting his hand on Zach's shoulder again and giving it a little squeeze, "how would you tell someone they should trust what you say—to believe—to only believe *without* seeing?"

"I don't know," Zach said. "I guess I'd tell them that they have to take my word for it. They'd just have to believe what I say."

"They'd *have* to believe you?"

"I guess they wouldn't have to. I'd hope that they chose to."

"There you go!" Kenneth said, taking his hand off Zach's shoulder and stepping around the back of the grave as if to leave.

"W-What?" Zach said, wishing he had never come to the cemetery but feeling, somehow, like the carpenter was abandoning him. "Where are you going?"

Kenneth let out a little laugh. "I have some errands to run. I still have to get my costume for Saturday."

"Saturday?"

"The harvest party at the church," Kenneth said cheerfully. He clapped his hands together and leaned over slightly to put his hands on the top edge of Andrew Hood's headstone. "Believing is a choice, Zach. You can't *force* somebody to do it. Does that make sense?"

Zach nodded in agreement.

"Amy is more alive than ever. More alive than you could ever imagine."

Zach stared into his eyes. There was no shade of dishonesty in the man. No sense of ego or anything bad he could identify at all. He swallowed hard. "I want to believe that, Kenneth. I really do."

The carpenter smiled. "Tough to swallow? Kind of like how people might respond if you tell them about the cross?"

Zach looked around the cemetery again. "Something like that. Yes."

"I have a quick question," Kenneth said, holding his hands out. "What do you call believing without seeing? What do you call it when you make the choice to believe—the choice to let everything else go that you thought you knew and just believe?"

"I'm not sure," Zach said. "What do you call it?"

The carpenter slowly walked toward him. Zach kept waiting for him to stop, but he didn't until their faces were only a foot away from each other. He felt a slight chill dance across his neck but conversely felt steadied, strong, assured. He looked into the man's eyes and waited for the answer.

"It's called faith, Zach."

Zach couldn't look away. The chill ran down his back, and what he tried to ask only came out as a whisper. "Who are you, man?"

"You know who I am."

Zach froze, and the carpenter's face was now within inches of his.

"Zach, I know it scares you, because it goes against everything *you* always believed."

The chill was gone. A warmth passed through him, as if he'd just wrapped up in a down blanket. He stood speechless as Kenneth took a few steps backward and then turned to walk slowly up the hill. The carpenter finally stopped at the top and turned around. He held his hands up in the air and shouted, "Only believe, Zach! Amy is more alive than ever!"

"Only believe," Zach whispered, his ankles and feet still feeling as if they were buried in wet cement. "I want to. But I can't."

The carpenter disappeared over the other side of the hill toward the cross, and Zach looked at his watch. He was now over an hour late. "Only believe," he muttered again.

He turned around and limped back toward the entrance.

"Don't forget your coat!" he heard. "You left it back there." It was the old man who'd been fiddling with the flowers, who was now sitting on the crumbled bench, pointing behind him.

"Thanks!" Zach yelled, waving to the old man before rotating around gingerly on his slightly twisted knee. He walked toward the grave, and when he reached it, he said to the back of the headstone, "I'll bet this is the first time you ever had on a $1,200 coat. Thanks for keeping an eye on it for me."

He stepped on top of the grave, picked the coat up, and folded it across his arm. "And I guess I probably owe you an apology too," he said, turning to face the tombstone. "I certainly didn't mean any—"

AMY ELIZABETH NORMAN
BELOVED DAUGHTER AND SISTER
SEPTEMBER 22, 1971–DECEMBER 18, 1981

Zach dropped the coat and blinked hard before quickly stepping backward off the side of the grave. He tried swallowing and couldn't. His cheeks felt paralyzed, and his mouth gaped open as he stared at the headstone.

"Amy," he finally said breathlessly, the faded black letters on the tombstone blurring and then slowly coming back into focus. "There you are."

He licked his lips and ran his hand across his forehead. He looked back to the old man on the bench. He was gone.

But then he felt it. Knew it. Knew it before he even looked.

The carpenter was back on top of the hill, arms at his sides, looking down the hill and straight across Amy Norman's grave into the eyes of her big brother.

Zach felt something creeping down his cheek. He wiped it away and could feel the wind cooling it on the back of his hand. It was a teardrop. There was another one, and then another. He lifted his hand to his face, choking on sobs long buried, and looked back up on the hill.

The carpenter was gone.

"Only believe," Zach whispered again, this time to the tip of the cross that glistened beyond the hill.

His legs gave out and he dropped to his knees on top of the grave.

Then Zach leaned his head against his sister's headstone and cried—for the first time in twenty-eight years.

✣ TWENTY-ONE

Despite the brief nap she had taken, Brooke was exhausted and couldn't remember ever being so tired. She tugged the sleeve of her sweatshirt down into her palm and gripped it tightly to wipe the side of her face. She sat up on the couch and looked out the window at three doves that had settled on the front porch's wooden railing.

"You feeling better?" Shirley asked, crossing the living room to lean over and kiss Brooke on the cheek.

Six years ago it wasn't really that difficult to explain to the Lindys the chain of events that led to her getting pregnant. But what was coming would be tough—the thought of finally chasing that skeleton out of its closet took her from euphoric relief to absolute terror and back again, banging off two imaginary borders like a tiny rubber pinball.

"So," Pastor Jim said, sitting back in the aged recliner. "I hear you're to meet with Alex's father? That was quick."

"Yeah," Brooke said. "He has the same cell phone number."

"When was the last time you saw him?" Shirley asked, perching on a rocker, coffee cup between her hands.

"I ran into him a few years ago at the movies," Brooke said, sitting up. "I'm lucky I got ahold of him. Other than the movies, I haven't seen him since I worked at the plant. I don't even know what I'm going to say." *Hey there. Funny thing. I forgot to tell you that you're a daddy . . .*

"What'd you tell him?" Pastor Jim asked, interrupting her hundredth conversation rehearsal.

"Just that we needed to talk and that it's important," Brooke answered. "He said he'll be back in town Thursday." She looked at the ceiling and shook her head. "Seriously. How do you tell someone something like this?"

"Just tell him the truth," Pastor Jim said. "And God will take care of the rest."

"Tell him Alexander is a gift from God," Shirley added. "He'll know that when they meet."

"And tell him he may lose a son he hasn't met?" Brooke whispered. "Isn't it . . . I don't know, sort of cruel?"

"That's not going to happen," Shirley said, walking into the kitchen, leaving a silence in the living room that seemed to hum.

"Leukemia," Brooke said. The word detonated like a little bomb, flooding the room with an invisible threat.

"It's not going to happen," Shirley repeated confidently from the kitchen.

Pastor Jim slowly leaned forward in the La-Z-Boy and laced his fingers tightly together. "Let's take a walk, Brooke, shall we?"

"Okay," she said. "Let me check on Alex real quick."

"They're out cold," Shirley said, walking back into the living room. "Down in the basement."

Brooke opened the basement door and lightly tiptoed down the steps to peek around the corner.

Charlie was flat on his back on the small couch, his legs folded over the end of it at ninety-degree angles with his feet flat on the floor. He was wearing a white T-shirt and his gray cotton sweatpants, and the big toe of his right foot was sticking out through a hole in his sock.

Alex was sprawled out across Charlie's chest. He was snoring lightly and appeared to be wrapped in a gray sleeping bag that was actually the matching top to Charlie's sweatpants. He had a piece of popcorn in his hair, and tiny beads of sweat dotted his forehead. His small body rose with each of Charlie's inhaled snores, and then slowly lowered as Charlie exhaled.

Brooke lightly touched the side of Alex's cheek, and then his forehead, noticing that the sweat that had dewed on her son's head was alarmingly cool. Alex lifted his head, mumbled something in his sleep, and then plopped his cheek back on Charlie's chest.

Brooke picked up a half-empty glass of cherry Kool-Aid, grabbed a pair of macaroni-and-cheese-stained plastic bowls off the coffee table, and headed back upstairs.

Pastor Jim was pulling a faded navy blue sweatshirt over his head that ultimately revealed *Carlson Rotary* emblazoned across his chest. "We'll be back in about an hour," he said to Shirley. He leaned his head toward Brooke. "Let's go, kiddo."

Brooke put the dishes in the kitchen sink and then returned to the living room to grab a rarely worn jean jacket out of the closet. She followed Pastor Jim out the front door into a light breeze and unusually bright autumn sun.

Both of them were quietly absorbing the news of the day, and neither of them said anything until they had reached the gravel of Church Road.

"Why don't you ever worry about anything, Pastor Jim?" Brooke asked. "Why doesn't anything ever seem to bother you?"

Pastor Jim continued to walk while pulling lightly at his ear. "My father once told me something when I was quite young. He told me that worry is disbelief in disguise."

Brooke crossed her arms and cupped her elbows with her palms. "So if you worry, that means you don't believe?"

"I'm really not sure," he said. "I think what my father meant was to give up control to God."

"I can't help it though," Brooke said. "I'm worried about Alex, and now I'm worried about Carla. She won't answer my calls. I called work to tell them I needed a couple weeks off to take care of Alex, and they said she didn't show up today."

"Hmm," Pastor Jim said. "Carla was pretty horrified about Tim. She'll get through it. And our little Alex will get through this too."

"I still don't see how you never worry."

"Oh, I have my moments of worry," he said with a frown.

"What do you worry about?"

"Charlie," Pastor Jim said without hesitating. "I worry about Charlie."

"Charlie?" Brooke asked. "Charlie always seems so happy."

He nodded. "That may be true, but . . ."

Brooke took his arm and they stopped. "But what?"

He turned his head away and then back to Brooke. "What is going to happen to him when Shirley and I are gone?"

Brooke didn't say anything, painfully imagining life without Pastor Jim and Shirley. "Don't worry about Charlie, Pastor Jim. I'll take care of him. He'd always have a home with me."

Pastor Jim held out his arm, which Brooke stepped under. He pulled her next to him as they continued to stroll. "You're wonderful, Brooke. But your whole life is in front of you—and Charlie isn't your responsibility."

"We are all each other's responsibility," Brooke said. "We're a family, and Charlie will always be part of the life that's in front of me."

"Yes, we are a family," he said, smiling. "Thank you, Brooke. Thank you for reminding me. And, honey . . . Alex is going to be fine."

"You seem so sure," Brooke said, looking at three doves on the side of the road in front of them. The same three from the porch rail? *That's weird . . .*

"Do you believe that the Lord sometimes works in unusual ways, Brooke?"

Brooke stopped walking. "I guess so."

"I've been meaning to tell you this since you got back," he said. "I think our construction worker friend may be blessed. And I also think he may have given me a word, intended for you."

"You're talking about Kenneth."

"Yes, I am," he answered.

"He sure seems to know a lot about other people. It's not just Tim that made Carla freak out. Something happened at the bar between her and Kenneth, and she was already . . . out of sorts. I've *never* seen her like this. Even when she used to drink *a lot.*"

"Why didn't she come talk to me?" he asked.

"I have no idea."

"Let's try to get ahold of her again when we go back in. Maybe she'll pick up my call."

"Okay."

Pastor Jim took Brooke's arm. "Listen, Kenneth told me something that I wanted to share with you."

Brooke hesitated. She wasn't sure she wanted to hear Kenneth's "word" for her. Would it set her off as it had Carla? But looking at Pastor Jim's face, she could tell there'd really be no way of avoiding it. "What is it?"

Pastor Jim looked like he was mulling it over. "Brooke, I have complete faith in God's ability to heal Alexander."

"What did Kenneth say?" Brooke said, narrowing her eyes. "Tell me."

"He quoted a Bible verse at the diner but changed it slightly," he said. "Brooke, I can't really explain it. But I just know that he was talking about Alex. It was as if he *knew* Alex was sick before any of us did."

"He couldn't possibly know," Brooke said. "What Scripture did he quote?"

"He said, 'Tell her to only believe and *he* will be made well.' What else could he possibly have been talking about?"

"It's obviously some kind of coincidence, Pastor Jim."

"Maybe," he said. "Regardless, we already believe with all our heart and our soul that God can heal Alex. Right?"

"I believe that," Brooke said.

"That's all you *can* do."

They walked for a time in silence, each deep in thought. Brooke looked over her shoulder, thinking about Alex sweating, but cold. And sleeping again. "Maybe we should get back, Pastor Jim."

"Of course, of course." They turned and went back the way they came. When they reached the edge of the driveway that separated the house from St. Thomas, Brooke stopped again. She crossed her arms and glanced up at the cross.

"What is it, Brooke?"

"Pastor Jim, do you really believe that people can know things? That they can give—I mean, really give—a 'word' from the Lord?"

"I do," he said. "But I'm not sure I ever really witnessed it until I met Kenneth." He smiled. "Take a look at that cross. Doesn't seeing that burned and broken, then whole, all within an hour make you a tiny bit more open to what he had to say?"

"Open to what he has to say . . . or just willing to accept amazing carpentry skills. He didn't claim it was an act of God. Why should we?"

Pastor Jim just smiled and turned toward the cross as if he could see it too. "Truly, Brooke. How can we not? Sure, God used a man. But he used him mightily—all we can ever pray that he would do with each of us. I would say the Almighty has placed someone special in our path, and we'd be wise to pay attention when he has a word for us."

Brooke took a deep breath and saw them out of the corner of her eye—the three doves. They were about thirty feet in the air and banking hard off the tree line on the other side of the church. She held her breath as they cut across the church lawn and then quickly pulled up, gracefully lifting their wings to softly land.

They landed on the cross.

She slowly tilted her head to the side and said, "What'd Kenneth say again?"

"Only believe," Pastor Jim said. "And he will be made well."

✢ TWENTY-TWO

"It's the salsa that makes this place famous," Kaitlyn said, dipping a warm tortilla chip into a bowl of Dos Hermanos's superhot salsa.

"Mm-hmm," Macey said, taking a sip of her margarita.

"You sure seem quiet," Kaitlyn said.

"Just thinking, that's all," Macey said, breaking a chip in two and dipping in herself.

"A quiet Dr. Lewis is like a Sasquatch or Nessie sighting," Kaitlyn added. "It's more than a little rare. What's wrong?"

Macey seemed to force a smile. "I don't know. You're going to think I'm losing my mind."

A pair of elderly mariachis began serenading three women a couple of booths down, and Kaitlyn hoped they wouldn't come their way. "For me to think you're losing your mind, it must be good. Lay it on me."

"Do you believe in God?"

"Wow," Kaitlyn said, surprised. Something about the way Macey asked it made her uncomfortable, as if a stranger had guessed her age or weight. But this was no stranger—this was Macey Lewis.

"Wow?" Macey echoed softly. "I get a wow?"

"Yeah," Kaitlyn said, squinting suspiciously. "One trip to church, and you're asking the ultimate question?"

"I'm sorry," Macey said. "You asked me what was wrong, and I'm telling you."

"What are you sorry for?" Kaitlyn said, noting that her friend was oddly serious.

"The God talk," Macey said. "I guess there's a reason people

179

don't talk about politics and religion. The topics can obviously create some discomfort."

"I'm perfectly comfortable discussing it," Kaitlyn said. "Even though I may not know what I'm talking about when the subject comes up, I'm still comfortable with it."

"Answer the question, then," Macey said, tapping her finger on the table.

Kaitlyn hurriedly drank some ice water. Her mouth burned from the salsa, and she tongue-parked a piece of ice against the inside of her cheek. "I guess I want to believe in God—that there is something more."

Macey ran her finger around the rim of her sweating glass. "What would it take for you to actually believe?"

"I guess I'm really not sure," Kaitlyn answered. She wasn't dodging the question; she kind of liked the idea that they were talking about God. "Is it safe for me to assume that going to church inspired this?"

"Of course," Macey said. "But it had a little more to do with the people we were *with* at the church."

"I agree," Kaitlyn said, readjusting the napkin on her lap. "It felt good to me just being there, like I was doing something right. It was like I was actually where I was supposed to be on Sunday mornings."

"Yes," Macey said, "but I'm not sure it was just being in church, per se; I think there are some really strange things happening around us. It's hard for me to explain. Some of it just doesn't make sense to me."

"Like what?"

"You saw that cross before they fixed it," Macey said, scraping the tomatoes off a pair of tacos on the plate in front of her.

"I'll take those if you don't want 'em," Kaitlyn said.

"Sure," Macey said, picking up her plate and sliding the tomatoes onto Kaitlyn's. She paused a moment. "Kait, something's going on, and I think Zach knows it too. Have you ever seen him as quiet as he was at the diner?"

"I thought he was sulking about me."

"Sorry to burst your bubble," Macey said. "But I think it's because he was totally overwhelmed. Zach *just* missed seeing whatever happened to that cross because he *conveniently* got that splinter in his hand. And that big guy, Charlie, saw it happen and peed his pants. He was terrified! Kait, I'm telling you that the construction worker did his thing to the cross in front of the minister who couldn't *see* it, and the big guy who couldn't *talk* about it, while the doctor was away."

Kaitlyn took a slow sip of her margarita. "So you're saying the carpenter made Zach get a splinter? Don't you think that's a stretch, Doc?"

Macey sighed and sat back, crossing her arms. "Any way you dice it up, something bizarre happened."

"Because the carpenter fixed the cross. Like he was supposed to."

"Kaitlyn. He. Fixed. It. Too. Fast."

"We don't know that! He does this *for a living*."

"C'mon, Kait!" Macey said, smacking the table with her hand and turning a few heads. "It was totally destroyed. You don't have to know anything about construction to recognize that. Even if he had a brand-new cross sitting there, he couldn't have planted it that fast!"

"But he did," Kaitlyn said, squinting at her friend, never having seen her so worked up over anything but a patient. "You said strange things were happening. What else?"

"How about Zach yelling 'Amy' in the phone when I called? I wonder if that had anything to do with why he was late for work today."

"Late?" Kaitlyn said. "He never came in."

"Yes, he did. He ended up coming in around two."

"Hmm. I didn't see him," Kaitlyn said. *He came in and didn't talk to me?*

"He made his rounds and left. In fact, I heard he spent more time with the kids today than ever."

"That must explain why I didn't see him then," Kaitlyn said.

Macey took a bite of her taco and stared at her. "Someone sounds miffed. Weird, for a girl who doesn't care anymore."

"Please," Kaitlyn said. "Now you are really talking *bizarre*."

Macey bit her lip and then paused. "You really want to hear something weird?"

"Go for it," Kaitlyn said.

"I also think Kenneth may have had something to do with Mary Springsted's recovery."

"How?"

"Before he came to see us at my office, when I was getting on the elevator, all of the elevators were stuck on five. And then, when I apologized to him for being late, I could have sworn he said it gave him a chance to visit an old friend *on the fifth floor*. I believe that friend was Mary Springsted."

The mariachis came to their table, and Kaitlyn politely waved them off.

Macey took another sip of her drink and continued. "Not to mention those words I've heard Kenneth say on more than one occasion."

"What words?"

"Only believe," Macey said. "He said it a couple times to me, and then Dr. Timmins said Mr. Springsted was shouting that same phrase."

"Check with the staff on five and see if he was up there."

"I did."

"And?"

"They said the only visitor she ever had was her husband."

"I think that about closes the case, then," Kaitlyn said. "Either that, or our magical carpenter had his magic carpet parked outside the fifth-floor window."

"I'm being totally serious," Macey said. "He was *there*. I know it. And quit looking at me like I'm crazy."

"What are you trying to say, then?"

Macey gave her a little shrug, fiddling with a chip. "I don't know. Only this . . . If Kenneth's a miracle worker, I can't wait to see what happens next."

✢ TWENTY-THREE

It'd been a couple of years since Carla had been this drunk, for this long. But no matter how much she drank, she couldn't find the freedom she was looking for . . . only emptiness.

Sitting here, on the edge of the Big Island Toll Bridge in the dark, her feet dangling over a hundred feet of emptiness, she thought it was somehow just right. *An empty girl, in an empty space. If I just let go, I might disappear. Maybe then I'll find freedom.* She stared down at the dark, swirling waters, catching reflections of the moon on the crests of the small waves. *Maybe I was never supposed to be here at all.*

Cars passed by her, but with a support beam directly at her back, she doubted any of them could see her. She adjusted her earbuds. Seals & Crofts's "Summer Breeze" ended, then Phil Collins started to tell her about something "In the Air Tonight." She looked down, and the frigid wind that bounced off the Detroit River hit her arms in a way that felt everything but summery.

Dark forms swept from the sky, and she was so startled, she almost slipped from the rail. Wings came so close to her face, she could swear she felt feathers. Ten feet away, three small owls landed and drew in their wings. The one closest to her stared at her with a wide, slow blink.

She stared back at them in amazement, wondering if that last rum and Coke was now giving her hallucinations. "Go! Shoo!" she said, waving her hand.

The closest one only blinked again and rotated his head to look at the passing traffic, then over to his two friends, then back to her.

Carla had never seen anything like them. She'd only heard owls in the night, never laid eyes on one. And now, here was a family of them. She frowned. The closest acted like a seagull, begging for scraps.

"Go on, now!" she tried again, moving as if she intended to jump up and grab him. "I don't have anything for you! Can't you see? I'm nothing. Worthless. Hopeless. A dirty drunk! Go! Shoo!"

But the owl remained where he was, with the two behind him nothing more than a pair of shadows, closing their eyes as if to rest. *Maybe this is their home,* Carla thought.

Her cell phone vibrated against her hip through her coat pocket. It buzzed three times, and she took it out and looked at it. It was Brooke again.

Carla had ignored all of Brooke's calls since they'd parted yesterday but decided to answer this one. The last one. It was time to say good-bye.

She pulled out one earbud, opened the phone, and listened without saying anything. She could hear Brooke.

"Carla?" There was a brief pause. "Are you there?"

Carla didn't know what to say. There were a lot of things she wanted to tell Brooke. She wanted to tell her the real reason why she was at the bridge, after all this time. She had always wanted to tell her, but never could.

That really didn't matter now anyway, so she decided to tell Brooke the only thing that really did. "I love you, Brooke."

"Carla? Carla, where are you? I'll come get you. Just—"

Carla closed the phone and rubbed the smooth surface with her thumb. She could almost see Brooke's face in it, Alex's too. The Lindys. "I'm sorry," she whispered. She held it straight out in front of her and let it drop, watching it fall away from her, over and over, then disappear into the water with a little splash.

She carefully wrapped her earbud cord around her iPod, still playing, and sent that to the depths too.

Just a little splash and they're gone. Like me.

The owl shifted, partially opening and closing his wings,

startling her. In her drunken haze, she'd kind of forgotten he was there.

"Hooo-hooooo," he cooed, the sound of it oddly comforting.

"Who?" she muttered. "Ain't nobody here. Or not for long, anyway."

She lit another Marlboro Light, took a deep drag off it, then looked straight up the river toward Detroit. In the distance, to the right of the Detroit skyline, she could see the Ambassador Bridge connecting Detroit to Canada. The upper supports of the bridge were lit up, making it look like the hills of a roller coaster that took people to another country.

Another country, she thought. *Another world. Another time.* Anywhere—anywhere away from the way she felt sounded good to her.

She rubbed her cheeks, numbed by the cold breeze. She looked off the north edge of Big Island into Canada and could see little fingers of lightning flickering miles away. She thought about where she would be when the storm finally came. *Where my body will be.*

Sometime between bar three and bar four, Carla had quit wondering why her life had turned out the way it did. *It's not unfair—it's all my fault. All of it. Every rotten thing. I'm a curse on people, always have been, always will be.* Except for Brooke and Alex and the Lindys. They were her sole bright spots. Everything else? Superficial. False.

Even Daddy . . . he didn't really love me. If he had, he wouldn't have—

"Hooooo-hooo," she heard.

"Who?" she said, with a humorless laugh. "Well, my dad, for starters." *I hate him for what he did. For all of it. For coming to my bedroom all of those nights. For blowing out his brains when I told Mama.* She blew out a long stream of cigarette smoke. Guilt washed through her. Familiar confusion. Doubt. Love.

"It's all my fault," she whispered in a frozen puff of air.

But that's okay, she told herself. *Because it's almost over.*

She thought about her mother, starving and drinking herself to death after Daddy died. Her fault too.

But that's okay. I'm about to make it right.

She thought about Brooke, and Alex and the Lindys, and how she'd disappointed them. How this final act would disappoint them.

But that's okay. I'll never disappoint them again.

She thought about Tim and how he hit Charlie at the diner, and how he used to hit her. As much as she tried, she was always screwing up every relationship she had. Making bad choices. Finding another bad seed.

But that's okay. It's over. No man will ever touch me again.

Carla took one last, big drag on her cigarette and scooted closer to the edge of the wide rail. She leaned over and looked straight down at the water. The river now seemed so close.

She thought about the little girl she'd met in the apartment last night. *This morning,* she corrected herself. It seemed like so long ago. And then she thought of herself as a little girl. It seemed like yesterday.

Then she thought about Kenneth one last time. She had absolutely no idea how he did it, but he knew her. He knew everything about her.

All of it.

That's . . . not okay.

And then she jumped.

✢ TWENTY-FOUR

J im used his left thumb as a bookmark and gently closed the Bible. He lowered the book to his lap and took a long, slow breath, struggling to digest what he'd just read. He pulled up on the lever on the side of the chair to lift the leg rest and lay back, closing his eyes, thinking on it.

He imagined the ancient prophets and their remarkable God-given abilities. He wondered about the possible existence of modern-day prophets, or those capable of "signs and wonders."

He wasn't quite sure who Kenneth was, but he knew for certain that he had never met anyone like him. He knew so little about Kenneth, and yet he felt like he'd known him his whole life. And the more he thought about the carpenter's indirect quote of Luke 8:50, the more he was convinced that Kenneth's words directly related to Brooke and Alex. He opened the Bible back up, thumbed his way to Deuteronomy 18, and then ran his finger diligently across a half page of braille until he reached verse 21. "And if you say in your heart, 'How shall we know the word which the LORD has not spoken?'—when a prophet speaks in the name of the LORD, if the thing does not happen or come to pass, that is the thing which the LORD has not spoken."

Jim took a sip of tea that had become a little too cold and thought, *Who are you, Kenneth? You didn't speak in the name of the Lord like the Bible says, but you quoted Luke 8:50 almost perfectly. Why would you say it if it didn't have anything to do with Alex? What else could you possibly have meant?*

Shirley walked into the living room from the kitchen. "Are you coming to bed?"

"I'll be there in a minute," he answered, closing his eyes.

"You are going to fall asleep right there in that chair, James Lindy."

"No, I won't," he said, opening his eyes dutifully.

"Yes, you will."

He smiled and picked the Bible up off his lap to set it on the side table. "What time is it?"

"Quarter past eleven."

"Okay. You're right. I'm comin'." Jim pushed the side lever down and lowered his leg rest. But he didn't rise. "What time are you guys going to the hospital in the morning?"

"They are doing the procedure at six forty-five," Shirley said, walking into the kitchen. He could hear her setting cups down in the sink. "I'm guessing we will leave here around six."

Shirley came back in and kissed him good night, leaving Jim to the silence of the living room and his big, comfy chair. He lay back again and closed his eyes. *Just five more minutes,* he thought, raising the leg rest again. *Just five more . . .*

Jim could feel someone tapping on his arm. "Charlie, is that you, son?"

"No, Pastor Jim. It's me, Alex."

Jim turned his head, realizing he'd fallen asleep in the chair. "Alexander? What are you doing up?"

"Mom and Charlie are sleeping," Alex answered. "I had a bad dream."

"Come here," Jim said, lifting Alex up into his lap. By the chill and quiet of the house, he knew it was very early.

Jim understood that Alex was fully aware that he had two dead grandparents, two unknown grandparents, and an unknown father. He also suspected that Alex had him pegged as all five wrapped up in one, and on more than one occasion had confided in him certain fears he didn't want anyone else to know about. Jim had a feeling one of those was coming right now.

"I was getting chased by the shot doctor from the hospital. He was in a painting. He was laughing and chasing me around the hospital with a *ginormous* shot in his hand."

"Then what happened?"

"I waked up," Alex said. "Can I tell you something else—and promise not to tell Mom?"

"I'll try."

Alex put his mouth next to Jim's ear and then surrounded it with his hands to whisper, "I'm afraid about tomorrow."

"Why is that?" Jim whispered back.

"I'm getting a shot. Don't tell Mom or Nurse Kaitlyn I'm afraid, okay?"

"Your secret's safe with me. I don't like shots either."

"Really?" Alex asked, and Jim thought he sounded a little surprised and relieved that he wasn't alone in his fear. "But you give yourself shots all the time for your beeties."

"That's right," Jim said. "For my diabetes. But I still don't like the shots, even though they only hurt for a second."

"I know," Alex said. "I had them before."

"Oh, that's right," Jim said. "You're a big kid now, and you know they only hurt for a second."

"Yeah," Alex said. Jim could feel him stretching out on the chair next to him. "Why was my mom crying today?"

"Don't you worry about your mother. She is just fine."

"Why was she crying, then? Was it because of me?"

"People cry for all sorts of reasons," Jim said. "The important thing to know is that she's okay." He gave the boy a little hug. "When was the last time you cried, Alex?"

"I don't cry as much as I used to," Alex said, sounding more like eight than five. "I'm growing up."

Jim chuckled. "Yes, you are, Alex. Yes, you are. But you still fit when you're cuddling with me." He leaned the chair all the way back and could feel Alex's head rest on his shoulder. "How about a story?"

"Can you tell me about the man in the fish?"

Jim smiled. "There was a man who lived a long, long time ago."

"How long ago?" Alex asked sleepily.

"A long, long time ago," Jim repeated.

Alex was asleep by the time Jonah boarded the ship.

With one hand, Jim ran his fingers over the cover of the Bible. The longer he thought about what Kenneth had said, the more convinced he had become.

"Tell her to only believe, and he will be made well."

He smiled and clicked his feet together. *It's no coincidence. The carpenter was definitely talking about Brooke and Alex.*

He closed his eyes and looked forward to talking with Kenneth at the harvest party on Saturday to confirm it. *Now to figure out what the 7:14 thing is all about . . .*

CARLA OPENED HER EYES.

She felt like that time Tim had shoved her against a wall as hard as he could. But this time, she could smell the river all over herself. *My clothes are soaked.* She could see the bottom of the bridge and the glow of headlights that spilled over the edge of the rails, but here, far below, she was in total darkness. She blinked, wondering if she could trust her eyes.

What am I doing here? What happened?

She took a deep breath and sat up, looking down the shoreline to her left, into the darkness. She thought she heard something behind her and looked back over her shoulder.

Nothing.

Carla stood on shaking legs and brushed the sand and pebbles off the bottom of her left arm and hip. She was cold, and the uncomfortable cling of wet jeans made her look up at the bridge again.

I was just up there.

I jumped.

And then . . .

Way to go, loser. You've even managed to screw up your own suicide.

She brought her hands up to her ears and shook her head in disappointment.

Now what?

She had no idea. *What's next? What now? It was all supposed to end!* Now that she was standing, she felt the full effect of the wind off the river as if it were bent on punishing her, making her pay for her sins. Carla turned her back to it and wrapped her arms around herself, trying to keep herself warm. She started walking down the shore, wondering if a good cold night might finish what she couldn't manage to complete, when she heard the voice behind her.

"Things are that bad, eh?"

Carla stopped immediately. The wind was gone and the side of her face warmed. She recognized the voice and that *feeling* on her neck. She turned around and could see Kenneth's silhouette against the lights of the city.

"Why are you here?" she asked.

"You can be forgiven, Carla," he said in that calm voice of his. He started walking toward her, and Carla noticed that with each step he took, that warm feeling spread a little farther across her body.

"No, I can't," Carla said. "What are you doing here?"

"Saving you."

Carla glanced out at the river and then at the carpenter. She lifted her arm and gripped her wet sweatshirt just below her elbow. Then she reached out to touch his arm. But his sweatshirt was bone dry. She jerked her hand away.

What? Did you think he dived in? Hauled you to shore?

"Why are you really here?" she asked.

"I already told you," he said, stepping closer. "Carla, there's an easier way. And it begins with forgiving your father."

Carla took a step back, gaping at him. "I knew it," she muttered. "You really do know everything about me. *Everything.*"

"Some might say that."

"Then you know you shouldn't be hanging out with a girl like me. A drunk. A loser nobody wants. I just want it *over.*" She pointed up at the bridge. "But I—I can't even kill myself without screwing up!"

"It can be over, Carla."

She gaped at him. "It can?"

"Just not in the way you were thinking. You can have a new beginning."

"What?" He was making no sense.

"Tell me why you were up there, Carla," he said calmly.

"You know *exactly* why I was up there. The night I met you, when you told me to forgive, I know you were talking about my dad. But I can't forgive him. I can't!"

"You must. It's the key to your own freedom. Let him off the hook, Carla. Forgive him."

"No. I can't. It's not fair."

"Does forgiveness have to be fair?"

"Please go away. Please just leave me alone."

"No," he said. "I'm staying. Right here, until this is done."

She resisted the urge to strike him, to try and drive him away. "I can't be forgiven! Not for what I've done! And neither should my father!" Hot tears came then, choking her. She swallowed hard and angrily wiped them away. "Some things, some decisions . . . make us what we are. You can't take the stripes off a tiger."

He was perfectly still in the dark. "Yes. Yes, you can."

"You're impossible!" she yelled, quickly turning and walking away. He came up beside her, easily matching her stride.

"I know you can forgive him," he said. "And you can be forgiven too."

"No, I can't! What I've done is terrible! And I can't forgive my father! Get it through your head!"

"Why can't you forgive your father?"

She stopped, turned to him, and crossed her arms and cupped her elbows as the wind blew against her. "Look, I've been to a counselor or two in my time. I know my dad's a big problem in here," she said, pointing to her head, wondering if he could see her in the dark.

"No," he said. He reached out and laid a gentle hand over her heart. "It's a problem in here."

Warmth spread out from where he touched her, and she resisted the urge to lean into him, to ask him to hold her, comfort her. Instead, she pulled away, as if breaking a magnetic force. She took two steps back and shook her head. "You don't understand. I can still see my dad standing in my bedroom doorway the night before he died. The day before he did that to himself. I see it, every day. It's why I drink. To block it out."

"To block what out?"

"To block out what he did to himself. What he did to *me*."

"What he did? Forgive him, Carla. Forgive him now."

"I said no. What he did was too terrible."

"Answer this for me," he said. Kenneth paused and the silence grew between them. "Is one sin greater than another?"

"Yes."

"You're wrong. Sin is sin. If *you* could be forgiven for doing what you think is terrible, why couldn't he?"

She paused, his words playing over in her head. "But who would forgive me?"

"Him," Kenneth said, pointing toward the sky. "That's all the forgiveness you'll ever need."

Carla thought about it and it made no sense. "How can he forgive me after the things I've done?"

"That is up to him, not you. I want you to forgive your father."

"No!" she yelled, the word echoing under the bridge. "It wouldn't be fair to forgive him! I'm glad my dad killed himself!"

Kenneth didn't say anything, and Carla closed her eyes. She remembered getting off the bus that day and tiptoeing into the house, hoping . . . *praying* her father wouldn't hear her come in. The empty beer cans that normally littered the kitchen counter weren't there. Neither were the ashtrays that always overflowed with cigarette butts and ashes.

The only thing on the counter was the case to her father's shotgun.

"Forgive him," Kenneth whispered. "The time is now."

"I love you, baby girl."

Why did her father have to say that the night before he killed himself? It was the only time she could remember him saying it. And he said it on the very last night, of all the nights he stood in her bedroom doorway.

Nights.

Carla wrapped her arms around herself, desperately trying to hold on to the flood of shame that had eaten away at her for so long, to keep it from overflowing onto the carpenter.

She couldn't hold it any longer. It was like he was *pulling* it from her.

"I can't be forgiven for the things I did with my dad."

"Yes, you can."

Carla couldn't look at Kenneth. Though she was sure he already knew, she still had to say it. What she wanted to yell was nothing more than a whisper. "I was only a kid. Only a little girl. He made me do those things."

Her shoulders dipped and she lowered her head. All she could hear was the water and a few cars passing over the bridge. And then Kenneth gently pulled her into his arms, his embrace nothing but brotherly, warm, protecting.

"I know," he said.

"I know." The only words she'd longed to hear. Understanding. Acknowledgment. And yet acceptance too.

"But how?" she asked, feeling the beat of his heart under her cheek, even as doubt began to creep into her own. "How could God possibly forgive someone like me?"

"You know how," he said.

Carla couldn't count the number of times she had heard Pastor Jim talk about it. She opened her eyes and gave Kenneth her answer.

"The cross."

The carpenter nodded.

Carla thought about Christ on the cross for her. "Why would he die for the sins of people like me and my dad? I still don't get it. It doesn't seem . . . it just doesn't seem—"

"Fair?"

"Yes," Carla said, as the word she used earlier took a little bite at her. "Why would he do it, then? Why such a sacrifice for people like us? What is the reason?"

Kenneth released her and stepped slightly away, but he still held her hands. She could feel the heat of his gaze. "Because God wanted this. Relationship. Unbroken relationship."

Was it possible? Really? That she might be not only forgiven, but sought after?

"He wants your heart, Carla," Kenneth said. "He loves you already. More than Brooke and Alex and the Lindys love you. More than all the people who've ever loved you, combined. And he will never fail you. Never leave you." He paused. "Close your eyes."

When she did, she could immediately see those two words that were painted on the side of the train. She remembered explaining to Brooke that there was something she needed to do, and if she just did that one thing, her mistakes would be forgotten.

"Tell me something," Kenneth said, dropping her hands. Carla could feel the warmth in his palms as they met the sides of her face. "Do you really believe that Christ died for you?"

"Yes," Carla said. She really did.

"Carla, did he die for your dad too?"

She hesitated. Swallowed. She didn't want to say it but had to. It was the truth. "Yes," she whispered.

"Was his sacrifice in vain?"

"No," she said reluctantly. But clarity strengthened her. "No!"

"Why?"

"Because he saved me."

"Yes, he did," Kenneth said. "Just as he died to save your dad. Because he loves you both. Completely. Forever." He paused. "Open your eyes, Carla."

She immediately knew that this was different from the first time they had met at The Pilot Inn. There was no more shame, guilt, or fear as she stood under his gaze. She now understood with absolute clarity what his eyes were telling her. She'd figured it out.

She knew she was loved unconditionally in a way that represented pure acceptance, regardless of what she had done. *Even whatever I do next.*

Carla began to sense a limitless form of strength building inside of her. It was building out of that perfect love she felt, and she knew it would allow her to do things beyond anything she ever imagined.

"You know what to do," the carpenter said.

"Forgive him," she whispered. "Forgive him as I've been forgiven."

"Do it now, Carla, as if your father were standing here before you." Kenneth continued to hold on to her, as if pouring his strength into her. And for the first time, Carla felt hope. A shiver of . . . possibility.

She closed her eyes again, seeing her dad stumbling toward her, close enough to see the lines on his face.

Drunk. Crying. Broken.

Broken, like me.

"Say it," Kenneth whispered, still holding on to her face.

In her mind, she reached out to touch her father's face just like Kenneth held hers. Seeing him. Acknowledging him, for all he was and all he was not. But loved, regardless.

"I forgive you, Daddy. I'm sorry—so sorry you were hurt and broken too. I forgive you."

Kenneth's hands fell away from her face, but she could still feel a measure of what he'd given her.

Power, through love. Never had she felt stronger.

Freedom. She felt ten pounds lighter.

And *hope.* A conviction that things really were going to turn out all right.

Carla opened her eyes and blinked.

The carpenter wasn't there.

She smiled and glanced back up at the bridge, never more certain of just one thing.

I'm not alone.

✛ TWENTY-FIVE

B rooke and Shirley were sitting alone in the small waiting room. Alex had just been taken away by both Kaitlyn and Dr. Lewis for a bone marrow aspiration, where they'd take a sample of marrow from either his leg or hip. Even though he was only in the next room and the procedure would supposedly not take that long, Brooke had never felt so far away and separated from her son.

She stared at the small pamphlet on the table in front of her without really seeing it.

"Why can't I be in there with him?" she asked, her protective instincts overflowing. "He probably wants me in there."

"Brooke," Shirley said passively. "You are going to have to trust Dr. Lewis and her team. They certainly seem to know what they are doing."

Brooke picked the pamphlet up and read it. *What to Know When Your Child Has Leukemia.* Her eyes couldn't seem to leave the last word. She didn't like the way it seemed to cruelly drown out the others.

Brooke dropped the pamphlet to her lap.

"You need to be strong," Shirley said. "Open that back up and read it, Brooke Thomas. I think you should know everything. I think you should do your best to understand what they are doing at all times."

Brooke closed her eyes and took a deep breath. She was muddled in a three-way tug-of-war between disbelief, denial, and reality. She struggled to hide the panic in her voice. "I don't know what to do, Shirley. I just don't know what to do."

"Remember what you told me about the doves?" Shirley asked. "About the train car?"

"I know," Brooke said. "If I only believe, Alex will get better." She flipped her cell phone open and thumbed to the text option. She highlighted Carla's name, and despite it being only six thirty in the morning, she began to type: *We can get through whatever is happening, Carla. Plz call me.*

As she studied the letters on the cell phone's small screen, the pit in Brooke's stomach told her that the text would not be returned—not that day, not ever. She knew something had happened to Carla, and whatever it was, she couldn't stop herself from somehow feeling responsible. She still hit Send, and the message was off. She bit her lip and slowly opened up the brochure.

Inside was an illustration of a little girl. Brooke guessed that she was maybe a year older than Alex, lying on her side with her bare hip exposed. She was smiling eagerly as if she were miraculously enjoying what was happening to her. Next to her was a doctor, who looked considerably older and much more experienced than Macey, preparing to draw bone marrow from the little girl's hip with an extremely long needle.

But Brooke knew her son. And if they were about to insert a needle like *that* in him, he wasn't smiling.

IN THE NEXT ROOM, MACEY GLANCED OVER THE EDGE of the small surgical theater that Kaitlyn had created. The three-foot-wide, two-foot-high curtained display spread across Alex's midsection, with bright-red drapes that closed around his belly button and lower back, making it impossible for him to see his lower body—or what was being done to him. Alex was smiling from ear to ear and seemed to be fully occupied by Mr. Brave, Kaitlyn's hand puppet. Mr. Brave's head bobbed back and forth over the top of the theater, and his shiny, black button eyes and sing-song "voice" were clearly making Alex remarkably less nervous.

Alex rested on his side, wearing only a small purple hospital gown and his SpongeBob underwear. Macey settled a warm blanket across his legs.

"You're going to like this part!" Mr. Brave said, as Kaitlyn performed the dual roles of nurse and puppeteer while applying more EMLA cream to Alex's hip to further numb his skin.

"Hey, Mr. Brave," Kaitlyn said calmly. "Ask Alex if he can feel that."

"I heard what she said, Mr. Brave," Alex said attentively. "Tell her it feels warm. Tell her I like it."

"He says it feels warm. He says he likes it," Mr. Brave reported back to the nurse in his high-pitched voice, bringing another grin across Alex's face.

"Isn't Alex doing well?" Kaitlyn asked the puppet as she massaged the cream further into Alex's hip.

"Well? *Well?!* He's *amazing!*" the puppet squeaked as the nurse tapped on Alex's leg.

Alex giggled.

"Can you feel that?" Kaitlyn asked, pinching on the loose skin of his tiny hip.

"Feel what?" Alex asked.

"Nothing," Kaitlyn said. "Nothing at all." It looked like he never felt the quick pierce of the needle numbing him further, and she gave Macey a quick nod.

Mr. Brave peered back over the curtain, and his fist-sized head teetered slowly back and forth. The puppet whispered, "Hey, Alex . . ."

"What, Mr. Brave?" Alex said, his eyebrows lifting curiously.

"It's time to be brave—real brave."

"Okay," Alex said, his eyes big and round in anticipation.

Macey winked at him and had a feeling he really wasn't interested in being any braver than he already was. But she was sure that he didn't want to let Mr. Brave or Nurse Kaitlyn down.

Kaitlyn looked over the edge of the curtain and said, "There is going to be a little pinch here, Alex."

"Are you ready?" Mr. Brave said loudly, soliciting a bolt of enthusiasm from the boy.

"Yeah!" Alex said.

Macey lowered the aspiration needle to his hip and could see Alex swallow hard.

Then his cheeks puffed.

Then he asked where Charlie was.

Then he wanted his mother again.

Then she removed the needle.

"Man, you did good!" Mr. Brave said, sliding across the top of the theater.

"Great job, Alexander," Macey said. "You did terrific!"

"Wow," Kaitlyn said, lowering her head next to Mr. Brave's. "You are so brave, Alex."

Alex laughed thankfully and took a quick wipe at his eyes. "I did do good, didn't I?"

"Yes, you did!" Mr. Brave affirmed. "Really good!"

"Am I done?" Alex asked, sounding not even remotely open to the possibility of the answer being a no.

"That's it for now," Kaitlyn answered, pushing Mr. Brave all the way over the curtain rod so the puppet could request a congratulatory high five from the boy. "Sit tight, and I'll grab your mother for you."

JIM POURED THE DREGS OF HIS COFFEE OVER THE EDGE of the front porch and took in a deep breath of early morning air. It was cold outside. He could actually feel tiny slivers of scented air banking off the walls of his lungs. He recognized the smell as the remaining hints of lacquer that the breeze had continued to pull off the cross. Birds were chirping their good mornings, and a car's horn beeped impatiently somewhere miles away. He thought about Alex and Brooke and closed his eyes for a quick prayer to give both of them strength.

The front door of the church opened and then banged shut. Charlie had gotten an early start on his chores and had ambled up the hill when Shirley, Brooke, and Alex had left for the hospital. By the sound of it, he was ruthlessly pounding on a rug with a broom handle, knocking the dust out of it and into tomorrow.

"About fifteen minutes, Charlie!" he yelled, letting his son know when it would be time to eat breakfast. In response, the church door opened and closed again. Jim crossed his arms, quickly warming them, took another breath of the cool fall air, and went back in the house.

Inside the kitchen Jim unwrapped two double-packs of blueberry Pop-Tarts and dropped them into the spring-loaded slots of the old toaster. He felt for the electrical outlet, plugged the toaster in, and pressed firmly down on the plastic lever that lowered the four pastries next to the hot coils. He rinsed out his coffee cup, put it in the sink, and took a big, delighted whiff of the Pop-Tarts warming. "Yes, my boy," he said, as if Charlie were already with him. "The finest breakfast known to man. And no *ladies* here to refuse me my double portion!" He rubbed his hands together in excitement.

Jim turned and reached up in the cupboard, feeling for and then retrieving two drinking glasses. He lowered them to the counter and then filled each with cool tap water. He quickly set the last one down, overcome by a sudden need to sneeze. He pulled out his handkerchief just before he let go of the biggest sneeze he could remember.

"Bless you, Lindy," he said with a little laugh of wonder, lifting the handkerchief to cover his nose before sneezing uncontrollably three more times.

"Wow," he added, wiping delicately at his nose, his chest expanding before sneezing yet again. "Good *grief*," he said, putting a hand to his chest, actually feeling *winded* from the episode.

He blinked rapidly, clearing the tears from his eyes. He dabbed at the sides of his face and then the inner corners of his eyes with the handkerchief. His body rocked as he sneezed yet another time. He chuckled. "Here we go again."

He covered his eyes with the handkerchief and sneezed twice more.

Jim braced himself against the counter, waiting defensively for another sneeze that wouldn't come. "What in creation?" he said to the empty kitchen, wiping his eyes again with the handkerchief. "I must be getting allergies in my old age."

He began to take the handkerchief away from his eyes and suddenly stopped.

What? No. It can't be!

But it was. It had really happened.

Lord? Lord! Is it possible? He spun in a slow circle.

He'd prayed for it, in the early years. But there'd always been bigger items on the prayer agenda. Prayers for provision. For his people. For Brooke. And lately, for Alex.

He'd thought he'd become content with the memories over the last twenty years.

Memories of Shirley's face. Charlie's.

He thought he'd become content with the sound of Shirley's voice and Charlie's laugh.

He thought he'd become settled with the mental snapshots of faces that he alone had personally assigned to Brooke and Alex. Faces he loved, but faces he'd never truly seen.

But right now, the thing he wanted most was to see . . . to truly see Shirley, Charlie, Brooke, and Alex. The people who made up his personal fortune, making him the luckiest man in the world.

Until he did, he wasn't sure he could trust this.

"Charlie!" he yelled. "Charlie!"

He continued to pull the handkerchief away from his face, watching it wave. He didn't need his son to know it. It had really happened. This was no dream.

He could see.

The handkerchief was white. It fell away from his hand like a parachute falling out of a navy bomber toward his feet.

His feet were covered by a pair of faded black slippers. He knew about the hole in the side of his left slipper. He had felt it for a long time. Its torn edge was drooping pathetically against the floor.

The floor was the same light brown linoleum he and Shirley had put in close to thirty years ago. It looked awful. It was beautiful.

The table.

The finger paintings that had obviously been done by a child posted on the refrigerator. They had to be Alex's.

The toaster.

The steam coming off the Pop-Tarts.

The cookie jar.

The digital clock next to the stove.

Jim walked dreamily to the sink and looked out the window.

The cross.

The church.

Please don't be a dream. I'm sorry. Please—not this time. He'd had plenty of those over the years. Dreams where he could see, and woke to blindness.

The toaster again.

The clock next to the stove.

The numbers.

The clock.

Lord? Lord!

The numbers on the clock. Kenneth knew.

Jim let go of the counter and stepped cautiously to the stove. He fell to his knees for the second time that morning, bowing low. *It's impossible! Isn't it? Isn't it?*

"Praise be to God," he said, knowing the full measure of *possibility.* "Thank you, Lord."

He gently rubbed his eyes with his fingertips, then slowly pulled himself up to peek over the front edge of the stove at the clock again.

Kenneth knew this was going to happen.

Gooseflesh ran across the minister's back and arms, and his heart raced. And then he began to weep uncontrollably as he stared at the three black numbers on the clock.

7:14

✢ TWENTY-SIX

Jim immediately recognized the man, even though he hadn't seen him in over twenty years. The hair was certainly grayer. The skin under the chin and along the neck seemed to have loosened a bit. He was late-fall tan, making the distinct creases coming off the corners of his mouth look like the thin cracks that appeared in sunbaked mud. The lines across the forehead were more pronounced and obviously permanent. The nose was the same, but he couldn't stop staring at the man's ears. They seemed like they had gotten bigger.

He smiled easily—loving it all—and leaned closer to the mirror for a better look. There was absolutely no doubt about it. His ears *had* gotten bigger.

Jim continued to stare. His Indian-brown eyes were shining, almost as if they were made of glass. Unwavering, fearless, unblinking. *My eyes.* They looked exactly as they had in his youth. *A young man's eyes in an old guy's face.* He grinned at his reflection.

"Lindy, you look a hundred," he said. He ran his hands down the sides of his cheeks, and they met at his chin in prayer pose. "But it's great to see you."

Jim headed down the hallway, looking curiously at the tops of his hands, noticing the wrinkles and spots, the puffy, age-thickened knuckles. Even the sight of them made him glad. Because they screamed of his miracle.

He knew without a doubt that miracles took place all the time, and that every one—without exception—was from the hand of God.

There were big ones. There were small ones. There were those everyone noticed, like surviving life-threatening illnesses and accidents. Then there were the many more that went unnoticed, like healthy children, something to eat, a roof, someone to love, birth, and sometimes, even death.

He wondered what the world would be like if people would just stop and take the time to look at everything they were given every day of their lives and be thankful—to offer thanks and try to realize where their personal miracles were coming from, and give credit to where it was rightfully due.

Jim walked into the kitchen and ran his finger along the tiny knit cross that hung like mistletoe directly above him. He knew he wasn't Lazarus from the book of John. He wasn't the lame beggar from Acts, and he wasn't the risen son of the widow of Nain. He was the blind man. He was the minister, James Lindy, from the small town of Carlson, Michigan. He once was blind, but now could see. "Oh, can I *see*, Lord!" he shouted to the ceiling, grinning. "How I can *see*! Thank you, Father. Thank you!"

Though he had always known, he now knew more than ever how truly amazing grace really was. He put his hand to his heart, overcome with the knowledge that God had chosen him, *him*, to touch. It made him feel as tiny as an ant, and as big as the earth, all at once.

What a better witness he would become. He didn't have places to go. He had people to see.

"To see," he said aloud. "Praise God!"

He picked up the phone and dialed Brooke's cell. It went straight to voice mail. He didn't leave a message and was glancing back at the digital clock next to the stove when the carpenter's words flitted through his mind again. *"And when it happens, promise me that you will never tell anyone about it."*

"Don't tell them, Kenneth?" Jim asked the clock, somehow expecting it to answer. "It won't take a detective to know I'm not blind anymore." He lifted the phone back up and paused. "I'm not supposed to tell anyone that you *knew* it was going to happen?"

The front door closed behind him in the living room, and Jim froze in anticipation. He couldn't move. He held the phone against his ear and leaned against the wall like he had stage fright, his heart racing triple-time.

Someone grabbed his shoulder lightly and stomped past him to the kitchen table, snatching up one of the glasses of water before stepping to the window to look outside.

Charlie turned sideways, not having any idea he was being watched.

Jim felt breathless as he studied his son. He didn't know what to say, where to start. Charlie was the most beautiful sight he had ever seen—the tight crew cut; the high Lindy forehead; the slow-motion blinks of his eyes; the innocent, trusting, and still incredibly youthful face.

Jim had not forgotten about his son's enormous size. His seven-foot height and bulk created a presence that was felt as well as seen.

Charlie sipped at his water, and Jim noticed that the glass had completely disappeared into a rounded hand that looked to be the size of a catcher's glove. Charlie held the glass to his mouth and looked right at him. Jim lifted his head off the wall and hung up the phone. Charlie grabbed the Pop-Tarts out of the toaster and put two each on the plates that had been set out earlier. Charlie then approached and tugged at Jim's sweatshirt sleeve, prodding him to the table to join him for breakfast.

Jim didn't move. Charlie tugged again, and he grabbed Charlie's arm, prompting him to turn around and look at him.

"Hello, Charles Paul Lindy," Jim said. "Hello, my son."

Charlie smiled. He always did whenever he heard his middle name. Charlie then took a giant step toward the table. He stopped, slowly turned around again, and looked at his father in a way Jim found peculiar. Charlie looked at his face—and then his eyes. He stepped back next to Jim and hunched over, lowering his face within inches of his father's. His head slowly swiveled back and forth, as if something seemed different to him.

He lifted his hand and waved a thick finger back and forth in front of his father's face.

Jim put his hand around Charlie's finger, which felt like the handle of a baseball bat. "I can see you, Charlie," he said, nodding. "I can see you."

Charlie squinted, as if confused, and Jim could do nothing but grin.

He heard a car door close then. Jim patted Charlie on the arm and went quickly to the living room and looked out the window. He held his hand against the glass as an attractive young woman lifted a young, redheaded boy out of the backseat of a small, four-door car.

"Hello, Brooke and Alex," he whispered, lowering his hand from the window.

There was an older woman closing the dented passenger door. She was saying something to the woman and the boy. She threw a floral-designed purse over her shoulder. She wore jeans that were pulled up a little too high, a hooded sweatshirt with the sleeves rolled to her elbows, and small, gold-rimmed glasses that formed perfect circles around her eyes. The top of her back was arched slightly forward, and she walked slowly, as if she were hurting. He knew it was her arthritis.

"Hello, beautiful wife," he said, his mouth hanging slightly in amazement.

The front door opened, and he faced the two strangers who walked in. Alex had his head on Brooke's shoulder, and he opened his eyes to glance sleepily at Jim. Brooke carefully put Alex on the couch and covered him with the green and white knit quilt that was folded over the top of the recliner. The boy promptly fell asleep.

"What happened?" Jim asked, watching Shirley through the glass, climbing the steps to the porch. "What did they say?"

"They did the bone marrow aspiration," Brooke said in a tone that Jim found surprisingly upbeat. Brooke walked into the kitchen. "Everything went well, and we go back tomorrow."

"Praise God," Jim said.

Shirley walked in, and he looked down and away shyly. He wasn't sure why.

Charlie was ducking under the kitchen doorway. He waved at his mother and pointed excitedly at Jim.

"Are you men having a good morning?" Shirley asked, looking to Jim to see what was up.

"I guess you could say that," Jim answered, slowly meeting her gaze. "It has certainly been a rare one."

Charlie took hold of Shirley's hand and pointed at Jim again.

"What is it, Charlie?" Shirley asked, looking up at him over the edges of her glasses. "Something on your mind?"

Charlie poked anxiously toward Jim.

"Okay," Shirley said playfully. "What are you two up to?"

Charlie's head bobbled, and he waved toward Jim again.

But Jim paused, no words seeming right to him. No words were magnificent enough to capture what had happened! So he just grinned.

"What's going on?" Shirley asked, turning to Jim. "What's Charlie trying to tell me?"

Jim raised both of his hands to the window and looked up at the ceiling. He slowly outlined a handprint on the window with his left index finger. "Sorry about messing up your clean window, Shirl."

Shirley's head pulled slightly back. "What did you just do, James Lindy? You know how I feel about people putting their hands on my clean windows!"

"I apologized to you," he answered. "I apologized for putting handprints on your window. It was so clean."

Shirley let go of Charlie's hand and took a couple of steps toward Jim. Her tone was trusting, but suspicious. "What are you trying to say, James? Out with it already."

He cleared his throat and continued to stare at the smudged window. *I can see smudges.*

"Your sweatshirt," he said. He had never forgotten about colors. "It's purple."

"How did you know that?" Shirley asked, looking down as if she'd forgotten what she'd put on. "Who told you?"

"Brooke's car," he said, lifting his hand back up against the glass. He tapped on the window and pointed right at the vehicle. "It's white, and there is a dent in the passenger-side door."

"You knew that."

"And over there," he said, nodding out the window to his left at the rhythmic steps of a deer that meandered down the driveway from St. Thomas toward Church Road. "There is a doe."

"How in the world do you know that?" Shirley asked, crossing her arms and looking out the window at the deer. She stepped to his side, and he looked away. "How do you know that, James Lindy?"

"Because God healed me."

"What?"

"Because I can *see*," Jim said, facing her. "I see *you*, Shirley Lindy. And you're more beautiful than ever."

Shirley looked into her husband's eyes, frowning in confusion and wonder, and her arms dropped to her sides like deadweights.

Jim smiled boyishly and hoped his eyes were sparkling. He hoped they shouted his love for her.

"James?" Shirley said faintly, still staring at him. He kept looking back, knowing what she was seeing. No longer were there milky patches of scar tissue that clouded the surface. They were gone. No longer were there frayed and jagged edges of detaching retinas. They were gone too. His eyes were clear and brown. They were the way they used to be. They were the way God had made them before. They were the way God had made them *again*.

"James?" she whispered, completely absorbed in the gaze of a long-lost friend. Her eyes began to well with tears.

"It's a miracle," he whispered back. "Something happened."

"What's everybody mumbling about in here?" Brooke asked, returning from the kitchen to find Shirley falling into Jim's embrace.

"Something wonderful has happened," Shirley said, her face nestled against Jim's chest.

"What?" Brooke asked.

Shirley wiped away her tears and grinned up at him.

"What is it?" Brooke asked again. But she wasn't looking at them; she was looking at Charlie, who was standing by the window. He wore a frozen grin, his small lower teeth exposed in pure joy.

Brooke inched next to him and looked out to the front yard. "He's looking at that deer like he's never seen one before. You all right, Charlie?"

Charlie's head bobbed back and forth, and his smile broadened further. He lifted his hands and began to clap ecstatically.

"Shh, Charlie, shh," Brooke whispered. "You'll wake Alex."

"What is it?" Jim asked.

Charlie clapped harder. His hands thundered together joyfully.

"Something sure has him going," Brooke said to Jim, then slowly did a double-take. "Pastor Jim?" She grabbed his arm and half squinted in apparent disbelief. "Your *eyes*."

Jim smiled at her, and Charlie shot out the front door, letting it slam shut behind him. He took an enormous leap over the porch steps and ran quickly out to the center of the front yard. He turned back toward the living room window and started clapping again, jumping up and down and pointing at the deer, which had turned around and was making its way toward him.

Alex stirred and then sat up, and Brooke pulled him into her arms.

"Crazy deer," Shirley said. "She's coming right at him! She better look out, because Charlie looks like he's fixin' to try and claim her as a pet or something."

"He looks like he has gone crazy," Brooke said.

Jim put his hand lightly around the back of Shirley's neck. "Heck. I'm starting to think I've gone crazy too."

"Poor thing," Shirley said, looking at the deer as it got closer. "What do you suppose happened to it?"

"I have no idea," Jim said, wincing. "Whatever happened, it sure doesn't seem to be bothering it much anymore."

The doe had stopped and turned its head toward the house.

Jim could see what looked like a thick, reddish-brown patch of dried blood that had clotted around a nasty wound across the edges of the doe's rib line.

Alex leaned out of his mother's arms. "Put me down!" he cried. "Put me down!"

"Be still! Your hip is gonna be sore!" Hastily, Brooke tried to set him down, but he was squirming so much, he fell heavily to his feet. Nothing seemed to bother him. He was out the door as fast as Charlie had been, slamming it behind him.

Brooke, Shirley, and Jim moved closer to the window, watching as Alex joined Charlie on the lawn. The big man took the little boy's hand, and the sight of it made Jim start to cry.

Charlie and Alex took three hesitant steps toward the deer and paused. They turned back to the living room window and smiled, pointing at the deer again like they were trying to tell them something.

Alex was shouting and lifting his hands. He sounded ecstatic.

"It's the deer," Jim said. "C'mon." He took Shirley's hand and led her out to the porch, Brooke right behind them.

They couldn't hear what Alex was screaming at first. But then he turned around and ran toward them.

"Don't you see?" Alex asked, clenching his hands full of bright red hair as if he wanted to pull it out. "Don't you *see*? The deer was dead! But now she's alive! She's *alive*!"

✦ TWENTY-SEVEN

Macey dropped the folded copy of the *Carlson Herald* on the coffee table in front of Kaitlyn. "Check it out," she said, sitting at her desk and grabbing a handful of manila folders. "Zach brought it by earlier."

"Already saw it," Kaitlyn said, leaning back on the couch. "Carrie Armstrong showed it to me down at the cafeteria. A lot of people down there were talking about it." She picked up the paper for another look and read the headline above the photo: "'East Shore Professionals Nurse Cross Back to Health.'"

"Isn't that a good picture?" Macey asked, opening one of the folders and pulling a red pen out of her desk drawer. "Zach must be eating it up."

Kaitlyn glanced at the photo again. She tried not to look at Zach and checked out Kenneth. She grinned. "I don't think God would ever look bad in a picture."

"Very funny," Macey said, pulling a sheet of yellow legal paper out of the folder. She crumpled it up and tossed it at Kaitlyn, missing horribly.

Kaitlyn tapped on the photo, feeling slightly bothered that Zach hadn't dropped the paper off to *her*. "It is interesting that Zach and that Kenneth guy are standing next to each other in the same picture, don't you think?"

"Why is that?" Macey asked, rising.

"One guy thinks *he* is God. The other guy, *you* think is God."

"I never said that," Macey said, snatching the newspaper out of Kaitlyn's hand and plopping down on the far end of the couch. "Why can't I ever be serious with you about things that aren't work-related?"

"Lighten up," Kaitlyn said, leaning her head apologetically toward the doctor. "I kind of thought you were suggesting that he was—"

"I didn't say that. I was just—I don't know—theorizing."

"Theorizing?" Kaitlyn asked, tilting her head slightly and knowing full well that her friend had been doing more than just *theorizing*. "You were dead serious."

"Okay," Macey said. "So what if I was?"

Kaitlyn smiled. "Well, it's not every day that your best friend *theorizes* about a higher power hanging drywall."

Macey crossed her arms. "Like it or not, and as weird as it sounds, I'm standing by what I said."

"Okay," Kaitlyn said, raising her eyebrows and hands. She sat up straight. "Subject change. I'm putting in an admin supply order. Need anything?"

"We don't have to change the subject."

"I didn't mean to hit a nerve," Kaitlyn said. "I'm sorry, okay?"

"You didn't hit a nerve," Macey said, and paused. "Okay, maybe you did hit a nerve. I'm probably being a little too sensitive about all of this, but it has certainly been a bizarre couple of days. It's not like me to talk religion. It's embarrassing."

"Sorry," Kaitlyn said again. She meant it.

"No, *I'm* sorry," Macey said. "I need some black pens. And white-out."

"You've got it," Kaitlyn said.

Macey picked up the paper again. "Kenneth certainly seems like a good guy, though, doesn't he?"

Kaitlyn grinned. "Oh, I would say almost . . ." She stopped at the risk of going overboard.

"Almost what?" Macey said with a hint of smile. "Say it, smart aleck."

"Heavenly."

"I knew it," Macey said, shaking her head.

"By the way," Kaitlyn said. "Other than him dropping off the newspaper, have you seen much of Zach today?"

"No," the doctor answered. "It's strange, though. A couple people told me how he spent extra time with the kids today. *Again.*"

The office phone rang, and Macey reached her desk on the second ring.

"Hello, this is Dr. Lewis."

Kaitlyn crossed her arms and looked back at the paper—mostly at Zach.

Macey snapped her fingers and pointed at the paper, wanting Kaitlyn to hand it to her, and she did.

"She called the paper ten times?" Macey asked. "The man of her dreams? Oh, man *in* her dreams. Which one was he?"

Kaitlyn watched as the doctor ran her finger across the page.

"On the far right?" Macey asked, squinting at the picture. "I, uh . . . I can't make any promises . . . Well, yes, I suppose I could try. What's her phone number?"

The doctor grabbed the pen off the desk and pulled off its cap.

"Go ahead and give me her number, Shannon. Got it. And her name is? *What?* You're kidding me . . ." Her last words were mumbled.

Kaitlyn watched the color drain from Macey's face.

"Okay," the doctor said, holding the phone tightly, her eyebrows huddling as if she was confused. "Thank you, Shannon." She promised to have Zach call her back and hung up.

"What's wrong?" Kaitlyn asked.

Macey was still staring at the phone. "That was Shannon from the *Carlson Herald.* The one who came and took our picture?"

"Yeah," Kaitlyn said.

"She tried to call Zach a couple of times today," Macey said, her eyes wide and staring.

"*Macey.* What'd she want?" She was freaking Kaitlyn out, acting so weird.

"She said there's a woman who keeps calling, demanding to

know the name of the man in the photo. She said he's the 'man in her dreams.' It's Kenneth, I just looked."

"So? Maybe she thinks he's cute."

"She wants Kenneth to call her."

"Well, there you go. Some girls just can't give in to eHarmony, it seems."

"Kait," Macey said, meeting her gaze. Her face had gone totally pale. "The woman's name is Mary Springsted."

✠ TWENTY-EIGHT

Good morning, everyone," Macey said, entering through the staff door of the room to a big smile from Alex. He was in Spider-Man pajamas and new Winnie the Pooh slippers, just a little too big for him, and sat between Brooke and Shirley.

"Dr. Lewis," Kaitlyn said professionally, "Mr. Alex has a question for you."

She bent down in front of him. "What is it, Superboy?"

"When do I get to take my sleepy medicine?" he asked, resting his chin on his knee.

"Can you wait a little bit longer?" she asked, surprised at how anxious Alex was to reap the benefits of the sleepy medicine promised to him by Kaitlyn. Maybe he thought it sounded like a dream adventure. Or maybe he'd rather sleep than fret. *I know I would* . . .

"Okay," Alex said, standing up and shuffling his feet. His new slippers swooshed on the carpet, and one slid partially off his heel. He bent over and pulled it back on.

"How's your hip feeling today?" Macey asked. "I'm guessing a little sore, maybe?"

"A little," Alex said, holding his tiny thumb and index finger a half inch apart from each other to indicate his measurement of discomfort. "That much." He tapped Brooke's leg for her to lift him to her lap. "Will it hurt, getting a pote put in me?"

Brooke kissed the top of his head. "It's called a *port*, little man," she said. She looked to Macey to answer him.

"That port is going to help us give you your medicine. And no, it won't hurt going in. That's why you're getting the sleepy medicine. You'll wake up and—wham!—it'll be in place."

"Okay," Alex said. "But where is Mr. Brave?"

"Mr. Brave took his sleepy medicine *already*," Kaitlyn said quickly. "He'll be asleep for a little while too."

"Alex," Macey said, pushing a wheelchair to the center of the room and then sitting in it. She grabbed the tops of the rubber wheels. "I want you to know what a great job you are doing so far. I'm super impressed."

"Thank you," he said, then moved over to whisper in his mom's ear.

"Ask her," Brooke said to him, nodding at Macey. "Go ahead."

Alex seemed hesitant to ask, as if he liked being the kid who had all the answers.

"He wants to know how long he will be asleep," Brooke said. Alex looked thankfully to his mother and then quickly at Macey.

"Not long," Macey said. "When you wake up, don't forget you may feel a little sore and a little sleepy, but both your mom and Mr. Brave will be there with you, all right?"

"All right," Alex said. "Can I have that sleepy medicine now?"

"When you leave here, the anesthetist will give it to you," Macey said, getting out of the wheelchair. "Can you say anesthetist?"

"Yeah," Alex said confidently. "Answerthetisist." He looked around the room as if proud of conquering that challenge.

"You ready, Alexander?" Kaitlyn asked, standing. She stepped behind the wheelchair and grabbed the handles. "You want to walk or ride?"

"Ride!" Alex blurted, sliding off his mother's leg.

Kaitlyn gestured toward the chair, and he hopped on it. She put down the foot pedals, but his little legs didn't reach them.

"Don't I get a hug, mister?" Brooke asked.

"I'll take one too," Shirley said. "Charlie is going to be wondering where you are all day."

"Tell Charlie I got a wheelchair ride, Mrs. Lindy!" Alex said excitedly, shimmying off the wheelchair. He gave his mother a quick hug and then wrapped his arms around Shirley's leg.

"We love you," Shirley said. "We'll see you in a little bit."

Alex waved toward Kaitlyn and Macey as he climbed into the chair again. "Hey, Mrs. Lindy, are you gonna tell them about Pastor Jim's eyes?"

Shirley smiled. "At some point, Alex."

Alex's left slipper fell completely off, and Kaitlyn picked it up and put it back on for him. She patted his head, winked at Brooke, and then looked down at Alex. "Tell Mom and Mrs. Lindy good-bye."

"See you later, alligators," Alex said. Macey held the door, and he dropped his elbows on the armrests as Kaitlyn pulled him backward out of the room.

"He is so cute," Macey said, closing the door. She walked over, sat next to Shirley, and then laced her fingers together and leaned forward. "Do either of you have any questions? About anything at all?"

"I don't," Brooke said. "Can you think of anything we should be asking, Shirley?"

"I think they have done a wonderful job of explaining things," Shirley said.

"I know this is a lot," Macey added. It *was* a lot, and Brooke had been dealing with the situation as well as any parent the doctor had seen. "Alex is off to a great start. Most kids constantly fight any type of process, and he has done absolutely incredible. Believe me."

"I believe Alex is going to be all right," Brooke said. "Just keep telling me what I need to do and I'll do it."

"All right," Macey said, standing back up. "Dr. Norman will be done with the procedure in about an hour, and then Nurse Kaitlyn or I will take you back there. Remember, you will see him with two bandages. There will be one on his neck and a larger one where the incision is on his chest. And plan on seeing a small amount of blood under or around the dressing on his chest. Don't let that alarm you."

"Okay," Brooke said.

"And you'll start his chemotherapy this afternoon?" Shirley asked.

"Most likely," Macey said, her doctor tone fading from her voice. "Mrs. Lindy, I know I'm going to be seeing a lot of you guys in the weeks to come, but I was wondering if I could somehow speak with Pastor Jim before Saturday's harvest party? On a personal matter?"

"Of course," Shirley said. "He'd love it. Come by anytime you wish."

"I could maybe stop by tomorrow evening, if that's convenient."

"I'll tell him you're coming," Shirley said. "And I actually had a question for you *about* James."

Macey sat back down. "Sure."

"An amazing thing has happened. James can see now, and I was wondering what the medical explanation might be. We were out and about, and when we came—"

"I-I'm sorry," Macey interrupted. "Did you say Pastor Jim can *see*?"

Shirley's smile widened. "Yesterday morning, when we went home from here, his eyes—all of the damage to his eyes—it was all gone. They look brand-new."

"What do you mean, brand-new?" Macey asked slowly, waiting for a punch line.

"James said that he was in the kitchen and that he had a sneezing fit. When he opened his eyes, he could see."

"From sneezing?" Macey asked, wondering how Shirley and Brooke could be so calm. They acted as if a scab had fallen off the minister's elbow. Regardless, something key was obviously missing from the story.

"That's what happened," Shirley said. "He's been healed. You can see it tomorrow for yourself."

Dumbfounded, Macey watched Brooke nod in agreement with Shirley's story and grinned. "That's what happened," Brooke said. "I'm guessing you don't hear *that* every day."

Macey stared at Brooke and then shook her head, not in dis-agreement, but to clear it. "Mrs. Lindy, maybe I should come by tonight instead of tomorrow. Would that work?"

"Of course," Shirley said.

Macey stood and crossed her arms. Her stomach was churn-ing in a tightly wound ball of anxiety for the third straight day. *Things keep getting weirder . . .*

Pastor Jim can see.

The result of a sneezing fit. That's not something you see in the American Medical Journal.

She brushed her palm nervously against the end of her pony-tail and faked a smile.

Wait 'til Kaitlyn hears this one.

Sneezing fit? I don't think so.

I think the guy in Mary Springsted's dream had something to do with this too . . .

✛ TWENTY-NINE

Kaitlyn waved back to Macey as the doctor disappeared behind the elevator doors. She was off to talk to the minister. The guy who could now supposedly see.

From sneezing? Kaitlyn thought. *Gimme a break.*

She drummed a pen across the top of the nurses' station and turned her head in the direction of Zach's office down the hall. He was still there. Not that she'd seen him. Was he avoiding her now?

The third floor had seemed eerily quiet to her over the past couple of days, almost too quiet. Down the hall she could hear a vending machine buzzing steadily from the waiting room. And then she heard a fresh batch of ice fall and crash in the ice machine before giving back into the dull silence. A closet door closed in the A wing, immediately followed by the stuttering laughter of one of the kids. And then there was nothing—nothing but the steady hum of the vending machine in the waiting room again.

But there was also something else.

Something beyond the vending machine was humming. It wasn't a buzz or hum she could hear, but one she could *feel*. Almost like a glow you could touch. Kaitlyn held her hand out in front of her face and pinched dreamily at the air, as if she were trying to capture a piece of it.

"What are you doing, Kaitlyn?" Harriet Jasper asked.

Kaitlyn snapped out of it and blushed as she looked at the other nurse. "Oh! Nothing . . ." She shook her head and yawned. "I'm obviously working too much. I'm practically seeing things."

Harriet laughed playfully. Layers of fat jiggled at the bottom of her arm like tiny water balloons as she imitated Kaitlyn pinching at the air. "You looked like Mr. Miyagi from *The Karate Kid* trying to catch a fly with chopsticks, except there was no fly and no chopsticks."

Kaitlyn wasn't all that amused but couldn't summon the strength to fake it. "Does it seem quiet to you around here lately, Harriet?"

"Lesia and I were talking about that earlier," Harriet said, sipping at her third mineral water of the day, a critical element of yet another diet. "Quiet and low maintenance. The kids all seem to be doing great."

"It's weird, isn't it?"

"You know how it goes. It'll be chaos before you know it," Harriet said.

Kaitlyn nodded and picked up her coat. "I'm outta here, Harriet. See you tomorrow."

"Have a good one," Harriet said.

Kaitlyn put her coat on and headed down the hallway toward the elevators.

She walked past the visiting room, thinking about Pizza Hut or Taco Bell. *Pizza Hut. Definitely Pizza Hut, and then a long bath, and then a good night's sleep.* That's what she needed.

There's that buzz again.

Her pace slowed until she finally stopped about fifteen feet from the elevators. She turned around and looked suspiciously back at the waiting room door. The buzz—that *presence.* It was coming from there.

She turned, went back to the waiting room, and had a look. It was practically empty, except for a few people. A young couple watched their two-year-old play with wooden blocks on the floor in front of them. The dad looked indifferent, sprawled out from the stained chair, his eyes on his phone. The boy's tiny left arm was in a cast, and the woman seemed to have the dark yellow remnants of a black eye that didn't exactly match the fresher and darker string of bruises at the base of her neck. She quickly looked away in what

Kaitlyn easily recognized as shame. Kaitlyn felt a shiver of rage and studied the man beside the woman, then moved on to the other guy in the room.

On the far side, a bearded old man stood in front of the aquarium. He turned around and offered a pleasant smile—one she found oddly familiar—and stroked the whitest beard she'd ever seen. He had a folded newspaper neatly tucked under his left arm, and the long, thin fingers of his wrinkly right hand seemed to be wrapped around what looked like—she studied it for a second—like an apple.

"I'm heading home for the night," she said. "You folks need anything?" Kaitlyn looked directly at the young woman, but she didn't meet her gaze. Then she looked at the young man and gave him a threatening look that she hoped said, *I'm onto you.*

He yawned at her and waved at the woman and child, muttering, "Car accident," with an innocent face that sickened her. He smirked, and she made herself turn and leave the room.

She made it to the elevator doors, pressed 1, and waited. She leaned back and glanced down the length of the empty hallway again.

So quiet. So weird.

Admissions were down. Remissions were up. The kids had been remarkably less irritable and unusually cooperative with treatment and medications. Johnny Lawson had actually gone three days without kicking any of the nurses, and the new kid on the block, little Alexander Thomas, took his first round of chemo like it was nothing and went happily on his way home.

Kaitlyn wasn't sure what was going on—not only with the kids, but also with some of the big people around her. Regardless, *something* was going on, and her interest slowly began to percolate. The elevator arrived, she got in, and the doors closed behind her.

Religion—the great unknown.

When Kaitlyn thought about religion, she thought about going to church as a kid. It made her remember how she and her older sister, Connie, used to hold back laughter as Mrs. Trotter sang brazenly off-key. She thought about all those boring sermons and constantly turning her wrist to see her watch, *praying* for twelve o'clock to come and the service to end so they could eat dry brownies and drink flat punch.

And then gradually, over time, other things seemed to become more important. Church became every other weekend, then once a month, then hardly ever.

Religion—the great unknown. She had made it that way. Now, however, religion appeared to be trying to nose its way back into her life. Macey was right. Something *bizarre* was going on.

Mary Springsted awakens from a coma. Unusual, but not impossible—act of God?

Cross is repaired, maybe a little too quickly—act of God?

Zach Norman is suddenly a little less of an idiot—act of God?

Blind minister can now see. Impossible, unless . . . Definite act of God. If it's true. She'd wait until she heard from Macey on that front. Or Zach.

Zach.

The elevator doors opened, and Kaitlyn didn't move. The five waiting visitors and staff members each gave Kaitlyn their individual looks and glares that all seemed to ask, *Are you going to get out or just ride the elevator all day? This is the ground floor . . .*

"I'm sorry," she said, stepping toward the rear. She knew, then, that she had to go back up and talk to Zach. She had absolutely no idea what she was going to say, but she knew she had to speak with him.

She got off the elevator and passed the visiting room. The old man was sitting and talking with the young couple.

She passed the nurses' station. Harriet had managed to find a twin pack of Twinkies to go with her mineral water and never even noticed Kaitlyn as she walked by and continued down the hall.

The door to Zach's office was open, and it was a little darker than usual. Only a spill of light from a desk lamp fell lazily out the door. Zach was sitting at his desk, eyes closed; his hands were together at the palms, and his index fingers formed a steeple directly under his chin.

Is Zach praying?

Kaitlyn tapped lightly on the door. "Knock, knock."

Zach's eyes opened, and he slowly turned toward her without saying anything.

"Hey, Zach," she said, in what she knew was the least threatening tone she had used with him in months. "I didn't mean to interrupt. I was just stopping by to say hi."

"Well, hello back," Zach said kindly—almost too kindly for her. "What's up, Kait?"

"I guess I wanted to say great job with Alexander Thomas today."

Zach cocked his head back and squinted curiously, almost in a way that suggested he knew the Thomas boy had nothing to do with her visit. "C'mon in, if you want."

"Oh, I was just taking off for the day," Kaitlyn said, spotting a Bible on Zach's desk. *A Bible?* "Just wanted to tell you that."

"Oh, right," he said, shifting to the side of his chair. "Though I don't blame you, Kait, you haven't complimented me or just stopped by my office to say hi in over a year. What's going on?"

She half-frowned and took a small step toward him. "Zach, I was going to ask *you* the same thing."

"Why is that?"

"I don't know," she said. She knew. The truth of the matter was that he was being almost too nice. He was acting like someone that she wanted to be with. "I guess I felt that you haven't been yourself the last couple of days."

Zach nodded and rose. He came around the front of the desk and leaned against it, as if he were trying to keep a respectful distance. "Hopefully I can keep it up."

Kaitlyn just stared at him. He was calmer and more reserved than he usually was. She was actually *comfortable* with him, at the moment. "Keep it up?"

"Yeah," he said. "I think I can keep it up. Keep from acting like my old self."

She squinted in confusion. "What's really going on, Zach?"

"What's going on is that I owe you an apology."

"Apology? For what?"

He looked down in a way that said he was embarrassed. He waited, and then he looked back at her and said, "I'm sorry for the way I treated you, Kaitlyn, when we were together. I really am. I'm sorry for the way I treated a lot of people. I guess I was focused on the wrong things."

"Like what?" she asked.

This wasn't the Zach Norman she knew. *He really seems sorry.*

"Just about everything," he said, still sounding apologetic. He slowly shook his head, almost as if he was a little confused. "But more importantly—"

"Are you all *right*, Zach?"

"More importantly," he continued. He quit shaking his head and stared at her. "I think I may have been wrong about something."

Kaitlyn could *feel* that buzz again. She could also *see* something. It was in Zach's eyes. He looked like a man who was close to finding something—something really valuable.

"Wrong about what?" she asked.

Zach brought his hands to the sides of his face and closed his eyes. He shook his head again, then reached behind him, grabbed the Bible off the desk, and lifted it toward her.

"About this, Kaitlyn. About this."

✛ THIRTY

Jim heard the front door to the church open. He lifted his head up from the Bible he was reading at the pulpit and watched as Charlie led a woman toward him. She had straight brown hair pulled back into a simple ponytail and a youthful, healthy glow that belonged, at tops, to a twenty-year-old.

Wait a minute. That's no twenty-year-old. I know who that is.

Charlie stopped at the fifth pew and turned around to head back out the door.

"Thank you for walking me up here, Charlie," the woman said.

Jim closed the Bible. He went down the carpeted steps from the altar and held out his hand. "I am certainly no Henry Morton Stanley, but—Dr. Lewis, I presume?"

"You presumed correctly," Macey said, shaking his hand and studying his eyes.

"Please, have a seat," he said warmly, pointing to the first pew. "It's certainly nice to see you, Dr. Lewis. Pun intended, I guess."

"Pastor Jim," Macey said, "when I heard the news, I didn't know what to think. But it's really true, isn't it? I don't know what to say. You . . . you can see."

"Yes, I can," he said calmly. "It's remarkable, isn't it?" He helped her take her coat off and folded it over the back of the pew. He caught her looking at—*examining*—his eyes.

"I am so sorry for staring," the doctor said. "Please excuse me. It's just . . . I mean, I'm no ophthalmologist, but I *guarantee* there is no medical explanation. And then there's the *look* of them—Mrs. Lindy was right. They really do look *brand-new.*"

227

"Yes, they do," he said confidently. "Only by the grace of God."

"Pastor Jim," she said, "I was going to see if I could come by this week and talk to you anyhow, but when I heard about your eyes, I just had to come today."

"You're welcome here anytime."

Her face went from pure amazement to youthful confusion. "I guess I'm not really sure where to start."

"I suppose you want to know what happened to my eyes? How I can see?"

"It's not only your eyes," she said. "There are other things—several things—happening around here lately that flat-out don't make a whole lot of sense to me. To be honest, I'm not really all that well versed on matters of religion, and I guess what I'm looking for is your help in understanding it all."

"Interesting," Jim said, smiling. "Why don't you tell me about some of the other things you've noticed."

"We recently had a patient come out of a twenty-two-week coma."

"Praise God."

"And then walk right out the door a few *minutes* after waking up. Her doctor described her as being in the best physical shape she'd been in for years."

"That certainly sounds unusual."

"It's more than unusual. It's impossible!"

"Improbable, apparently. But not *impossible*. Her family must be thankful."

Macey sighed. "And then there's your cross. If you'd *seen* it . . . It was unfixable. When we got here, we looked at it and knew there was no way anybody could do anything with it other than haul it to the dump and get a new one. But *he* did. He *fixed* it."

She started to ramble, and Jim wanted to slow her down. He held up his hand as if he were stopping traffic and said, "You are talking about the carpenter?"

"Yes!" she blurted excitedly. "He fixed it, and your son saw him do it."

"He was right there," Jim said. "I know he saw it."

"Pastor Jim," she said, "feel free not to answer this, but does Charlie have any history of incontinence?"

"What?" Jim was a little surprised and then understood where Macey was going. "You're referring to Charlie's accident that day, aren't you?"

"I'm sorry for asking," she said. "But yes."

"No," Jim said. "I don't remember him doing that since he was little. Are you concerned that something may be physically wrong with Charlie?"

"Not at all," she answered. "I believe he saw what happened, and I think it scared him enough that he wet himself."

"Saw what, though?" he asked. "Kenneth fixing the cross?"

"I'm not really sure. But I think what scared him wasn't the cross itself, but rather *how* it got fixed."

"Charlie was clearly afraid," Jim said. "The carpenter even told us to step back for a second. I could hear some peculiar sounds, like wood bending and snapping. Charlie panicked, picked me up, and carried me away from the site. And then he was through."

"How long did it take him?"

"I'm not sure how much was done up until Dr. Norman left, but the noise only lasted a matter of seconds."

"A matter of seconds," she repeated. "To do the job. *The whole job.*"

Jim paused, remembering. "I think Kenneth said it'd be done quickly."

Macey brought her hands to her cheeks and exhaled in agitation. "Pastor Jim, hardly anything was done up until Zach left. I'm telling you that something quite unusual happened—something that most people would consider impossible. Why don't you tell me how anything he did on a *cross* could possibly scare Charlie that badly?"

"Good question."

"I know," she said, shaking her head, practically frowning. "It just seems like the carpenter is at the center of all these things that are happening."

"What'd he have to do with your coma patient?"

"I think he was in her room before she woke up."

"Why is that?"

"The woman called the paper because she saw his picture. She wanted to know who Kenneth was—said he was the man from her dreams." Macey took a deep breath and covered her eyes like she was counting for hide-and-seek. Then she lowered her hands and glanced back at Jim. "Something is going on around here, Pastor Jim, something big. Bigger than some children's story of Noah's ark."

Jim grinned. "Why would you call it a children's story?"

"I'm sorry," she said, looking contrite. "I hope that wasn't offensive."

"Not at all," he said. "I was just curious."

"I don't know," Macey said. "I guess I always thought a four-hundred-foot ark with two of every animal on it was a bit of a stretch."

"A bit of a stretch?" Jim repeated. He put his hand on her shoulder. "Just remember that we're talking about *God* here. He made the world. He made you. He made me. When you can do that, you can do things that may appear a *stretch*. You can do things like help with the ark, help with a woman coming out of a coma, heal a blind man, or even help fix a cross. And I'm using the word *help* a little loosely."

She stared at him for a long moment. "I came here thinking that Shirley and Brooke were confused—traumatized by all that's going on with Alex . . ." She tossed him a rueful look. "I didn't expect it to be real."

He simply smiled back at her.

"This all should be documented," Macey said. "I am an oncologist, not an eye doctor. But I know the body, and I know medicine." Her head dropped, shook, and then she rose suddenly and pointed at him, as if frightened. "What has happened to your eyes . . . *It just does not happen.*"

He pointed an index finger at each eye. "It just did, Macey. I asked the Lord to heal me, and he healed me. It's that simple."

Macey laced her fingers together and then lifted them, bouncing them lightly off her forehead. "It can't be that simple. I saw the damage to your eyes the other day. And now it's gone."

"I don't know what else to tell you. The Lord did it. Let's call it a *stretch*, shall we?"

"So you just woke up yesterday morning, asked God to heal your eyes, and *poof*—they were brand-new?"

"Not exactly," he said. "I haven't prayed for my sight in a good ten years."

"Ten years? And it finally happens now? I'm sorry. Now I'm prying."

"Yes," he said. "It just happened now. In his perfect timing. When he has your attention."

Macey smiled. "You seem too nonchalant about it. You can see, for Pete's sake!"

"I am a man of faith," Jim said, giving her a little shrug. "It's not a stretch. Regardless of what you believe, Macey, once again, look at me. It *really* happened."

"So if God heard your prayer, isn't he answering it a little late?" Macey asked, shifting her head closer.

"All prayers are answered," he said. "People just sometimes get confused because they don't get the answers they want. I figured he'd heal my sight in heaven, if nothing else. It boils down to trusting in our Maker and his ways, even if his ways don't appear to match up with ours. Make sense?"

"I guess." But she didn't look sure at all.

"Let me give you an example," he said, tugging down on his maize and blue sweatshirt. "Three Saturdays from now, Michigan will be playing football against Ohio State."

"Biggest game of the year," she said.

"Only if Michigan wins," he added with a perfectly straight face. "Regardless, I am extremely confident that before the game, there will be players and fans from both sides praying for a victory. Right?"

"Sure."

"Well," he said, "both prayers will be answered."

Macey looked at him and said, "Even if the answer is no, it is still an answer."

"Right," Jim said, tapping her on the shoulder. "What we need to understand is that it isn't about what *we* want. It's about what *God* wants for us. It's about God's plan and God's will. And if we want something and pray for it, we will get it if . . ." He tilted his head toward the doctor, inviting her to answer.

Macey's eyebrows arched. "If it is God's will?"

"That's what I believe," he said. "And I believe it was God's will for me to see again."

"I think I understand," Macey said. She paused again and looked up toward the altar and cross. "I like it here. I think I'm going to start coming on Sundays."

"Praise God," he said.

"Now the other reason I came," Macey said. "That's if you haven't had enough of me today . . ."

"I've got all the time you need," he said. "Let me have it."

She stared at the cross. "This might sound really strange to you, Pastor Jim."

Jim waited patiently as she searched for the right words.

"He's here," she said calmly. "I think God is here."

"Yes, he is," Jim said with a smile. "This is his house."

"No, Pastor Jim. I mean here in Carlson."

"He is everywhere, Macey."

She looked back at the cross, and her voice sounded like it went up an octave as she whispered, "He brought that woman out of her coma. He fixed the cross. And he made you see."

"Yes, he did," Jim said, a warm glow filling him. "And praise be to him."

Macey turned her head and faced him. "I don't think you understand what I'm saying. He is here. He is *really* here."

"I understand," he said. "And when we learn to—"

The front door opened behind them. They both turned around. A woman was standing there—tall, sharp features, very pretty, and a little rough around the edges. Jim guessed that she was having a bad day. The woman smiled, but he didn't recognize her.

"Can I help you?" he asked, his voice resonating throughout the small church.

The woman began walking slowly up the aisle. "You always do when I need you."

Jim stood. He knew the voice.

"Carla. Where on earth have you been?"

"YOU CAN'T BELIEVE HOW GLAD I AM TO SEE YOU," JIM whispered, returning Carla's hug. "In more ways than one."

"I need to talk to you when you can," Carla whispered back. She glanced apologetically at Macey. "I'm so sorry for interrupting you guys."

"It's okay," Macey said.

Carla hugged Jim again. She backed up, but her hands still rested on his shoulders. She looked in his eyes and said, "When Brooke told me, I couldn't believe it. It's not every day that someone gets their eyesight back."

"That's for certain," Macey said, standing and shaking Carla's hand. "Pastor Jim is the miracle man. I know *I* certainly can't explain it. How are you doing, Carla?"

"I'm not sure if I've ever been better," she said, "even though I've probably had the most unusual couple days of my life."

"Never been better?" Jim asked.

"Yes," Carla answered. "And I just left the house. Shirley's making peanut butter fudge, and she wants you both to come get some when you're done talking."

"Oh, I really should be going," Macey said. She sounded like she didn't want to go anywhere, and Jim had a feeling she had more to talk about. "I've taken up enough of your time."

"You have to hang on, Macey," Jim said. "For two reasons."

"Oh?" the doctor said, sounding surprised.

"One," he said, holding up his index finger. "You haven't truly lived until you've tried Shirley's peanut butter fudge. Even though I shouldn't, given my diabetes, I always have to have a little."

Macey shrugged. "Well then. How could I possibly turn down the opportunity to truly *live*?"

"And two," he continued, "I think there is something that you still want to discuss?"

"Yes," Macey said. "More like *someone* I want to discuss. I want to talk about Kenneth."

"That's strange," Carla said. "That's exactly who *I* wanted to talk about."

"Now isn't that *another* coincidence?" Macey said, her tone playfully sarcastic.

"Could be, could be," Jim said, winking at the doctor. "Since Kenneth is on both of your minds, let's head over to the house and talk some more." He rose and rubbed his hands together in anticipation. "Nothing greases the conversation wheels like peanut butter and chocolate."

BROOKE AND MACEY WALKED BACK IN THE KITCHEN after checking on Alex, who was sleeping.

Jim set the pan of Shirley's fudge on the table and looked at Carla. "So Kenneth just showed up out of nowhere?"

"Yes," Carla said. "I know it seems weird, but he said he is there all the time."

"Under the Big Island Toll Bridge?" Jim asked. "At night? At the exact same time you happened to be there?"

"Yeah," Carla said. "What are the odds?"

"Carla," Jim said, "what in the world were you doing out near that bridge so late at night?"

"I used to go to the bridge a lot when I was a teenager. You know, to think about things. I went there to think about my dad."

"There is something up with Kenneth," Brooke said. "It's one thing after another with that guy."

"I agree with you there," Macey said, picking up another piece of fudge. "I really *hadn't* lived yet, Mrs. Lindy. This fudge is ridiculously addicting."

"Oh, aren't you kind?" Shirley said.

Charlie took five individual pieces of fudge and stacked them one by one on top of each other on his plate. He grabbed them all between his index finger and thumb and shoved them in his mouth like a tiny burger. His cheeks puffed, and he looked at Macey. He covered his mouth and bashfully smiled at her.

Macey grinned at Charlie and then looked back at Brooke. "Why do you say that something is up with Kenneth?"

"Because," Brooke said, "from the time we first met him, he has said a lot of interesting things."

"Like what?" she asked.

"Like he knew that Alex was sick," Brooke answered, nodding at Jim. "Tell her, Pastor Jim."

Jim paused, worried that they were all taking this too far. But there was a lot of truth to what they were saying too. "Kenneth made a biblical reference that was quite timely in relation to Alex's illness. It was from Luke 8:50."

"He knows the Bible well, does he?" Macey asked, arching a brow.

"You might say that," Jim said, pausing to glance at the clock near the stove.

"What else?" Macey asked. "What else has he said?"

"The first day I met him," Carla said, "he told me to learn to forgive."

"Kenneth said that?" Macey asked. "Pretty intriguing statement from a man you just met. A carpenter."

"Yeah," Carla said. "And we talked about it again near the bridge. Actually, it was near the shore."

Jim wrapped his hands around a glass of milk. "Want to tell us more about that, Carla?"

The kitchen became silent. Carla rested her hands lightly on the tabletop. She took a deep breath and exhaled slowly before looking back at Jim and Brooke. "After that incident at the diner, I slipped a little further off the wagon."

"I was worried," Brooke said, biting her lip.

"It all seemed to come crashing in on me. Everything from the last few years. And then . . . further back. Stuff I hadn't really dealt with."

They all waited, silent, encouraging.

"I was sitting on the edge of the bridge," she said. "Ready to end it."

Shirley gasped and reached out to grab her arm, as if she were ready to jump, right then. Carla gave her a tender smile.

A pair of tears ran down Brooke's face. She covered her lips with her fingers. "Then what?"

"I think I jumped. I was really, really drunk. I remember dropping my iPod in, watching the water. And then I was on the shore, below, soaking wet. But not alone. I was with Kenneth."

They all stared at her.

"He told me that I was forgiven."

"Oh, honey. Did you accept it, then?" Shirley asked.

"I did," Carla said. "I finally decided to turn everything over." She smiled. "I turned everything over to God, Kenneth left, then I walked home and practically slept all day." Carla turned her head toward Jim and suddenly seemed distracted. "Pastor Jim, I'm pretty sure Kenneth knows God. In fact, I know he does."

"He always seems so calm," Brooke added. "So confident, like he's got it all under control."

"I don't think you know what I mean," Carla said. "This may sound a little crazy, but when I say I think he knows God, I mean he *knows*-knows him. Like he has personal access to him."

"You're not the only one that thinks that," Macey said, reaching out to put her hand over Carla's before repeating herself. "You're not the only one."

✢ THIRTY-ONE

Ian Tobias sat patiently in the back corner booth of Kamren's Grove, casually sipping at the last couple ounces of a draft beer. He was staring at the second page of the fall dessert menu as different thoughts of Brooke continuously invited themselves into his head. Though his mind registered listings such as Obscene Chocolate Cake, the Peanut Butter Fudge Cookie, and Granny's Apple Crisp Surprise, all his mind's eye could see was her. He hoped she was all right. She sounded pretty serious on the phone, so he agreed to meet her as soon as he got back in town from Milwaukee.

It'd been just about forever since he'd talked to her, but he'd immediately recognized the number on caller ID. It was good to hear her voice again. She always seemed like such a nice person, and they'd become pretty decent friends before that night . . . when they'd made a really bad decision and ruined it all. She'd been a great employee. It practically broke his heart when the cutbacks came and he had to lay her off from the plant, particularly after she had her little boy. Just about everybody at the plant missed her after she left. Especially him.

"Sweetheart, would you like another?" the waitress asked. She had to be almost eighty years old, and her smile showed off what seemed like a brand-new pair of flawless dentures. He glanced at her name tag and pushed the glass in her direction.

"Ruth, darling, I'll bet you run around here and call all the guys *sweetheart*, don't you?"

"Only the handsome ones," she answered quickly.

237

"You made my day, Ruth," he said. "If I were ten years younger, you would be in a heap of trouble. Let's have another Budweiser."

"You better cut him off after that one."

He knew the voice. He turned around and there she was.

"Hello, Brooke," he said, standing.

"Hey, Ian," she said, sounding not quite as enthused as he was.

"You want something to drink, sweetie?" Ruth asked.

"A Coke, please," Brooke said.

Ian gave her a hug, and it seemed like she was having a hard time hugging back. She quickly sat down across from him in the booth and immediately started fiddling with the saltshaker, almost like she was afraid to look at him.

"So what've you been up to?" he asked. Not the most original line to break a few years of ice with, but it would at least make a dent. "Where you working?"

"I'm doing nails at the mall," she said.

"I missed you after you left," he said. "We had a great crew when you were there."

"Yeah," she said distantly. Ian thought an *I missed you too* would have been kind of nice, but she clearly didn't seem to be herself.

Ruth was already back with the Coke and the Budweiser. Ian never saw her approach the table and imagined her arriving through some secret Kamren's Grove trapdoor. She called him "sweetheart" again and wanted to know if they wanted an appetizer, which they declined.

"I've got you figured out, Ruth," Ian said, grinning. "You keep calling me 'sweetheart,' thinking I'm going to fatten your tip, don't you?"

"Am I that obvious?" She laughed.

"Shameless," Ian said.

"You always were such a flirt," Brooke said.

Was she really taking him to task for teasing an old waitress? He could flirt with anyone he wanted to—he was a free man. Divorced. Single. Somehow he had to let her know. Part of him had wondered if she'd heard and that's why she'd called.

He cast about for another topic to discuss, waiting for the opportunity to work it in. "Whatever happened to that friend of yours who got drunk and fell off the stage singing karaoke at the Best Western over in Woodhaven?"

"Carla," she said. "I see her all the time."

Ian smiled. "She was halfway through 'Summer in the City' and did a back dive into the speakers. But she was so far gone, I don't think she felt a thing."

"That was her in the old days," Brooke said, shaking her head and now tapping her finger on the ketchup bottle. "She's come a long way."

Ian nodded and took a sip of his beer. "How is your little boy? He's gotta be about five or six by now, isn't he?"

"Almost six," she said. "His name is Alex."

"Growing like a weed?"

"Yeah."

Brooke still hadn't looked at him and hadn't touched her Coke either. He figured the emergency that prompted their get-together either got her tongue or had been falsely categorized.

He waved his hand to get her attention. It worked, and she finally looked at him with those pretty green eyes. Now maybe he could get her to string more than two sentences together.

"What's on your mind, Brooke? Why the call, after so long? You said it was an emergency."

"Alex has leukemia," she said quickly. "I just found out."

It was only two sentences, but Ian wasn't about to complain. He suddenly felt like taking his turn playing with condiments, but he couldn't look away. He could see the lost look in her eyes and wanted to help her. What'd she need? Money?

"What's going to happen?"

"A lot of stuff," Brooke said. "He's gonna have to go through chemotherapy and have lots of tests. It's gonna be a tough road, but I know we're going to make it."

"Of course you will," he said. "You have insurance?"

"Yeah. Thankfully."

He breathed a sigh of relief. Lots of people, once they got laid off, had insurance for a while, but after COBRA ran out, they did without.

Brooke took a sip of her Coke and her cell phone rang. She reached in her purse and, instead of answering it, killed the call. Ian suspected he was about to find out what she really wanted.

"You know, Ian," she said. "It's kind of a coincidence that you brought up the night that Carla fell off the stage at the Best Western. The second I saw you, I was already thinking about that night."

Ian didn't really need the funny little look she was giving him to remind him of what else happened that night. He'd had a hard time thinking about anything *but* that since she called.

"Carla wasn't the only one who was bombed," Brooke said. "So were we."

"Everybody was," he said with a shrug. "It kinda ended up being an interesting night."

"You can say that again," she said, pausing. "You know something, Ian?"

"What's that?"

"We never once talked about what happened between us that night."

"I know," Ian said, realizing how uncomfortable she seemed. "I'm sorry I even brought it up. I wasn't thinking."

"It's all right," she said.

"You should know," he said, "that I'm divorced." He lifted a hand. "I don't want you to think I'm running around behind my wife's back."

"Oh," she said, her eyes widening a bit.

"I mean . . . because we . . . That was a onetime thing for me."

"For me too," she said, looking miserable at the memory.

"I don't want you to think . . ." He sighed. "Whatever. I was drunk. You were drunk. We made a mistake. But other than that, I was a stand-up guy. Unfortunately, my wife went looking for greener pastures."

"I'm sorry," she said dimly.

He was totally screwing this up. It wasn't going at all the way he'd hoped. He leaned forward. "I've wanted to call you, Brooke. I've thought about you a lot."

"W-wait," she said, lifting both her hands slightly off the table. "You think . . . ? Look. I actually came here to talk about Alex."

"Oh, right," Ian said. "Of course." He felt the slow burn of a blush at his jaw and hoped she wouldn't notice in the dim light. He searched his mind, wondering why the hundred hours of useless HR training at the plant hadn't covered how to ease the minds of former employees who'd just found out their kids had a life-threatening disease.

"You know how I told you they were going to be doing a lot of tests on him?"

"Yeah."

"They're also gonna be testing me and Alex's father to see if either of us are a bone marrow match for him. I guess it's a long shot, but we're potential candidates for a match."

"You never know," Ian said. "Long shots can happen."

"I need your help with something, Ian."

"Sure. Anything."

"And it's the only thing I'll ever want from you, Ian. I swear."

He stared at her. What was she trying to ask him? "Go on, Brooke," he said, frowning. "Ask me. I'll do whatever I can."

"I hope you can. I hope you're a match for Alex. And that you'd be willing to do whatever it takes to save him."

His mouth went dry. "Ex-excuse me?"

"Ian," she said carefully, "Alex is your son."

"SHH," BROOKE SAID AS SHE AND ALEX WATCHED Charlie. They were hiding near the foot pedals of the piano, both of them peeking out, trying desperately not to be noticed. Alex was totally into the game, but Brooke's mind kept wandering back to Ian and the expression on his face last night.

Charlie was it, and Alex found it difficult not to laugh at him as Charlie peeked over each of the individual pews in his effort to find someone. They turned on every light possible to get Charlie to play with them—convincing him that it wouldn't be nearly as dark as during the storm.

He started toward the fellowship hall to hunt down Carla when Alex yelled out to him, "Charlie!"

Charlie spun around. His eyes widened and his mouth rounded as he ducked back under the door. He laughed, covered his mouth, and then tiptoed halfway up the center aisle. His head tilted to the front and then to the back of the church before he resumed his walk back toward the altar. Something bumped near the front door. It was Carla. Charlie stopped and turned his head back toward the main entrance as if he suspected she was kneeling behind the stack of folding chairs in the corner.

"Go save Aunt Carla," Brooke whispered. "She's toast. He's gonna get her."

"I'm gonna scare him," Alex whispered back, crawling out and crouching out of Charlie's view.

"Not too bad," Brooke warned. "Be sweet."

Charlie reached the edge of the stack of chairs and was leaning slowly over the top to peek down at Carla. He began to smile.

"Boo!" Alex yelled, hurtling himself toward his friend and wrapping his arms around Charlie's leg.

Charlie had gasped and jumped, sending Alex into a bout of laughing hysterics. Charlie bent over and quickly picked him up, tickling him.

"Careful with the port, Charlie!" Brooke yelled, walking toward them.

"Aww, it's okay, Mom!" Alex said. "He's not hurting it. I got you, Charlie! I scared you!"

"Is it safe for me to assume that I am found?" Carla asked from behind the chairs.

"Yeah. Come on out, Aunt Carla!" Alex said, taking notice of the odd way in which Charlie was looking at him. "He's worried about me now, Mom. You got him all a'scared."

Charlie squinted and then protectively lowered his chin to the top of Alex's head. He cradled him and then rocked him back and forth.

"You're so sweet, Charlie," Carla said, leaning her head on his massive arm.

"What are you doing, Charlie?" Alex asked, sounding embarrassed at Carla's sentiment. "I'm not that sick. I'm okay."

Carla's head lifted off Charlie's arm. She squinted and looked up toward the front of the church. "I think your cell phone is ringing, Brooke."

"I think you're right," Brooke said, running up to the first pew and pulling the phone out of her purse. "Hello." She glanced back at Carla and held up her hand.

It was the call she had been waiting for.

Ian was there.

IAN SAT IN HIS GRAY FORD EXPLORER IN THE PARKING lot of St. Thomas. He stared up the hill at the light pouring through the glass of the church's front doors.

He looked at his watch for the fifteenth time. Six thirty.

Time to head up.

He stepped out of the Explorer, buttoned up his coat, put his hands in his pockets, and started slowly up the stairs, deciding to abandon all of the lines he had just rehearsed.

He stopped in front of the church doors. The last time he'd been here, he was with David Mills for sixth-grade Vacation Bible School. He had correctly memorized all of the books of the New Testament and had won a fancy Bible. He remembered taking the Bible home and reading it for three hours until the novelty of it wore off in the middle of a blockade of Old Testament names.

He opened one of the doors and stepped inside. The door shut behind him with a loud click that seemed to echo in the mostly empty hall. Four people turned around as one to stare at him from the first pew.

Brooke and Carla both stood. And then there was the big guy he remembered from Bible school. But his eyes were on the small boy kneeling on the pew with his elbows on top of the backrest, looking back at him. He realized that he'd been thinking about Alex like something he'd forgotten and had to go and collect. But the little kid wasn't a pair of gloves he'd accidently left at the airport, a watch he'd missed packing in some hotel room, or a putter he'd not grabbed at some golf course. This kid was his son.

But I didn't know.

Brooke and Carla walked down the aisle, and Brooke gave him a hug. He and Carla exchanged an awkward smile, but his eyes were on his son. *My son.*

"Did you tell him?" Ian asked, pointing up at Alex.

"Not yet," Brooke answered.

"And what's the big guy's name? I remember him from when I was a kid."

"Charlie," Brooke said. "He and Alex are best friends."

"If you don't mind, I would like to tell Alex myself," Ian said, unbuttoning his coat. He took a deep breath and ran his hand across his forehead. "Wow. This is crazy."

"Everything is going to work out," Brooke said, taking Ian's arm. She sounded more confident than he felt.

"It has to work out," he said.

"It will," Brooke said.

The three walked up to the front of the church and stopped at the first pew, where Alex and Charlie were sitting. They both looked up at Ian.

"Charlie, this is Ian," Brooke said. Charlie stood, and the awe was no less for Ian than it had been twenty-five years ago. The only difference was that Charlie had gone from maybe six foot six to nearly seven feet tall.

"It's good to see you, Charlie," Ian said, smiling and holding out his hand. He suddenly remembered from VBS that a response wasn't likely to come. *He's only fifteen? Look how tall he is. Hey, guys—the big kid can't talk.*

Charlie took his hand gently and then let it go.

Brooke gestured toward Alex. "And this is Alex."

Alex looked up at him, and Ian's first instinct was to hug him. But he couldn't. He recognized the boy's hair. He'd also seen the small button nose and the acceptably oversized Tobias ears. He had seen this child before, because he was looking at a five-year-old version of himself. He remembered one of his mother's favorite photographs, the one where he was sitting on Santa's lap at the Kiwanis Christmas party. He looked at Brooke and then back to Alex—back to his son. Ian squinted, and his mouth slowly opened and closed like he was a fish out of water. The resemblance was uncanny. That little boy had jumped out of his mother's favorite photo and onto the first pew of St. Thomas's sanctuary.

He turned to Brooke, who looked like she wanted to cry, but Carla beat her to it. Brooke kneeled in front of Alex and said, "This man wants to talk to you, Alex."

"About what?" Alex asked. "Is he a doctor too?"

"No, baby," Brooke said.

"Why is Aunt Carla crying?" Alex asked. Carla edged away.

Brooke took Charlie's hand. "Aunt Carla, Charlie, and I are going to go sit in the back so you two can talk. Okay, buddy?"

"Why?" Alex asked.

"Ian has something to tell you, Alex."

Alex shrugged and looked at Ian. "Okay."

Ian took his coat off and sat down next to Alex as the others moved off. "I'm really not sure what to say to you, Alex."

Alex stared back at him. "Who are you?" he demanded, looking suspicious.

Ian found it interesting that Alex's question seemed to pierce the heart of the matter. He leaned closer to his son and tried to answer. "I am friends with your mom." He lifted his hand and held it out. "Let's start with a handshake, okay? My name is Ian Tobias."

Alex shook his hand and looked up at him. "That's a funny name."

"I agree with you," he said. "I don't want you calling me that though."

"Okay," Alex said in a way that Ian felt was a bit indifferent, almost as if the boy was already losing interest in him. Alex looked back at his mother and then to Ian. "What do you want me to call you?"

"How about Dad?"

"I don't have a dad," Alex said, turning quickly back to his mother again. "I don't have a grandma and grandpa either."

Reading bedtime stories, playing catch, playing baseball, teaching a child how to ride a bike—things a father was supposed to do—danced through Ian's mind like single frames of a black-and-white movie. He put his hand on Alex's shoulder. "Yes, you do."

"I do?"

"It's me, Alex. I'm your dad."

Alex propped himself up on the heels of his palms. "Really?"

"Really."

Ian noticed the peculiar way in which Alex stared at him. The boy's eyes suddenly rounded as if a five-dollar bill had just dropped out of a birthday card. Alex stood up on the pew cushion and yelled, "Hey, Mom! He's my dad!"

"Yes, he is, buddy," Brooke said, putting her hands on top of the pew in front of her and rising to join them again.

Alex pulled down the top of his shirt and pointed to his port. "I have this for my medicine."

Ian smiled at Brooke as she approached, and then at their son. "Yes, you do, Alex."

"I have leukemia and get chemo syrupy."

Ian dared to put his arm around Alex, pulling him a little closer. He wished he could pull him into his arms.

"Are you all right?" Brooke asked.

"Yeah!" Alex said excitedly, clearly not realizing Brooke was talking to Ian.

"How about you?" Brooke asked, trying again and nodding at Ian.

Ian looked up at her and then over to Alex. "Never better," he said. And deep down, he knew he meant it.

✢ THIRTY-TWO

There was absolutely no doubt in Jim's mind. He knew exactly who Kenneth was and wasn't the least bit shy about telling him. "You are Jesus."

Kenneth stared at him for a few long seconds, then finally nodded in agreement. "I didn't think it would take you long to figure it out, James."

Jim smiled into Kenneth's eyes. "Shirley had you pegged too."

The carpenter grinned and then gave a little tug on Jim's tie. "And you make a good Fred Flintstone. Better lay off Shirley's fudge."

"Can't. Wilma makes the best in the county," Jim said.

The two had just sat down in the last pew of the church, and Jim could hear Bobby Boris Pickett's "Monster Mash" entertaining the partygoers over in the fellowship hall. The second he had spotted the man wearing the ridiculously cheap brown cotton beard, T-shirt, blue jeans, terrycloth bathrobe, and sandals, he couldn't wait to invite the carpenter for a little chat.

"Best costume goes to Charlie, though," Kenneth said. "It's kind of hard not to vote for a seven-foot tin man."

"I don't know. I kind of liked Dr. Norman's Elvis," Jim said, "but I'm a little partial, so I'll make mine a swing vote."

Jim thought about how Alex had laughed when Charlie had his turn at "Pin the Tail on the Donkey." It had become "Pin the Tail on the Donkey Eight Feet to the Right of the Donkey." Just remembering his hysterical giggles made Jim smile; he was thankful they could have this party and bring so many people together for good family fun. But he had bigger things on his mind.

"You know, Kenneth," Jim said, "you have some people around here, myself included, thinking some pretty unconventional things."

"Unconventional, huh?" Kenneth asked, pulling the beard down below his chin and scratching his upper lip. "I personally like the unconventional."

"Me too," Jim said. "More and more."

Kenneth narrowed his eyes and smiled. "Something specific on your mind, James?"

Jim shrugged, then fidgeted with his tie. "I think you are blessed. I believe you have a gift."

Kenneth picked up a hymnal and leafed through the pages. "Everyone's blessed, James. Everyone has gifts."

"You know what I'm speaking of," Jim said, his tone slightly chiding. "Seven fourteen? How could you possibly know when I would see?"

Kenneth's smile grew.

"It was no accident. And I believe that you were talking about Alex and Brooke with Luke 8:50. Correct?"

"Time will tell, right?"

Jim studied him, a little disappointed he couldn't get the man to directly answer him. "Macey said there was a woman at the hospital who came out of a coma, and she seems to think you were somehow involved. Then, both she and Zach, two very smart people, think that the cross couldn't possibly be fixed . . . and I think that maybe Charlie was trying to tell me the same thing. Then last night, even Carla . . ." He paused. "I'm sorry, I'm blabbering."

"No, not at all," Kenneth said. "Please go on."

"Look. I am a man of God," Jim said after taking a deep breath. "And I'm not sure what to say to these people when they ask me about the *things* that have been happening. Christ himself said, 'Unless you people see signs and wonders, you will by no means believe.'"

"Not you," Kenneth said quickly. "Not you."

Jim shook his head. "I'm surprised you didn't tell me which verse that was."

"John 4, verse—"

"I know you know the verse," Jim said, shaking his head in humility. "Why do you think the Lord allowed me to see? I mean, kids are sick. Kids are dying. There is a war going on more often than not. There are so many things happening that are more important than I am."

"Says who?" Kenneth asked, leaning forward to rest his elbows on his knees, hands clasped.

"Says me," Jim answered. The sounds of the party seemed to fade as Kenneth stared over at him, connecting with him.

Kenneth tugged at the beard again, exposing the thin rubber band that ran up his cheek into his thick brown hair. "You are an incredible witness, James—with or without your sight. You are, and always have been."

"Who are you?" Jim asked, wanting—*needing*—to know how the carpenter seemed to be at the center of all these happenings. "How do you get the visions? How do you know what's going to happen? Does it come straight from the Lord?"

"I guess you could say that," Kenneth said calmly.

"Why didn't you want me to tell anyone that you knew what time I would be able to see?"

"Because that isn't important."

"But I want to tell the whole world about God's glory. I want to talk about the Lord's incredible works."

"You already do," Kenneth said.

The earnest look in his eyes took Jim's breath away for a second. *It's like I'm really staring into the eyes of Jesus. The man is touched. Gifted by God. I can see it in his eyes!*

"I would give up my sight right now for Alex's health," Jim said. "Right now, this very second."

"I believe that," Kenneth said, leaning toward Jim and lowering his voice. "But you don't have to do that. Tell her—tell Brooke to only believe, and Alex will be made well."

"She does believe. I know it, Kenneth, I know it."

"Yes, she does," Kenneth said.

"How do you know?" Jim asked.

Kenneth smiled. "I just do."

"Praise God," Jim whispered.

Kenneth nodded. "Praise him, indeed." He smiled again. "Should we get back to the party? I saw some Special Dark bars in there."

Jim laughed under his breath. "I'm talking with a man who has the most incredible gift I have ever seen, and all he wants is some dark chocolate?"

"Best thing on earth," Kenneth said, rising.

"Not better than a good Reese's cup," Jim said, standing too. "But can I ask you one more question?"

"Of course," Kenneth said.

"You sure seem to be taking quite an interest in a lot of people around here."

"Yes," Kenneth said. "And?"

Jim opened one of the fellowship hall doors, and the noise from the party seemed to bounce off them. He raised his voice so the carpenter could hear him. "Carla said you were there at the bridge when she was saved—literally saved. And Macey . . . well, she actually thinks that you—"

"Macey Lewis," Kenneth interrupted, scanning the crowd for her. "She sees things as they are. She is very intuitive, very perceptive. Maybe even more perceptive than you are, James."

Jim wasn't offended by his words. They gave him hope for the doctor. "I think it's great that you're using your gift to be a witness for the Lord. That you're establishing personal relationships with all of these people, myself included. We're really glad you're here." Jim felt something strange race through his chest as the carpenter looked at him with his warm green eyes.

"That's all I've ever wanted, James," he said, pulling his beard back into place and smiling. He rested a hand on his chest. "It's all I'll *ever* want."

✢ THIRTY-THREE

Brooke sat next to Carla on the couch, only partially listening to her chat with Ian, as everyone else in the house slept.

It had been a draining, strange couple of weeks since the harvest party, with Ian coming by every day, sometimes twice a day, to be with Alex and go to chemo treatments and other appointments.

Ian hadn't been shy about letting everyone know he didn't have the faintest idea what he was doing when it came to being a father. But the general consensus was that he was doing a pretty good job, and Brooke found herself wondering if maybe Ian was a little *too* good at it.

All she heard lately was "Dad this" and "Dad that."

Alex was crazy about his father, and last week when her son, *their son*, had refused to let her tuck him in for the night and insisted that Ian do it, the only thing that eased the hurt was the look on Alex's face when Ian came into the bedroom. Stubborn as she was, nothing melted her heart like Alex's joy. Especially now.

But that didn't keep her from secretly hoping that Ian would do something that Alex didn't like. Maybe it would bring the hero worship down a notch or two. Make a little room for her again.

She thought about the questions that kept her on guard. How could she possibly let Alex be around a man whose morals were loose enough to allow him to have an affair on his wife? But she knew how many it took to tango. She was as much to blame as he was. And if she was a different woman now, couldn't he be different too?

She looked at Ian as he sat in Pastor Jim's La-Z-Boy. They had agreed that neither of them wanted to be a couple, but she knew they both wanted to be good parents.

Parents, Brooke. As in plural.

Alex now had two. It was harder to get used to than she thought it would be. Half of her had expected him to give his sample to see if he was a match and then run. Becoming a dad? An involved dad? That really hadn't entered her mind. And as much as she was struggling with it, she knew it was good—really good—for Alex.

My issue. Not his. Don't make it his.

"Thanks for being here, Ian," Brooke said softly, interrupting the conversation.

"Will you quit saying that?" Ian said, giving her a playful frown. "I want to be here."

"I know you do," Brooke said, trying to hide a small sigh with a fake yawn.

"So, let me get this right," Carla said. She tossed a kernel of popcorn in her mouth and passed the bowl to Brooke. "They're gonna do a platelet transfusion if the chemo lowers Alex's white blood cell count too much?"

"Yes," Ian answered. *That's another good thing about him being here.* Ian asked lots of questions, and he seemed to understand practically everything Macey talked about, even when she was going a million miles an hour.

"So we should be scared if they have to do that?" Carla said, pulling her feet up on the couch and wrapping them in a quilt.

"No, not at all," Ian said. "Macey says it happens all the time."

Brooke heard the bathroom door click shut, back in the hallway.

"I guess I really don't understand all of it," Carla said. "But either way, from what everyone says, it sounds like Macey is the perfect doctor for Alex."

Brooke leaned forward and listened for the bathroom. She had a feeling it was Alex.

"I just wish they could get his white blood cell count down to where they want it."

"What did Macey say about that?" Carla asked.

"She said it wasn't that unusual," Brooke said.

"Okay," Carla said. "So what's next?"

"They're changing up his regimen slightly."

"His regimen?"

"Yeah," Ian said. "They changed the combination of drugs they're giving him to lower his white blood cell count, and if it knocks it down too much, that's when they will give him the platelet transfusion."

"I think I get it," Carla said. "How long are they going to keep doing all the chemo and testing?"

Brooke answered, "That's what we're still not sure about."

Ian looked over his shoulder. "Is that Alex in the bathroom?"

"I think so," Brooke said. "I'll give him another couple minutes."

Carla turned to Brooke. "Didn't you say you guys are both getting tested for something Friday?"

"To see if either of us is a marrow match," Brooke answered. "That's what Kaitlyn told me. But I guess the odds of me or Ian being a match for Alex are like a gazillion to one." Brooke glanced back at the empty hallway. *What's taking him so long?*

"Want me to check on him?" Ian asked, following her gaze.

"I got it," Brooke said, pushing back a wave of irritation. *He's just trying to help.* She went down the hallway to the bathroom door. "Is everything okay in there, Alex?"

There was no answer. She knocked lightly on the door. "Alex, are you in there?"

"Yeah," a small voice said, muffled behind the door.

"What are you doing, buddy?" Brooke asked. "Are you okay?"

"Yeah," Alex said faintly. "I'm trying to go potty."

"You sure have been in there awhile. You want me to come in?"

"I'm okay," he said softly. "Are Dad and Aunt Carla still here?"

"They are," Brooke said, pressing her ear to the door. "Are you sure you're okay?"

"Yeah."

"Yell if you need me. Okay?"

"All right."

Brooke walked back into the living room and dropped on the couch. "It's Alex."

"Is he okay?" Ian asked.

"I think so. I'll give him a few more minutes. I'm getting tired."

"Me too," Ian said. "I should probably get going."

Brooke turned to Carla, who was staying the night. Carla had been spending a lot of time with Pastor Jim, probably talking about her newfound sobriety and direction. "You need to be up at any certain time?"

Carla grabbed the bowl and scooped up the popcorn that had spilled on the couch. "I work at nine. But I'm sure Pastor Jim will be doing his 5:00 a.m. rattling thing in the kitchen, waking the whole house up."

"You're probably right," Brooke said, smiling.

Carla leaned over and gave Brooke a quick squeeze, then smiled over at Ian. "Everything's going to be all right, you guys. Remember what Pastor Jim said?"

"Only believe," Brooke said.

"I like that," Ian said.

Brooke hugged Carla tightly, stood, then headed back down the hall. The bathroom door was still closed. She tapped on the door. "Alex?"

"Yeah," he answered. He sounded younger this time.

"What are you doing, buddy?"

He didn't say anything.

"Alex, I'm coming in." She tried the door, but it was locked.

"Are they still here?"

"Yes, honey. Unlock the door."

"Are they with you or in the living room?"

"In the living room. Unlock the door."

He fumbled briefly with the doorknob, and then she could hear the lock turn. Brooke slowly opened the door and noticed that the only light was the soft glow of a night-light that was plugged in near the bottom of the wall.

Alex was by the bathtub with his head down and his hands at his sides.

"What's wrong, buddy?" she asked, still not approaching him. "You don't feel good?"

"It feels like I sunburned my head and . . ." He stopped and covered his face as if he were ashamed. She noticed his shoulders had started to bob. He was crying.

"Alex," Brooke said, kneeling down and hugging him. This was the first time she had seen him cry since he had begun his treatment. The needles, the port, the prodding, the constant orders to be still, the chemo . . .

Everyone had marveled at how well he was taking things. How well he was doing. How brave he was. But he was also only five. "What, baby? Tell me what's wrong."

"Close the door," he whispered into her shoulder.

"Okay, sweetie," she said, swinging the door shut behind her.

"It's happening," he whispered.

"What, buddy? What's happening? Tell me."

"Turn the . . ." He paused and lifted his head. "Turn the light on."

Brooke flipped the switch, and they both squinted against the light.

"See it?" Alex asked, climbing the step stool in front of the sink.

Brooke looked in the mirror at their reflection. She couldn't see anything out of the ordinary. "I don't know what you're talking about, Alex. What is it?"

"Really?" he asked, sounding hopeful.

She rose and glanced back in the mirror. There it was. Now she could see it. She looked down at her chest, where Alex's head had been.

"Look," he said, pointing up at her. She could see the hopelessness in his eyes. "See it?"

"I do, baby," she whispered.

Tiny shreds of reddish-orange hair clung to her shirt between her chest and shoulder. She glanced back in the mirror at Alex's reflection and could see a small tear angling across his cheek. At the base of his neck and around his shoulders, more hair had fallen out, virtually covering the collar of his Spider-Man pajamas.

"I don't want Dad to see it."

"Baby, it's okay."

"Can you tell him that it's because of the chemo syrupy?"

She picked him up and hugged him, feeling his wiry arms wrap around her neck, his legs around her torso. She leaned in, inhaling the scent of him, and swallowed the lump in her throat. *You have to sound brave, Brooke. Strong. Positive.* "Remember what they told us, buddy?"

"What?" he said, nestling against her shoulder.

"They said it would grow back. Remember?"

"Are you sure it will grow back?"

"Yes, I'm sure."

"You promise?"

"Yeah, baby," she said, rubbing his back and kissing the side of his face. "I promise."

✤ THIRTY-FOUR

I'm still trying to figure out which genius chef keeps putting green beans on the same plate as pizza," Kaitlyn said, sitting in front of Macey at the East Shore cafeteria. She studied her plate in partial disgust, making absolutely sure that none of the beans had the gall to touch either of her two slices.

"What are you, ten years old?" Macey asked, laughing and stabbing at the beans on her plate with her fork. "Ever try eating one? They are actually pretty good for you."

"I have no problem with green beans," Kaitlyn said. "I just can't get used to them being served with pizza. It's like ketchup and ice cream. Certain things don't belong together. It's food taboo."

"Look. I'm eating it," Macey said. "It doesn't bother me."

"I've also seen pictures of you diving out of a perfectly good airplane. So that explains that."

Macey turned to face the cafeteria entrance as a rowdy cluster of construction workers trampled through the hallway and then out the main door. "So Zach asked you to go somewhere with him this weekend?"

Kaitlyn nodded as she completed the separation between the beans and the pizza. "Just when I was completely prepared to give him his newfound space, he asked me to go."

"Space? Like the space you gave him at church on Sunday? Not exactly beans and pizza, Kaitlyn. You were sitting right next to him."

"Shush, Lewis."

"What are you guys going to do?"

"I'm not sure," Kaitlyn said. "But he told me it would explain some things. He also said to wear old clothes."

"Explain some things?" Macey asked. "Like what?"

"I'm not sure."

"I knew you were going to go out with him again," Macey jabbed.

"It's not a date."

"No, it's not a date," Macey agreed. "It's a romantic weekend away."

"With separate rooms."

Macey smiled. "Quit being so defensive! I'm allowed to harass you."

Kaitlyn put down her fork, but she wasn't smiling. "I didn't think I'd ever want to spend time with him outside of the hospital again, Macey. I was sure of it. I know it hasn't been that long, but something's different about him, don't you think? It's like some type of switch was flipped."

"You won't get any argument from me," she said. "He's way more focused on the kids here, less self-centered. And who would've ever guessed that he'd be in church three weeks in a row? Heck—*once*, for that matter?"

Kaitlyn agreed. "Who would've ever guessed that *we* would be there three weeks in a row?"

"Kenneth," Macey said. "That's who."

"Here we go again," Kaitlyn said, rolling her eyes lightheartedly. But she smiled. "I wonder why he wasn't there on Sunday?"

"Are you two talking about me again?"

They were both startled but not scared, recognizing his voice. They looked up, and Kenneth was casually standing next to their table, dressed in his usual construction outfit of jeans and flannel shirt.

"Hello, Kaitlyn," he said. "Hello, Macey."

"Kenneth!" Macey said, choking on her swallow of soda. "Hi."

Kaitlyn looked back up at the carpenter and oddly felt like a child hanging out with a favorite parent.

He is the buzz.

"We were just saying that we didn't see you at church on Sunday," Kaitlyn said, finally finding her voice.

"Interesting," Kenneth said as several hospital employees looked over at them. "I was there on Sunday."

"We didn't see you," Macey said curiously.

"You're right." He nodded, quickly stepping back. "Listen, guys, I didn't mean to interrupt. I saw you two in here, and I wanted to swing in and say hi."

"You're welcome to join us," Macey said.

"Thanks, but I better be going," he said. "The superintendent doesn't really approve of us being in here."

"We have you covered," Kaitlyn offered, her confidence and comfort slowly coming back to the table. "Please join us."

"I really have to leave," he said, cocking his thumb back over his right shoulder. "But I hope to see you guys again on Sunday. And I'll make sure you see me too." He gave them each a smile, then turned and made his way out the door.

Both women watched as he disappeared around the corner.

"I feel like an idiot," Macey said, tossing her crumpled napkin on the table. "I really didn't know what to say to him."

"I was waiting for you to say something," Kaitlyn said. "He probably thinks we are a couple of gossips. Of *course* he walks in right as we're talking about him."

Macey shook her head, grabbed the napkin, and then picked up a piece of pizza. "I don't think he thinks that at all, Kait."

"Maybe," Kaitlyn said, trying to read the strange look on Macey's face. She leaned closer so she could lower her voice. "He makes me feel like a little kid when he's around."

"Me too," Macey agreed.

"Did he just say he was there on Sunday?"

"Yes, he did."

Kaitlyn quickly sipped her Diet Coke. "Don't you think if he was at church, we would have seen him? There were more people than ever, but we would've seen him. Right? Since we were both looking?"

Macey paused. "Not necessarily," she said lowly, giving her a conspiratorial look.

"C'mon, Macey," the nurse said.

Macey lifted her elbows to the top of the table and leaned forward. "Maybe we weren't looking hard enough. In the right *way*."

"What do you mean?" Kaitlyn asked.

"He said he was there," Macey said quietly, sitting back. "You know exactly what I mean."

"Here you go again," Kaitlyn said, looking over her shoulder and around to see if anyone was overhearing their crazy talk. "Don't even say it."

"Fine." She looked miffed.

"Listen," Kaitlyn said, lowering her voice. "We don't want anybody knowing that the best doctor here thinks that God is a dues-paying member of the local carpenters' union. They'll send you to the eighth-floor psych ward instead of letting you keep working on the third."

Macey looked away dismissively and then back to the nurse, a smile twitching at her lips. "Dues-paying member?"

"Yes," Kaitlyn said. "But if you do end up on the eighth floor, I'll visit you every day. I promise."

"Ha-ha," Macey said. "But back to the church thing. I want to keep going. In fact, I'm going to call Pastor Jim and see if our little group wants to go back to that Pilot Inn for lunch after church this Sunday, my treat. You in? Oh, that's right. You'll be gone. With *Zach*." She tossed her a teasing smile.

Kaitlyn gave her a sassy look back, thinking about the standing-room-only crowd at St. Thomas. *The happily standing crowd.* "Your treat? I'm sure they can probably afford it now. There were more people there this week than last. I figured the hype would've died down."

"Blindness just doesn't up and go away," Macey said. "People want to know what happened. They want to be around a miracle. And then they tell people who tell more people. And Pastor Jim isn't half bad at preaching."

"I guess you're right," Kaitlyn said. "The day we went for the cross, there were probably twenty people there, tops. How many do you think were there Sunday?"

"Two, maybe three hundred," Macey answered. "Those people in the back stood for the whole hour."

"Pastor Jim keeps them on their toes, though, doesn't he?"

"Yes, he does. He makes me want to try and make more of my life. Live it differently."

"Me too," Kaitlyn said.

Macey finished off her first slice of pizza. "Just like Zach, I'm going to try. I really do want to do better."

"Just like Zach," Kaitlyn repeated in disbelief. "Go figure."

ZACH LOWERED THE VOLUME ON THE RADIO AS HE AND Kaitlyn turned off the Van Horn exit of I-75, a little over a mile north of Carlson. "You ever wonder what it's all about, Kait?" he asked, waving his hand in a sweep across the breadth of the windshield.

"What?" Kaitlyn asked, giving him a little puzzled frown.

"Life," he answered. He rolled the driver's side window down a few inches and lifted his cheek closer to feel the crisp air. "It's a perfect day, isn't it?"

It is a beautiful day, Kaitlyn thought. She smiled over at him, as interested in the man beside her and the changes she saw in him as she was in the bright blue sky outside. "To be honest, Zach, I've actually been thinking a lot about it lately."

"Anything specific?"

She paused, studying him. He'd never shown an interest in anything deep before, let alone sought her opinion. Now he seemed more alive to her. "Like you, Zach."

"Like me?" he asked. She thought he was surprised—maybe even a little pleased—by her sincerity.

"The way you have acted over the last couple of weeks is . . . well, it's inspiring."

"Thanks," he said. "I appreciate that. The truth of the matter is that I've been more than inspired. I think I'm changing." He shrugged. "In fact, I don't just want to believe, I think that maybe . . ."

She could see his smile. It wasn't forced, like the Dr. Norman smiles she'd become accustomed to. "I think it's part of the reason I'm with you today. I see the change in you."

"And I want to keep it up," he said. "Do you remember when Pastor Jim was talking to all of us about the past, the present, and the future? And how he pointed out that too many of us are so wrapped up in worrying about things we can't control that we ignore our obligations and blessings in the present?"

"I'm that way sometimes," Kaitlyn said. "I think about the future all the time."

"There's nothing wrong with that," Zach said. "But the way I see it, *worrying* about the future is where we get into a problem. We should plan, but *start* with planning to do the right things— right now. The things we're called to do, deep down. For me, it's spending more time with each of our patients rather than just seeing them as names on my to-do list. And it's made each day so much more . . . meaningful."

"I see that," she said, thinking he'd really never looked handsomer than he did today.

"If we do those things first, the rest will work itself out. The future too. Don't you think?"

"I do," she said, wondering if he'd missed his calling. He had made his point every bit as well as the minister had. "Zach. What's got into you?"

He glanced over at her, his eyes somber, contemplative. "I'm in the present, rather than working over my past."

"What do you mean?" Kaitlyn asked carefully.

"We all make mistakes. All of us. I made a hundred with you," he said, giving her a rueful look. "Someday I hope you can forgive me for those. But I had to go further back to deal with something in order to break free of it." He slowed the car down and tapped on the steering wheel. "I wasn't smart enough to realize the obvious."

"What?"

"That there's nothing we can do about the past. The past is over. We can't go back and fix it. We can only accept what it was. And what it wasn't."

She nodded. "You're right—blown careers, divorces, opportunities that we missed or didn't handle quite right. It's so easy to live every day dwelling on our mistakes that we eat up the now."

"Exactly," he said, nodding, thinking. "And the *now* is our only opportunity to be aware—to change. We only have today, and hopefully tomorrow. And we need to do the right things—do the right things not just for ourselves but for those around us."

She studied him again. Was he even the same person anymore? "What was it, Zach? The thing in your past? Can you tell me?"

Zach pulled the car over onto the left shoulder of the road and rolled into some high weeds. They were in the middle of nowhere. She thought he was just wanting to focus before he told her what it was.

He put the car in park and turned off the engine. "You of all people deserve an explanation."

"An explanation for what?" Kaitlyn asked.

"For the way I was," he said. "And I figured while we were here, we could fix something up a little bit, if you don't mind."

Here? Kaitlyn leaned across the front seat to look out the driver's side window. "A *cemetery*?"

"C'mon," he said, giving her a gentle smile. "There's something I need to show you."

✢ THIRTY-FIVE

For many, it was almost too loud at The Pilot Inn.
   Not for Jim.

The sound of it all, the *sight* of it all—he loved every second of it.

In the diner there were older couples, younger couples, some of their children, and what seemed to be quite a few of their children's children. They laughed, smiled, and mouthed words over small wicker baskets of french fries, chicken strips, hamburgers, and clear plastic pitchers of different-colored sodas.

Returning from the restroom, he saw that the areas around the pool tables, dartboards, and jukebox were primarily clusters of college-age kids and other twentysomethings who wielded single bottles of beer or mixed drinks. His smile weakened as he looked up at the bar and the backs of the patrons who *had* to be there—the regulars. These were the ones who gave up their lives to an alternative higher power. *Lord, help them*, he thought, glancing up at the faded lights along the mirror behind the bar, mercifully dimming the reflections of the ghosts who hopelessly stared back at it.

Carla had been one of them. A shiver ran down his back, thinking of her here and what it had driven her to—

"Man, we suck!" someone yelled in a hoarse voice behind him.

Jim turned around and watched a replay of the pass that had put the Detroit Lions down fourteen to zero only five minutes into the game. He looked up at the TV. It wasn't the one-handed catch that amazed him. *Look at the size of that television.* And then he walked under it and through the swing doors, returning to the dining room.

"Isn't this fun, James?" Shirley said simply, taking his hand as he sat down beside her again. "What are you looking at?"

"Everything," he said, looking around at the table full of loved ones as well as those beyond them. "Absolutely everything."

"Do you want to say grace?" she asked.

"Of course," he said, surprised he hadn't noticed the food had arrived in his absence. "Shall we give thanks?" He lifted his hands. Shirley took his left hand again, and Macey took his right. The rest of the table followed suit, and they all dropped their heads.

After church, they had anonymously dropped off four carloads of food, clothing, and a generous envelope to Mick Solack's food bank over in Rockwood and now sat with hot burgers and chicken fingers awaiting them all.

Only Macey, Shirley, Brooke, and Kenneth could hear him saying the prayer in the bustling diner, but it didn't matter. Every one of them felt it, Jim believed. Down at the far end, Ian, Carla, Alex, and Charlie looked up a moment after they'd said their amens.

We're so blessed, Lord, he thought. *So blessed. Thank you, Lord. Whatever comes, thank you for this day.*

"QUIT PATRONIZING ME," MACEY SAID PLAYFULLY. JIM looked to his right over Macey's shoulder at Kenneth. The carpenter wasn't talking. He was nodding his head and listening to the young doctor. Macey had told Jim that she was going to ask Kenneth some interesting questions; apparently, she'd already started.

"What?" Kenneth said. "You asked me how I fixed the cross, and I told you."

Macey rocked in her seat. "I need a better answer than 'God-given ability.'"

"What else would I need?" he asked. "It seems like you've been given an ability in your line of work."

"I studied to learn what I do," Macey said. "I think what you did was a miracle."

Kenneth threw his hands up. "It was."

"Will you please stop?" Macey said. "It's driving me crazy how that cross went up so fast."

"Will I please stop?" Kenneth said, repeating her question and nudging her with his shoulder. "I don't think so."

Macey nudged back. "Seriously, Kenneth, you seem to be at the center of the miracle fest. Of everything that is good."

"That's because I am—"

"Oh my goodness!" a smoke-rasped voice barked from only a few feet inside the front door. Tim Shempner had just entered the diner with a couple of drunken buddies at his side. "Lookie, lookie here. Look who is back! The Pilot bimbo and her band of Coke-drinking Jesus freaks!" He took a step forward. "Where is the big retard today?"

Jim froze. Kathy and her baseball bat were off for the day, so Shempner had dared to return.

The diner quieted as Shempner walked up behind Carla and tugged sharply at the back of her hair. He looked like he'd been up all night and reeked of booze and sour body odor. He and his friends slid into an empty booth, right behind Carla.

"Where's the waitress?" he shouted. "We need some menus!"

Jim pulled back his seat to stand up and approach the drunken man, but Kenneth put his hand on his shoulder, suggesting he stay put.

Carla turned around and faced Shempner with a confidence and sense of peace that Jim had never seen in her before. "Why do you have to be this way? Stay and eat, but remember this is the *family* side of The Pilot Inn . . . not the bar."

"Shut up," Shempner said, belching. "I don't need your permission for anything."

A waitress tentatively came over and handed three menus to the guys. She took their order for drinks and hurried off to the kitchen.

Carla turned around with a heavy sigh and fiddled with a french fry as Shempner and his buddies hunched together, talking.

Shempner rose and leaned over Carla's shoulder, took a fry, and popped it into his mouth, giving the rest of the table an insolent look.

"Tim, please."

"Please what?" he said, taking another fry.

"Please leave us alone."

"And if I don't?" he sneered, leaning down and pushing her hair over her shoulder, looking at her neck like he wanted to kiss it. "Kathy isn't here to save you today!"

"She doesn't have to be here to save me," Carla said, brushing aside his hand. "Now I'm going to ask you nicely. Please stop."

"*Pleeeaaase . . . pleeeeaaaase,*" Shempner whined, mocking Carla. "I'll make you say—"

"That's enough!" someone yelled.

Jim looked up. It was Ian.

He was about five feet from Shempner. Charlie and Alex had followed him back from the video games and were standing right behind him.

"And you are?" Shempner asked.

"I'm Ian Tobias. And I think you're leaving."

"Only after I kick your butt!" Shempner ground out, stepping toward him.

"I love getting my butt kicked," Ian said, a confident smile creasing his lips. "Let's go outside."

Shempner paused. He clearly heard the cackle and then the muted sound of laughter to his left. His buddies were making fun of him. He still hesitated.

"That's what I thought," Ian said quietly. "Such a big man with *women*. But not so ready to take on another man. Now apologize to Carla and to everyone at our table. No. Make that the whole diner." He turned to pick up Alex.

Shempner grinned. It was the opening he needed. He lunged forward and kicked Ian's back. Ian's head snapped back and his arms fanned out, sending him sprawling helplessly forward. His arm hit Alex's chest, and the boy went flying backward.

"No!" Brooke screamed, jumping up from the other side of the table.

Panic flooded across Charlie's face. He quickly dropped to a knee and put his hand behind Alex's head, who was gasping for the air that had just been knocked out of him.

Ian brought himself to one knee as Macey and Carla raced to Alex's side opposite Charlie. "We've got him now, Charlie," Macey said. "We'll help him. Don't worry." Charlie rose and backed away.

"Look at my finger, Alex," Macey said, calmly holding her hand up in front of his face to check his eyes. "Look at my finger. Look right here."

"Alex?" Carla said.

"He's all right," Macey said, sensing pressure from the circle of bystanders that had formed around them. She pulled the top of Alex's shirt back down. "The port's okay."

"Please," Jim said, trying to create some space. People were spilling over from the bar side to gather around. "Please, friends, please. She's a doctor. Pull back."

"He's going to kill him!" a young woman yelled. "Help!"

"Somebody do something!" another voice cried.

"James!" Shirley shouted from behind him. *"James!"*

Jim turned from Alex and looked at the center of yet another circle that had formed. It was something he'd never imagined. *No.*

"Charlie!" he yelled, working his way quickly through the crowd to the edge of the other circle. "Charlie, no!"

Charlie's lips were coiled back and his teeth were gritted. His exhales were not breaths, but intermittent growls that were clearly frightening people. His arms were perfectly straight in front of him and vibrated only with the hopeless thrashing of the weight they held.

Charlie had Tim Shempner by the throat.

Shempner's boots kicked and dangled helplessly in the air as Charlie served as both executioner and gallows. Shempner clawed at Charlie's hands until they bled, desperately seeking release.

"No, son!" Jim said. "Charlie, no!"

Shempner's face became a light shade of purple as Charlie lifted him higher into the air.

"Charlie!" Jim yelled again, reaching up and pulling down on Charlie's arm. He could see the veins pulsing in his son's hands and forearms, as well as his temples.

"Alex is okay!" Shirley yelled, coming to his other side. "Look, Charlie! Look!"

"Alex is okay!" Jim echoed, still pulling on Charlie's closest arm with all his weight, desperate now. *Please, Lord, don't let him kill him. Please, Lord . . .*

Charlie looked down at his father, then at his mother, and then back toward where Alex was. Alex was now on his feet, standing between Ian and Brooke. Carla handed Alex his ball cap, and Alex put it back on. Alex then rubbed the tears from his eyes and shook his head in disapproval at Charlie.

Charlie stared back at Shempner, giving him a message that words could never say. Shempner's hands dropped to his sides, and he was slobbering at the corners of his mouth when Kenneth reached up and took Charlie by the wrist.

"It's *okay*, Charlie," the carpenter said. Charlie immediately let go, and Shempner fell to the floor like a rag, bringing his own hands to his throat and gasping for air.

"Way to kick his butt, big man!" somebody yelled.

"Please, no," Jim said, holding up his hands. "Please."

Charlie turned toward Alex, and everybody got out of his way. He walked over and Alex held out his arms for a hug. Charlie picked him up, and Alex rested his head on his shoulder. Charlie lowered his cheek to the top of Alex's head, and they both closed their eyes as if they were equally glad it was over.

MACEY AND KENNETH SAT BACK AT THE TABLE. SHE realized her hands were trembling when she reached for her glass of water. "Unreal, huh?" she said to him.

"Looked pretty real to me," Kenneth said calmly. "Nice work with Alex."

"He's lucky. *Very* lucky."

"What if he wasn't?" Kenneth asked, taking a sip of his own water as everyone began to return to their own tables.

"What's that supposed to mean?" Macey asked.

"What if you couldn't help him?"

"I don't know," Macey said, frowning. "What kind of question is that?"

"What if your best wasn't good enough, Macey Lewis? What would you do?"

"Are you messing with me again?"

"I wasn't messing with you before," Kenneth said. "I thought maybe you should think about that."

Macey squinted and tilted her head. "Don't you think that's kind of an odd thing to say?"

"No, Macey," Kenneth said. He stood and walked around the other side of the table. "Kaitlyn saying I took a magic carpet to visit Mary Springsted is an odd thing to say."

Macey glanced up at him. "What did you just say? Can you say that again?"

He put his palms flat on the table and smiled. "I think you heard me."

"But there is no way you could have possibly . . ." Macey stopped and then just stared, stone-faced, as the carpenter turned and walked out the door.

✦ THIRTY-SIX

Macey stepped into the consultation room, and the first thing she saw was Ian, who was confidently balancing Alex on his left knee. Like father, like son—the two of them wore matching smiles that reminded her of a ventriloquist act. She was pretty sure Ian would make up for his unknowing absence in Alex's life. He already had, in an important way.

"Good morning, guys," Macey said. She shook Brooke's hand and then Ian's. "How is your back feeling?"

Ian reached his hand around his side and tapped it. "It only took three days, but it's like new."

Macey tilted her head and gave him a look that said she knew better. "That was quite a kick you took. Are you pressing charges?"

"Nah," Ian said. "Everything turned out all right. I think Tim Shempner has enough problems already. And if I press charges, he might retaliate by pressing charges against Charlie."

"I don't know," Macey said, lifting a copy of *Highlights* off a seat before sitting down. "Carla should do something about that guy. He's clearly dangerous."

"She did," Brooke said. "He can't come within five hundred feet of her."

"She got a restraining order?"

"Yeah," Brooke said. "Thank God."

Macey agreed. "That may be in everyone's best interest for now—particularly until he gets the help he obviously needs."

Ian looked at Brooke in a way that said he was more than okay with the outcome. "Maybe what he most needs is Charlie's kind of help."

"Yeah," Alex said attentively. "Charlie kicked his butt, huh?"

"Alex!" Brooke said.

Ian swallowed a grin and tapped on Alex's baseball cap. "Hey, you."

Alex looked up at his father. "That's what that man said at—"

"We don't talk that way, partner."

"Okay, Dad. I'm sorry."

Brooke smiled at Macey, who winked back at her. The doctor figured it was probably the six hundredth time that Alex had used the word *dad* in just under a week. And those were only the ones she was around to hear.

Macey leaned forward in her chair and put her elbows on her knees. "And how about you, Mr. Alex? How're you feeling?"

"I'm pretty good," Alex said.

She could see that he appeared a little more drawn than usual. Despite his upbeat tone, he was a bit pale—almost peaked. "It's okay if you're not feeling well. You can tell me."

"I'm a little sleepy sometimes," he said.

"That's okay," Macey assured him.

"He hasn't been himself the last couple of days," Brooke said. "He also threw up last night."

Macey nodded, not surprised, and said, "I have some news for you guys."

"Lay it on us," Ian said, wrapping his arms around Alex.

"We already have Alex's results back from today. We also have the parental blood test results back."

"Okay," Ian and Brooke said together.

"First," Macey said, "Alex's white blood cell count came down, which is encouraging. So we will go ahead today with the same regimen." She smiled at Ian. "And second, even though it's extremely rare, and we still have to do a few more tests, we believe we have a marrow match for Alex. It's also convenient that this person is local—really local."

"Kind of like you're-lookin'-at-him local?" Ian asked calmly, his eyebrows slowly bunching together.

"Are you serious?" Brooke said, her mouth dropping open.

"Yes," Macey said. "Congratulations."

"That's good news for us, partner," Ian said, pulling down on the bill of Alex's cap, who quickly readjusted it.

"Yes, it is," Macey said. "We are extremely fortunate to have you as a potential match. Having a marrow transplant as an option is an incredible advantage. If needed, that is."

"Thank you, God!" Brooke said, squeezing her knees together and looking thankfully at the ceiling. "Thank you, God. Thank you, God."

"Thank you, God," Ian repeated. He lowered his chin to the top of Alex's head and met eyes with the doctor. She guessed that he was thinking about the last five—almost six—years, and about all the gifts he'd never given Alex.

And now he had the one his son may need the most.

Thank you, God, Macey thought.

A WEEK LATER IAN JOINED PASTOR JIM AT THE WINDOW in the Lindy living room. It was starting to get dark, and the year's first snow was fluttering straight down in thick, quarter-sized flakes.

"It's beautiful," Pastor Jim said. "I haven't seen snow in such a long time."

Brooke and Shirley entered the living room. They'd been with Alex.

"How is he doing?" Ian asked.

Shirley joined them and looked outside. "The chemotherapy seems to be hitting our little man a bit harder this week."

Charlie came into the living room, and Ian noticed that even the big guy seemed stressed.

Ian turned and went down the hallway to the bedroom to check him out for himself. Alex was lying on his side, asleep. He looked milky and appeared thinner than he had a week earlier—for that matter, since just that morning. Ian quietly sat in the chair next to the bed, stared at him a moment, and then closed his eyes. It was hard to believe that less than a month ago, he'd been sitting in that little pub back in Milwaukee, swapping divorce horror stories with some bartender he'd never see again. They'd gotten into a big discussion. About important things. Topics he couldn't remember now.

About things I thought were important. Then.

He ran his hand across the top of Alex's head, wondering how his son had coped all this time without a dad. He'd had Pastor Jim, which made Ian thankful. *But it's not the same.* It wasn't fair for the kid to have to go through all of this, but that was going to change. He was going to help Brooke give Alex the life he was meant to have.

"Fatherhood," Pastor Jim said quietly, standing in the bedroom doorway, startling him. "It's good stuff."

"Yes, it is," Ian said.

"He's a little sicker than normal, eh?"

"Looks that way," Ian said, pulling the blanket up to Alex's shoulders.

"He'll be made well," Pastor Jim said. Ian liked the way he said it. It sounded like it was already done.

"Pastor Jim," Ian said, "can I talk to you about something?"

"Sure. Anything." The tall man took a seat on a kid-sized stool and Ian smiled at the sight of it. But Pastor Jim looked like there was no place he'd rather be.

"I remember you from when I was eleven or twelve years old," Ian said, keeping his voice down so he wouldn't wake Alex. "And I certainly couldn't forget Charlie."

Pastor Jim smiled. "He's hard to forget, isn't he? In more ways than one."

"I know a *lot* of people aren't going to forget him at The Pilot Inn. It's not too often that a grown man is picked off the ground by his throat."

Pastor Jim nodded disapprovingly. "I really don't know why,

but Mr. Shempner has never been too kind to Charlie. And obviously, Charlie never did anything about it . . . until then."

"He was just protecting Alex."

"Absolutely," Pastor Jim said. "Though I don't condone what happened, I suspect Mr. Shempner won't be coming up to our table for a while."

"I think you're right," Ian said. He would never admit it to Pastor Jim, but a part of him—a really big part of him—got a nice charge out of the look on Tim Shempner's face when Charlie was serving up some payback.

"So on to what you wanted to talk about," Pastor Jim said. "Is it about your situation?"

"My situation?"

Pastor Jim gave Ian a wise, fatherly look. "I'm guessing you feel a little morally awkward about your, ah, *situation*," he said, waving between Alex and Ian, "particularly when you're around me. Because of my profession. Is that right?" Ian could tell he was being cautious with his words in case Alex woke up and heard them.

"Yeah," Ian said. "That's exactly it. I feel *really* awkward."

"And you're wondering what a man of God thinks about your responsibilities as a father, especially when your son is living under his roof?"

"Pastor Jim," Ian said. "You've gotta know that I plan to do my best to help Brooke and Alex. And I know how this all must look, but believe it or not, I generally try to do the right thing and—"

"The right thing?"

"Yes," Ian said. "I try to do the right thing. But knowing I have Alex changes so many things. I just arrived and I feel like I'm supposed to be Dad of the Year or something." He rubbed his temples. "It's happening too fast."

Pastor Jim smiled. "I already know you're going to do the right thing."

Ian looked at him. The old-fashioned and morally *right thing* to do was marry the mother of his child. "So you think I ought to marry Brooke?" he whispered, soft enough that he was sure Alex couldn't hear.

"Are you serious?" Pastor Jim asked, arching a brow.

"I figured you wanted me to . . . you know . . . the whole 'having a child out of wedlock' thing . . ." He thought back to meeting up with Brooke again. And thinking about anything but a wedding . . . It seemed like a lifetime ago. Was he even the same man?

"Little late for the dance on that one, don't you think?" Pastor Jim said.

Ian stole a quick look at him, then let out a breath he didn't realize he'd been holding. "I guess so. In fact, we aren't even planning on dating." He dared to look at him again.

Pastor Jim leaned forward and rested his forearms on his knees. "Ian, always seek God's guidance for your life. And be the best father you can be to Alex. That's the *right thing* to do. I'm just thankful you're here now. Our little guy is happier than I've ever seen him, even sick as he is."

Ian looked over at his son and thought about what Pastor Jim said. If he only did what the minister said, he'd be doing the *right thing*.

Seek God's guidance. Be a good dad. *I can do that*, he thought with relief. *That, I can do.*

✢ THIRTY-SEVEN

M acey leaned against the windowsill in her office as she waited for the results of Alex's weekly blood test. Despite the eleven inches of snow that blanketed the Detroit area, the construction of the hospital's new wing was moving along swiftly, finally nearing its much-anticipated completion.

She glanced down to the parking lot, once again seeking out the old F-150. Though she couldn't see it, she knew it was out there. She knew *he* was there—whoever *he* was.

She stepped back to her desk to open her e-mail and read the test results.

Flat. She was surprised. Alex's white blood cell count had not gone up or down much at all. She closed the screen, grabbed Alex's chart, and headed toward the consultation room, where she knocked quickly on the door before entering.

Ian and Brooke were on either side of Alex, whose appearance suggested that he had gone through a rough week. The balance of his hair was nothing but a sparse collection of short orange threads; he appeared exhausted and pale, with purplish-blue circles under his eyes. He'd obviously lost weight.

"What if you couldn't help him? What if your best wasn't good enough?"

As Kenneth's words from The Pilot Inn flitted in and out of her head, another voice—this time her own—told her that a race had begun, and they were beginning to fall behind.

She shook it off. Alex wasn't going to lose. She wasn't going to lose. They weren't going to lose. She was Macey Lewis, and her best had always worked—always.

She just needed full control. 24/7 control. *Admit him.*

"Hello, everybody," Macey said confidently. "How are we doing?"

"Not so great. Alex's appetite has been way off," Brooke said without preamble. "And what he has eaten, he's had a hard time keeping down."

"Add to that a week of diarrhea," Ian said, "and the poor kid is miserable. I thought you said he'd be feeling better by now."

Macey was used to this stage with parents—they felt the weight of the treatment too. They often got mad at the doctors and nurses, wanting to cast blame. It was just part of the process. She lowered herself to one knee. "Not feeling too well, Alex?"

Alex lifted his head off Brooke's shoulder barely long enough to shake it.

"We're going to make you better, okay?" Macey said. She straightened. "He's pretty dehydrated."

"Well, *yeah*," Brooke said. Alex looked at her with almost sad eyes and nodded listlessly before dropping his head again on Brooke's shoulder. "Sorry," Brooke said. "It's been . . ."

"I know," Macey said. "It's a lot. Hang in there." She opened Alex's file. "We got the test results. Alex's numbers were relatively unchanged."

"Is that bad?" Brooke asked.

"I was looking for a bit of a decrease," Macey admitted. "But now I'm hesitant to ramp up his regimen because he's struggling. I think we should do another week of the same treatment, but this time in-house. That way we can monitor him more closely. As well as keep this dehydration business in line."

"You want to check him in?" Ian asked, casting an alarmed look at Brooke. Macey recognized the sound of parental fear.

"It's simply precautionary," she said. "We need to make sure he is getting proper rest and nutrition, and I can also monitor him a bit more closely."

"Was there something we should have done differently?" Brooke asked.

"Not at all," Macey said, holding her hand up. "You guys are doing an excellent job."

"How long?" Brooke asked, giving Macey a panicked look that the doctor had seen hundreds—maybe thousands—of times from parents before.

"Let's plan on a week and see how he responds," Macey said. "It's where he needs to be, and you can be here 24/7 if you want."

"Okay," Brooke said quietly. She poked lightly at Alex's leg. "You want to stay at the hospital tonight, buddy?"

Alex hunched his shoulders indifferently.

"Mr. Brave will stop by almost every day," Macey promised, prompting a tiny smile from Alex.

"When do you want him?" Ian asked.

Macey stood, opened the manila folder she had been holding, and then jotted something quickly on its inside cover. She looked at Alex, then collectively at all three of them. She snapped the folder closed. "Right now."

"I SEE THAT ALEX HAS JOINED US," ZACH SAID, STICKING his head into Macey's office. "It's a little early for that, isn't it?"

Macey turned around and looked blankly at the other doctor. She couldn't tell him how she felt. She had conditioned herself. *I don't get nervous, I don't get worried, and I certainly don't show fear. I have all the answers. I've been told I'm the best because I am.*

Then why am I freaking out?

Zach stepped into the office. "Macey? We see kids this sick in treatment every week of the year. What's up? You need to talk?"

She knew he was sincere. For starters, he'd never asked her if she needed to talk, but again, she'd never really needed to before. Now she did—not just about Alex, but about a lot of things. She didn't know where to begin. All she could do was stare at him.

He gave her a compassionate look and then quietly closed the door. "May I?" Zach asked, pointing at the couch.

"Please," she muttered, putting her elbows on her desk and her head in her hands.

He sat on the arm of the couch. He leaned forward with his left elbow on his left knee and his fist under his chin. "As Kaitlyn would say, 'You look like your dog is missing, Dr. Lewis.'"

"*Something's* missing," Macey said. She looked down, bit gently on her lip, and then sheepishly raised her head to him. "I'm concerned."

"About Alex?"

"Yes," she answered. "I believe it's aggressive—extremely aggressive."

"Okay," Zach said softly. "You know what to do. You've seen this before."

"Not like this, Zach. Regardless of what I do, he's not responding as expected."

"Macey, you know how this goes. You take your best stab at the regimen, adjust, and try again. It's what we do, week in and week out."

She took a deep breath and blew it out. "I don't know. I can't put my finger on it, Zach. There's just something . . . different."

"Different in the numbers?"

"In the numbers, in his appearance . . ."

"Every kid is different," he said.

"I know," she said. "I just have a bad feeling about it."

Zach stood up and walked around the desk, grabbed a chair, turned it around, and sat down on it backward. He perched his elbows up on the back of the seat and looked at her with the quiet understanding of a big brother. "Macey. Are you too close to this one?"

"No," she said, right away.

"With you getting close to Brooke, the Lindys—"

"No, Zach. I'm okay. Really." It would be the worst if he forced her to give up the case. "I mean, obviously, it makes it trickier, knowing them. Coming to love them. But I'm not doing anything for Alex that I wouldn't do for any other patient."

"Except admitting him a good two months before most other patients."

She sighed heavily. "It's my gut, Zach. My gut tells me he should be here."

"Then you know you have my support," he said. "With all that's been going on around here lately, I'm beginning to understand following the lead of a power higher than mere medicine."

"Thanks, Zach."

They shared a smile, then Zach grew more serious. "Listen, Macey. Any way you dice it, if my son was sick, I'd trust him to no one but you."

Macey nodded thankfully, because she knew he meant it. And because it was the first time that they'd ever had this kind of conversation. "I appreciate it, Zach. That means a lot to me."

"You're welcome," he said. "Now just do your best. And say a few prayers."

She smiled. "That's exactly what I was doing when you came here."

"That's good," Zach said, rising. He set the chair back in place and moved toward the door.

"Listen to us," she said. "Can you believe you and I are talking about *praying*? It's weird, huh?"

"Bizarre." He put his hand on the knob. "But what's more weird is that I think I like it." He gave her a wink.

"Zach," she said as he opened the door. "One more thing, if you don't mind."

"Of course. Shoot."

Macey stood and walked halfway across the office. She stopped and lifted her hands to the sides of her face as Zach stood in the doorway. "I know this may sound strange, but something has me concerned." She lowered her hands from her cheeks and crossed her arms. "He asked me what I would do if my best wasn't good enough."

"Who said that?"

"*Him*," Macey answered, lifting a brow.

Zach ran his hand across his chin. "Kenneth?"

"Yes," she said. "And if he meant what I *think* he meant, I almost feel like it's an uphill battle—like he knows something is going to go wrong with Alex."

"*Kenneth* asked you what you would do if your best wasn't good enough?" Zach repeated, obviously thinking it through, giving it weight.

"Yeah," Macey said. "And if it were anyone but him saying that—I mean, *anyone*—it wouldn't bother me." She could see he agreed. It made her heartbeat speed up.

Zach looked away, then back to her. "Are you sure he was talking about Alex?"

"Yes."

"Let's hope you're wrong," he said.

✢ THIRTY-EIGHT

The little girl's long, brown hair dipped down her back as she tilted her head up. Her eyes rounded in amazement, as if she were looking up at a living skyscraper. "How tall are you, mister?" she asked in a small but curious voice.

Charlie just smiled at the girl and ducked out of the elevator onto the third floor at East Shore. Ian followed behind, smiling. He turned around as the doors slid shut. "Almost seven feet," he whispered.

The little girl's eyes widened.

Charlie and Ian made their way past the visiting room and then past the nurses' station before taking the first left down a brightly lit hallway to Room 364.

"Knock, knock," Ian said, tapping on the door and pressing it open.

He and Charlie each stepped around a navy blue curtain with a three-foot SpongeBob SquarePants embroidered in the middle. Alex was curled up on the bed, sleeping with his mouth slightly open. He had an IV in his arm, and his head was propped up on a pillow that had been folded carefully in two. His small right foot stuck out the end of his blanket.

Brooke was also asleep. She was lying on a reclining chair to Alex's right, and like her son, she had dark circles under her eyes.

Charlie walked up to Alex's left and removed a portable lunch tray that held a Styrofoam cup of water and a barely touched plastic container of Lucky Charms beside the little boy. He reached over and touched Alex's forehead lightly with the palm of his hand. Alex's eyes opened and were little more than a tired pair of slits. They widened when he saw Charlie. He looked at Charlie's hand and then at the Tic Tac it held. He barely shook his head and then struggled to clear his throat. "I'm not allowed, Charlie."

Charlie gave Alex a puzzled look and then popped it into his own mouth.

"Hey, partner," Ian said quietly from the foot of the bed.

"Hi, Dad," Alex said. Spoken at full throttle, the words only came out as a weak whisper. "We missed church today."

"I know. We missed you there."

Brooke's eyes opened and she stretched.

"Hello, sleeping beauty," Ian said. "Why don't you go home and let us take over? You need a break."

Brooke yawned. "Did you call Clippers for me?"

"Carla did," Ian said. "They said to take as much time as you need and that you and pip-squeak here are in their prayers. It didn't hurt that she offered to cover a bunch of your shifts for you."

"Oh, that's so nice of her," Brooke said. "She must be working eighty-hour weeks lately."

"I don't think she minds. It gives her a way to help you."

Ian turned his head and could see that Charlie had lowered his face within a foot of Alex's. They were studying each other with perfectly straight expressions.

"Do you know that this is the longest they have gone without seeing each other?" Brooke said. "They've never been apart for longer than a day."

"What are they doing?" Ian asked.

"First one to smile loses," Brooke said faintly. "It's one of their games."

An IV alarm beeped rudely next to Charlie's head, startling him and causing him to jump. Alex lifted his head, started laughing, and then proceeded to cough up a tiny patch of vomit, which slowly dribbled down his chin.

"I've got it," Ian said, grabbing a washcloth folded on the

sink to wipe Alex's chin. "There ya go, partner. It's like it never happened."

"That's the third time today," Brooke said. "And he still has diarrhea."

"Has Macey been in?" Ian asked.

"Oh yeah," Brooke said. "She and Kaitlyn have been in and out continuously since he was admitted. It's like he's getting preferential treatment."

"Did somebody say my name?" Kaitlyn asked, bouncing into the room. "Excuse me there, big guy," she added, stepping around Charlie and pressing her thumb firmly against a green button on the machine next to Alex. She removed the empty IV bag, turned around, and looked up at Charlie. She took off her glasses. "How are you, Charlie?"

Charlie smiled.

Kaitlyn put her hand on top of Alex's. "You sure seem glad to see Charlie. I see you have perked up all of a sudden."

"I just throwed up again," Alex announced.

"That's okay, honey," Kaitlyn said.

"Where is Mr. Brave?" Alex asked. "I think Charlie would like him."

"I'm not sure, but hang on a second," the nurse said, stepping back around Charlie and then disappearing around the navy pull curtain.

"Hey, Charlie, look!" Alex said, pointing at his IV. "I forgot to show you this." He tugged at the tape around the needle in his arm. "Look, Charlie, this doesn't even hurt!"

"Alexander, stop pulling on that!" Brooke said.

Alex's head flipped back at his mother. "But it doesn't hurt, Mom."

"That's cuz he is so brave!" a high-pitched voice said from behind the curtain. They all turned around.

Alex laughed and pointed at Mr. Brave. The puppet's head arched around the corner of the curtain.

"Man, are you ever a big guy!" Mr. Brave said in a tone of awe. "Are you *Charlie*?"

Charlie's mouth opened, and he smiled at the puppet as Alex laughed heartily. Charlie held up his index finger to Alex and then slowly tiptoed to the edge of the curtain to peek around it. He grinned at Kaitlyn with an *I-know-it's-you* look on his face.

"He's looking at you, Nurse Kaitlyn," Mr. Brave said. "Charlie sees you."

The nurse came back around the corner and smiled at Ian and Brooke. "It looks like we've found some additional therapy for Mr. Alex, and it's called Charlie."

Brooke agreed. "Alex seems ten times better. That sparkle is back in his eyes, and his coloring even looks better with his BFF in the room."

"The *best* of all medicines," the nurse said, lifting Alex's head and adjusting his pillow. "Is Charlie your best friend forever?"

"Heck yeah," Alex said, grabbing his Styrofoam cup and sucking in a straw-full of water.

Brooke stood up and stretched. "I'm going to go grab a shower. I'll be back in a couple of hours."

Ian hugged her, and then she hugged Charlie. "You're good medicine for him, Charlie. Thanks for coming to be with him."

Charlie nodded and then returned to Alex, while Ian and Brooke stepped outside with Kaitlyn.

"How are things looking?" Ian asked her.

Kaitlyn looked down at his chart. "Dr. Lewis wants to keep him here for a few more days. And then we're going to check his blood again."

"And then what?" Ian asked.

"Then we'll see where we are," Kaitlyn said carefully.

"Shouldn't his numbers come down?" Ian asked.

"They certainly should," Kaitlyn said. "But it's equally important to see how the rest of his system responds to his treatment. Macey wants him eating more, retaining it, and she also wants him better hydrated."

"When is she going to check his blood again?" Brooke asked the nurse.

The nurse flipped through a couple pages in the chart and ran her finger down to the center. "Looks like Wednesday."

ON WEDNESDAY, JIM THOUGHT THE SUN GLISTENED ON the snow like a blanket of tiny diamonds. He put his arm around Shirley as they looked out over the snow-glazed pines that bent around the back of the church.

"It's pretty, isn't it?" Jim asked.

"As a picture," Shirley said.

Jim was thinking how quiet it was, inside and out. "Do you know that Sunday was the first service Brooke and Alex missed since they came into our lives?"

Shirley didn't say anything. She gave his arm a little squeeze and walked over to the sink.

"You know," Jim said, "if it warms up a little, it'd make great packing for a snowman. I'll see if Charlie wants to make one for Alex to greet him when he comes home Saturday. We could build a doozy."

"Let's *hope* he comes home Saturday, James."

Jim had never met another person with Shirley's faith, and that faith never made her hesitate to speak plainly. He stared back at the snow-laden branches. Alex had lost seven pounds and had been in the hospital for almost a week now. He knew there probably wouldn't be a snowman in the yard this weekend.

"I'm kind of surprised Kaitlyn and Zach are joining us tomorrow," Shirley said.

"I'm glad. It will help it seem less lonely."

Jim looked back out the window and took his turn at not saying anything.

It was hard to believe tomorrow was Thanksgiving. *Help me concentrate on the blessings, Lord. The amazing blessings. And not what I'm missing.*

ALEX TAPPED THE ROOF OF HIS MOUTH AND THEN THE inside of his cheek with his tongue. It all burned, and he wanted to cry. He was hungry, but it hurt when he ate. He was thirsty, his head hurt, and the thing in his arm was getting sore. He blinked lightly at his dad, who was standing at the side of the bed.

Maybe Dad can make it all go away.

"I know this isn't much fun for you," Dad said, taking Alex's hand and rubbing the top of it gently with his thumb. "What can I do for you, partner?"

"I don't know," Alex said, hunching his left shoulder. It slid out of his Spider-Man pajama top. "I'm a little hungry, but it hurts when I chew."

"Let's try some of this," Dad said, peeling the top off of a tiny container of cherry Jell-O that was on Alex's tray. "Do you want some water too?"

"Yeah," Alex whispered, carefully licking his bottom lip. "Can I go home today? Please?"

"I'm not sure, partner," Dad said, moving around to the side of the bed, trying not to wake Mom, who had fallen asleep in the chair she'd been glued to for most of the week. They were waiting for Dr. Lewis, who was supposed to come back with the test results.

"But I want to go home for Thanksgiving tomorrow," Alex said. "I want to see Charlie. If I don't, who will eat the other turkey leg?"

"I want you home too," Dad said, holding a cup of water in his palm and bending the straw for him to take a drink. "I'll see if the Lindys can save you a turkey leg. And I'll see if I can get Charlie up here tonight or tomorrow to see you, okay?"

"Okay," Alex said. He drew in a little taste of water. It soothed his mouth, making it feel cooler. It also felt like he could breathe better. He went for more, this time taking in too much. He choked for a second, coughed, and water streamed down the sides of his mouth.

"Slow down, buddy," Dad said. "Slow down."

Dad held the back of his hand to Alex's forehead. "You are a little warm, partner."

Alex gazed at his dad, wondering if he could maybe fix it.

"Does the water make you feel better?"

"Yeah," Alex said, opening his mouth slightly while Dad gave him half of a plastic spoonful of Jell-O. After only two bites, Alex shook his head. He didn't want any more. It tasted funny. Everything tasted funny ever since he started chemo syrupy.

Dad finished the rest of his Jell-O and went back around to the foot of the bed. Behind him on a shelf was a box of those funny rubber gloves. Dad pulled one out and then dangled it under his chin like a rooster's beard, making Alex smile a little. He then pulled it to his mouth for three quick puffs that quickly blew it up, making it look like a fat, bodiless hand. He held it over his head and then let it go, making it rattle and then fly in a funny circle above the bed before bumping against Mom's forehead and landing on her shoulder.

Alex let out a laugh that made his throat hurt superbad. But he smiled, looking at the dead glove on Mom's shoulder.

"What's so funny?" Mom asked in a lazy voice, her eyes still closed. "What's up with you two?"

"Nothing," Dad said, looking over at Alex.

"Nothing," Alex echoed. He felt like crying again. He didn't want to be here anymore.

Dad came up beside him and felt his forehead again. "I'm calling Kaitlyn," he said to Mom.

"I want to go home," Alex said, half crying. His mouth still burned, his eyes hurt, and his throat now felt as if he'd swallowed broken glass. He had to go to the bathroom, he was on the verge of throwing up again, and the back of his neck was going *boom, boom, boom*.

"I know, buddy," Mom said, looking at him like she knew just how he felt. She kissed his cheek and then looked up at Dad. "He's warmer than usual." Her eyes looked all big and scared, which made Alex more scared.

"I know," Dad said. "Macey is supposed to be in any minute."

Mom offered Alex some water, but he turned away.

The drape pulled back, and Dr. Lewis entered the room. "Hi, everybody," she said. "How are we doing today?"

"Not so great," Mom said. She looked like she was gonna cry, which made Alex feel like crying too. Alex noticed that Dr. Lewis wasn't carrying the manila folder that she normally held under her arm as she stepped right up next to the bed and looked at him.

Nurse Kaitlyn came around the curtain, wearing her standard smile. She scooched in beside Dad and pressed the same button that he'd used to have her come to the room. "How are we doing? It looks like somebody turned Alex's temperature up, huh?"

"That's normal, though, right?" Mom asked, her voice all high and squeaky-like. "The fever?"

"He's okay," Dr. Lewis said, sounding like she knew. She looked down at Alex. "I know you don't feel well, Alex. We are going to fix you up, okay? You're doing great."

Alex nodded.

"Let's pull our chairs over here for a few minutes," Dr. Lewis said, gesturing past the blue curtain into the other side of the room. "Kaitlyn, can you entertain Mr. Alex while I speak to Mom and Dad for a few minutes?"

"Sure!" Kaitlyn said. "How 'bout a visit from Mr. Brave?"

Alex shrugged. He knew Dr. Lewis was going to talk to Mom and Dad about him, but he didn't feel good enough to care. And today he didn't really care if he saw Mr. Brave ever again.

I just wanna go home.

IAN WASN'T A DOCTOR, BUT ONE THING THAT HELPED him move up the ranks of the plant was his ability to read people. *Something's definitely wrong.* With one look at Brooke, he knew she knew it too. They all sat down, and Macey leaned toward the edge of her seat and laced her fingers together.

"There's a problem, isn't there?" Ian asked.

"Ian and Brooke," Macey said, "all kids are different. They all have different treatments, and they all respond differently."

"Tell us," Ian said. He didn't like the tone of the doctor's voice, confirming his suspicions. "Straight up."

"I wouldn't do it any other way," Macey said. "Here it is. Alex's white blood cell test came back, and his count went up."

"That's bad," Brooke said.

Macey nodded somberly. "The cancer's very aggressive."

Aggressive.

Ian didn't like that word. It had tiny fangs that carried poison—poison that could make the heart skip beats and then pound with sickening cold flashes.

Brooke beat him to the punch and repeated it. "Aggressive?"

"Yes," the doctor said.

"What's the plan, then?" Ian asked. "What do we do?"

"Like I said, all kids are different. They all respond differently. As tough as Alex is, I'm concerned about the toll his treatment is taking on him. With that being said, I believe we need to move on against the disease."

"You're worried about the toll it's taking?" Ian asked. Reality had an interesting way of constantly redefining itself. *I have a son. My son has leukemia. The leukemia is both aggressive and taking its toll.*

Macey nodded yet again. "He's now down eleven pounds in a little over a month. He is still not eating well, and at this pace, we're going to have a hard time keeping him comfortable. We need to move forward before he loses more ground. There are some significant hills to climb ahead of us."

Brooke looked like she was in agony. Their little boy was going to suffer some more. It was like sending a wounded soldier back to the front.

"How aggressive is it?" Ian asked, standing up and looking around the edge of the curtain. Alex was perfectly still, his small hand in Kaitlyn's. She lifted a finger to her lips. He was asleep. Ian sat back down and asked the same question. "How aggressive?"

"It's early in his treatment," Macey said. "But I know we are now looking at a high-risk leukemia—one where regular treatment is not effective enough to keep the cancer away."

"High-risk?" Ian said.

"He is going to be okay," Brooke said, taking a deep breath. She tilted her head toward the ceiling and closed her eyes. "He is going to be okay. He is going to be okay. Only believe. Only believe."

Ian put his hand on Brooke's shoulder. He knew she was scared. He was scared too, but something about Macey's confidence had earned his trust. He looked back at the doctor. "What do you plan to do next?"

"Treating leukemia is sometimes like playing a game of cat and mouse. You treat and then test, treat and then test again, constantly adjusting until you get consistent results, with the ultimate goal being remission."

"And with Alex," Ian said, "it's like chasing a very fast mouse."

"You could say that," Macey said. Her eyes flicked from Ian to Brooke and back again. "You wanted it straight . . ."

"Let's have it," Ian said.

"I believe with just chemo, the cancer will keep coming back, making it more difficult to treat, because the cancer itself can develop a drug resistance."

"So what do you do then?"

"We up the chemo. Try to kill it before it can outrun it, in a sense."

"So then," Brooke said, "why aren't you doing that?"

"We could," Macey said. She rose and walked to the window, putting her hands in her white coat pockets. "It's definitely an option."

"But you're hesitating," Ian said. "Because?"

Macey turned around, took a long step back toward them, and crossed her arms. "Because it could kill him," she said quietly.

"No," Brooke said, bringing her hand to her mouth and shaking her head. "You have to help him. Before it gets to that point."

Ian reached over and took Brooke's hand. "What's your best plan, Macey? What would you do if this was your kid?"

"We need to go in and knock it all out," she said. "Fast."

"How are you going to do that?"

"The transplant. It's our best chance. And that chance is inside of *you* right now, Ian."

"Best chance?" Brooke asked.

Ian gently put his hand under Brooke's chin and had her face him. "It's gonna be okay, Brooke. Macey knows what she is doing."

"I know," Brooke sniffled. "He is going to be made well, remember? He is going to be all right. I believe—I believe."

"That's right," Macey repeated, the increasingly familiar words providing comfort in a clearly uncomfortable moment. "Only believe."

But there was something in her eyes that made Ian think she didn't.

✤ THIRTY-NINE

W hat a day," Jim said, sitting down in his La-Z-Boy. "We get to eat turkey *and* watch Thanksgiving football on television. It has been quite awhile for me. Praise God."

"Good for you," Kaitlyn said, sitting on the couch next to Zach and Charlie. She nudged Zach with her elbow to look at Charlie.

Charlie was wearing headphones that could only reach his ears by being put on from the back of his head instead of from the top. He was listening to Brooke's iPod. Kaitlyn smiled, watching as his lips rounded in amazement. His head slowly moved back and forth as he pressed the mystery button—the button that magically changed the songs he was hearing.

Shirley came out of the kitchen and handed Jim a soda, and Carla trailed right behind her. Carla sat down on the floor, resting her back against the edge of the sofa. "So you said that it went pretty well at the shelter this morning, Pastor Jim?"

"It went really well," he said, reaching over and grabbing a handful of potato chips out of a plastic bowl on Charlie's lap. He held his hand out to Carla, and she took one. "A lot of people showed up to help."

"Many from St. Thomas?" Zach asked. "I know Kenneth was there."

"We had quite a few, and he was," Jim said. "Did you talk to him today?"

"Sort of," Zach said dismissively. He tapped Charlie on the leg. "You ready for some turkey, big man? It smells like it's getting closer." He rubbed his hands together in anticipation and smiled at the rest of them. "I've had way too many Thanksgiving dinners in the hospital cafeteria. This will be a serious treat."

Charlie took the headphones off, nodded like he understood, and put the headphones back on.

"I'm thinking the big guy would pass on his turkey to have his little buddy back home," Kaitlyn said.

"Undoubtedly," Jim said.

"Dr. Norman?" Carla said. "When would you expect Alex to be out of the hospital?"

"It depends," he answered. "Each patient is different. And when are you going to start calling me Zach?"

Carla grinned and grabbed some more chips. "So they are doing some more tests on Ian today?"

"On Alex too," he answered. "Dr. Lewis wants to make absolutely sure they are both ready for the transplant."

"They're both in the best possible hands they could be in," Kaitlyn said.

"I know," Carla said. "But when do you think they will do the bone marrow transplant? In a couple of days?"

"Oh no," Kaitlyn said. "It will be longer than that."

"And Alex will be in the hospital for quite a while," Zach said. "The bone marrow transplant will allow Macey to get more aggressive with the cancer through chemo, radiation, or both. We want to wipe it out and then make a replacement with healthy marrow. Make sense?"

Jim laced his fingers on top of his lap. "So out with the old and in with the new?"

Zach leaned forward on the couch. "More like out with the bad and in with the good."

"How long do you think it will take?" Carla asked.

"That's a good question." Zach smiled, and the sight of it did Jim good. The man was changed. Even if Jim went blind again before the game, he'd know the change in the man. He thought back to the day he'd met him, when he came to help with the cross, to now. It was like he was a totally different man. He'd been freed.

Zach stood and walked over to the window. "It takes as long as it takes the team to kill whatever residual cancer cells remain in Alex, while making sure his immune system doesn't reject the new marrow from Ian."

"How dangerous is it?" Jim asked. "Macey told Ian and Brooke that there are risks."

"Practically none for Ian."

"And for Alex?"

"Like Kaitlyn said, we have to trust that Alex is in the best of hands."

"He is. He's in God's hands," Jim said.

"He *really is* in God's hands," Zach repeated. Jim was surprised by the way he said it. He actually sounded a little sad.

Shirley came in from the kitchen. "James Lindy, I'd like to ask you something I haven't asked you in a long, long time."

Jim swiveled around in the La-Z-Boy. "What's that, hon?"

Steam from the potatoes was still disappearing from Shirley's glasses. "Would you like to carve the turkey?"

"If I can remember how," he said, smiling and rising to his feet.

"Charlie," Shirley said, pulling off his headphones. "Would you come and mash the potatoes for me, please?"

He nodded.

"Put me to work too," Zach said. He gave Kaitlyn a kiss on her cheek and followed Charlie into the kitchen.

CARLA TOOK ZACH'S PLACE ON THE COUCH. "I HOPE Zach wasn't mad that I started asking those questions."

"Not at all," Kaitlyn said, sensing that something was weighing on Zach's mind. She wasn't sure what it was, but she knew it wasn't Carla's questions. "Don't worry about that, Carla. It's perfectly normal to ask questions at a time like this."

Carla glanced over her shoulder and then whispered to her, "It's just that Brooke made it sound like the bone marrow transplant was their only option." She paused. "Is Alex in that bad of shape?"

"He's really sick," Kaitlyn said.

Carla shook her head. "But Kenneth told Pastor Jim . . ." She caught herself and shook her head. "Never mind. Somehow, I think it will all be okay. It's just so scary."

"Tell me about it," Kaitlyn said. "It's my life. But for obvious reasons, little Alex is the patient that holds our hearts."

"Come to the table, you two," Shirley called.

The two women entered the kitchen, and Kaitlyn found herself stopping before she sat down. She looked around the kitchen, from the table, already loaded with food, to the people, still scattered. Pastor Jim was humming an upbeat tune she couldn't recognize, working on carving the turkey. Shirley directed Zach to bring the cranberries as she placed a steaming dish of mashed potatoes on the table, and Charlie had the iPod on again. Shirley walked behind him, took the headphones off, and set them aside, squeezing his shoulders. She sat down at one end of the table and smiled at Kaitlyn. "Well, I think it just might be all done. You begin the day wondering . . ."

"I can imagine," Kaitlyn said. "Someday I'll have to try my hand at it."

Shirley's eyes widened. "You've never made a Thanksgiving meal?"

"Not yet," Kaitlyn said. "Most years I seem to draw the Thanksgiving shift card. By some miracle I didn't this year." *By some miracle*, she repeated silently, wondering who just uttered those words. But oddly they didn't *feel* foreign, really. They felt right.

Kaitlyn sat down next to Zach, and Pastor Jim came to the table with a silver platter stacked with thin slices of turkey. He placed it at the center of the table and then sat down at the opposite end of the table from Shirley. He pointed at the turkey and then lifted his hands. "The Ginsu master has performed his magic. This bird is carved."

"You haven't lost your touch," Shirley said.

"Looks perfect," Carla added.

Kaitlyn knew that these truly were people of God, continuing to embrace *life* despite facing adversities. There were plenty of families at the hospital even now, walking the halls, wringing their hands, weeping in fear. But Alex's people weren't worrying; it was like they all had a peace about him. Momentary worries for sure, as with Carla, but overall, a peace. It was so remarkably different from anything she'd ever experienced before, she found it kind of stunning.

Carla looked over at Kaitlyn and smiled as she sat next to Zach. Carla kind of had a glow about her lately. Kaitlyn would have to ask her about it one of these days. What was up, what had changed.

"Shall we pray?" Pastor Jim asked, still holding his hands up.

"Let's do it," Zach said.

They all joined hands, and Pastor Jim led them through a prayer. Kaitlyn listened carefully as the minister thanked God for looking over Alex. Then he thanked God for bringing them together and for the food. Next he thanked God for the growth of the church before finally asking God to remember those less fortunate.

Kaitlyn noticed that there was something peculiar about the tone of Pastor Jim's voice when he prayed for Alex. He didn't pray as *if* God were going to take care of the boy. He prayed as if God had *already* taken care of him.

They all said, "Amen," and Kaitlyn glanced around the table one more time at the faces of these genuinely good people. She was glad they were now part of her life. She looked up at Zach, beside her, and it was then that she knew.

She nudged him on the side of his leg and whispered in his ear, "I think I've fallen in love with you again, Zach Norman."

Zach pulled his head back, looking surprised. He smiled, paused, and then leaned over to whisper back, "I don't think I ever stopped loving you."

Kaitlyn poked at Zach's arm, then nodded for him to look over at Charlie. He already had a mouthful of turkey and was putting three rolls' worth of butter onto a single roll.

She bit lightly on her lip and thought, *Don't you worry, Charlie. We'll have your friend home in no time. Nothing is going to happen to him. Nothing at all. Because clearly, God has his hand on this house.*

✢ FORTY

Brooke walked quietly into the fellowship hall, hugged Shirley, and then plopped down on the couch without saying a word.

"Honey, you look so tired," Shirley said, wearing the motherly face that Brooke had seen quite a bit of lately. And she had to admit, it looked good to her.

"I am *so* tired," Brooke said, her eyes straying past Shirley and back to the doors that separated them from the sanctuary. She raised her hands to rub her eyes. "Today is Saturday, right? How long was I at the hospital?"

"Yes, today is Saturday," Shirley answered, unplugging an extension cord from the vacuum and winding it around her arm. "And the answer is four days. You have been at the hospital for four straight days. Remember what Dr. Lewis told you about not neglecting your own health during this?"

"I know, I know," Brooke said. "I'm going to head back down to the house and take a shower."

"Did you eat while you were up there?"

"Probably not enough, but I'll be okay. It's hard to eat when your stomach is constantly in knots." Brooke slid up to the front of the cushion and stretched her arms over her head to yawn. "Somebody is in the sanctuary."

"It's probably James," Shirley said.

Brooke sighed. "I haven't talked to Carla today. Have you seen her around?"

"Unless that was her in the sanctuary, or she's at Clippers, she's likely still down at the house," Shirley said, picking at a snag on the corner of the couch and then sitting down. "She's been trying to keep Charlie company in Alex's absence."

Brooke smiled. "That's sweet of her. Is it working?"

"Not really," Shirley said. "You know how my son is about yours."

"I know."

"So you said they put a catheter in Alex?"

"Yeah," Brooke answered. She was disappointed in herself for answering so casually. She wondered if she was getting numbed by the ongoing struggle. "Zach did it this morning. It's something called a Hickman catheter, which is an intravenous line."

"What's it for?"

"It's to get Alex ready for the bone marrow transplant. It allows him to get the medicine and blood stuff he needs, and it allows the staff to withdraw a bunch of blood samples from him without having to poke needles in him all the time."

"Ian went back to the hospital this morning?" Shirley asked. "For the same thing they did yesterday?"

"Yeah," Brooke said. "It's the stuff that's supposed to help boost Ian's marrow stem cells before he makes his donation to Alex." Brooke yawned again, causing her eyes to water. "They were giving him more of that today when I was leaving the hospital."

"When are they actually going to do the marrow transplant?"

"Pretty soon," Brooke said. "Kaitlyn said they may go in as early as tomorrow to harvest Ian's bone marrow. I guess they have to do a few more tests. But like I said, it all depends on when Macey thinks Alex is ready to go."

"The sooner the better," Shirley said. "Let's get through this and get Alex home."

"He's going to be in the hospital for eight more weeks," Brooke said. "*Two more months.*"

"Eight weeks?" Shirley said, sounding more than a little surprised. She slowly took her glasses off and then pulled a piece of tissue from her pocket to rub the lenses. "My goodness, honey. Why so long?"

"It takes time to see if the procedure was a success," Brooke said. "The radiation is going to knock his immune system down to practically nothing. That way, Alex's immune system doesn't reject Ian's bone marrow. And then it takes time for it to be able to reproduce on its own—I think Macey called it *engraftment* or something like that."

"He's going to be all right," Shirley said, standing up. She put her glasses back on and leaned toward Brooke. "I need to get up there and see Alex myself. It's been a couple of days and I miss him. I can tell Charlie wants to get back up there too."

"You should probably go tonight, then," Brooke said. "And bring Charlie if you want, because Macey says she may only want us in there one at a time after they do the transplant."

"Why is that?"

"She said that when they knock his immune system down that far, he will have very little defense against even the most common things. She also said that they want to keep him in the most sterile environment possible. He can't even have gifts like plants, fruit, flowers—nothing like that. They don't want him in contact with anything, and it sounds like that may even include some of us."

"That poor little thing," Shirley said. "God love him."

Brooke suddenly wanted more than ever to get back to the hospital, pick Alex up, and hold him. "I guess when we're in the room with him, we are going to be wearing masks, gloves, the whole nine yards."

"Well, if that is what has to be done to get him well, so be it," Shirley said, holding out her hand. "C'mon, let's go to the house. You need to get some rest."

Brooke took Shirley's hand and stood. "It's going to be tough on him, Shirley, and I feel so helpless."

"He is going to get through this," Shirley said. She pulled Brooke into her arms.

"It's so much on his little body." Brooke sighed, pulling away. "Macey said on top of him being vulnerable to infections and viruses, he may also bleed a lot. And then he is going to be taking all kinds of medications, getting blood transfusions—it's just . . ." She paused, wondering for the umpteenth time why it was happening to Alex, why it was happening to her, and why it was happening *to them*. She closed her eyes and slowly exhaled a lungful of stress-tainted air. She gave Shirley an exhausted look and then continued to convince herself, *He is going to be okay. He is going to be okay. He is going to be okay . . .*

Shirley held one of the fellowship hall doors open and pointed into the sanctuary. "I'm telling you he will pull through this. We will all get through this. All of these things that they are doing now—this is how Alex gets better."

"I know, I know," Brooke said. "It just seems so unfair, Shirley. And I'm sick of saying that, and I'm sick of thinking that."

"Come here," Shirley said, stopping and putting her arm around Brooke as they reached the last pew. "This will pass, honey. I just know our little Alex will be made well."

"Eight weeks," Brooke said, laying her head on Shirley's shoulder and wiping at her eyes with the pad of her thumb. "He missed Thanksgiving, and over the next eight weeks, he's going to spend his sixth birthday and then Christmas in the hospital. It's not fair."

"Let's sit down again for a second," Shirley said, motioning Brooke to the pew seat.

"If I sit down again, Shirley, I'll fall asleep," Brooke said. She brought her hands up to her cheeks. "I don't want to lose him. I can't lose him. I'm not going to lose him."

"No, you are not," Shirley said, putting a hand on each of Brooke's shoulders. "Honey, look at me."

Brooke did.

"Brooke, I *know* the feeling of being a mother and being totally helpless. I know what it is to hear that voice inside you, telling you to help, telling you to do *something*, but you can't."

She was talking about Charlie. When he was a baby. "I still can't imagine Charlie ever being small," Brooke said.

"And then you start to ask yourself why? Why is this happening to him? Why is this happening to me? And you want to believe . . . and more often than not, you do believe. I think it's important to know that if we didn't experience pain and hardship, we would never know the full measure of triumphs and joys."

"I don't know, Shirley," Brooke said, giving her a small smile. "I might settle for a half measure of joy and triumph if I could bring my boy home tomorrow."

Shirley returned her smile. "I know, honey. I know all about it. But trust me, down the line, you'll be glad you held out for the full measure."

"I'm trying to believe," Brooke said as they walked toward the church entrance. "I don't know how many times I've told myself, 'Only believe,' since we found out Alex was sick—since Kenneth said that to Pastor Jim."

"Yes," Shirley said. "I know it's tough not to worry, but trust that God will see it through. Now let's go get you something to eat. A little food, a little nap, a little shower, and you'll feel like yourself again."

"Thank you, Shirley," Brooke said, taking her arm as they walked down the hill. "I really don't know where I'd be without you guys."

"We don't know where we'd be without you guys either," Shirley said. "So let's get through this and bring Alexander home."

✢ FORTY-ONE

Macey hooked her index finger under the Hickman catheter, and Alex's eyes followed her every move as his father's bone marrow flowed through the thin tube into his fragile body. Alex kept very still and looked very small in his bed, temporarily located in the Bone Marrow Transplant unit.

"How you feeling, Alex?" she asked through her mask.

"Okay," he said faintly.

"Remember what I told you?"

"I think so."

"If you start to feel funny, I want you to tell me." She drew a circle in the air a few inches above his chest. "Especially in here, okay?"

"Okay."

"Good job," she said. "I'm going to bring your mom and dad in."

"Okay," he said again.

Macey went beyond the curtain to the far side of the room and went through a small door to where Ian and Brooke sat anxiously waiting. She pulled down her mask and removed her gloves. "He is going to be hooked up for a while. Are you guys ready?"

"I think so. Is everything going okay?" Brooke asked.

"As well as can be expected," she answered, nodding at Ian. "How's your hip feeling?"

"Feels fine," Ian said.

Macey grinned. "That's interesting. People compare making a marrow donation to getting hit in the hip with a baseball bat, or having a really hard fall on the ice."

"I feel fine," Ian said. "I really do."

"I'm starting to see where Alex gets his bravado from," Macey said, winking at Brooke.

"Alex looked so tired earlier," Brooke said. "Does the radiation do that?"

"He *is* tired," she said. "All of this is very taxing on the body, particularly little bodies. It is important that you understand that it's every bit as psychologically tiring as it is physically. And, as we discussed, it's going to get worse."

"Eight weeks' worth?" Brooke asked.

Macey reached behind her and grabbed a pair of surgical masks. "He is going to have good days and bad days, but once we get over the hump, you will notice quite a difference for the better." She clapped her hands together and pointed toward the curtain. "Masks, gloves, and caps. Once you're suited up, you can see him."

ALEX THOUGHT IT WAS FUNNY SEEING MOM AND DAD with all of the hospital stuff on. He was starting to feel a little bit funny in his tummy and his neck, but he still didn't want to say anything to Dr. Lewis.

"You are doing it, buddy," Mom said. "You are doing so good."

"Yeah, you are, partner," Dad said. "Just be still and relax, okay?"

Alex tilted his head slightly, and despite the warm, almost burning feeling in his neck, he remained still, only moving his eyes back and forth to whoever was talking. His mouth still hurt, and he wanted to go home. He knew it had snowed outside, and he wanted to make a snowman with a carrot nose with Charlie. He thought about the last time he and Charlie had made a snowman and how one of the deer had eaten the nose off the next day. He remembered how Mrs. Lindy had given them another carrot for another nose and how the deer had eaten it again.

He also wanted Charlie to pull him on that funny sled again. He tried to think of the name of it. *A botagan?* Then he wondered how it was now feeling warm inside his tummy but suddenly so cold on the outside of his body. He tried not to think about it, but it was getting worse. He remembered when Charlie was pulling him on that—*toboggan, not botagan*—and how Charlie slipped and fell down. He remembered how hard he laughed when Charlie got up, brushed himself off, took one step, and fell down again. His eyes shifted back to his dad, and he wondered if he would get more Christmas presents now that he had a dad. His arms were starting to hurt a little, but not enough to cry. He was tired, but he didn't want to sleep.

"We have a little surprise for you, Alex," Dad said. "We can't have too many people in here, so I'll be back in about half an hour."

Alex watched as his dad went around the other side of the curtain. This one was a plain white curtain. He liked the SpongeBob one in the other room lots better. He wondered why his dad left and also wanted to know what the surprise was. He felt a prickly feeling in his legs, and he was getting colder—not on the inside, where it was warm, but on the outside.

"I think somebody is getting the chills," Dr. Lewis said, gently raising the blanket to cover as much of Alex as possible without interfering with any of his several connections. "That feel better, Alex?"

"Yeah," he whispered.

"Good," Dr. Lewis said. "I'm going to leave for a little bit too, while you get your surprise. But I'll be back in about ten minutes."

"Okay," he said.

Dr. Lewis looked at Mom and said, "Kaitlyn will be here in a minute."

"Sounds good," Mom said.

Alex watched as Dr. Lewis touched that machine next to him and then started writing something down in the folder. And then she walked away and disappeared behind the curtain.

"You feeling okay, baby?" Mom asked, her eyes looking funny between the mask and the cap.

Alex didn't answer. He didn't feel as cold as he had earlier, but his skin felt prickly, and his neck and stomach were hurting him even more. He wondered if he could go home right after this was done.

Nurse Kaitlyn appeared at the corner of the curtain.

"We have a surprise for you, Alex," she said.

Mom smiled as Nurse Kaitlyn counted. "One—two—and three." Nurse Kaitlyn pulled the curtain back, and Charlie was standing there with a mask on. He had what Mom called "surgical caps" taped over his big hands instead of gloves, his mask looked like a small white nose, and the cap on his head fit like something a real swimmer would wear.

Alex laughed as Nurse Kaitlyn pulled the big chair from the other side of the room to the foot of the bed. She guided Charlie to the chair, and he waved at Mom before sitting down. Nurse Kaitlyn patted Charlie on the shoulder and pulled out Mr. Brave, who was also wearing a tiny cap and surgical mask. Mom laughed real hard.

"We need you to stay right there," Nurse Kaitlyn said. "Okay, Charlie?"

"He won't move," Mom said.

"I know he won't," Nurse Kaitlyn said. She held the puppet up and Mr. Brave said, "Everything is going great, guys!"

"Okay," Alex said.

"Who is your bestest best friend ever?" Mr. Brave asked.

"Charlie!" Alex said.

As Nurse Kaitlyn and Mr. Brave left the room, Charlie leaned forward and waved his hello. Then he looked over at Mom, who looked sleepy.

Alex noticed the lines that ran across Charlie's forehead and knew that there were things Charlie didn't understand. There were things that he probably was curious about.

"You want to know why I'm here, don't you, Charlie?" Alex asked, yawning. He guessed that Charlie also wanted him back home to watch TV, play hide-and-seek, and eat bologna sandwiches.

Charlie held up his hands with the masks on them and lightly patted them together.

"I gotta get this bone marrow stuff in me," he said. "So I can get better. Then I can come home."

Alex looked over at his mother, who was sleeping. Sleeping seemed like a really good idea. He smiled again at Charlie and closed his eyes.

BROOKE'S HEAD JERKED, AND HER HEART FELT LIKE IT kicked in her chest, popping her out of sleep. As she caught her breath and the room swung in and out of focus, she could see that Macey had returned and was standing behind Charlie. *Yes, Brooke... you're at the hospital. Alex is sick. This is really happening.*

"I didn't mean to wake you," the doctor said, stepping to the other side of the bed to toggle a switch on one of the machines that was attached to Alex.

"Oh, it's fine," Brooke said, a little embarrassed she'd dozed off. She looked at Charlie, who seemed like he hadn't moved since he arrived. It was like he was Alex's personal bodyguard. She sat up in the chair and wondered how long she was out. It could have been five minutes or five hours. All she knew was that she was still exhausted.

"Excuse me one second," Macey said, coming around to Brooke's side of the bed. The doctor leaned behind Alex and adjusted a pair of knobs on a different machine, adding an almost soothing hum to the room, making Brooke even sleepier.

Brooke rubbed her eyes and took a deep breath. Alex had shifted his head on the pillow away from Charlie and was facing her. The dark circles under his eyes had become more apparent, and it almost seemed like he was smiling in his sleep. Brooke smiled back at him. He was a little angel. He practically looked like a doll. *He is going to get better*, she thought. *In fact, he is getting better right now. Please, Lord, make him better!*

"One more second," Macey said, putting her foot on the side rail a little closer to Brooke. "Sorry about the intrusion here."

"No problem," Brooke said, unable to take her eyes off of Macey's tennis shoe—the way her foot was positioned on the rail and the light blue Nike logo.

"That should do it," Macey said.

"Are those the same tennis shoes you spilled the coffee on?" Brooke asked. It reminded her of something . . .

"Yeah," Macey said. "I threw them into the washer, and that one came out faded. I don't mind, though. I'm not trying to make a fashion statement."

The shore. That was it. It was on the shore at the park.

"Carla and I were walking along the lake awhile back, and we found a single Nike tennis shoe laying in the sand. It looked just like yours."

"Only one shoe?" Macey asked, letting out a little laugh.

"Yeah," Brooke said.

"I've seen one on the side of the road before," Macey said, "but never at the lake." She walked back around Brooke and stopped next to Charlie. "It's good to see Alex, isn't it, Charlie?"

Charlie smiled at her and nodded.

"I'll be back in fifteen minutes or so," Macey said. "Everything is going smoothly, okay?"

Brooke was looking back at Alex. She didn't answer.

"Did you hear me, Brooke?" Macey asked.

It was right near the Nike tennis shoe—the tennis shoe with the faded Nike logo.

"I'll be back in about fifteen minutes," Macey repeated.

Brooke just kept staring at Alex. One of his eyes opened and looked at her, then closed.

"You all right, Brooke?"

"The doll," Brooke said dreamily.

"The doll?" Macey asked. "What do you mean?"

Brooke could feel the tears dampening her surgical mask.

"What doll?" Macey asked, coming back around Charlie and kneeling next to Brooke's chair. "What's wrong?"

Brooke couldn't take her eyes off of Alex, nor her mind's eye off the doll. The baby doll she and Carla had seen, near the tennis shoe. She remembered that most of its hair had fallen out. She remembered how the lake water had stained dark circles under its eyes. She remembered how one of those eyes seemed pasted shut and how the other eye had just stared at her. It looked dead.

"Brooke?" Macey said. "What is it?" She took her hand.

"I'm okay," Brooke muttered, still crying. But she wasn't.

She remembered thinking about the little girl who lost the doll. Wondering how the little girl must have felt, knowing she'd never see her baby again. Wondering how long the little girl must have cried, hopelessly wanting to hold her baby just one more time.

But she didn't get to. Her baby was gone, carried away in the water . . .

✣ FORTY-TWO

I'll call you in about an hour," Zach said, kissing Kaitlyn on her cheek before she made her way out of the fellowship hall. He turned and waited for Pastor Jim to finish talking to an older couple.

"You look like a man in deep thought," Pastor Jim said.

"Thoughts," Zach said, feeling like a man with a secret. "And it won't cost you a penny to hear some of them."

"Let's head back to the office," Pastor Jim said. He gestured toward the narrow hallway that led to the back of the church.

"Okay," Zach said, following him.

"Are you going to be at the hospital this afternoon?" Pastor Jim asked. He stopped in the hallway and turned the thermostat down. "Shirley and I were going to run up there around three-ish."

"Not today," Zach said. "Kaitlyn and I both have the day off, and we were going to head up to Birch Run for a couple of hours and shop."

"Ah, Frankenmuth," Pastor Jim said. "Haven't been there in years. It's beautiful."

"Yes, it is."

Pastor Jim opened the door to his office and flicked on the light switch. "With us heading over to see Alex every night, I hope you guys don't run out of those masks and gloves."

Zach smiled. "Well, prepping Charlie *is* like outfitting five people, but I think we'll be okay." He paused, thinking about how faithful the Lindys had been. A visit every night since Alex's blood marrow transfusion, almost a week ago, and many days before then. They truly embodied the meaning of *extended family.* "You have all been incredibly supportive of Alex, Pastor Jim."

Pastor Jim smiled. "Ahh, it's the least we could do. By the grace of God, they say he is doing well and everything seems to be going as planned."

By the grace of God? Zach thought. *As planned?* He could still see the look on Macey's face when she shared what Kenneth had asked her about her best not being good enough. That single look had let him know that her normal mountain of confidence hadn't just been reduced, it had been eliminated.

And Macey was right, wasn't she? Had it been anyone but Kenneth who had said it . . .

"Have a seat," Pastor Jim said, clearing off the top of his desk.

"Nice office."

"I used to spend a lot of time in here," he said, stacking books he had just taken off his desk onto a small table behind him. "Excuse the mess. I was going through these, trying to get organized, and in the process became more unorganized."

"I certainly know that feeling," Zach said, pointing at a photograph on the wall. "Who is that good-looking couple?"

"Forty-three years ago," Pastor Jim said, smiling and running his finger across the wood that framed his wedding picture. "I am lucky. To me, she's every bit as beautiful today as she was then."

"You are both lucky. You seem very happy."

"We are," Pastor Jim said, sitting down and closing the Bible in front of him. "You and Kaitlyn certainly seem to be hitting it off lately, but I'm guessing you're not here to discuss my marriage services."

"Not yet," he said, pausing. "It's that obvious that something's bothering me?"

"I'm not sure if *bother* is the word I would use," the minister said. "Preoccupied, maybe?"

"More than maybe."

"Let's give it a whirl," Pastor Jim said. "What's on your mind?"

Zach put his hands flat on top of the desk. He was more than comfortable with Pastor Jim, but still wasn't quite sure where to start. "I'm new to a lot of this, Pastor Jim. So please bear with me."

"You can say whatever you want in here, Zach. Take your time."

"You see, I've experienced something that's allowed me to be very confident in my knowledge of God's presence. But despite my confidence, I guess I still have questions about the Lord and the way . . . well, the way some things end up happening."

"You're not the only one," Pastor Jim said, his kind and patient smile bending his lips. "Maybe we can help each other."

"I want to know more about why God allows things to happen. Bad things. Like this, with little Alex. I meet up with kids like him every day."

"God has a plan," Pastor Jim said. "And everything does happen for a reason. In fact, Paul tells us to 'know that all things work together for good to those who love God, to those who are called according to His purpose.'"

"But then why do bad things happen to good people?"

"His promise isn't that bad things don't happen, Zach. His promise is that God can turn every circumstance into something good. *Every* circumstance. Sometimes we just need to look." He sighed heavily and lifted one eyebrow. "Sometimes it takes a lot of time to see it. Sometimes we don't get to see it at all—but somehow our suffering aids others. The key is trusting the Master through it all."

Zach thought about Amy. About how he'd been striving so hard, and for so long, to somehow make up for her death. To pay penance for a crime he did not commit. And then he thought again about Macey's best not being good enough for Alex, and how she might have to soon come to a similar realization. *Some things are out of our control.*

"Make sense?" Pastor Jim asked.

"Yes." He took a deep breath. "But then why pray at all? For healing? For change?"

Pastor Jim gave him a gentle smile. "Because he loves to hear from his children. You and me. And you never know if he simply wants us to ask before he grants it to us." He tapped his lips. "In really simplistic terms, it's kind of like a kid asking for a cookie. If it's the right time, not too close to a meal, then sure, we say yes. But if it's going to spoil a meal, or if the kid has had nothing but junk to eat all day, we say no. Right?"

"Right."

"But the kid can't really see that. All he can see is the cookie, and how yummy it looks, and how he wants it right now. Only someone with a greater perspective can make the wise decision. And the wise kid accepts and trusts that person."

"I understand," Zach said. "But what if we're not talking cookies? What if we're talking someone's *life*?"

Pastor Jim seemed to hesitate, and their eyes met again. "Are you talking about Alex?"

"Yes. And others . . ."

Pastor Jim sighed. "Obviously, the stakes are totally different, but the principle applies. Regardless of what the outcome is, Zach, and as much sense as it does or doesn't make, we really are not capable of understanding it all. We're left with one decision: to trust or not to trust. Because we are not in control, as much as we'd like to be. I mean, we're to use our God-given brains, follow where God leads. But we're sinful, fallible people in a fallen world. There are a ton of dynamics in play."

Zach stared at him for a long moment. "It's strange. But I do have this weird feeling that everything is going to be okay, Pastor Jim. Regardless of what happens. *I know it.*"

"That's all that really counts here," Pastor Jim said. "Let go, and let God take care of it, no matter how it feels at the time."

Kenneth's words to Macey ran through Zach's mind again, speaking to him as much to her, it seemed.

What if your best wasn't good enough?

Zach stood. "But what I really want is for everyone . . ." He stopped, and the images of people flitted in and out of his mind, like a slideshow in his head—first there was Kaitlyn, then Macey, Brooke, Ian, Shirley . . . and finally Charlie. "What I really want is for *everyone else* to know that whatever happens, it really is all for a reason. I want everyone to believe that. I just want them to have—"

"Faith?" Pastor Jim interrupted calmly.

Zach looked at the cross on the wall behind Pastor Jim. He wanted everyone to feel the way he did . . . at peace, and secure with whatever was to come. He brought the tips of his fingers to his forehead and thought about Alex and how the boy fit into that equation.

"Faith?" Pastor Jim asked again.

"I don't know," he said.

"Think about it. Something tells me you do."

Zach looked away from the pastor, to the cross. A lot of things had happened in his life for reasons he couldn't understand. Maybe he never would. But somehow, it was still okay. He'd been freed from making it all make sense, freed from making Amy's death—and the patients he'd lost—count. Because their God had already counted them. It was up to Christ to save them, not Zach. *Not me. Not me! And not Macey either . . .*

Even though it had taken him close to forty-one years, it was at that exact moment that Zach Norman knew he had something he never had before. He looked at Pastor Jim.

"Yes, Pastor Jim," he said. "Faith."

✢ FORTY-THREE

I'm just a little tired," Alex said, rolling carefully onto his side. It hurt to move much. He scratched right above his belly button and ran his tongue around his top gums. He was tired of feeling tired, and even though the inside of his mouth was sore and the inside of his nose was feeling scratchy, he did feel pretty good today. He had been in the room for a long time, close to a month, Mom had said, and he was hoping maybe he could go home today. Mom promised that it was gonna be pretty soon.

Maybe if I pretend I'm okay, they'll let me go, he thought. But even the thought of pretending made him sleepier still.

"Do you want me to turn the DVD off, then?" Dad asked, pointing up at the small television mounted on the wall. "You look like you need to take a nap."

"No," Alex said, making his eyes open wider. Willy Wonka had just walked out of his factory.

Aunt Carla was sitting in the chair next to Dad, playing cards. She set down a card. "If you ever try to pause, stop, or change a movie with Alex or Charlie in the room, you do so at your own risk."

"Yeah, Aunt Carla," Alex said playfully. He licked his lips again. "Hey, Aunt Carla?"

"What, Wonka boy?"

"My nose hasn't bleeded today."

"That's great," Aunt Carla said, her mask making her eyes really blue.

"It's okay even if it does, partner," Dad said. "You're doing really good."

"Yeah, I know," Alex said. "Does that mean I can maybe go home?"

"We still have a little bit to go, partner."

"Okay," Alex said. That didn't seem like too long.

"Hello, Mr. Alex," Nurse Kaitlyn said, entering the room. She pressed the buttons and wrote some numbers in the same folder that Dr. Lewis carried. "I just saw your mother outside."

"Unbelievable," Dad said, smiling and shaking his head. "Brooke can't stay at home for longer than a couple of hours, can she?"

"And I think she wants to see *the boss* as soon as possible," Nurse Kaitlyn said, tilting the edge of the folder at Alex.

"I'm the boss?" Alex asked. He liked that idea.

"Yes, you are, Alex," the nurse said. "You sure seem chipper today."

"Yeah," Alex said, not having any idea what Nurse Kaitlyn meant. Based on her smile and the way she said it, he decided that *chipper* was something good.

"Is Brooke here by herself?" Aunt Carla asked.

"No," Nurse Kaitlyn said. "Shirley is out there with her." The nurse closed the folder and looked at Alex. "Hey, Bossman, you sure have a lot of people who care about you."

"That's good," Alex said, wondering, *If I had a candy bar with a golden ticket, could I go to meet Willy Wonka?* He didn't ever remember seeing a golden ticket before, just the silver wrapper part that he and Charlie tore in two pieces when they shared.

"Why don't we run down to the cafeteria and get something to eat?" Dad asked Aunt Carla. He checked his phone. "Then I gotta head over to work."

"Okay," Aunt Carla said. "Then I can come back up and take Shirley home in an hour or so."

"That'll work," Dad said as he and Aunt Carla stood.

"I'll see you in a couple days, Alex," Aunt Carla said.

"Okay, Aunt Carla," he responded. He always felt a little sad when any of them left. He wanted to be home with all of them. All the time.

Dad rubbed his head. "I'll be back tonight. You get some rest. Deal?"

"Deal," Alex said. "And then maybe you can take me home."

"Not yet, partner. But you'll be home before you know it."

"THIS FOOD REALLY ISN'T THAT BAD," CARLA SAID, STAB-bing her fork into the East Shore cafeteria's version of chicken Caesar salad.

Ian nodded and then took another bite of pepperoni pizza. "Brooke and I've been down here probably four or five times with Kaitlyn. She continuously steers us toward the pizza as some type of precautionary measure. But it's not all bad."

"You spending the night here tonight?"

"Probably," Ian said. "They have only been letting one of us stay, and Brooke needs a break that's longer than two hours."

"Yeah, she does," Carla agreed. "But will she agree to it? That's the question."

"I think so," Ian said. "I think she finally believes that Alex is stable. And that she can trust me to watch him sleep." He tossed her a wry grin.

Carla smiled, closed her eyes, and rested her cheek in her palm. "I just want this to be over so they can both move on. I feel so bad for him, lying up there, hooked up to all those things. And for Brooke, fretting over him every day."

"They're both troupers. They'll get through this. We all will."

"You really think everything's going to be okay?" Carla asked.

"It has to be," Ian said. He took the napkin off his lap, folded it neatly, and placed it on top of the table.

"You're a lucky man," Carla said.

"I know," Ian said. "In more ways than one." He thought about all that'd happened to him—he'd gained a son, some true friends, and for the first time, something that resembled a relationship with God.

"God is good," Carla said, smiling shyly. "Everything good comes from him. It's awesome."

Ian's cell phone chirped and he answered it by the end of the second ring.

"*What?*" he said, standing quickly. He felt like ice water was pouring down the inside of his chest. "We're on our way."

"What?" Carla asked, dread on her face.

"Alex is having a seizure," he said, and then he turned and ran.

✤ FORTY-FOUR

I an and Carla raced past the third-floor nurses' station and down
the isolated hall that led toward the BMT corridor. They slowed
at the solid double doors that led into the unit, and Ian slammed
his fist against the shiny metal square button on the wall that auto-
matically opened them. Ian could see Shirley and Brooke standing
down the hallway. Brooke was crying and had her face buried in
Shirley's shoulder; the two women stood outside of the door that
led to yet another hallway and then to Alex's room.

"What happened?" Ian asked. "Where is he?"

"It was terrible," Brooke said, lifting her face and then letting
go of Shirley to hug Ian. "His eyes rolled back, and he was shaking
so hard. And then . . ."

"And then what?" Ian asked, pulling back and looking at Brooke
as he held her out in front of him by her shoulders. "Brooke, *is he
all right?*"

"And then they put all of these ice packs on him . . ."

"They said he is going to be all right," Shirley said. "Try to—"

"I want to know what happened!" Ian said, putting his hands
on his head. "He was fine just a second ago! Where's Dr. Lewis?" he
bellowed down the hall, toward a nurse.

"Please, Ian," Shirley said, taking a step toward him. "They said
for us to stay out here. Macey's in there with him."

"I'm going in there!"

"Please, Ian," Shirley said again, blocking his way. "We're not—"

"He needs me!"

"Yes, he does," Shirley said. "But he needs *them* more right now."

Ian glanced at Brooke, who seemed to agree with Shirley. He tilted his head up to the ceiling and closed his eyes. He had never felt so helpless.

"C'mon," Shirley said, holding out her arms as if she were talking him off of a ledge.

"I don't understand it," Ian said, running his hand through his hair again. "We just left here, and he seemed fine."

"He was fine," Brooke said, her eyebrows wilting as she glared back at the door. "And then all of a sudden, his hands went into little fists and his eyes rolled back." She paused, noticing that the door was moving. Macey came out and pulled down her surgical mask.

"Is he all right?" Ian asked. "What happened?"

"It's called a febrile seizure," she said. "He's okay. It's caused by an abrupt increase in body temperature."

"But how in the world did that happen?" Ian asked. "All of the things he is hooked up to. You can read his temperature right there on the machine. We just left the room about—"

"Ian," Macey said, holding up her hand. "Febrile seizures can happen in a matter of seconds. We are prepared for when things like this happen. What's important is that he is stable right now."

"But why—what caused the increase in his temperature? I don't understand."

"There are several things that could have caused it."

"Like what?"

"Ian," Macey said again, this time putting her hand on his arm. "It may only be a side effect of the transplant, but we are taking blood cultures right now to make sure."

"Make sure of what?"

"That it's not something else."

"When can we go in there?"

"When they're done," Macey said firmly. "I don't want you in there right now."

"Why not? Why can't we go in there?" The more she said he couldn't, the more he wanted it.

"Because," Macey said in a way that entertained no argument, "he's going to be very uncomfortable while they take those cultures. You guys are his protectors—"

"Exactly. As his protectors, we—"

"*No*," Macey said, lifting her hand. She took a deep breath and dropped her hand. "These cultures are going to be painful for him. It's this simple: I don't want him to watch you watch *us* hurt him. There's nothing you can do to help him, and trust me, he won't understand."

"Oh," Ian said, glancing at Brooke and regretting that he'd asked. Now all he could imagine was Alex screaming, reaching out for him, begging him to make it stop. *Dad.*

"They're probably done already, okay? Just hang tight for a minute. I'll be right back."

She opened the door and then pulled it closed behind her.

Brooke began to weep again, and Shirley pulled her into her arms.

"It's probably over already," Ian said, desperately repeating Macey's words, failing his crash course in helplessness.

"He's going to be okay," Shirley said. "She said he's stable. That's the important thing."

"Stable?" Brooke said through choking tears. "If you could've seen him, Ian . . . His back arched off the bed, and the sound of him choking on his tongue . . . They all came running in and put their hands over the bed rails so he wouldn't thrash against them."

The door opened back up, and Kaitlyn stepped out.

"He's all right," she said, motioning with her hand to Brooke and Ian. "But he wants to see you two."

Ian and Brooke followed Kaitlyn through the door and into the small area where they put on their masks, gloves, and caps.

Macey stepped out from behind the curtain, and even though she had on a mask, Ian recognized that her game face was still on. "We've asked Alex to be still for a bit," she said. "We'll come back in a little while to remove the ice packs, then we'll see if we can get him to take a little nap. He has to be exhausted. So let's all stay real low-key, okay?" She looked at both of them.

They quickly agreed and pulled back the curtain. Alex was lying there with ice packs around his groin and under his armpits. Ian felt his chest constrict at the sight of Alex's face, pasty and pale. The few strands of hair he had left were now sweaty and glued to his head like fresh scratches. It looked like his freckles had disappeared. His eyes were sunken, darker, and more hollow. His cheeks were puffy, and both sides of his nose were tear-soaked. He had clearly been crying—and crying very hard.

"Oh, Alex," Brooke said. "I'm so sorry you had to go through that, baby."

Alex's eyebrows huddled together, and his bottom lip covered the top one. He looked disappointed, like he didn't want them to know he had been crying.

"Hey, partner," Ian said.

Alex tried to talk and cleared his throat, wincing in pain. He swallowed delicately and paused. "Does this mean I don't get to go home pretty soon?" A new tear was forming at the corner of his left eye.

"I don't think so, buddy," Brooke said.

Alex's eyes shifted to his father, and Ian knew that he hoped for a different answer from him. The sharp teeth of helplessness bit once again into the edge of Ian's heart as the tear slowly cascaded down Alex's cheek. It made *him* want to cry.

"Just try to rest, partner," Ian said, trying to force cheer and confidence into his voice. Alex seemed easily ten times—no, a hundred times—more sickly than when he'd seen him an hour ago. He looked like a little old man, and what tugged even more at Ian's heartstrings was the fact that Alex appeared to be ashamed of himself. Like he'd failed. And there was something else, something he couldn't quite identify.

And then, looking at Brooke, he knew what it was.

It probably was plain as day on his own face too.

His brave little man, less than a week away from his sixth birthday, could neither fight it nor hide it any longer.

Alex was scared.

✢ FORTY-FIVE

I know you're out there," Macey said, gazing out of her small office window over the parking lot and into the construction site. "And I know you hear me."

She turned the small crank to crack open the window and was slapped by a gust of crisp and blustery December air. She looked down at the muddy, slush-banked puddles that littered the parking lot like hundreds of tiny lakes and guessed it was no more than ten degrees outside.

Where are you?

She lifted her elbows to the windowsill and cradled her head in her palms as she began to diligently survey the fenced-in area that was reserved specifically for the construction crew. She noticed the mounds of plowed snow, dirtied from exhaust, along with the three different plywood walkways that had been assembled over the icy muck that led from the parking area to the different entrances of the new wing.

A half dozen men stood outside a foreman's trailer, sipping coffee and listening to a heavyset man who wore coveralls that were way too clean. He pointed in all different directions, and their heads followed his finger as frozen puffs of air came out of his mouth with every word.

"So you think you're the boss out there?" she said to the heavy man, having a sneaking suspicion that at least one of his employees had a more impressive résumé.

"Who are you talking to?" Kaitlyn asked, standing in Macey's doorway.

"Myself," she said, her eyes quickly running down a row of cars and trucks that had all been glazed by a powdery film from winter roads. She turned around and clapped her hands together, trying to snap herself out of her preoccupied mind-set. "Whatcha got?"

"Good news," Kaitlyn said. "Dr. Mueller said no growth after twenty-four hours for Alexander."

"That doesn't surprise me," Macey said, taking a copy of the e-mail from the nurse. "I never thought that this was a bacterial infection."

"What are you thinking, then?"

Macey took her hair out of its ponytail and let it fall across her shoulders. She sat at her desk and tapped her fingers nervously on the arm of her chair and then suddenly stopped. "I'm thinking he doesn't look good, Kaitlyn."

Never, ever, had they shared such words. A peculiar silence separated them, and then the nurse said it: "No, he doesn't."

Macey's heart sank. Kaitlyn had *a lot* more experience on the pediatric oncology wing than Macey. If she agreed, then . . . *It really is bad.*

"What's your plan?" Kaitlyn asked, coming to sit down.

"No growth after twenty-four hours with the first culture is good news," Macey said, backing up, thinking it all through for the hundredth time.

The nurse nodded.

"And I have to respect the test results. But I have to treat the patient, not the test results."

"What are you saying?" Kaitlyn asked. "Even though the culture looks good . . ."

"I'm saying something's wrong, Kaitlyn. Something isn't right here."

"You'll get it," the nurse said supportively. "That is what we do. We fix things that aren't right. And I've never seen a doc better at it than you. If it can be fixed, you will do it. Just stay focused."

"But," Macey said, feeling like she couldn't breathe, "what if it can't be fixed? What if it's out of our hands, Kait? What if there is nothing we can do about it?"

"That happens in our business too, Macey," she said somberly. "All we can do is our best. You know that as well as—"

"Our *best*?" Macey interrupted. Kaitlyn's words seemed to slap her in the face. She sat back in the chair, trying to get her breath. Then the carpenter's words shot through her and exited her back. *"What if your best wasn't good enough?"*

"I'm going to run down and get something to eat," Kaitlyn said, frowning. "Do you want to go?"

"No. You go ahead. I need some time."

"Want me to bring anything back up?"

"I'll take whatever you're having, with a Coke," Macey said. "Why don't you bring yours up and we'll both eat here?"

"Okay, I'll be right back," Kaitlyn said, pointing at the office door. "Open or closed?"

"Close it, if you don't mind, Kait. Thanks."

Kaitlyn left, and Macey wandered distractedly back to the window. She felt like she had dipped her toe in the same pool that Ian had taken a few laps in earlier—*helplessness.* Her head cleared momentarily, and she found herself mechanically scanning a couple more rows of cars and pickups.

"I know you're out there," she said. "I know it."

Newer truck—newer truck—car—car—car—vacant spot—newer truck with a huge dent in the driver's side door.

Down another couple of rows. And then a few more.

Car—car—older truck—car—older truck—empty parking spot with a stack of wet cardboard surrounded by orange cones—newer truck—car—car—dumpster—back end of a truck.

There. An older pickup truck.

Macey squinted and pressed her forehead against the glass as she looked straight down and to her left at the rear of the older truck.

The truck.

A confusing flash of relief and fear rounded through her stomach. Part of her felt like she had just found a lost set of keys. The rest of her felt as if she had spotted the school bully from a distance and was desperately kidding herself that she had time to hide.

A knock sounded at her door, three times. *Kaitlyn? Back so fast?*

Macey went to open the door and gasped.

Kenneth was standing in the hallway.

Her shoulders flinched upward, and she felt like an ice-cold mallet had struck the side of her heart. Her mouth closed, muffling her shriek, and she instinctively stepped backward.

"Hello, Macey," he said gently, his eyes filled with compassion. She stood there, speechless, her heart hammering away.

"Sorry to frighten you," he said, hooking his thumbs casually into the tops of his front jean pockets. "I was just down the hall, talking with Zach, and thought I would pop in and see how you're doing."

"You know how I'm doing," she said, finding her voice. "Why bother?"

Kenneth tilted his head. "Think so, eh?"

Macey nodded. "Yeah, I do. And so far it looks like my best really isn't good enough with Alex. What do I do now? Just quit on him?"

"Why would you do that?" He gestured to the center of her office, and she waved him in. He quietly shut the door behind him.

"I knew you were talking about Alex when you said what you did to me at the diner—about my best not being good enough."

"Tell me why you would quit on him."

"Why don't *you* tell me?" she asked, not really sure how comfortable she was with her own audacity. "You are the big man with the plan."

Kenneth smiled casually, and she didn't like it.

Macey crossed her arms and stepped even closer. "You are the big man with the plan, and the rest of us are nothing more than puppets on a stage, going through the motions."

He smiled again, but it seemed a little different to her. Their eyes met, and he said, "You make it sound like you have no free will. Like you really have no control over your actions."

"No," she said, maintaining their eye contact as she took yet another step toward him. She lifted her hand and pointed at his chest. "What I'm saying is that I have no control over what *you* do."

"That's true," he said matter-of-factly.

"What do I tell Alex's people?" she asked, taking a step back. "What do I tell those good, *Christian* people? Maybe I will just tell them that I'm doing everything I can, but someone *bigger* and *badder* than us wants Alex dead."

He stood deadly still, as if her words had wounded him. *Good,* she thought. *Good!*

"I'm not the enemy, Macey."

"Aren't you?" she asked. "Aren't you the one who basically told me my best wasn't good enough?"

"Does that make me your enemy?"

She shook her head, pushing her hair from her face. "I'm telling you I'm going to fight you on this."

"Fight me?"

"I know I can't win, but I'll still fight."

"I'm sure you will."

She wasn't about to give up. She had a feeling she'd already crossed a line with him, so she figured she might as well stay there. "I can beat the cancer, and I can beat whatever caused that seizure yesterday. But I can't beat destiny. I can't beat you and your will, but I'm going to try."

"I believe you."

Macey turned and shook her head as she walked toward her desk. She spun back around. She wanted just one answer and knew there would never be a better time to ask. "Why a little boy? Why Alex?" She thought about Zach and the age-old question. "That's the least you can do for me. Tell me why God lets children suffer and die? Why the little ones, Kenneth?"

"You are all little ones. Every one of you."

She clenched her fists and banged them at her sides. "But he is *five years old*! He is only five, for Pete's sake. He will be six in only a few days."

Kenneth went to the window and looked out, saying nothing for the span of a minute. "Macey, you said you can't win. *Win* is an interesting word, don't you think?"

"I know I can't win," she muttered. "Deep down, I know that." She rose and walked away, wanting some distance from him. He was just too . . . close.

Kenneth turned around and didn't say anything.

"The odds have been stacked against this kid from the get-go," she said. "Right?"

He didn't answer, just stared at her.

"I've studied case after case," Macey said. "I've prepared for every possible situation. I've done things with kids that other doctors call miracles. I want to help. I want to make a difference, but with Alex, it's all about you, Kenneth. All about that mystery plan of yours. Cancer doesn't move this fast, and that seizure you gave him—and I want to reiterate the fact that *you gave it to him*—knocked three-quarters of the wind out of that kid's sail yesterday. Why don't you squeeze his kidneys a little today and make sure he suffers some more? And don't kid yourself. He *is* suffering."

Kenneth crossed his arms and let her words hang in the air between them. "Let's say I am who you think I am."

"You *are* who I think you are!" she snapped.

"Let's say that is the case," he said, stepping around the desk, leaning against it. "If that's true, tomorrow morning a beautiful little boy will be without suffering, without pain, in that proverbial perfect world—a perfect paradise—and he will be there forever. How do you lose in that, Macey? How is that not winning?"

"He is a little boy!" she shouted. "And you can save him!" This wasn't going how she'd envisioned. She wanted his help, and she wanted it right away. "The cross. Mary Springsted. Pastor Jim's sight. Zach's faith. And my faith. These are all miracles. I'm asking you for one more—just one more."

He remained where he was, still, listening, and she took a few steps toward him.

"I see what you wanted me to learn. That it's not all up to me.

That people's lives are ultimately in God's hands alone. If you'd only stop now," she pleaded. "The way Alex is right now, I can fix him. I can make him better. I know I can. Please, Kenneth."

The carpenter uncrossed his arms and lowered them to his sides. "I'm sorry, Macey."

She stepped back from him, fighting tears. "Why this little boy?" she asked. "You know it all. You've already seen it all. You have all the answers. Tell me *why*. Why Alex?"

"You wouldn't understand."

Kaitlyn knocked on the door behind the carpenter and then opened it, holding a white paper bag in her left hand and a cup holder in her right. Her eyes widened. "Whoops. Sorry."

"It's okay, Kaitlyn," Kenneth said, "I've gotta get back to work now."

"Why'd you even come?" Macey asked, sinking to a chair as defeat washed through her. "Seriously . . . why'd you even bother coming?"

Kenneth approached and looked down at her. "Because you wanted me to."

She paused and then reluctantly looked up into his face, hating the fact that he was right. "I'm still going to fight you on this."

"I know you'll do your best," he said, turning and heading back to the door. He looked over his shoulder. "But don't prolong it."

Kenneth nodded at Kaitlyn, who quickly stepped aside as he went out the door.

The nurse peeked curiously back down the hallway and then turned to Macey. "Whoa. What was *that* about?"

Macey stared blankly at the open door.

"C'mon," Kaitlyn said, setting the bag and drinks on the table. "Out with it. What'd the magic carpet man want?"

"Tomorrow," Macey muttered, looking out the window.

"What's tomorrow?" Kaitlyn asked.

"Alex," she said sadly. "Kenneth just told me he will be dead in the morning."

✦ FORTY-SIX

I f you need anything at all, just let one of us know."

"Thanks," Brooke said, unable to remember the nurse's name. There had been so many different ones in and out of the room that day. She pointed at Alex as he slept. "As long as he is okay, I'm okay."

The nurse's cheeks lifted above the top corners of her mask as she smiled. Brooke recognized the smile as a fellow mom's. The nurse clicked her pen closed and hooked it over the upper edge of what Brooke and Ian had labeled *the* manila folder. Alex's file. His chart. It had been passed back and forth between them like a medical baton in a relay race that Brooke desperately wanted to end—in a good way.

The nurse glanced over at Pastor Jim, who was seated at the foot of the bed, and then back at Brooke. "Kaitlyn will be back in a few minutes."

"Very good," Pastor Jim said as the nurse made her way out of the room. "Thank you."

"Pastor Jim," Brooke said, "I can't remember what that nurse said her name was."

"Diane," he said.

"I like her."

"They're all doing a fine job."

"But there are so many of them today. Even before you got here, since around two this afternoon, there have been all kinds of extra nurses taking turns coming in and out of here. Even Macey and Kaitlyn have been in here ten times more than usual."

"Our boy's in good hands," Pastor Jim said, scratching at his left ear and adjusting his surgical cap. He leaned forward on his chair and dropped his elbows on top of his knees as he stared at Alex. "I'm thankful for all of the help he's getting."

"Me too, but I don't like the idea of an infectious disease specialist, or whatever he was called, being here either."

"They just want to be sure nothing else caused his seizure," Pastor Jim said. "And from what you said, the results of that first culture they took looked pretty good."

"Yeah, but I still don't understand how it's possible for whatever they are looking for—the bacteria, or whatever it is—to *not* be there after twenty-four hours, but to still be able to show up after forty-eight or seventy-two hours. It doesn't make sense to me."

"Me either," Pastor Jim said. "But whatever they're doing is all part of how he will be made well. That I know."

"Why can't he be well now? How much more does he have to endure?" Brooke asked.

"I'm really not sure," he said, speaking softly. He waved his hand in a small circle above the bed. "But I would like to tell you how I feel about some of this, if that's okay."

"Of course," Brooke said. "I always want to know what you think, Pastor Jim."

Pastor Jim's eyes stayed fixed on Alex. "You know, Brooke, I sit here and look at Alex, and I remember the day he was born. He's made such a difference in all of our lives—your life, Charlie's, and of course, mine and Shirley's." His head never moved, but his eyes shifted to Brooke, and they stared at each other for a few seconds.

"You're gonna make me cry, Pastor Jim."

"Go ahead and cry, then, sweetie. I may join you."

"I've never seen you cry," she said, swallowing hard around a ball in her throat.

Pastor Jim looked back at Alex and rested his hands on the edge of the bed. "It's hard for me to describe the way I feel, Brooke. All that I'm thinking."

"Go ahead and try. I'll listen."

Pastor Jim turned to Brooke and lowered his voice. "We have an enemy with us, honey. We live in a very fallen world and still experience so many consequences like sickness and even death, but I look at Alex—"

"Don't say death, Pastor Jim," she whispered, fresh tears streaming down her cheeks. Was he saying what she thought he was saying? *Please, God, no . . .*

"Don't get ahead of me. Just hear me out," Pastor Jim said, his hands lifting back off the bed. "I look at Alex right now—I look at him the way he is right this second—all of those things hooked up to him, how pale he is, how thin he is, and how his hair has fallen out. As hard as I look, I just can't see his spark right now—you know, that spark of his that lights up every room he goes in?"

"Yeah," Brooke whispered, her heart pounding. She knew exactly what he meant.

Pastor Jim pointed back at Alex. "And there he is, exactly where I would never want him to be, looking the way he is, and still . . . there is absolutely no doubt in my mind . . . I really can't explain it, but I am *certain*, Brooke."

The growing strength of his tone encouraged her. "Certain of what?" she whispered, wiping her eyes.

"That God is going to make him better."

"I like when you say that, Pastor Jim."

"I wouldn't say it if I didn't believe it. The Lord has never given me so much confidence about anything in my life, Brooke. I'm not talking about wishful thinking here. To me, it's a certainty. I have no doubt at all. Not a shred."

"Not a shred?" Brooke repeated.

"None," he said. "And I want God to give it to you. I want you to be the one without any doubt that Alexander will be made well."

"How about both of us having it?" Brooke said.

"Only believe," Pastor Jim said.

"Yeah."

"Never forget that," he said, nodding at Alex, who had just opened his eyes. "Let them do their work here, and the Lord will do his."

"Hey, sleepyhead," Brooke said to Alex. "That was another short nap, mister."

Alex's left eye was only half as open as his right. He licked his lips and then closed his eyes again.

"They are bringing you some more ice chips for your mouth, Alex."

Alex squinted at the food tray on the side of the bed and then fell back asleep. Brooke wondered if the lining of his mouth and the area behind his eyes still hurt him, or if his stomach still felt funny. She wanted to know what he was thinking about. Maybe it was about his new baseball mitt and how his dad had promised to show him how to play when the snow melted. Ian had even given him a hint about a new bike for his birthday—one that Alex insisted not have baby wheels on it.

Kaitlyn slid the curtain open, and Alex's eyes opened a bit again.

"Here you go, Mr. Alex," she said, stepping to the side of the bed and handing Brooke a Styrofoam cup of ice chips. "Feeling a little warm still?"

Alex's eyelids bobbed up and down, and then he nodded sadly.

"He keeps falling asleep and waking up," Brooke said. "He hasn't stayed awake longer than a few minutes all day long."

"He's wiped," Kaitlyn said. "Not unusual after what he's gone through."

"He falls asleep even with *Charlie and the Chocolate Factory* on," Brooke said, scooping a few ice chips to the tip of a small plastic spoon and holding it out in front of Alex. "Even with Willy Wonka on, huh, buddy?"

"He's still running a low-grade fever," Kaitlyn said, glancing at Alex's food tray that had been basically untouched.

Alex's bottom lip dropped, and Brooke tipped a pair of ice chips off the spoon into his mouth. He dabbed at the ice with his tongue, and his bloodshot eyes watered. He tried to say something, but Brooke could only make out a couple of the words.

"What, buddy?" she asked, lowering her head within a few inches of his mouth. "See Charlie what?"

"See Charlie," he whispered.

Brooke forced a smile. "Maybe when you wake up next time, Charlie will be here with those caps on his hands."

Alex had trapped a few ice chips between his tongue and the inside of his cheek. As they dissolved against the roof of his mouth, he fell back asleep.

"There he goes," Brooke said. "There he goes again."

"Let him rest," Kaitlyn said, glancing at a monitor behind Alex. "He needs it."

"There's blood on the spoon, Kaitlyn," she said, trying not to panic as she looked at the bright-red against the bright-white plastic.

"Low platelets," the nurse said. "I want all three of you to try to relax, and I'll be back in a few minutes."

Brooke lifted her feet up to the edge of her seat as Kaitlyn left. She crouched forward and rested her arms across her knees.

"Why don't you go ahead and take a little nap?" Pastor Jim said. "You look exhausted, Brooke. I'll do nothing but stare at our boy and pray over him."

"Thanks, Pastor Jim. I'm glad you're here."

"Me too," he said.

Brooke watched as Pastor Jim pulled out a pocket-sized New Testament. St. Thomas had been fortunate enough to recently receive two hundred of them from the Gideons, and he hadn't been able to resist the temptation of keeping one for himself.

Brooke slid her hip against the lower part of the chair's right armrest and tried to get comfortable. Her sleep had become nothing more than a series of interrupted dozes, each loaded with its own dream sequence where none of this had ever happened. Each of the dreams took her to places like Lakeside Metropark, where Alex and his full head of bright-red hair swung daringly on the swings, or to Church Road, where a healthy and vibrant Alex—a boy with a *spark*—threw rocks at invisible monsters. Other times the dreams would allow her to watch as Alex played with Charlie behind the church or irritated everyone by accidentally resetting the TV remote control in the basement. Regardless, the dreams were nothing more than teases, disappointingly dashed when she woke up to reality.

Invisible monster? she thought, lifting her head and glancing at Alex over the bed's side rail. *Keep fighting it, buddy.*

She lowered her head again and peeked back at Pastor Jim as he flipped through the tiny Bible. He put it back in his pocket, stood up, and lowered his head while stretching his arm out over the end of the bed toward Alex. He began to say the Lord's Prayer, and the tranquility of his voice made Brooke sleepier.

Her eyes fell closed again. She was back at the Metropark and could see a flock of geese flying over her head. They now seemed dark and were practically flying in slow motion.

"Hallowed be thy name . . ."

The lake was like black glass. It was perfectly still except for the reflections of the three geese as they headed toward Canada. *Three? There were just twenty or thirty of them. And where did Carla go? Wasn't Carla just there?*

She kept walking, and Pastor Jim kept praying. She could hear his voice like a narrator in a movie.

"Thy kingdom come . . ."

She continued to walk down the shore. The sand felt like cool flour between her toes, and the only thing she could hear were the sounds of her own breath and heart. She looked up the bank and then up the hill to where Charlie had just picked Alex up out of the leaf pile. They weren't there. There were no leaves, no more swing sets, no more playground. It was all gone.

"Thy will be done . . ."

She could hear something. It was coming from above her. It was faint, and it had a pulse. Little flashes of light behind the solid gray sky beckoned her. She looked farther down the shoreline. Someone was standing there, waiting for her. It was a man.

She walked toward him. With each step the pulse grew stronger. Its buzz became louder and more pronounced. It was an old man—a very old man with a beard and shiny white hair. He was holding something.

She kept walking, and the buzz got louder with each step she took. But she kept going, knowing that whatever the old man was holding, she wanted it. It was the reason she was there. It was why *they* were there.

She was no more than twenty feet from the old man when she stopped. Something about him looked familiar. She felt comfortable, as if she knew him, as if she'd always known him. She knew he wanted to show her something.

He turned his head toward the sky and pointed with his left hand. That light in the sky grew brighter and flashed in perfect unison with each pulse of the vibrating noise, the noise that now came in hollow booms, outwardly warning her of something. She closed her eyes and covered her ears. The noise was unbearable.

And then it stopped.

She opened her eyes, and the old man was smiling at her. Yes, it was a familiar smile—a smile that told her everything was all right. It told her that everything was going to be okay.

The old man lifted his arms straight out in front of him. In his hands was the doll. The doll from the lake.

It was brand-new.

Both of its eyes were glassy and bright, and its thick red hair shined. The man held it out a little farther, offering it to her, and Brooke stepped forward.

The buzzing sound was back and grew louder and louder . . .

Brooke's head slid off the armrest, and she sprang up in her chair. Kaitlyn was hitting a switch that killed an alarm at the other side of the bed. The nurse then removed something that was attached to Alex's finger and thumbed at another button on a machine next to Alex's IV bag. Kaitlyn immediately wrapped a Velcro cuff around Alex's small arm and began to take his blood pressure manually.

"What's wrong?" Brooke asked, gripping the sides of the seat and questioning herself as to whether this was real or yet another bizarre dream.

"Alexander was sleeping, and that alarm went off," Pastor Jim said, looking stricken. He was on his feet.

Diane appeared from behind the curtain and gestured to Brooke. "Brooke, I need you back here for a minute."

"What's wrong?" Brooke said. "Why are you doing that, Kaitlyn?"

"Diane, call the code," Kaitlyn said sternly, beginning chest compressions on Alex.

"What's happening?" Brooke asked again, her mouth dry. She tried to move closer to Alex before being held back by Pastor Jim. "Why are you doing that? Is he breathing?"

Macey and two other people rushed into the room and took their places beside the bed.

"I'll take the lead," the tallest one said.

Brooke cringed. *The lead of what?*

"Brooke, Pastor, please come with me," Diane beckoned again.

"No!" Brooke said. "Tell me what happened!"

"Brooke, you gotta let us do our job," Kaitlyn said.

Pastor Jim grabbed Brooke and pulled her out of the room as the code team continued working on Alex.

And as the door finally closed, the last thing Brooke saw was the expression on Macey's face.

It wasn't good.

✛ FORTY-SEVEN

Just under an hour had passed before they could hear the monotone hum of muffled voices behind the door.

Ian stopped pacing.

Brooke lifted her head off Carla's shoulder.

Pastor Jim opened his eyes and stood up, away from the wall where he'd been leaning.

When the latch finally clicked open, they watched as the youngest of the nurses pushed the door all the way open and then held it against the wall. Diane was next, slowly backing out and pulling at the foot of a gurney while the tall one at the far end stared straight ahead and pushed forward.

"Alex," Brooke said, rising. Ian stood next to her as the team wheeled him by. He'd been stripped of his Spider-Man pajama top and was flat on his back, with his arms motionless at his sides. Two other members from the code team flanked the gurney, one of them managing a pair of IVs, and the other holding and squeezing one of those breathing bags Brooke had seen on television over Alex's face.

Macey was right behind them and waved to Ian and Brooke. "You two only. C'mon."

"We'll be in the waiting room," Carla called as Brooke hurried to catch up with Ian, who was already right behind Macey.

"Where are you taking him?" Ian asked.

"We're going up to the ICU," Macey said, her voice now that of someone on a mission. They paused at the thick, gray doors that led out of the BMT unit and waited for them to open.

341

Brooke turned around and looked at Pastor Jim.

No doubts, Pastor Jim?

He nodded as if he could hear her, and Brooke turned and followed Alex and the team out.

They stopped in front of an elevator marked AUTHORIZED PERSONNEL ONLY. Brooke stared at it, anxious to look at anything but Alex, looking like he was still battling for his life as the nurse squeezed, and squeezed, and squeezed the bag . . .

Macey took Brooke by the arm and then grabbed Ian's, leading them into the elevator first, and over to the corner, out of the way. "When we get up there, you guys are going to have to wait a little longer until they get him situated. I'll come right out and sit with you in the waiting room to go over all that's happened."

The tall nurse pressed 4 on the first row of numbers, and the doors closed. The elevator was uncomfortably quiet, with the exception of the puffing sound that came from the bag over Alex's face. Brooke's boat of confidence was taking in water, and she could tell by the way Ian was looking at the gurney that his was too.

She forced herself to glance down at the side of Alex's face, which had been practically consumed by the mask. His small jawline was more pronounced than ever, and she reached her hand out, because his little eyelids looked so pink and were—

"Please don't touch him, Miss Thomas," the tall nurse said, causing Brooke to pull her hand back as if she had grazed the side of a hot stove. The nurse gave her an apologetic smile. "It's good for him to hear you, though." She gestured forward. "Please say something to him."

Brooke swallowed hard. "Alex, baby, I'm here," she said. "So's your dad." She felt like she was talking to a picture of Alex. What was before her wasn't her son, not her vibrant, bouncy boy . . .

Ian brushed away a tear like he hoped no one saw it. "Hey, partner. You gotta get better so we can go shop for that bike you want."

The elevator door opened, and they swung a right and made it past a nurses' station that Brooke guessed was three times bigger

than the one down on the third floor, with nurses who disappeared behind banks of computers. The code team led them to
another corridor, obviously knowing exactly what room they were
headed to.

Macey slowed down and then pointed to a crowded waiting
room. "Please wait in there. I'll be back in a few minutes."

Brooke watched the gurney make its way down the hall. Ian
was already sitting in the waiting room and had his head tilted
back with his hands over his eyes. She went in and sat next to him,
and he glanced over at her.

"You okay?" he asked.

"It's almost like this isn't really happening," she said, absorbing
the tension reserved specifically for ICU waiting rooms. It was as
if the twenty to thirty people in there simultaneously realized that
their priorities had always been out of order. "How about you?"

"It's like the worst nightmare I've ever had. It won't end, and it
keeps getting worse."

"He's going to get better," Brooke said, trying to stop hyper-
ventilating. "He has to."

"He will," Ian said. But Brooke thought he sounded only half
sure.

Macey entered the room and pulled up a folding chair to sit
in front of them. "Only a few more minutes until you can see him,
you guys."

"What happened, Macey?" Brooke asked.

She licked her lips and then looked them both in the eye. "Alex
quit breathing."

A shiver ran down Brooke's back. *He quit breathing? As in,
never to begin breathing again?*

"Is he going to be all right?" Ian asked, his voice faint.

"We're doing everything we can," Macey said. "Now we just
have to wait."

Brooke felt light-headed. The words sounded powerless. *Doing
everything we can. As in, there's nothing else we can do. It's up to
somebody else. Somebody else.*

A nurse showed up at the waiting room door. She pointed at Brooke and Ian, and Macey nodded back.

"Ah, here's Alex's new nurse," Macey said. "The intensive care unit has its own nurses, and she's one of our best."

"Hello," the nurse said, holding out her hand. "I'm Talia." Her Indian-brown hair was pulled off her forehead and wrapped neatly into a shoulder-length ponytail. The resilient look in her dark brown eyes and the firmness in her handshake let Brooke know that it was all about business on this floor and that Talia had the confidence it took to be up here.

Which was fine with Brooke.

"Listen, Mom and Dad," the nurse said. She lowered her voice so only the three of them could hear her. "Before we go back, I want you to prepare yourselves, okay?"

"For what?" Ian asked.

"First of all, Alex is unconscious, and he's on a ventilator, so you're going to see a tube in his mouth. Beyond that, there are a few different machines that help us monitor him, so you're going to see wires running in all different directions. It can be tough seeing your son this way. Don't let it alarm you, and try to keep in mind that all of these things are necessary, all right?"

Brooke looked at Ian and then at Talia. "Okay."

"Do we know when he will wake up?" Ian asked, nervously glancing at Brooke as he waited for the answer.

He doesn't know, Brooke thought, a shred of panic sliding down her throat. *Ian really doesn't know whether or not Alex will be okay.*

"We don't know that," the nurse said. "But I will be here with you all night." She smiled confidently.

"Why don't we head back?" Macey said.

Talia led them down the hallway, and Brooke tried to figure out exactly what it was about open hospital room doors that made her want to look in them. They were like eye magnets, and when she did look, it almost always seemed like someone was looking right back at her.

They went through another set of thick double doors beneath

a sign that read CORRIDOR C, signaling to Brooke that Alex was once again in some type of isolation. The nurse took them into another room, where they all put on their masks, gloves, and surgical caps, confirming Brooke's suspicion. They walked down to yet another room that had the block letters CUBE with the number 9 attached to the door. The nurse opened that door, and they all went in.

There was a bathroom to their immediate left, followed by eight to ten feet of solid beige wall, and then a thin white curtain—not unlike the room he had just left. Talia pulled the curtain back, and they saw Alex lying there.

Ian gasped.

"Oh, buddy," Brooke whispered as thousands of tiny pinpoints danced nervously across the lining of her stomach.

The back portion of the bed had been slightly elevated, giving the impression that Alex was sitting up. His head was perfectly still and cocked back at what looked like an uncomfortable angle. Just looking at the tube that his mouth was taped around made Brooke want to gag. Alex's thin, bare chest was crisscrossed with more tape, which held down countless wires that tailed off toward machines to his left. His right arm was tucked under the sheet, and his left arm was draped off to his side. His little legs stuck out at forty-five-degree angles from under the blanket as tiny drops of urine skittered slowly through a catheter into a drainage bag on the side of the bed.

Despite Talia's words of warning, it was still too much.

Ian stepped in front of Brooke, blocking her view. He slowly turned around and looked at her. She recognized the hollow helplessness in his eyes. *You are helpless*, she thought. *And so am I.*

"Come on," Macey said softly, inviting them to sit down.

"There are chairs over there," Talia said, pointing toward the side of the bed.

"Talia, I'm going to stay here with them for a bit," Macey said.

"Okay," Talia said. "I'll be back shortly."

Brooke firmly gripped the armrests and looked at the white

piece of tape stretched across the top of Alex's tiny right hand. *My buddy's little hand.* Brooke wondered how many times she'd gone into the basement with a wet paper towel and found Alex sleeping. It was that same little hand she'd lifted and wiped clean of Cheetos, popcorn butter, melted chocolate, or anything else he'd eaten while watching TV. It was the same little hand he held up to her last summer as Charlie carried him, running across the front yard toward the house, the swell of a bee sting forming a tiny red mound between his two little knuckles. He'd howled at her, tears racing down his face, wanting her to *please fix it,* to *please make it all better,* to *please make the stinging stop . . .*

How many other times had she bandaged and soothed that little hand?

Now she couldn't help. There was nothing she could do.

Brooke looked back to Alex's small face and knew that he was somewhere in there, quietly crying for her to come, wanting her to somehow help him—to make him better. To *please make it all go away.*

The sickening feeling of helplessness throbbed between her chest and stomach. She closed her eyes and thought of the look Pastor Jim had just given her downstairs. And then she remembered his words.

It's what he wanted her to do.

It's all she could do.

Only believe.

✦ FORTY-EIGHT

The Lindys and Carla reluctantly went home when it was apparent that nothing immediate was going to happen, but they'd been sitting at the house for nearly six hours, staring at a plate of untouched cookies and drinking Jim's especially strong coffee, as if they'd set up their own waiting room. Intermittently, they prayed. They were hoping for something that even resembled favorable news in the periodic updates they were getting from both Ian and Brooke.

So far, good things were not coming to those who waited.

"What did she say?" Jim asked, tilting forward on the La-Z-Boy when Shirley came back from answering the phone.

Shirley sat on the couch, and Carla joined her. As Jim awaited Shirley's answer, he could sense a tiny bubble of hope that fluttered invisibly around the room, bouncing back and forth between his unwavering faith that Alex would be made well and Carla's increasing conviction that things were getting progressively worse.

"The same thing," Shirley said. "She said the same thing that she told you an hour ago."

"Alex still hasn't woken up?"

"He hasn't moved an inch on that bed."

"Did the new nurse say anything? What are the doctors saying?"

"Macey just left," Shirley said, removing her glasses and gently rubbing her eyes. "She's been there this whole time and will be back up there around five thirty in the morning."

"What time is it?"

Shirley looked at her watch. "It's 11:50 p.m."

"And Macey just left?"

"Yes."

"God love her," Jim said, his eyebrows rising in admiration. He stood and started toward the front window. "How did Brooke sound?"

"She sounds exhausted," Shirley said. "And I'm sure Ian is too."

Jim stood at the window. In the reflection he could see Shirley and Carla and Charlie behind him, all staring at him, waiting for him to say the right words. He looked out the window and down the snowy driveway into the darkness that led out to Church Road. There was another face—another expression—that came to his mind. It was Brooke's. He could still see the glance she gave him as they took Alex away to the intensive care unit. He knew that Brooke had always trusted what he told her—and more importantly, he knew she trusted in God. Still, that look she had given him let him know that she wanted just one more nod of reassurance. And he'd given it to her. *Because Alex is going to be okay.*

Jim tensed and then relaxed as his eyes settled on St. Thomas. Even in the dark, there it was. He could see it perfectly clear—the outline of the cross in front of the church.

"Tell her, James . . . Only believe, and he will be made well."

He turned around. "I feel like I need to be up at the hospital with them."

Shirley crossed her arms. "They won't let us in the ICU at this hour, James."

"I feel like I need to talk to them," he said. "To tell her again. To tell them both."

"Tell them what?" Shirley asked.

"Tell them what?" Carla echoed, shaking her head impatiently. "Let me guess—to only believe?"

"Yes," he said. "To only believe."

Carla stood up from the couch and took her turn at the window. She put her hands on top of her head and then slowly looked up at him. "Pastor Jim, you've been telling Brooke that all along."

"I know, Carla," he said. "And Brooke does believe. I know she does."

"I know she does too," Carla said, pausing as if trying to choose her words carefully. "But . . . aren't we *all* ultimately made well? If we only believe?"

Jim frowned, a cool sliver of fear poking at his heart, but Carla continued.

"Ian is scared," she said. "And he doesn't seem like the type of person who gets scared. You should hear his voice."

Jim stepped closer to her and held out his hand. "Carla, we have no control over what is happening, and it's important that—"

"And I'm scared too," Carla interrupted, her voice skipping and her lip beginning to quiver. "I have a really, really bad feeling about this. *Really* bad."

He put his hand on her shoulder. "Carla, what is important is that—"

"Can you please answer the question?" she pleaded, almost like she was ashamed to ask. "My faith is stronger than ever, but, Pastor Jim, aren't we all—all of us—ultimately made well *if we only believe*?"

"Yes," Jim said wearily. She was entirely right. "The answer is yes."

Carla was silent for a long moment. "Brooke's hung her hat on what you told her since the day she found out Alex had leukemia."

Jim glanced over at Shirley, and he could tell by the expression on her face that she was fighting an unwelcome notion that had begun to dance uninvited back and forth across her mind—the idea of life without Alex.

"Tell me," Carla whispered. "Tell me *where* we are all made well if we only believe."

Jim settled his hands on Carla's shoulders but struggled to say what he had to. He looked back at Shirley, who had tears forming in her eyes.

"Answer her, James Lindy," Shirley said bravely. "You know the answer to that question."

Jim closed his eyes. Kenneth was right. Carla was right. And now, Shirley was right.

Why hadn't he seen it?

Jim knew where believers were made well. He pulled Carla closer and hugged her, sickened as he whispered the two words he never thought he would regret saying.

"In heaven."

✦ FORTY-NINE

I sn't it pretty?" Brooke asked.

"Yeah," Ian said.

Neither of them had said a word in close to three hours as they sat side by side next to Alex's bed. Out the window and beyond the hospital parking lot was the southern edge of North Jefferson Avenue and the small business district of downtown Carlson. Even though Brooke's cell phone read 5:07 a.m., the Christmas lights that the Rotary Club had draped across the town's storefronts and streetlights were still on. They pumped an artificial sense of life into the empty streets.

"Did you sleep at all?" Brooke asked.

"A little," Ian said. "I was out for an hour or so. You?"

"I don't know," Brooke said, glancing over at Alex. "I think I did, but I'm really not sure."

Ian considered what she said and he began to second-guess himself, not sure if he slept after all. He sure didn't feel like he had, and if he did, it was not beneficial. He knew he'd gotten up to use the restroom and that Talia had come in and out of the room maybe fifteen times in the last few hours to check on Alex. *Fifteen times?* he thought. *Or did I dream that?* It was hard to tell. He was a notch past exhausted, and part of his subconscious was trying to convince him that none of this was real. It was all one big dream— or maybe he was an actor in a depressing movie or playing a part in a video for some sad song.

"Cat's in the Cradle."

Ian looked at Alex's profile—nothing more than a still

shadow—and thought about the ball mitt he'd just bought for him. You would have thought he'd handed Alex a bag of gold or had given him a brand-new car. His son had watched in amazement as he performed the age-old ritual of properly breaking in the baseball glove. First, he'd rubbed half a jar of Vaseline into the glove's pocket, then he put a baseball in it, and finally, he wrapped a shoestring around it before tossing it under a mattress—Alex's mattress—the same day they'd admitted him to the hospital.

The respirator inhaled and clicked, then exhaled and clicked. As Ian watched his son, the respirator seemed to get louder as the part of his mind that had muted it for the last eleven hours took a much-needed break.

"Can I ask you something?" Brooke asked. "And I want you to be honest with me."

"Sure, Brooke," he said, closing his burning eyes.

She pulled her leg up on the chair and rested her chin on her knee. "What is going through your head right now?"

It wasn't the exact question Ian expected, but a distant relative. He hesitated and then answered honestly. "What's *not* going through my head? That might be a better question."

"I know," Brooke whispered. "It's too much."

Ian's mind drifted back to where it had spent most of the night—not in and out of what he thought was sleep—but in the middle of a cruel tug-of-war between pure sadness and wishful thinking about Alex. He agreed with Brooke. It really was too much. "It's almost like I can't breathe."

"Like you're being suffocated?" she asked, then nodded, as if answering her own question.

"Exactly," Ian said. "It's like a giant glass has been placed over my life, and I'm trapped here in a new world. I feel like I can't take a full breath until Alex gets better. And like we're running out of air—like time is running short—and I want to pick him up, break that glass, and take him with me. But I can't. All I can do is sit here and watch, drowning in the knowledge that there's nothing I can do—nothing at all."

He leaned forward and put his hand up on the side rail and pointed at Alex. "Since I met him, I envisioned so many things that we were going to do. Reading to him, teaching him how to ride a bike, coaching him at football, basketball, golf—anything he wanted to do. I was dying to—"

Ian stopped and glanced over at Brooke, wanting to erase the word he'd just used. "I was *wanting* to spend time with him. Make some memories together. Make up for some of our lost time."

Ian could faintly hear the words to that sad song coming from some distorted channel playing in the back of his mind.

"You can still do those things with him, Ian. You still can."

He put his hand on the side of her arm. "Nothing else matters to me more than him getting better, Brooke. Nothing. And I don't want to say this, but—"

"Don't say it," she said wearily.

Ian dipped his head back toward the floor and waited. "Maybe we need to realize that—"

"Ian, *no.*"

"Brooke, there's a good chance he won't get better." She had to get ready, be prepared.

"Please don't say that, Ian. I don't want to hear that. You shouldn't even be saying that! Here! In his room, where he can hear you!"

He looked at Alex, his tiny chest inflating and deflating, all due to the ventilator. Was he even in there anymore? Was he coming back to them? "Brooke, I know we aren't supposed to think like—"

"Can I tell you something?" Brooke interrupted. "And I really have no idea what made me think of this, but I want to tell you."

"Okay," Ian said reluctantly.

Brooke pulled her other foot up on the chair and rested her arms across the tops of her knees. "I remember when I worked at the plant. Alex was a little over a year old. It was a Friday, and Pastor Jim and Shirley had taken Charlie to the doctor's office with an ear infection, so I took Alex to work with me. It was the only time he ever went there. Remember the nurseries there?"

"Yeah," Ian said.

"They were pretty fancy too," Brooke said. "Among the six rooms, there were probably one hundred to two hundred kids."

"That's a heckuva lot," Ian said.

"Yeah," Brooke agreed. "They really did a good job trying to accommodate single parents. And it was free. I just never took him there before." She paused and then said, "I was only an hour or two into my shift, and I kept imagining I could hear Alex crying. After around ten minutes, I knew I wasn't imagining it. The strange thing about it was that he was on the other side of the plant—not to mention that the production noise was so loud I couldn't hear the worker next to me talking. But still, I knew it was Alex who was crying. I could hear him."

"Kind of a motherly instinct thing?"

"I guess." Brooke nodded. "You were my supervisor that day, Ian. And you let me go check on him. When I got there, I realized that part of that wing had a power failure, and three of the nurseries were filled with kids who were freaking out about the dark, including Alex. Among all those crying kids, in the midst of all that noise, I could still hear his cry, and I knew which room it was coming from. I remember opening the door to the nursery. It was still pretty dark, and they had a little emergency generator light on that barely lit anything, and guess what?"

"What?"

"Alex was right there. Right near the door, leaning against a little fence, holding his arms over the edge. He quit crying and he said, 'Mommy.'"

"So he was already at the gate like he knew you were coming?"

"Yeah," Brooke said. "It's one of those connections, I guess, that mothers can have with their kids."

"I've heard about stuff like that before."

Brooke glimpsed at Alex and bit her lip. "But I know what you're probably feeling. Why you're saying . . ." She shook her head and wrapped her arms around herself. "Because I can't—I just can't feel that connection right now. I look at that bed, and I don't know where he is. That's my son there. That's *our* son right there. That's really Alex. This is all real."

"Too real," Ian said.

"But there's another connection," Brooke said, her composure changing. "There's something else that I feel." She hesitated.

"Go on."

"God's going to make Alex better. I know it." Brooke dropped her feet back on the floor and pointed at the bed. "Pastor Jim told me to believe, and he'd be made well. What I feel is something I simply can't explain. But just like I knew Alex was crying at the plant, I know God is going to make him better. *I know it*."

The door opened on the other side of the curtain, and Brooke and Ian turned to see who it was.

"Good morning," Macey said, stepping around the curtain and standing at the foot of the bed.

"Good morning," Ian said. The doctor looked like she hadn't gotten much more sleep than they had.

"Why don't we go out in the hallway for a minute?" Macey asked.

Ian looked at Brooke and then at Macey. A bit of that instinct that Brooke was just talking about was telling him that things had gone from bad to worse. "What's wrong?"

"Something *else* is wrong?" Brooke asked. "Is something happening?"

"Let's step out in the hall for a minute," Macey repeated. She walked out and they followed her.

Macey crossed her arms and paused. "I just met with Talia and Dr. Kelly. We are *very* concerned."

Ian felt Brooke gripping his arm, and he put his hand on top of hers.

"We've had him on two relatively heavy IVs for his heart and blood pressure."

"Yes," Ian said. "And?"

"And he's not responding like we hoped he would."

"What does that mean?" Ian asked.

"We're concerned that his blood pressure has been down so long that maybe there hasn't been adequate blood flow and oxygen getting to his brain."

"Charlie's brain didn't have enough oxygen," Brooke said. "Is Alex going to be—"

"Brain-damaged?" Ian asked.

"I'm not prepared to say that," Macey said, holding up her hands. "But we have a tech on his way up here that is going to run an EEG in a little bit."

"How long does it take to get the results?" Ian asked.

"It will take him probably twenty minutes to set it up and then thirty to forty minutes to record. We have a neurologist making a special stop by here at seven to read it."

That glass over Ian's life had suddenly gotten smaller. "What are we supposed to do? What can we do?"

"Pray," Brooke said.

Macey nodded in agreement. "Why don't you two run down and get something to eat? The cafeteria just opened."

"I'm not leaving him," Brooke said.

"Me neither," Ian added.

"Please," Macey said. "I'll be here with him."

Ian and Brooke looked at each other, and then Ian took Brooke's arm. "C'mon. Let's go down for a little bit. We're probably going to be here for a while."

"Okay," Brooke conceded. "But I want to go back in the room real quick before we go."

They went back in and Ian looked at Alex. He was doing everything he could to make that connection with his son that Brooke had talked about. As hard as he tried, he just couldn't feel it. *Where are you, partner? I know you're in there. Where are you?*

Brooke stroked Alex's arm and bent down to kiss his head. "We'll be right back, buddy." She turned to walk out the door and Ian went to grab her coat. He paused at the window, overlooking downtown Carlson. Something seemed different out there, and whatever it was somehow managed to sadden him even further.

What is it?

He made his way to the door and stopped. He turned around and went back to look out the window.

"What's wrong?" Brooke asked.

"The Christmas lights," he said.

"What about them?"

"Nothing," he said, quietly staring at Alex's reflection in the window.

The lights had gone off.

✦ FIFTY

D r. Monica Kelly rubbed the edges of the photograph and then tucked it neatly back into the small leather planner in her desk drawer. The picture served as her daily reminder. Every morning before heading out to the floor, she not only checked her normally unpredictable schedule but also counted her blessings.

This morning she was counting a little more.

As head intensivist at East Shore's ICU, Dr. Kelly was the first to see the results of Alexander Thomas's EEG that had just arrived from Neurology. She stepped away from her computer and grabbed a copy of the report off the printer in the far corner of her office. She put the report in a blue folder and slid it tightly under her arm before returning to the desk. She picked up the phone.

"Talia, can you grab Dr. Lewis? I'll be out in about two minutes."

"She's right here," the nurse answered.

"I'll be right there."

Dr. Kelly hung up the phone and stared at the desk drawer.

She opened it back up and took the photo back out of the planner. It was a little over five years old. She held it and looked at her two children—her two *healthy* children—as they played on the swings in the backyard. Jennifer was seven in the picture and was pushing little Jack, who would have been two. He was smiling from ear to ear, hanging on for dear life, not caring in the least about the purple Kool-Aid that had stained both sides of his mouth and the front of his T-shirt.

Dr. Kelly was going to give them each an extra hug tonight when she got home. She kissed the photo, put it back, and left her office.

As she turned the corner of the hallway, she saw Talia and Dr. Lewis standing side by side against the far end of the nurses' station. As Dr. Kelly marched down the corridor toward them, she purposely looked at the floor, not wanting to knock the legs out from underneath what little hope Dr. Lewis had left. Not yet.

"GOOD MORNING," MACEY SAID.

"Good morning," Dr. Kelly echoed, handing the blue folder to Macey, who quickly opened it. It didn't take long for one of the words at the bottom of the report to jump off the page and punch her in the gut.

Flat.

Macey's head pulled back in disappointment, and she could feel a heavy cloak of sympathy from the other two. She shook her head and closed the folder.

"I'm sorry," Dr. Kelly whispered.

Macey glanced at the ceiling. "I've got to go tell the parents."

"I'm sorry, Dr. Lewis," Talia added.

"So am I," Macey said sadly. Even though this was an inevitable part of the business, no other doctor or nurse had *ever* told her they were sorry, and it made her feel uneasy.

There was nothing I could do.

"Are you all right?" Dr. Kelly asked.

"He's a good kid," Macey said. *Was a good kid.*

"Of course," Dr. Kelly said softly.

Macey closed the folder again. "It's a good family."

"I'm sure they are," Dr. Kelly said. "We'll still run another EEG in twenty-four hours, and then we'll see what the family wants to do."

"All right," Macey said.

Talia tapped Macey's elbow. "Do you want me to go with you?"

"I've got it," she said. "Thank you, though, Talia." Macey turned and slowly walked away. Uneasiness began shifting back and forth between her stomach and her throat, growing with each step closer toward Alex's room.

"Dr. Lewis?" Talia said.

She stopped. It felt good to stop. She turned around. "Yes?"

"Dr. Lewis, I want to show you something real quick," the nurse said, tilting her head toward Dr. Kelly as if she were asking permission. The doctor nodded toward her.

Macey walked back to the station, and Talia flipped open yet another folder and made a circle with her finger around a series of blood pressure readings. "Look right here."

She studied the numbers. They didn't make any sense.

"Look at what we were giving him—what we're *still* giving him. Alexander has been on maximum dosage, and his blood pressure hasn't even entertained the idea of staying up. I've never seen anything like it."

Macey glanced suspiciously at Dr. Kelly and then back to the chart.

"Me neither," Dr. Kelly said, lifting her eyebrows and giving her head a little shake. "Not quite like that."

Macey stared at the numbers, reading them three times, then four. "Nor have I. I guess sometimes the cards are stacked against you."

"I know I can't erase your disappointment," Dr. Kelly said. "And I would never say that he had *no* chance. But it certainly looks that way here."

You have no idea, Macey thought.

Dr. Kelly put her elbows on top of the station counter and made a proposal. "We could put him on bypass if you want. He's not the best candidate, but I'd back you on it. See if something changes."

Macey closed her eyes and pinched lightly at her forehead. She shook her head, thinking about Alex—what was left of Alex—hooked to a machine for the next five, ten, or twenty years.

"Don't prolong it."

She could hear the carpenter's perfectly calm voice again.

"Don't prolong it."

"No way," she said, dropping her hand on the countertop. She had no interest in playing God with Alexander Thomas. There was too much competition hanging out at East Shore.

"No way?" Dr. Kelly repeated.

"No way am I putting this family through that. Particularly with these EEG results."

"Of course," Dr. Kelly said. "I respect that decision."

"Are you sure you don't want me to go with you?" Talia asked, looking at her with concern.

"Thank you," Macey said. "I think I've got it."

She turned again and made her way down the hallway to corridor C. She finally stopped and wasn't sure how much time was passing as she stared at the 9 on the door. Would this ever get easier? Giving parents the worst news possible?

But Brooke and Ian were not simply the parents of her patient; they'd also become good friends. She knew she was in no way ready to run through that door with this bomb strapped to her back.

C'mon, Lewis. Let's go. There's no such thing as ready. There's only willing. She opened up the door, walked in, and gently pulled back the curtain.

Ian immediately propped up in his seat, looking eager for good news.

The bottom of Macey's heart felt like it had been dunked in cold water. She looked in Ian's eyes, knowing what a good father he was. And how little time he'd had to try his hand at it.

Brooke was still looking at Alex, and Macey joined her. His head had been turned since the EEG was taken. He was now facing them, and the thick tube that led out of his mouth into the respirator had been replaced and freshly taped.

Macey pulled a chair to the foot of the bed. She ran her hand uncomfortably along the side of her face and then crossed her arms. The respirator seemed like it was the only sound in the room. Inhale—*click.* Exhale—*click.* Inhale—*click.* Alex's little chest went up and down.

"What did the EEG say?" Brooke asked.

"It's not good, you guys."

"What do you mean?" Brooke asked, crouching forward. "It's not good?"

"It was flat," Macey responded, her voice light and apologetic. "The EEG came back flat."

"What does that mean?" Brooke asked in a way that suggested she wasn't quite ready to panic.

"It means . . ."

"He's brain-dead," Ian said numbly, looking back at Alex. "That's what it means, right?"

Macey frowned, watching the shades of sorrow spread across his face. "We are going to do another EEG tomorrow morning. Until we have that report—"

"Brain-dead?" Brooke said, the pitch of her voice heightening. "No, that's impossible. It's not supposed to happen like this. I want to talk to Pastor Jim. I need to talk to Pastor Jim!"

"We'll call him, Brooke," Ian said. He put his arm around her and then turned back to the doctor. "What do we do now?"

"Wait," Macey answered. "All we can do is wait."

"Wait for what?" Brooke asked.

Macey couldn't answer the question. Not yet, anyhow. All she knew was that she had to get to the window.

"Wait for what, Macey?" Brooke repeated.

Macey glanced at both Ian and Brooke. She had done nothing for them, in the end. Everything she had ever worked for—everything she had ever done—was crashing into this one moment of failure. She was at God's mercy and couldn't do anything about it.

"Macey?" Ian asked.

God's mercy.

"Excuse me," she muttered, walking over to the window to look outside.

This time there was no overweight boss, no searching the vast construction site.

He was right there.

The first vehicle she looked at was the truck, and Kenneth was standing in the center of the bed with his arms crossed, looking right up at her.

"Macey?" Brooke asked, wanting an answer to her question. "What is it?"

Macey stared straight down at the carpenter.

Let me ask you something, big man. Mary Springsted, the cross, Zach Norman, Pastor Jim's eyesight—you hold the power. You know all the answers to every question ever asked. I'm going to ask again. Why these people? They are some of your biggest fans. Why this boy?

Kenneth didn't move.

"Macey!" Brooke shouted, crying now. "Why aren't you answering me?"

But Macey could only put her head closer to the glass. *What are we waiting for, Kenneth?*

Kenneth just stared.

I'm not a quitter. I did my best. But I can't win. I can't beat you.

Kenneth lowered his arms to his sides and then tilted his head to his right. Macey could feel his stare running right through her.

I'm not prolonging this. I did what you said. You're prolonging it. Why?

Kenneth stepped off the back of the tailgate onto the ground.

"Tell us," Ian said. "Go ahead and tell us. We know why you're hesitating. Why you don't want to say it."

I didn't prolong it, Kenneth. Why are you? Tell me. Please, tell me.

Brooke was sobbing.

Kenneth turned and walked toward the new wing.

"Don't you walk away from me," Macey gritted out, belatedly realizing it was aloud.

Ian rose and joined her at the window, just as Kenneth slipped behind a construction trailer.

Brooke was choking, she was crying so hard. Ian turned to kneel beside her and missed Kenneth appearing on the far side of the trailer, heading down the wooden walkway.

Macey's face was an inch from the glass and her inner voice screamed at a fevered pitch. *Tell me, Kenneth! What are you waiting for?*

Kenneth stopped in his tracks, and Macey held her breath. She waited, and he still didn't move. Behind her, the respirator continued to raise little Alex's chest, then let it fall. As it would for hours, days, months . . .

"You win," she whispered.

Kenneth slowly turned around. There was something different about his stare this time. It didn't run through her. It *filled* her.

"You win," she repeated.

"Who are you talking to?" Ian asked.

Macey pulled back a little farther from the window and waited. And then she did something she never thought she would be capable of doing. She let go. She surrendered.

She waited a moment longer, and she and the carpenter continued to stare at each other. She took a deep breath, paused again, and then she finally said it.

"Take him."

The oxygen saturation alarm sounded, wailing and turning Ian's head.

"What is that?" Brooke screamed, trying to get around Ian to Alex.

The blood pressure alarm was next.

"No!" Brooke screamed. "No! Please, no!"

The heart monitor went off last.

Macey spun around and yanked a white spiral cord on the wall, calling the Code Blue. The last one.

"I want to talk to Pastor Jim!" Brooke cried, drowned out by the chorus of alarms as she clung to Ian. "Please! Please!"

Within thirty seconds five ICU members were working on Alex. Two more showed up and failed to usher Brooke out of the room. Ian had to pick her up and carry her out into the hallway, with Macey right behind them.

"What are we supposed to do now?" Ian asked.

Macey answered him with a question and felt like she was handing him the nails to a tiny coffin. "How long do you want to do this?"

"What are you talking about?" Brooke asked, clinging to Ian's arm. "It's not supposed to be like this! I want to talk to Pastor Jim!"

"How long?" Macey repeated. "Until you let him go?"

"What are you saying?" Brooke asked, trying to catch her breath. "We can't let him go! God is going to make him better!"

Macey shook her head. "No, Brooke. We can keep his body going, but . . ."

"Well you just keep him going!" Brooke screamed.

Macey felt like she had switched into autopilot. Feelings were gone, and words just came. "The part of Alex's brain that lets him breathe can go on for years, Brooke. *Years*."

"What are you suggesting we do?" Ian asked.

"Listen to me," Macey said. "Please listen to me. Even if Alex were to somehow come out of this, he won't be the same little boy you knew."

"No, no, no!" Brooke cried. "He is gonna get better. He's *supposed* to. I believed. I believed!" She put her fist to her mouth, staring at Macey like she was a monster. Behind her, another nurse and orderly ran into Alex's room. "I want to call Pastor Jim."

"I want you to call him too," Macey said, taking Brooke's arm. "I want you to call him and have him come up here right now with Shirley, Carla, Charlie, and whoever else you want."

"What do we do until then?" Ian asked.

"Please do something, Macey," Brooke said. "I love him so much."

"I know you do," Macey said, emotion suddenly returning to the stage and forcing her to fight off her own tears. "Brooke and Ian—I love Alex too. I love that little boy. But he isn't here anymore. And he won't be." She dropped her voice. "Please, you guys, please."

"Please . . . what?" Brooke asked, dread in her eyes.

"Please do the right thing."

"What's the right thing?"

Don't cry, Macey Lewis. Don't you dare cry.

Macey closed her eyes and then struggled to slowly open them back up. "Let him go," she whispered.

Brooke stepped back as if she'd been slapped. She looked up at Ian.

"He's already gone," Ian said, his own eyes beginning to well.

Brooke quickly covered her ears and looked at Macey.

The doctor knew that Brooke was completely lost and searching for another answer that wouldn't come—ever.

"I am sorry," Macey said. "I'm so sorry."

"Don't side with her, Ian. Help me," Brooke pleaded, cringing and making fists that pounded at her sides. "We have to stand up for Alex!"

"Exactly," Macey said. "Stand up for him by doing what's best for him." She reached out to put her hand on Brooke's shoulder.

"No," Brooke said in a child's voice, edging away. She then went completely silent.

"Brooke," Macey said. She held her arms open, waiting, and Brooke broke then, looking as if she was going to collapse.

Brooke stepped slowly forward, her arms at her sides, and leaned against the doctor. Macey wrapped her arms around her.

"Let him go," Macey whispered.

Ian put his arms around both of them and repeated Macey's words. "He won't be the same little boy we knew . . ."

"But he was so excited," Brooke said, sniffling and shifting her head on Macey's shoulder. "He was so excited about getting a bike that didn't have training wheels. And he wanted a lunch box with a thermos in it, because he was going to go to school on the big kids' bus for the whole day, and he—"

"It's time," Macey said softly. "It's time to free him."

There was a pause. Macey could feel Brooke's heart thumping against her ribs.

"My baby is gone," Brooke muttered. "He's gone already, isn't he?"

"Yes," Macey whispered.

Brooke shifted her face from Macey's shoulder to Ian's chest. He held her, and then they both turned and looked at Alex's door, clinging to each other.

"Go ahead, buddy," Brooke said, closing her eyes. "Go ahead."

Ian nodded at Macey as his lip quivered. "Let him go."

Macey put her arms around them and watched as the tears began to race down the sides of Ian's face.

"I'll go inform the team of your wishes," she said.

✢ FIFTY-ONE

B rooke hadn't said a word in over fifteen minutes, and she knew for certain that she wasn't all there at the moment. Neither was Ian.

The big capital *E* in the East Shore sign on the wall kept coming in and out of focus as she stared dreamily down the hallway. There wasn't any sound. Everything was fuzzy and moving slowly.

Whatever was in her brain that was now cushioning her from the blow of Alex's death had transformed Corridor C into a colorless, emotionless wasteland. She didn't cry. She couldn't seem to form words. She couldn't seem to care.

Her head stayed glued to Ian's side as the last two members of the code team finally came out of the room. To her, they were like faceless apparitions, characters from an ongoing nightmare, gliding past. She clung to Ian's arm and turned her head back toward C-9. The door was still open, and inside was her dead child.

Dead child. Alex is dead.

She could already imagine Alex in that bed, and the thought of it added another drip of the natural painkiller that made things blurrier still.

Macey came out from around the door, and Brooke knew it was time.

She lifted her head off of Ian's arm. Every movement took effort, as if her body had been cracked open and filled with sand.

"Did you get ahold of Pastor Jim?" Macey asked, looking with compassion from one to the other. Brooke focused in on her face long enough to see that she was hurting too.

"They should be up here any minute," Ian said.

"Do you want to wait for them?"

"No," he said, looking down at Brooke. "I think . . . I think it'd be good for us to see him alone first."

Brooke nodded. Not because she agreed. But because dimly, she thought it would be what was expected of a mother. *Why can't I feel anything?*

"All right," Macey said, holding the door open. "I'll come with you."

They walked into the room and stood behind the curtain. Brooke momentarily panicked, thinking they'd all forgotten to don masks and gloves, but then remembered they weren't needed.

Not needed. Not needed. Not needed . . .

Macey began to slowly pull the curtain back, but Brooke looked away, out the window at snow floating down in thick, wet flakes into the parking lot below. Alex loved to play in the snow. Brooke had bought him a new sled for his birthday . . . It was in the garage.

Who will I give that to now? Can I return it? Maybe Charlie wants it . . .

The sound of the top curtain rings moving drew her attention, the only sound in the room. There was no longer any soft beeping or chirping coming from the monitors. There was no more puffing and clicking from the respirator. It was quiet.

Quiet, so quiet . . .

The curtain slid open enough to expose the machines to the right of Alex's bed, all off now, their flickering numbers replaced by blank and dull gray screens. *Time to watch over another patient.*

Another patient. Not Alex. Never again, Alex.

Macey finished opening the curtain and stood on the opposite side, waiting. Brooke knew she should look down, force herself to look at Alex, but she couldn't.

I can't. I can't. I can't.

She looked up and to her right at Ian. She tried to take in the empty look on his face as he stared at what she knew was their dead son. Slowly, she turned her head back toward the bed, and there Alex was.

The breathing tube had been taken out of his mouth, and his IVs had been removed. The back of the bed was propped up, and the side rails were lowered. Alex's head was positioned straight forward, centered on his pillow, with his chin tilted up slightly. The sheet had been pulled up to just below his shoulders, barely exposing the port in the top of his chest. His arms were draped straight down to his sides, and his tiny hands were flat on the sheet. His mouth was slightly open, and a small voice inside of Brooke said, *Wake up, buddy, wake up. The Pop-Tarts are done. Charlie's waiting for you. He wants to watch a show.*

Ian stepped to the side of the bed. He just stood and stared, almost as if he were on guard, frozen by the brutal, blunt unfairness of what was before them.

On legs that didn't feel like her own, Brooke walked past Macey and went to the other side of the bed. She wasn't sure how long it took her to get there. Alex's cheeks were a little puffy and stretched into a dark pink color from the tube that had been in his mouth. A new bruise was starting to appear on the side of his neck, and she could see a sliver of an opening in his right eye. Still, he looked like he was sleeping, and she sadly wondered if he'd finally met her parents . . . *his grandma and grandpa.* She hoped they'd find him. Maybe he was already parked on one of their laps, talking about all that had happened over the last five years.

Six. He was going to be six on Saturday.

"Go ahead and sit on the bed if you want," Macey said.

Brooke put her hand on the sheet and then quickly pulled it back.

Ian stepped closer. "I want to touch him. Can I, Macey?"

"Yes," Macey said, prompting Ian to put his hand on the side of Alex's face. "Go ahead and hold him, if you want." Brooke thought she heard her voice crack.

Brooke sat her hip on the edge of the bed, and Alex moved slightly up and down with her weight. For a moment she thought he had moved on his own and her heart leaped. She imagined for a second that they were all wrong—that he was still there—that he'd been made well because she really had believed.

But her skyrocketing hope came crashing down as Ian cradled the side of Alex's neck in his hand. Ian's face didn't light up with joy. Instead he silently bent down and tenderly kissed Alex's head.

Brooke looked back at Macey. It now seemed as if they were each playing their little parts in this big nightmare—or was it big parts in a little nightmare? She wanted to cry it out, but the tears just wouldn't come.

"They're here," Macey said quietly, looking toward the door, then at Brooke and Ian. "Do you want them to wait?"

Brooke just stared at her, not able to decide if she cared at all. Ian answered, "Have them come in."

Macey stepped back and gave way to Pastor Jim and Carla, who both gave the doctor hugs before stepping around the curtain to the foot of the bed. They both looked at Alex, and it was immediately too much for Carla, who covered her eyes with her hands and leaned against Pastor Jim. Pastor Jim put his arm around her and glanced at Brooke as she blinked heavily without saying a word.

Ian came and held Carla, who had started sobbing uncontrollably. Pastor Jim touched the side of Ian's face, and their eyes met. Ian merely nodded.

Pastor Jim came to Brooke's side then, and she stood and stared up at him. *You said. You said it. You said if I only believed . . .*

"I'm sorry, honey," Pastor Jim whispered. "I didn't mean to mislead you."

Brooke's lip quivered, and the words melted away at the back of her mind.

Only believe.

Pastor Jim hugged her, but she wasn't hugging back. Her arms dangled loosely at her sides. She looked to the door and saw Shirley step through it.

Charlie was with her.

Shirley guided Charlie by the arm and took him to the

opposite side of the bed. Charlie's expression went from one of cautious obedience—one that knew not to touch anything and to stay out of the way—to one of uncontrollable joy when he saw Alex. He'd noticed that Alex no longer had the wires plugged into him, so he must have thought that good things were happening. Charlie slowly lifted his finger up to his lips, making a *shh* motion for everyone to be quiet, as if he didn't want anyone to wake his friend up.

"Does he know?" Ian asked, his voice strangled.

"We told him," Shirley said, embracing Brooke, "but it will take him a bit to accept it. To understand." They watched as Pastor Jim placed his hand on the side of Alex's head and then bowed his own.

Carla tried to stifle her sobs and came around to hug Brooke. "I'm so sorry," she whispered.

Brooke didn't say anything. She wanted to talk. She wanted to cry. But she couldn't.

Pastor Jim turned around and took Brooke's arm. "I know you believed. And I need you to believe me, honey. Alexander *has* been made well." He tilted his head toward Alex. "I want you to take Alex's hand." He guided her back to the edge of the bed. "Everybody, please join me."

Brooke lifted Alex's right hand, waiting in vain for him to move.

They joined hands all the way around the bed, and Charlie followed suit, providing the last link by reaching down and picking up Alex's left hand. They all bowed their heads.

"Lord," Pastor Jim said, pausing, "we want to thank you for welcoming Alex—"

"Hang on, James," Shirley whispered.

"Charlie?" Carla said. "It's okay, Charlie."

Charlie had let go of Alex's hand and stepped back from the bed. He looked at his mother and then his father. He reached down with two fingers and lightly tapped at the top of Alex's hand. He glanced up at Brooke, ran his hand across his chin, and then picked Alex's hand back up. Brooke knew that Charlie didn't like the way Alex's hand felt.

Charlie turned his head toward Pastor Jim. He tapped again at Alex's hand, pressed his thumb against it, and rubbed it in a tiny circle. He looked over at Ian, who was shaking his head and weeping, and then looked at Shirley and Carla, who'd begun to cry again.

Charlie crouched over the edge of the bed and put his arm above Alex's head. He touched the side of Alex's cheek and then dipped his shoulder and head next to Alex's face. He gently tapped at Alex's forehead with his finger and then patiently waited.

Brooke just stared. *He wants to see who smiles first.*

No more smiles. No more smiles. No more smiles.

Charlie glanced desperately at Pastor Jim when Alex didn't respond. It was at that moment that Brooke knew Charlie realized Alex was gone. Not sleeping, but gone forever. Charlie's eyes rounded sadly as he stood, pulled a Tic Tac container out of his pocket, and then picked Alex's arm back off the bed. He took Alex's hand, opened it, and put the Tic Tac in his palm. He then coiled Alex's hand around the candy and carefully placed Alex's arm back at his side.

"Take his hand, son," Pastor Jim said.

Slowly, reluctantly, Charlie did as he was told, completing their circle.

"This is not the last time you'll hold his hand, Charles Lindy," Pastor Jim said. "Someday, when you're reunited in heaven, you'll hold it again. I promise." He looked around the group. "Let's pray. Father, we thank you that even in our sadness, Alex is experiencing total joy right now. We ask that you comfort us as we mourn his loss and yet celebrate in the knowledge that he is with you . . ."

As Pastor Jim prayed, Brooke looked up and around at all the people who loved Alex best. Behind Carla and Shirley, at the foot of the bed, Macey, Kaitlyn, and Zach stood, heads bowed. Macey's lip was trembling, and tears were running down Kaitlyn's face.

Pastor Jim finished his prayer and nodded to Zach and Kaitlyn. "Thanks for being here, friends. Would you join us in the chapel?"

Brooke noticed neither of them answered. They were both just staring at the bed, as was everyone else.

Charlie had lowered himself to one knee and was leaning against the side of the bed. His left arm was draped across Alex's chest, and his enormous head was resting on her dead son's bare shoulder. Charlie's eyes were closed, and Brooke could see the pair of tears that was slowly heading down his cheek. She couldn't help noticing that with each breath Charlie took, Alex's head shifted ever so slightly on the pillow.

"Please excuse me," Macey said, stepping back to the other side of the curtain.

Brooke went quietly to the foot of the bed and edged around the curtain too.

Macey was standing at the window. Brooke remembered how Macey had stared out that window . . . right before Alex died. And right now, looking anywhere but at Alex was what Brooke needed most. She stepped up beside Macey, and the doctor wrapped her arm around her waist. Together, they looked out into the snow.

"It's gone," Macey said softly.

What's gone? Brooke wanted to ask. But she couldn't make her lips form the words.

"His truck," Macey said dully. "Kenneth is gone."

Then the doctor turned and left the room.

✦ FIFTY-TWO

The AUTHORIZED PERSONNEL ONLY elevator beeped three times, and then its door hummed and closed smoothly behind her. Macey was back on the third floor and felt fortunate that nobody was in the hallway. She glanced sadly to her left through the small window of the gray double doors that led back to the Bone Marrow Transplant unit. Down on the right-hand side, she could see the door of the room Alex had been in before they took him up to the ICU.

She closed her eyes and then sighed as a dose of sorrow filtered through her like water through sand. She turned and made her way down the hallway. She didn't want anybody to see her. What she really wanted was to go home and stick her head under her pillow. She wanted to let it all out. But she couldn't do it here.

Anywhere but here. Don't you dare cry here, Macey Lewis. All you have to do is get to your office. Just make it there.

She passed the nurses' station unseen and then started down the hall toward her office. She'd almost made it when she heard Zach's voice behind her. "Macey!" he called.

She stopped and froze like a teenager whose late-night plans of disappearing out the back door had just been thwarted. She stood in front of her office and didn't respond to Zach. *I have to get inside, because I'm about to lose it.* She opened the door and went inside, almost making it to her desk when she heard Kaitlyn's voice.

"Macey?"

She couldn't answer. She only gasped for breath, widening her eyes, trying to hold on just a little longer . . .

375

She knew both Kaitlyn and Zach were in the doorway, but she couldn't face them. They already knew the truth.

"He was right," Macey said, keeping her back to them. She frowned and bit her lip. "My best wasn't good enough."

"You gave it everything you had," Kaitlyn said. "That's all anyone could ever ask."

"Macey," Zach said. She could hear him come into the office. "You have to believe me when I say that Alex is in a good place—the best place. I know for a *fact* that he is all right."

"I know *you* know," she said. She leaned forward and put her palms flat on her desk, holding herself up. She shook her head and paused. "What I don't know is about all of *this* anymore."

"All of what?" Kaitlyn asked.

"The hospital. My work. How do I know I'm making any difference with these kids here? Any difference at all?"

"What do you mean?" Zach asked.

Macey lifted her arms and put her hands behind her head. She took a deep breath and turned to face them. "I'm not in control of anything here. I always thought I was saving kids' lives. That's why I became a doctor—to do just that. But now I know—and I think you two also know—that we really aren't the ones in control of much at all."

Zach studied her. "I understand. I became a doctor to save kids' lives too—mostly to make up for the one I couldn't save." His sister. He was talking about his sister. Kaitlyn had told her about their visit to her grave site and Zach's experience there with Kenneth.

"It doesn't seem fair," Macey said. "It *isn't* fair. At the end of the day, regardless of what we do here, if a certain *Somebody* thinks a child's life on earth is over, there's absolutely nothing we can do about it."

"Looks that way," Zach said. "We do our best. But ultimate power is not our own."

Macey crossed her arms. "And you accept it just like that?"

"Yeah," he said, with the hint of a peaceful smile.

It irritated her, his peace. "Pastor Jim was blind for twenty years," Macey said. "Charlie has never said a word, and did you know that Brooke's parents were killed in a motorcycle accident?"

"Yes," he said.

"And now this," she added, preparing to ask the question once again. It was the same question that was without an acceptable answer. "Why? Why these people? These people who do good things for God? And more importantly, what does God have in store for them *next*?"

"I don't know," Zach said.

Her shoulders slumped, and she shook her head. "Alex was five years old. He was a good kid, a good son, and a good friend to somebody who doesn't have a whole lot of friends. Now he's gone. Does a loving God let things like that happen to people?"

"Yes, he does."

"Why? Tell me why."

"I said I don't know, Macey. But I know that someday we will."

"I could have saved him, Zach. If God had let me. And if he won't let me . . . why even bother?"

"Look at me," he said, stepping closer to her. "There's something you need to know."

"What?" she asked, crossing her arms.

He took her by the shoulders and spoke quickly. "Alex won't be the last patient you'll ever lose. I promise you that. But God will still use you, Macey. He smiles whenever any of us use the gift he's given us. And he's given you a doozy. There are kids here who need you, Macey, and you better believe there will be more. Do you hear me?"

She turned away.

"Don't you dare give up, Macey Lewis," Kaitlyn said, stepping closer. "We *all* need you here."

Macey swallowed hard, then covered her face.

"Don't hold it in," Zach said. "I know how you feel. It's okay, Macey. Let it go. Let it go now."

"What?" Macey asked. "Let what go?"

"Play tough all you want," he said. "But there's something else I want to tell you. Turn around and look at me."

Hesitantly, she did.

"Here is why you'll keep doing it, regardless of the heartache," Zach said. "Guess what God does with the kids he isn't quite ready for?"

"What?" she said.

Zach grinned, and then his smile slowly faded. "He puts them in your hands, Macey Lewis. Your hands."

"You don't know that."

"Yes, I do."

She looked back at him. "How?"

"Because Kenneth told me. He told me to tell you that. And he also told me that I would know when to say it. And that time is now."

"God puts them in my hands?" she asked in a tiny voice, her head lowering.

"Yes," Zach said. He put his finger under her chin and gently lifted her head. "And don't you ever forget that."

Macey just stared at him. She could still hear Alex calling her "Docca Lewis" and constantly asking her when he could go home.

It was at that moment she realized that he already was home. She then became perfectly still and lowered her head again. She took a deep breath and could feel her shoulders start to shake—and then her bottom lip. She closed her eyes tightly, desperately fighting the first tear from coming.

"It's okay," Zach said, holding out his arms.

Macey slowly looked at Kaitlyn, then to Zach. When their eyes met, she could somehow feel Zach's faith and knew he was right. It really was okay. She leaned forward to hug him, sighed, and began to cry uncontrollably.

Kaitlyn joined them and the three of them clung together, shaking as they all wept.

✛ FIFTY-THREE

The small chapel at East Shore was located on the first floor, directly through the main entrance and past the greeting center. It was tucked neatly between the gift shop and the main elevators, and its exterior was bricked in a deep brown, both separating and identifying it distinctly from the light tan drywall and paneling that ran the balance of the same hallway.

Brown double doors with thick black handles led to an interior that was carpeted in light beige. Twelve darkly stained pews were perfectly angled inward, split by an aisle that ran from the entrance to a two-step, rounded platform, which held a small altar and standard pulpit.

A dark wooden cross that matched the pews was mounted on the front wall, dramatically lit in the otherwise shadowy pulpit area. It instantly evoked a spirit of contemplation, perfect for those who often came here with desperate requests, or those reeling from bad news, seeking a place to anchor.

Jim was standing at the pulpit, looking at Brooke in the first row between Ian and Carla. Her cheeks were overly pale, and he hadn't heard her say a word since seeing Alex dead. She was staring vacantly at the floor with her hands in her lap and her head on Carla's shoulder. Directly behind them were Shirley and Charlie, who were only a few feet from Kaitlyn, Zach, and Macey.

Jim rested his arms on the pulpit and closed his eyes. *Lord, thank you for blessing our lives with Alex, and thank you for welcoming him into your kingdom. I ask that you give us strength and ask that you give me the right words to—*

He heard the creak of the floor and opened his eyes. Zach was up on the landing and walked right past him. Jim turned around and, in amazement, watched Zach kneel before the cross and bow his head. *Thank you, Lord,* Jim prayed silently. *How far you've brought this man—*

Charlie stood and stepped out into the main aisle. He ran his hand across the top of his head and down along the side of his face as he went up on the curved platform and took three huge steps to join Zach. They all watched as he went to one knee and dipped his head, imitating Zach. Zach and Charlie shared a long look, and Jim could see the tears that had begun to stream once again down his son's face. Zach put his hand on Charlie's shoulder and then squeezed the base of his neck. Then they both bowed their heads again.

Shirley joined them, right next to Charlie.

Kaitlyn nodded at Macey, then they stood up and walked up the aisle and onto the dais. They kneeled to Zach's left.

Jim could see Carla saying something to Brooke. Brooke didn't respond; Ian nodded for Carla to join the others, and she did.

Jim watched Ian pull Brooke closer, wrap his arm around her, and put his chin on top of her head. Then he whispered in her ear. It still didn't look like Brooke said anything; she just leaned forward, and Ian helped her to her feet. They seemed stiff and sore from the weeks of bedside vigil, but Jim knew that pain would soon go away, leaving only their sore hearts. They walked like an old couple up the two steps, and Ian held Brooke, guiding her as they slowly angled to the right side of the huddle to kneel next to Shirley.

Jim left the pulpit. He went up behind the others and took a knee, purposefully wedging himself between Shirley and Brooke. Brooke's arms were at her sides, and she was staring at the carpet. She slowly turned her head and glanced up at him, and it pained Jim to see that her eyes no longer held the certainty, the unwavering confidence in him, that she'd long shared with him.

"I'm sorry," he whispered. He knew it wasn't enough, but it was all he could say. He wanted more than ever for her to say something back.

Brooke just stared at him for a few seconds. Her mouth barely opened, and Jim knew she was about to say something. She turned her head all the way toward him and then suddenly stopped and leaned back to look past him.

Jim looked over his shoulder, and Kaitlyn was patting at the sides of her face.

Zach lowered his hand and put it on her back. "You okay?"

Kaitlyn slid her hands across the back of her neck. She shook her head and loudly said, "I can feel it. I can feel that buzz. I can feel him."

"Who?" Zach asked.

"He's here," Kaitlyn said.

"Who is here?"

"Him," she answered. The nurse stood and turned around, looking toward the back of the chapel.

Kenneth was standing near the back door.

They all stood and turned to face him.

Jim noticed that the snow that had fallen on the shoulders and arms of the carpenter's coat still hadn't melted. His hair was matted and wet, and he ran his fingers through it, moving it straight back off his forehead. He just stood there, and it became clear to Jim that Kenneth was staring at Brooke.

Kenneth finally slid his hands into his coat pockets, and as he slowly walked up the aisle, droplets of melting slush slid off the top edges of his tattered work boots, leaving a trail of water spots on the carpet behind him.

He stopped between the first and second pews, never taking his eyes off of Brooke. It was utterly silent as the two stared at each other. Brooke finally broke her silence.

"I believed."

Kenneth didn't flinch.

"Did you hear me?" she said, loud enough for a tiny echo. "I *believed*."

Kenneth didn't move.

"You told Pastor Jim that if I only believed, Alex would be made well."

Kenneth took his hands out of his pockets and walked to the base of the first step, directly before her.

Jim suddenly thought about Alex. He wondered if his body was still lying up in the hospital room, or if his body had been taken to the morgue. "Alex is with God, Brooke. Kenneth was right. He *has* been made well."

She ignored him, focusing only on Kenneth. "What am I going to do without Alex?" Brooke asked, tears filling her eyes. She stepped out from under Ian's arm toward the carpenter and crossed her arms. "What am I supposed to do now?"

"Continue on," Jim said.

Kenneth looked up at Carla, Shirley, the doctors, and then Kaitlyn. Zach nodded at Kenneth, but Kenneth just turned his head back to Brooke once again.

Brooke threw her arms up and let them drop. She lifted one back up and pointed at the carpenter. "I thought you *knew* God, you know that? There are people in this room who actually thought you were something bigger than just a carpenter. They, *we*, thought you had a direct line to God! But I guess not. In the end, it turns out you're just a carpenter."

They all seemed to wait for Kenneth to say something. He didn't.

"It's my fault," Jim said. "I misunderstood what Kenneth said. He was right. I was wrong."

"Thank you, James," the carpenter said calmly. "Thank you."

Jim held his hands up. He had no idea what the carpenter was talking about. "Thank you for what?"

"You tell them what to do," Kenneth said. "They rarely do it, but you certainly tell them, and you always have. I thank you for that."

"And you," he added softly, nodding at Brooke. "I thank you too. You were told to only believe."

"But I was also told he'd be made well. What about that?"

"James," Kenneth said, pointing at the pulpit. "You didn't read it."

"Read what?"

Kenneth's head didn't move. His eyes looked away from Brooke to Jim. "Verse 7:14."

"No, my friend," Jim said, lifting his hands again. "The verse was 8:50 that told her to only believe. It was 7:14 when I could see. You somehow knew that."

"Why are you doing this?" Ian growled, clearly fed up and taking a step toward the carpenter. "What's your point, man? Our son just died."

"Right there," Kenneth said in an even voice, pointing to a Bible on the top of the pulpit. "It's right there. I was hoping you would read it for us, James."

"Please stop," Brooke whispered.

"Why are you doing this?" Ian asked, taking another step.

Brooke put her hands back over her face and started crying again, and it seemed to make Ian even angrier.

Kenneth reached over and gently started to pull Brooke's hands from her face, and Ian laid hold of the carpenter's wrist, looking like he was about to punch him.

"It's all right, Ian," Kenneth said, placing his other hand on top of Ian's.

Ian squinted and looked bewildered. His hand fell limply to his side, his mouth dropping open.

Kenneth nodded at Ian and then lowered Brooke's hands. "You were told to believe, Brooke."

"I already told you," Brooke cried, her hands in his. "I really did believe, and now Alex is gone."

"Yes, you did," Kenneth said. The smallest hint of a smile creased his lips. "Your belief was real. It was beautiful. It was without the slightest reservation."

"But it didn't do him any—"

"You believed Alex would be made well as if he already was—as if it was a given. You did your part, Brooke."

Brooke cried harder.

"James," Kenneth said, still looking at Brooke. "The verse was 8:50."

"I know," Jim said. He wasn't sure why the carpenter was finally agreeing with him.

"But that is only part of the reason why I am here," Kenneth said. His eyes shifted back to Jim, and he held up his hand. "Verse 7:14 is also from the book of Luke."

Jim cast a confused glance at the others on the landing. "But Luke 7:14 doesn't have anything to do with someone getting their sight back. I know the verse, Kenneth."

"I know you do, James."

Jim thought about the verse, and the back of his neck suddenly warmed. "But, Kenneth, Luke 7:14 is where—"

"I do my part," the carpenter said, locking eyes again with Brooke.

"Will you please stop?" Brooke said. "Haven't we gone through enough? You're making it worse . . ." She broke off into crying.

Jim stepped back to the pulpit. "Kenneth, I don't think you really understand what that verse actually says. That is where—"

"Please read it," Kenneth said.

Jim opened the Bible and thumbed quickly to the verse.

"From the book of Luke," he said, looking almost obediently at Kenneth, "chapter 7, verse 14." Jim looked over at Shirley and then down at the Bible and began to read.

"Then he went up and touched the coffin . . . and those carrying it stood still. He said, 'Young man, I say to you, get up!'"

Jim stopped and looked at the carpenter, and Kenneth nodded and then repeated part of the verse.

"Young man, I say to you, get up."

"Stop it!" Brooke cried.

"Let him be," Ian said, his eyes glued to the carpenter.

Kenneth kept his eyes on Brooke. "Please keep reading, James. The next verse."

Jim battled for air. He gripped the sides of the pulpit and read on:

"The dead man sat up and began to talk, and Jesus gave him back to his mother."

Jim lifted his head again, his heart thundering in his chest.

"One more verse, James," Kenneth said calmly.

"Please," Brooke cried. "Please, please stop. I can't . . . I can't keep listening to this."

Kenneth pointed at the Bible. "Read it, James. Keep going."

Brooke covered her face with her hands, and Jim continued to read:

"They were all filled with awe and praised God. 'A great prophet has appeared among us, they said.'"

"Leave!" Brooke screamed, hysterical now. "Just leave!"

"Keep going, James!" the carpenter said, the urgency in his voice rising. "Please finish the verse!"

Jim's eyes scanned what followed. The words seemed to jump off the page. His stomach tightened, and then he cautiously glanced up from the Bible toward Brooke and the carpenter. He couldn't look. He tried again, but he just couldn't look at Kenneth.

Good Lord.

Jim turned toward Carla and then looked at the two doctors. Next to them, Kaitlyn was rubbing at the back of her neck again, and Jim couldn't stop himself from doing the same thing. Jim picked the Bible up and walked directly behind Brooke with his head down. He tried again and failed to look at Kenneth. The verse was perfect. Now it all made sense.

"Pastor Jim? Please, Pastor Jim," Brooke cried. "Make him go. Why aren't you making him go? What's he doing here?"

"Answer her question, James," Kenneth said. "Answer it. Read the answer."

Jim didn't have to read it. He already knew it, but he opened the Bible back up and read it anyhow.

"God has come to help his people."

They all looked at one another and the room became quiet, except for Brooke's sobs.

She finally broke the silence. "God is not here," she said, shaking her head. "If he were here, he—"

Jim covered her mouth with his hand and then slowly took it away.

Kenneth stared up at Charlie for a good ten seconds and then slowly lowered his head.

The room had gone quiet again. Even Brooke quieted. It was as if they all held their breath, none of them clear on how this could possibly turn out.

Except for Jim. Jim could *see* it.

One tear trickled down the center of the carpenter's left cheek. It worked its way down to his jaw and then fell to the front of his coat.

Kenneth looked up at Jim and spoke slowly. "James, I want you to tell them that everything happens for a reason. And you tell them that even in those times when it seems like God isn't listening . . . that they need to give up control . . . and they just need to know that they don't *have to know* why God does things . . . or why he allows things to happen . . . and that they should just continue to do as you have. Tell the people that God is trustworthy. Tell them that every single thing he does is for only one reason . . . and that is *the* reason."

Jim waited, absorbing the carpenter's words. He looked at the others, then back to Kenneth. "*What* is the reason?"

Kenneth turned his face up to the ceiling, hands outstretched. And then he began to cry. After a long minute, he looked straight back at Brooke, who continued to cry with him.

Zach stepped around Kaitlyn, as if to console Kenneth, but the carpenter lifted his arm for the doctor to be still. Kenneth stepped up closer to the altar. He then turned around and lifted his arm and pointed it right at Brooke.

"What?" Brooke pleaded. "What are you doing?"

Kenneth continued to hold his arm out straight at her. They all waited.

"What?" Brooke repeated.

Kenneth pulled his hand back and wiped another tear off his cheek. He studied it for a second and then lifted his arm up and pointed right back at her. He nodded at Brooke, and then he slowly swung his arm back to the chapel entrance. They all turned and looked.

Alex was standing there.

Brooke collapsed and Charlie caught her. Ian froze. Carla hugged Shirley as Kaitlyn and Macey clung to Zach. Jim could feel a tiny pool of sweat growing in his palm, affecting his grip on the Bible.

He has come to help his people.

Jim dropped to his knees, as Shirley had done.

Alex had his arms wrapped around himself as if he were cold, and he was looking down at the floor. He was still wearing his Spider-Man underwear. The port that had been in his chest was gone. His hair was back. He rubbed at his eyes with tiny fists and then dropped his arms to his sides, exposing the thin ribs of his small chest.

Charlie helped Brooke regain her feet.

Jim held his hands up toward the ceiling. "Praise God," he whispered. Then he said it over and over, getting louder each time, shaking his head in utter wonder.

On shaking legs, Brooke moved to the center aisle and kneeled, holding her hands out. "Bu-Buddy?"

Alex's head shifted from the floor to his mother's voice, and he grinned at her as if he'd not known she was there. But then his eyes shifted to the man behind her. He ran in a full sprint up the center aisle and right past her to leap into Kenneth's arms.

The carpenter picked him up, hugging him close. Jim watched the carpenter smile at Brooke as Ian helped her rise. And then he smiled again, this time at Macey, who had her hand over her mouth. Kenneth held the back of Alex's head, kissed it, and then put him back on his feet.

Alex wouldn't leave him. He lifted his arms until the carpenter laughed and picked him back up. Alex clung to him, burying his face in his neck.

Tears raced down Brooke's face as she held out her arms. "Please," she whispered. *"Please."*

Kenneth ran his hand through Alex's thick red hair, kissed him again, and walked over to Brooke. He handed the boy to his mother, who held him tighter than he'd ever been held before.

Charlie wrapped his enormous arms around Brooke and Alex as everybody else quickly huddled by.

Nobody said a word as Kenneth stepped off the platform. The room had gone quiet yet again, and they all just watched in silence as he walked purposefully down the aisle toward the chapel entrance.

"Thank you," Jim said.

The carpenter stopped a few feet short of the door. He didn't move.

"What is the reason?" Jim asked, bowing his head.

Kenneth waited for a few seconds. And then he turned around.

"Look at me, James."

Jim looked at Kenneth. "Can you tell us the reason why God does everything he does?"

Kenneth held up his fists and then slowly fanned his arms out to his sides. "You know the reason, James Lindy."

"I know," Jim said. "But I was hoping everyone could hear it from you."

The carpenter nodded and then uncoiled his fists, exposing his palms.

"The reason is God loves you."

✢ FIFTY-FOUR

"You're gonna need a bigger boat," Zach said, talking to Pastor Jim and passing a clear Tupperware bowl filled with pretzels to Ian on the other side of the couch in the Lindy living room. Ian grabbed a handful and then dropped them into his other palm.

"What's that?" Pastor Jim asked, looking puzzled. "A bigger boat?"

"It's from *Jaws*," Ian said. "The boat they were using wasn't big enough to get the job done. You don't remember that?"

Pastor Jim threw his hands up in the air in surrender and then dropped them to his lap. "You know what? I've never seen *Jaws*."

Zach shifted to the edge of the couch and grinned. "What I'm trying to say is that we're going to need a bigger church."

"I'm hoping you're right," Pastor Jim said. "But *we* are the church, Zach. Our message is not confined to any four walls. God wants his message to spread. He wants everyone to hear."

"Believe me," Zach said, "they're hearing about it already. All of the chatter about Alex around the hospital isn't going to stop there. People want to know more. Lots more."

"Praise God," Pastor Jim said.

Shirley popped her head in the living room. "We're going to sing to the birthday boy now."

"Okay, honey," Pastor Jim said. The three of them stood and went into the kitchen.

Macey was sitting next to Kaitlyn and Shirley on one side of the table. Opposite them were Charlie and Alex, and they were all wearing cone birthday hats with the number 6 on them. Zach sat down and had to smile when he looked again across the table. It was obvious that the rubber band attached to Charlie's hat didn't even come close to reaching under his chin, so he had tried to put it on a different way. The hat was on his forehead, pointing straight out, the band around his ears, making Charlie both the tallest and only unicorn in the room.

"Look at Alex," Kaitlyn whispered, leaning her head on Zach's shoulder.

He kissed her cheek and whispered back, "Look at Brooke."

Brooke's face was one of pure joy as she carried the birthday cake from the counter and set it in front of Alex. She took out a lighter, lit the candles, and then stepped back.

Charlie wiggled in his seat in growing anticipation, waiting for them to sing and for Alex to make his wish. There was no doubt that he wanted a piece of that cake and then to help Alex open presents.

Alex closed his eyes for no longer than three seconds, cocked his head back, and then tilted forward, blowing as hard as he could across the candles that formed a small circle at the center of the chocolate cake. All six of the tiny flames leaned away and then slowly recoiled back toward him before they went out. He straightened his back, lifted his chin, and threw his arms up in victory as little trails of smoke headed toward the ceiling. "Look, Charlie! I got 'em all the first time!"

"Good job, buddy!" Brooke said as everyone surrounding the kitchen table applauded—with the exception of Charlie, who'd gotten distracted by the smoke from the candles.

"What did you wish for, Alex?" Carla asked.

"I'm not sayin', Aunt Carla!" he answered, grabbing a party favor and blowing into it, uncoiling it's snake-like paper tongue rapidly into the side of Charlie's head. "I'm not 'posed to say, right?"

"That's right, Alex!" Ian said, drawing a broader smile from Carla. "Don't tell her."

"Alex probably doesn't want to open his presents while we eat cake," Brooke teased.

"Yeah, I do, Mom!"

"You sure?" Brooke asked.

"And Charlie is gonna help me open them, huh, Charlie?" he said, turning to Charlie just in time to see Charlie's cheeks puff on his own party favor and launch his retaliatory strike-off of Alex's small chin.

"Get him, Charlie!" Brooke yelled.

Alex squealed and took off running, Charlie lumbering behind. As Brooke sliced the birthday cake, Pastor Jim came up beside Zach. "There's something here you should see." He handed him a folded newspaper, the morning's *Carlson Herald*.

Zach lifted a brow and took the paper from the pastor, wondering if the media had finally heard about Alex. *He probably wants me to be ready*, Zach thought. He could see the future frenzy of reporters in his mind, gathering in front of the hospital or this little house at St. Thomas. *What will Macey say? What will I say?* How did one explain it, other than as a miracle?

That's all I'll say, he decided. *God did what we could not.*

Zach excused himself for a moment and stepped quietly back into the living room. He unfolded the paper and his eyes widened, immediately recognizing the battered Ford F-150. He quickly read the article under the photograph.

Driver Missing from Train Crash

CARLSON—Investigators are looking for the driver of a vehicle that was struck by a northbound train early Friday morning.

Carlson police said the crash was the first in over forty years at the Old Gibraltar Road central crossing, despite the site's not having crossing gates to protect drivers.

Police said, "Early indications lead us to believe that a collision occurred shortly after 3:00 a.m. with an unregistered 1996 Ford F-150 that was heading east toward Gibraltar. It is believed, at this stage, the truck was forced some 220 feet north into the old McLouth Steel property. The locomotive engineer has confirmed the truck was moving across the tracks prior to impact, leaving us to believe it was occupied. We are extremely concerned for the welfare of the individual operating that vehicle."

Anyone who may have information regarding this crash is being asked to notify the Carlson Police Department.

Detroit-Access Rail was not available for comment.

There were no other witnesses.

"No other witnesses," Zach whispered. "We'll see about that."

His eyes climbed up the page to the photo of the mangled F-150 lying next to a telephone pole in a dark ditch off of Old Gibraltar Road. Behind it, two train cars were visible, covered with graffiti. And then he saw it. The two words, in blocky tagger printing. He laughed aloud and glanced out the window and up the hill at St. Thomas just in time to see three deer prance playfully around the front corner of the church. They slowed near the cross. He remembered the first time he'd seen the cross and how hopeless he thought it was. But it had risen. It had been made new.

Zach looked back at the photo one last time and the words on the boxcar.

He closed his eyes and thought about those words and what they meant to him. About how he'd come to know love, true Love, and all that had helped him overcome. When he finally opened his eyes, he wiped away a tear and looked up again to the cross. It was there that his life had truly begun.

"And where I'll stay," he promised in a whisper, nodding. And then he said the two words that had been so neatly painted on the side of the train.

"Only believe."

✢ EPILOGUE

"S omeone is here to see you, Timmy."

He didn't feel like answering. Even if he did, she wouldn't be able to hear him. The old bat couldn't hear half the things he said from five feet away, so why bother answering now?

"Timmy?" she yelled from the base of the stairs.

Her voice was warbly, and he figured with the disease that made her shake all the time, that white-haired head of hers was probably bobbling all over the place. What a pain she was becoming.

"Timmy? Are you asleep?"

Not anymore, you idiot.

He could hear the creak in the stairs. Must be important, because she was on her way up. He glanced at the clock. It was 11:39 a.m., and he knew with that miserable back of hers, it would take her just about forever to get up to his room. *I'll just grab a little more shut-eye before she gets here . . .*

There was a knock on his door and Tim Shempner woke back up, startled. *I actually did go back to sleep,* he thought with a laugh under his breath. He rolled over in bed and looked at the clock. It was 11:43 a.m. It took her four minutes to get up the stairs. He hoped it hurt, so she wouldn't bother to do it again.

"Timmy?"

"Not now, Grandma!"

The door handle turned, and Shempner could see those crooked blue fingers that were holding the side of the door as his grandmother struggled to push it open over the carpet, against a mountain of dirty clothes. Even though it was her house, she had *a lot* to learn about respecting his privacy.

"Someone is here for you," she said, giving him that disappointed look that was *really* starting to get on his nerves. She shook her head, and it was the shake she actually had control of. "Timmy, honey, I asked you not to smoke in the house. Are you smoking up here again?"

"No, Grandma."

"What do you want me to tell those men downstairs?"

"Who are they?"

"I'm worried that they may be the police. Are you in trouble again?"

"No, Grandma. Tell them I'm sick."

"I'm not going to lie," she said. "I'll tell them you are tired."

"You do that, Grandma."

She grimaced as she pulled back on the door and suddenly stopped. "Do you think that you could get around to cutting the grass today?"

No, but I might get around to hiding your heart medicine.

Shempner covered his head with the sheet and ignored her. She finally gave up and closed the door.

He sat up and reached for his pack of cigarettes on the nightstand. It was empty, but there was a good half of one, a little bent up but still smokable, resting in the ashtray. He lit it and looked out the window.

Things had to get better.

It had been pretty close to a year since Carla had the big retard attack him at The Pilot Inn. Between the restraining order that drunk whore put on him and the constant humiliation from everyone in town, he figured his best play was to get out of Dodge for a while and come out to Arizona and mooch off Grandma for a bit.

Though it was normally a couple hundred degrees in this hotbox she called home, it hadn't been that hard for him to make ends meet. She didn't charge him any rent, he ate for free, and between his unemployment checks and the occasional ten- or twenty-dollar bill he'd lift out of her purse while she dozed off in her chair, he wasn't in any real hurry to get a job.

Grandma had also told him that she'd decided to include him in the latest version of her will. It wasn't but a couple weeks ago that he'd actually thought she'd punched out in the middle of one of her naps. He had already been counting the money as he held a mirror under her mouth to see if she was breathing. She practically gave *him* a heart attack when her eyes popped open and she asked him what he was doing.

It was all good, though. She was eighty-seven and hopefully it wouldn't be much longer. *If this heat keeps up, it'll help*, he thought. Old people died in the heat all the time. And Tim had been encouraging her to save money and keep the air-conditioning off . . .

He thought he heard a man's voice. Apparently, Grandma wasn't going to be able to fend them off. He snubbed out his cigarette and put his jeans on to go see what they wanted. He figured it probably had something to do with not paying his court costs and fines back in Michigan, but wasn't quite sure if they could even issue a warrant out here for that.

He went downstairs but only found Grandma, sitting in her chair. He shoved back a wave of irritation. He'd gotten up for nothing? "Were they cops, Grandma?"

"I asked them if they were the police, and they said no."

Shempner sat on the couch. "Then who were they?"

"I don't know," she said. "There were three of them, and the one who did all the talking left something for you. I put it in the kitchen."

Good thing it wasn't the cops. He needed more legal problems like he needed cancer.

"What did they leave me?" Shempner asked. A pile of tickets? Court paperwork? "They made you sign for it, right?"

"What? No. Oh, Timmy, it's beautiful," she said. "You just have to see it."

Shempner shook his head. Getting a straight answer out of the crazy old coot was like pulling teeth. He stood and made his way into the kitchen.

He immediately saw it and stopped.

Shempner squinted, and his mouth opened slightly. The side of his neck was becoming uncomfortably warm, and the strength was pouring out of his legs. He swore under his breath. *What's happening to me?* He leaned heavily against the refrigerator, but his hand slid slowly down the cool stainless steel of the refrigerator door as he sank to his knees, that warm feeling attacking every inch of his body.

He tried to lift his arms. He couldn't.

He tried to look away, but the whole time he was in the kitchen, he just couldn't take his eyes off it.

Over on the table.

It was the single most beautiful thing he'd ever seen.

It was *perfect*.

It was an apple.

✤ AUTHOR'S NOTE

Two little red wagons . . .

I can vividly remember walking down a hallway at a Detroit hospital back in early 2004. To say that things needed to be put in perspective for me at that time may be the greatest understatement of my lifetime. I had just gone through a divorce, I was in the middle of some activities that were hurting a lot of good people—activities that would ultimately lead me to federal prison—and my oldest daughter had just been diagnosed with type 1 diabetes. I guess I was more than a little self-absorbed, and found I was drowning in the middle of my own pity party.

That's when I saw the first one.

A young boy—I'm guessing maybe two or three years old—was being pulled in a little red wagon. He was wearing superhero pajamas, and his hair had fallen out. He looked awful. Both his mother and father were clearly exhausted and experiencing a level of stress that to this day is something I can only imagine. At that time, I had no idea that I was looking at Ian, Brooke, and Alex. I can still see that little boy looking up and smiling at his parents, and when they smiled back, nothing else in the world seemed to be happening. Their exchange was one of the most beautiful things I had ever seen. I wanted those smiles to be a result of something—of anything—and I wanted them to last, because in too many cases, they don't. That's when the idea for this book danced through my head.

Like so many inspirational moments, the promises I made to myself that day didn't last. I still couldn't be the better person I wanted to be. I had arrived at another one of those proverbial forks in the road and had somehow convinced myself that I could dig my way out of an enormous hole that I had created. I made the same terrible choices over and over again, and as I tried to fix a problem, I inevitably created more.

I continued to head in the wrong direction over the next few years and brought a lot of unknowing participants with me. In the middle of that destruction, I had somehow managed to scribble here and there writings to the tune of over one thousand pages about a stranger who shows up at a hospital in the small town of Carlson, Michigan. I guess I wanted him to do more than fix sick little kids—I wanted him to fix me. The problem was that I really didn't have the faintest idea who this stranger was, so I ended up tossing the story in a drawer.

In May of 2007, while on pretrial for wire fraud and money laundering charges, I was allowed to visit an uncle of mine in North Carolina. I had gone down there with a friend, and we were sitting in a restaurant just south of Asheville, waiting for my uncle to meet us for breakfast. He was going to lead us through the winding roads into the mountains where he lived.

That's when I saw the second one.

There were a few rows of booths in that restaurant, and in the row to my left, there was another young boy who was sitting in another little red wagon. He had a full head of hair and had one of those piercing laughs that came from nothing other than pure joy and an appreciation of being alive. I initially found it a little odd that his mother was spoon-feeding him. The kid continued to laugh and didn't seem to have a care in the world. He also didn't have any arms or legs. I didn't say anything about the little boy to my uncle or my friend, and I suddenly realized I had spent my whole life worrying about the wrong things. I was a little over six months from heading off to prison, and I felt like the luckiest man in the world. Needless to say, I thought about the kid in Detroit again and about my unfinished story. The book and its author were about to get a three-year overhaul.

On December 4, 2007, I reported to the United States

Penitentiary–Hazelton, in Bruceton Mills, West Virginia. Prison is something I would never wish on anyone, but at the same time, there are few things I would trade for the experience. It was a much-needed "time-out" that gave me the opportunity to not only figure out who I really was but also to figure out what was important—and what was missing in my life. The same thing that was missing in my life was also absent from the earliest version of the book, and I started to make some changes. When I refer to something missing, I'm talking about that "buzz" that Kaitlyn Harby felt. There is no doubt in my mind that the Cause of that buzz is, in fact, very real and isn't just there when you need it—it's always there. You just have to be open to it and trust that it doesn't have to be found in a prison, a cemetery, a little bar, or the parking lot of a hospital. It can be found anywhere. I hope that makes some sense.

When I was released, I was lucky enough to be given the opportunity and the time (a word I now respect more than ever) to take all the changed pieces and try to put them together. The one thousand pages (despite adding a few characters) quickly became eight hundred. I was fortunate to be able to work with editor Chris Cancilliari, who helped me knock it down to the five hundred pages that ultimately went to the publisher to become what you are holding. Chris—how many phone calls and e-mails did we exchange? I never knew the difference between three dots and an em dash, but I hope to harass you more in the future. Thanks for tolerating my OCD and for turning my drivel into something that made sense. It was truly a lot of fun, and I hope to do it again.

I have a lot of other people to thank. This book has been on a journey, so please be patient with me.

Thank you Ginny Simpson, Norm Fenton, and Jack Kelly—I couldn't have done this without you.

Brooke, thanks for your help with Carla's character and for explaining what love is and isn't.

I also want to thank everyone that read the earliest version of the book, particularly: Bob Deragisch, Kim Falkowski-Lewis, Debbie Vendlinski, Rich and Leann Hedke, Judi McNair, Liz Zeller,

Jacqueline Lynch, Rose Williams, Helen McCord, Lorene Miller, Dawn Overstreet, Aunt Paulette Pedigo, Cousin Susan Shelton, Ray Johnson, Uncle Bill Sirls, Janet Krust, Yvonne Cancilliari, Kathy Marcum, Kimberly Brown, Jim Steere, Patti Hogue, Mike Stedman, Tom Ayers, Russell Bradley Fenton, Tim Cooke, Brian Noble, and Mark Drew. Sometimes you can't see the forest for the trees, and you guys were incredible.

A very special thanks to Chris Sonksen, lead pastor at South Hills Church in Corona, California. I appreciate the guidance you gave me on the book and for sharing your thoughts on the twenty-third Psalm. It was the single most amazing sermon I have ever heard.

Thanks also go to the team at Westbow, including Joel Pierson, D. Spindler, Jamie Brazel, Megan Schindele, Andy Mays, Stefanie Holzbacher, Jeremy Weddle, Amanda Parsons, Richard Robertson, Shelley Rogers Landes and Chris Bass. Professionalism and good people are a great combination.

I can't forget my buddy with the English accent, Alan Bower, from Author Solutions. Alan is in the publishing business for the right reasons. He loves publishing and loves authors. Thank you for your advice, voice of reason, and your friendship. Thanks also go to his better half, Erica Dooley-Dorocke. What a difference you two truly do make.

I want to thank my friends from Thomas Nelson. I remember when Allen Arnold called me and asked me if I would be interested in talking about Thomas Nelson publishing *The Reason*. When this happened, I felt like I was ten years old again, wearing a brand-new ball glove, playing catch in the backyard with my dad, and *boom*, the New York Yankees were on the phone, wondering if I wanted to go pro. It was an incredible feeling knowing that the story would be in the best possible hands it could be in, and I am truly blessed to have met and worked with Allen and the rest of the team at Thomas Nelson. Thanks to Allen, Ruthie Dean, Katie Bond, Ashley Schneider, Eric Mullett, Ami McConnell, Amanda Bostic, Becky Monds, Jodi Hughes, and Kristen Vasgaard. You guys are seriously an amazing group of people, and it is so easy to see God working through you to both entertain readers and bring people closer to Him. Please keep doing what you guys do.

Pete Nikolai. Thank you for handing a copy of the Westbow galley to Marjo.

Marjo Myers. I can't thank you enough, so I'll do it again here. I'm thankful that a copy of the book somehow landed on your desk at Thomas Nelson. And I'm thankful you read it. Who knows what it will lead to?

Natalie Hanemann and Lisa Bergren. You have taught me more about writing than I have learned from everyone and everywhere else combined. There is nobody that I would rather have helping me with my storytelling than you. You've pushed me to get better, and I'm very lucky to have your help. Thank you.

I have two beautiful daughters and a family I love very much. I thank you for being you and for your patience. I'd mention your names here, but I've already done that, haven't I?

I want to apologize once again to the "31." You deserved much better than what you got from me. I don't know if I can ever make it right, but I promise you it won't be for lack of effort.

Finally, I want to thank the reader. I hope you enjoyed reading this as much as I did writing it—and that it somehow makes a difference in your life.

William Sirls
Rockwood, Michigan
March 4, 2012

✛ READING GROUP GUIDE

If your reading group of 7 or more members is interested in having William Sirls call in for a book discussion, please contact him through his website: www.WilliamSirls.com.

1. In chapter 2, Kenneth hands Carla an apple and asks her what would happen to it if it had a big worm inside of it. What do the apple and worm represent?

2. Early in the book, Zach Norman calls God a bully. If God allows something bad to happen, does that mean it is part of God's will? Why?

3. Pastor Jim encourages his congregation to spend less time worrying about what they don't have, and just be thankful for what they do have. Do you find yourself doing this? What has God given you that you are most thankful for?

4. Do you know anyone that harbors ill will toward someone who has harmed them? How would you help someone forgive another human being? Is it possible that sometimes we forgive others to let ourselves off the hook?

5. Pastor Jim explains to Brooke that God doesn't keep us from tests and trials, but he helps us get through them. What are your thoughts on this?

6. At what point do you think Zach Norman knew he had faith? Why? Can you describe the moment you knew you had it?

7. If we pray for something and it doesn't happen, does that make the prayer unanswered?

8. What lesson did Macey Lewis need to learn?

9. Do you believe that God smiles when we use the unique gifts or abilities that he has given us? Take a few minutes and think about what your gift or gifts may be. Are you putting your gift to use? How do you feel when you do?

10. How could God make something good come from the death of a child?

11. Who is the old man with the beard?

12. Who is Kenneth to you?

13. In the epilogue, who are the three visitors that Tim Shempner's grandmother encounters? Are they anywhere else in the book?

14. Who do you believe is the main character in the book? Why?

✢ AN INTERVIEW WITH WILLIAM SIRLS

THOMAS NELSON: This is your first novel. What was the rockiest section of road on this publishing journey?

WILLIAM SIRLS: Beyond the normal bumps in the road, writing this story was an incredible learning experience, as well as a lot of fun. Even though I'm getting better, something I have wrestled with my whole life is patience, so if I had to pick something about this particular journey that I struggled with, it would have to be the initial delay in the story's release as we transitioned it from a self-published galley to where the book is now. When we were first contacted by Thomas Nelson in the summer of 2011, we were only a couple months away from releasing the original version of *The Reason*. I was pretty excited about some of the feedback we had received from advance readers and was really anxious to get the book out there. At the time, postponing it for a year seemed like an eternity, but it went by quickly and I'm really glad we waited.

TN: Do any of the characters in the book closely resemble you?

WS: I would say Zach Norman because we both spent

a great deal of our lives worried about the wrong things. We both had the big house, the big car, the big job, and it wasn't until we were each in our forties that we realized that even though an incredible price was paid for it, the most valuable thing any of us could ever have is absolutely free—and that is a relationship with God. Zach just happened to discover this in a cemetery. I was in federal prison.

TN: How have your past experiences played a role in the telling of this story?

WS: I remember how different the world looked to me that golden moment when I knew I had faith. To me, faith is that absolute sense of certainty that God is who He says He is, that He is going to do what He says He is going to do, and that even guys like me had access to that through His Son, who died for all of us. Through my faith and the faith of others, I began to learn valuable lessons involving forgiveness, understanding, patience, and grace. It became important to me that I share some of these things that I learned, so I figured what better way to do that than to sprinkle them among the characters in the book.

TN: Do you have a favorite character?

WS: That's kind of like asking me to pick a favorite child. I kind of like them all, but again, I'm a huge fan of the author. If nobody was listening, I would say Zach Norman. If God can turn around guys like me and Zach, He can turn anyone around.

TN: If you had one piece of advice for someone out there struggling with grief, what would it be?

WS: God doesn't keep us from tests and trials. He helps us get through them. Ask Him for comfort and guidance and let your reaction to adversity be such a demonstration of strength and faith that it draws others to His kingdom.

TN: Who is Kenneth?

WS: Kenneth is an instrument of God's glory. I've heard readers call him an angel, a prophet, Jesus, and even God himself. One of them is correct.

TN: Does the phrase "Only believe" have any personal significance to you?

WS: Even though I always had the time, prison gave me more of it to pray, read the Bible, and experience fellowship with other Christians. It also taught me to be more patient and watch what happened when I did these things. It really opened my eyes to who I was. Prior to that, I had always allowed an internal competition between logic and faith. I was the type who constantly tried to pin things down I didn't understand. In all of my efforts to create different arguments to either prove or disprove different aspects of Christianity, I always came back to the irrefutable truth that we are simply incapable of understanding it all. At some point, we have to let go and make a conscious decision to either believe or not. It's a pretty important choice. So does the phrase "Only believe" have any personal significance to me? My answer is yes. When it's all said and done, I think we will find that everything else, in fact, is pretty insignificant.

TN: Is there anything else you'd like readers to know about this story?

WS: I would like them to only believe that everything in this book could happen.

✢ ABOUT THE AUTHOR

Author photo by Erica Dooley Bower

Over the course of his life, William Sirls has experienced both great highs and tremendous lows—some born of chance, some born of choice. Once a senior vice president at a major investment firm, he was incarcerated in 2007 for wire fraud and money laundering, where he learned a great deal more than he ever bargained for. Life lessons involving faith, grace, patience, and forgiveness are evident in his writing. He is the father of two and makes his home in southern Michigan. *The Reason* is his first novel.

You can reach William at WilliamSirls.com, on Facebook, or on Twitter (@WilliamSirls).